FEMALE INTELLIGENCE

"[Heller's] observations about men are dead-on and hilarious."

—*Booklist*

"A breeze to read, full of laughs, and solidly built upon an intricate, suspenseful plot."

—*Library Journal*

NAME DROPPING

"Jane Heller is feisty, funny, and fully in control . . . A great story."

—*Boston Globe*

"As much *Sex and the City* as *I Love Lucy* . . . Saucy heroine and screwball plot add up to a romp."

—*People*

SIS BOOM BAH

"If you loved *Divine Secrets of the Ya-Ya Sisterhood,* pick up *Sis Boom Bah!*"

—*Newark Star-Ledger*

"If you ever wanted to kill your sister, this is the novel for you . . . just the book to pass on to anyone's sis when you finish."

—*People*

ALSO BY
JANE HELLER

BEST
ENEMIES

JANE HELLER

St. Martin's Paperbacks

BEST ENEMIES

Copyright © 2004 by Jane Heller.

Library of Congress Catalog Card Number: 2003061063

ISBN: 0-312-99676-4
EAN: 80312-99676-5

Printed in the United States of America

St. Martin's Press hardcover edition / April 2004
St. Martin's Paperbacks edition / March 2005

St. Martin's Paperbacks are published by St. Martin's Press, 175 Fifth Avenue, New York, NY 10010.

10 9 8 7 6 5 4 3 2 1

For Susan Tofias,
who did the locomotion with me in junior high
and has been my friend ever since

ACKNOWLEDGMENTS

I couldn't have written this book without the professionals: my editor, Jennifer Enderlin, and my literary agent, Ellen Levine. Many thanks to them for their intelligence, creativity, and unwavering support. Thanks, too, to those who were willing to brainstorm with me, especially: Ruth Harris, Dara Marks, Brad Schreiber, Marty Bell, and Michael Barrett. Thanks to Amy Schiffman, John Karle, Sallyanne McCartin, Renee Young, and Kristen Powers for helping to spread the word about my books. And thanks to my husband, Michael Forester, for schlepping around the country with me, holding my hand on airplanes, smiling in the back row at book signings, and being an all-around great sport.

BEST
ENEMIES

AMY

1

Two weeks before I was to be married in front of a hundred and fifty guests on the lawn of a precious little country inn in Connecticut, I caught my fiancé in bed with another woman. To add insult to injury, the woman was my best friend. To add further insult to injury, she was the one on top when I walked in on them midcoitus. She was crying out, "Take me home, Hondo!" even though my fiancé's name is the far less studly-sounding Stuart, and she was riding him as if he were a horse, even though he is hung like a very small dog.

They were both horrified when they discovered me standing in the doorway of the bedroom Stuart and I had shared—they must have assumed it would take longer for the dentist to tame the inflammation I'd developed in my lower left gum, a condition brought about by the stress of the wedding, according to Dr. Ronald Glick, D.D.S. Stuart tried to say something to me but could only stammer, being the gutless wonder that he is, and I tried to say something to him but could only lisp, thanks to Dr. Glick's liberal use of novocaine. My best friend, on the other hand, though clearly upset (she was the one who burst out crying, while I was too catatonic to shed even a single tear), was able to speak for the two of them. She climbed off Stuart, covered herself modestly with the bedsheet (never mind that I had seen her naked in countless department store dressing rooms over the years), and went on and on about how much they both cared about me and respected me and thought I was *special,* but that, in the end, they couldn't deny that they had fallen in love. "I swear we never meant to hurt you, Amy," she added between sobs. "These things happen."

Well, she was right, as it turns out; these things do happen. Statistics show that when a man strays, the person he most often strays with is the best friend of the person he strays from. I don't know why this is, other than that men are lazy. Why should they go out of their way to hunt for someone to cheat with when their beloved's gal pal is right there in plain sight? The more puzzling question is, Why does the gal pal go for it? Are women really so desperate to find a guy that they can't just say no in sticky situations? Can't summon up some good old-fashioned willpower? Can't tell him, "Look, big boy, I'm lonely and I'm horny and, if you must know, I'm a little envious that my best friend has a man and I don't, but I take the friendship seriously, so get lost"? Is that really asking too much?

"Stuart was planning to talk to you tonight," she continued as I leaned against the wall so I wouldn't fall down. "He was going to tell you that he was having doubts, that he couldn't marry you knowing he had feelings for me, that he had to call off the wedding. It wasn't supposed to be like this. You weren't supposed to walk in and find us together. Oh, please, please try to understand, Amy. I know you must be dying inside—how could you not be?—but hopefully, after some time and distance, you'll come to accept the situation and forgive us."

I looked at Stuart, who had forgotten to cover himself with the sheet and whose privates had shriveled to giblets. I hated him for his treachery; hated him because he was jilting me at the altar, give or take a few days; hated him because he was forcing me to rethink every minute we'd ever spent together. But in time, I did forgive him—well, not forgive him, exactly, but I did stop fantasizing about his death. I realized that he had done me a favor by dumping me; that I'd never really loved him, either.

It was my best friend I couldn't forgive, she who became the object of my enmity. How could she have done it? How could this seemingly decent, although self-absorbed, human being have done this dirty rotten thing to me?

As I staggered out of the bedroom that day, my mind ran a little black-and-white montage of the highlights of our friendship, sort of a quickie golden-oldies reel. There we were as ten-year-olds, comparing the haircuts our mothers made us get for summer camp. There we were as thirteen-year-olds, discussing braces and pimples and whether tongue-kissing a boy was great or gross. There we were as sixteen-year-olds, comforting each other over our mutual failure to pass our driving test the first time around. There we were as eighteen-year-olds, graduating from high school and promising to stay friends, even though our colleges were three thousand miles apart.

We did stay friends through our twenties, although not with the same intensity. As we moved into adulthood, we got jobs, made new friends, and discovered we didn't have as much in common as we did when we were kids, but we continued to get together on a regular basis because, no matter what, we shared a history. You can't just write off the person who taught you how to inhale cigarette smoke up your nose, after all.

And so, while there were other women I saw more often, it was she whom I'd considered my best friend, she whom I'd asked to be my maid of honor at my wedding, she whom I'd trusted above all others. It was she whose betrayal sent me careening into therapy, which I paid for by selling my diamond engagement ring.

For three years, I spent Tuesdays at noon on the cracked leather sofa of Marianne Ettlinger, a Manhattan psychologist who is not of the old school, where the shrink just sits there and nods, but of the new school, where the shrink tells you so much about her own problems that you're tempted to remind her it's your dime. Her chattiness aside, Marianne is wise and smart and extremely compassionate. She helped me conquer my demons. She helped me let go of my feelings of rage. She helped me understand that there had always lurked a pattern in my relationship with my best friend, a pattern of my giving and her taking, but that I couldn't get on with my life unless I abandoned my obsession with exacting revenge. I pledged that I would do just that—stop obsessing about paying my best friend back—even after I'd heard from various high school classmates that she and Stuart had gotten married and moved into an enormous Tudor in Mamaroneck . . . on the water . . . with a guest house . . . and a pool and cabana. Talk about hard to stomach. Part of me still wanted her to suffer, not prosper, but Marianne and I worked on that. "Focus on you, Amy, on what you want out of life, not on how your life compares to hers," she said during a break in her anecdote about her ongoing rivalry with her sister. "It doesn't matter how she and Stuart are faring. What matters is how *you're* faring and whether you feel centered." Marianne was big on the notion of feeling centered. When I left her office after our final session, I did feel centered—but only temporarily.

What happened to throw me off center was this: On a prematurely warm Saturday afternoon in April, the very weekend after I'd ended my therapy, I ran into my best friend. I hadn't seen her in nearly four years, not since the day she was straddling Stuart, and I was undone, absolutely caught off guard. For one thing, Marianne and I hadn't rehearsed what I would do or say if such an occasion arose. For another, my hair was filthy, since I'd just come from a strenuous workout at the gym, I wasn't wearing makeup, and I was in midbite of the bagel and cream cheese I'd picked up at Starbucks, the cream cheese, no doubt, smeared across my front teeth.

And so when my best friend approached me, looking incredible (perfect clothes, perfect jewelry, perfect everything), there was good news and bad news about my behavior. The good news was that, thanks to my therapy, I did not feel the urge to slap her across the face or hit her over the head with my backpack or stomp on her five-hundred-dollar Jimmy Choo shoes, nor was I moved to give her the silent treatment or hurl obscenities at her. The bad news was that, although physical and verbal abuse were out of the question, I felt compelled to do *something* to her. I'm embarrassed about what I did, sure, but it felt right at the time. Well, not "right," of course, but satisfying, like an itch that got scratched.

"Amy, how *are* you?" my best friend said in that way people say it when what they mean is, How do you manage to get up in the morning, you poor, pitiful person?

"I'm great," I said, gulping down the mouthful of bagel and standing up straight. I wasn't great, but, up to that point, I'd been pretty good. I had a career and people to hang out with and enough money to take vacations in the Caribbean every now and then. There was only one thing missing: I wasn't in love with anybody, didn't have a steady, wasn't *involved*—a fact I had come to terms with but was suddenly, as I stood there facing down the woman who'd stolen my man, regarding as a spectacular source of shame.

"I'm happy to hear that," she said. "You know, I thought about calling you a thousand times, but I didn't have your number, didn't even know where you lived." I told her that I lived in a two-bedroom apartment in a doorman building on East Seventeenth Street between Third Avenue and Irving Place. I also told her I was the publicity director at Lowry and Trammell, the publishing company that had just released the autobiography of Ozzy Osbourne's wife.

"You work at Lowry and Trammell?" she repeated. "That's an amazing coincidence, because—" She stopped herself. Perhaps she was about to brag about having slept with Ozzy Osbourne before deciding to sleep with my fiancé instead. "So you're doing okay, Amy? You really are?"

Well, now she was pissing me off, because it was obvious she still felt sorry for me, still viewed me as this pathetic creature who couldn't hold on to a prize like Stuart.

"I'm doing more than okay," I said, trying not to sound defensive, even though I could hear the slight edge in my voice.

"I'm glad. So am I," she said, and out came the gory details: the waterfront estate, the famous interior designer she'd hired to "do" the house, Stuart's fabulous job as chief operating officer of his family's chain of gourmet food markets, her fabulous job as the host of some obscure local radio show in Westchester County, and—this was the worst—their recent decision to "get us pregnant." I was puking, mentally.

"But enough about me," she said with a hearty laugh, as if she honestly thought I would laugh, too. "How's your love life? Are you seeing anyone?"

I couldn't say no. I just couldn't. Not only did I not want her to rush back to Stuart with the headline that I was still pining for him but, as I indicated, I felt the need to do something to her, to punch her without punching her, scream at her without screaming at her, hurt her the way she'd hurt me. And so I answered her question by telling her a big fat lie. Marianne would have termed what I did passive-aggressive and ordered me back into therapy for another three years, but, therapy or no therapy, I had to show my best enemy that I was doing just as well as she was, that I had rebounded courageously in the romance department, despite the vicious blow she'd dealt me.

"You bet I'm seeing somebody," I said with a smile and a jaunty toss of my head. "I'm engaged." Oh, why not, I figured. I'll never see her again after today, so the lie can't come back to haunt me.

"That's wonderful," she said in a tone that felt patronizing, even if it wasn't intended to be. "When's the wedding?"

"In six months," I announced. "I'm very excited."

"Of course you are," she said. "Who's the lucky guy?"

"No one you know," I said, not bothering to mention that he was no one I knew, either.

We made a few more attempts at chitchat—she actually suggested we have lunch sometime, if you can imagine it—but no phone numbers were exchanged, and after an awkward beat or two, we went our separate ways.

It occurs to me that I've neglected to tell you the name of my former best friend. It's Tara. Tara Messer.

As I walked away from her that day, I smiled to myself,

replaying her look of surprise when I'd told her I was getting married. She'd lied to me and now I'd lied to her, and it felt like justice, the kind women understand. Tit for tit, if you will. But *justice* implies an ending, and I don't want to mislead you: The story of my tortured relationship with Tara is just beginning.

2

So you lied. Big deal. It's not exactly the crime of the century," said Connie Martino, a thirty-eight-year-old editor at Lowry and Trammell and my closest confidante at the company. A blunt, no-nonsense Brooklyn native who ripped you if she didn't like you and went to the mat for you if she did, Connie had one of the great New Yawk accents. I was born and raised in New York, but there were times when I needed a translator to figure out if, for instance, she was saying *saw* or *sore*.

"I know it's not," I agreed as we sat in her office eating lunch from the deli around the corner. It was two days after I'd bumped into the dreaded Tara. I'd had forty-eight hours to digest what had "gone down," as they phrase it in the mysteries and true-crime books Connie edited, but I was still shaken up by both the sight of my nemesis, so ostentatiously gorgeous and happy and successful, and by the desperate manner in which I'd handled the situation. "I just wish I'd taken the high road instead of stooping to her level."

"Look," said Connie, biting into a dill pickle, "she was your best friend and she ran off with your guy. She deserved much worse than being lied to. I'dliketobreakherjaw."

"What?" The other reason for needing a translator was that Connie talked fast and tended to run her words together.

"I said, I'd like to break her jaw."

"Oh. Well, you'd need a ladder." While Tara was as tall as a high-rise and built just as solidly, Connie was petite—just five two and barely tipping the scale at a hundred pounds. It was only her long, teased-up black hair that was tall, and she kept it that way with enough spray to paralyze trees. Between the hair and the layers of black eyeliner and mascara she painted on every morning, she looked like she should be working street corners, not poring over manuscripts, but she was a tough cookie with a soft, gooey center. What's more, she was terrific at her job and her authors adored her, as did her husband, Murray, a painter of abstract art that was so abstract, he sold insurance for a living.

"Still, somebody should whack her for what she did to you, Amy. How long did you say you've known this piece of . . . work?"

"A long time." I sighed, thinking back on the fateful day I'd struck up a friendship with Tara Messer on the playground of our elementary school. "It was winter and we were in third grade. She was crying because one of the other girls had swiped her wool scarf."

"Whatta baby."

"Maybe, but I didn't need the scarf my mother made me wear to school, so I walked up to Tara and said she could have mine."

"And you've been handing things—and fiancés—over to her ever since."

"Apparently. I didn't see it that way, though. Not for years. Tara had a way of spinning the relationship so it always felt like she was doing me a favor by being my friend."

"Why did you buy into that?"

I shrugged. "I was a dopey, insecure kid who was thrilled just to be in the orbit of someone as cool as Tara Messer. From the beginning, it was set up that she was the bestower of all good things and I was her ever-grateful recipient. Her parents were rich, so she'd take me along on family trips. She was more sophisticated than I was, so she taught me about big-girl stuff: how to dress, do hair, make it look like we had boobs." I smiled wistfully as I remembered the night

I slept over at her house and we raided her father's dresser drawer and stuffed our bras with his socks. "And—this was key—she was beautiful, Connie, even then, so she was wildly popular. By being her friend, I was popular by association. She got the cute boys, and I got her rejects."

She shook her head. "You make it sound like you were the only one who benefited from the friendship. She must have benefited, too; otherwise, she wouldn't have kept you around."

"Oh, she benefited all right. I finally understand that after three years of therapy. I was her handmaiden, her acolyte, her trusty sidekick. I gave her my class notes and ran errands for her and took care of her dogs, whatever she needed, and in exchange she let me be her best pal. But mostly, she kept me around because I was zero competition. This will come as a shock to you, Connie, but I wasn't the incredible babe that I am now."

We both smiled. I am not a babe now, incredible or otherwise, but I'm not a horror show, either. I grew into my looks, blossomed as I moved through adolescence into adulthood. At age thirty, the nose I used to think was as big as my fist is now well proportioned to the rest of my face, which is rather attractive in an understated, nonthreatening sort of way. I have large brown eyes and lustrous brown hair and a tight little body, thanks to my workouts at the gym. You wouldn't spot me in a crowd and go, "Oh my God! Put this woman on the cover of *Vogue* immediately!" But if you studied me closely, you'd probably think, She's really pretty. That's what Stuart told me the night we met at a party—that I was "really pretty." Little did I know that, within months, Tara's beauty would trump my prettiness and that not only would the guy I wanted want her instead but that she would want him, too. That's the part that gnawed at me—the fact that she could have seduced just about any man on the planet and yet she had to spread her mile-long legs for mine.

"What made Tara's treachery all the more painful," I told Connie, "was that I thought I'd finally found an honest guy for a change, a guy who would restore my faith in man*kind*. Talk about an oxymoron."

"Talk about a moron, period."

Actually, Stuart wasn't a moron. He was smart, well read, up-to-date on current events, eager to take the reins of his family's business. In fact, it was his stability—his maturity—that had won me over. He'd seemed so different from the other guys I'd dated—the ones who couldn't commit or couldn't get a job or couldn't get it up. Yeah, I'd had my share of losers before I met him. According to Marianne, I kept picking men who weren't relationship material because I suffered from low self-esteem. Ironic, huh? Thanks to Stuart, my self-esteem dipped so low, it practically flatlined.

"You must have been really traumatized when he turned out to be a rat," said Connie, echoing my thoughts.

"I was, because I just didn't see it coming, didn't see Tara coming. By the time he and I had gotten engaged, she wasn't a huge part of my life anymore. She had become sort of princessy and shallow, not that she was ever particularly deep, but at least she used to be fun. When I asked her to be my maid of honor and take part in my wedding, it was mostly because we'd known each other for so many years. She'd been my best friend and my oldest friend, and I thought introducing her to Stuart and including her in our special day was the right thing to do."

"The right thing to do would have been to keep her slutty ass out of your damn business."

"Yeah, well hindsight is twenty-twenty," I remarked, then cringed. I hate that expression. It's right up there with "six of one, half a dozen of the other." Tara's favorite was "the whole enchilada," and I was such a twit, I used to think she was worldly and hip for saying it.

"I'd love to continue to trash the bitch," said Connie, "but I've got an editorial meeting in five minutes. Sorry."

"Don't be. I've got to work the phones. I'm trying to get the news magazines to do a feature on Georgette Peterson. Her new novel is brilliant, but she's not a household name."

"If anyone can make the media pay attention, it's you, Amy. They should fire Betsy and make you marketing director."

"I don't want her job. I just want her to let me do mine."

Forty-year-old Betsy Kirby was my boss at Lowry and Trammell, overseeing the publicity, promotion, and advertising departments. A seasoned veteran of the business, having worked at three other publishing houses, Betsy had a reputation as a taskmaster, and it was well deserved. She'd sit on you, badger you, hound you until you accomplished whatever impossible goal she'd set for you, and then, once you accomplished it, she'd take the credit. So frustrating. What's more, her social skills were suspect at best. She was relentlessly chilly, distant, remote—under no circumstances could you and she have a girlie conversation involving men or makeup or menstrual cramps—and we all wondered if she behaved differently with her husband, or if she was the ice queen with him, too. There was no way to tell, since she was so closemouthed about her marriage. All we knew about it was that her husband was Armenian and that he traveled a lot and that the two of them rarely saw each other. We assumed, given the data available, that they never had sex, which was why Connie had dubbed Betsy "Celebetsy." Did I want her job? Yeah. But I wasn't ready to admit it.

"Now, do you promise you'll calm down about this Tara thing?" Connie said as she gathered her notes together in preparation for her meeting.

"I'll try, although I'm still sort of amazed at what I said to her. I don't know where I got the nerve."

"Hey, you saved face by telling her you're getting married in six months. It felt right at the time, didn't it?"

"You bet it did."

"Good. Now you can forget about it, which should be easy, since the chances of you two laying eyes on each other again are slim to none."

I nodded, thanked her for the reality check.

Our lunch break over, I went back to my office and Connie went off to her editorial meeting. A couple of hours later, I was on the phone, in the middle of my pitch to the book editor at *Newsweek,* when Connie walked in with an odd expression on her face. I couldn't tell if she was sick or sad, or both. She sank down into one of the two chairs opposite mine and waited for me to finish up my call. When I did, I said, "What is it? You look as if you just lost your best friend."

She shook her head and pointed at me. "Not mine. Yours. But you didn't lose her. That's the problem."

"Connie, what are you talking about?"

"The evil Tara, the one you'll never see again. You're gonna see her again all right. Again and again and again."

"Don't even joke about that."

"No joke. It came up in the meeting," she said.

"What came up?" What was coming up at that moment was my lunch. The conversation was suddenly making me queasy.

"Your old pal has sold us a book—some ridiculous 'How to have a fabulous life' book—and you'll be overseeing the publicity for it."

I stared at Connie, forcing myself to process this hot news bulletin of hers, forcing myself to absorb the fact that L and T would be publishing a book by the person I resented most in the entire world. I couldn't believe it. Could not believe it. Why hadn't Tara told—

I stopped, remembering our exchange in more detail. She *had* told me. Or, rather, she'd been about to tell me. Yes, when we met on the street and I mentioned where I worked, she said, "You work at Lowry and Trammell? That's an amazing coincidence, because—" And then she muzzled herself. Oh God, so it was true.

"In other words, you'll be seeing her again, Amy, like it or not," Connie was saying. "Well, not just seeing her. Taking her to dinner. Brainstorming over the phone. Figuring out how to make her look good to the media. That's gotta be your idea of hell, right?"

Now I felt genuinely ill. I was nauseous, light-headed, tight in the chest, numb in the hands and feet. For a second, I wondered if I might be having a heart attack. But I wasn't. I was having an anxiety attack at the very thought—well, at all the very thoughts. The thought of Tara writing a book instead of being content with her dinky radio show and her vulgar mansion and her lowlife of a husband. The thought of her selling this so-called book to a reputable publisher like Lowry and Trammell and making more money than I did. The thought of having to interact with her on a regular basis or else risk losing my job. The thought of calling the book editor at *Newsweek* and pitching him on a feature about *her*.

"And then there's your supposed fiancé and your supposed engagement and your supposed wedding in six months," Connie reminded me, as if I didn't have enough to worry about. "You'll have to deal with all that, now that she's back in the picture." She rose from her chair, blinked at me with her raccoon eyes. "It's lucky you're creative, Amy. That's all I can say. Most people wouldn't have a clue what to do in a situation like this, but you're a publicist. You're good at putting out fires. It'spartofwhatyoudoright?"

"What?"

"I said, It's part of what you do, right?"

"Right." Yeah, I felt ill, really ill, and getting worse by the minute.

3

I went to see Celebetsy. Since she not only sat in on the editorial meetings but also had a say in the marketing viability of each book we acquired, I figured she might be able to tell me more about Tara's, specifically: why we bought it, how much we paid for it, when we were publishing it, and—here was the crucial question—whether there would be a publicity budget for it or whether it was one of those books we'd drop in our schedule and ignore, allowing me to pretend it didn't exist.

She was on the phone when I entered her corner office, which wasn't lavishly decorated, considering that she was a corporate vice president, and lacked even a hint of its occupant's private life. There were no framed photographs of her husband, no knickknacks or souvenirs indicating their trips or hobbies, not even a potted plant or two. There were only shelves of books—our books—and they were stacked randomly, haphazardly, not organized or displayed, as if Betsy had only just arrived at L and T and hadn't had time to unpack, when, in fact, she'd been my boss for over two years.

"I hope I'm not interrupting," I said after she hung up.

"What do you want?" she said, as opposed to "No, of course you're not interrupting, Amy. Come right in." She wasn't the boss from hell, exactly. She was just missing the gene that enables people to treat one another with civility.

As for her physical appearance, she was attractive, although her look was as brittle as her personality. She was model-thin, with the cheekbones to match. Her stick-straight, chin-length brown hair had a blunt, severe cut. And her complexion was pale, excessively powdered, the only color coming from her lips, which were a slash of ruby red. And speaking of her mouth, she had a great smile—one of those wide grins that can really light up a face—but she hardly ever used it, except when she was sucking up to an important author.

"I wanted to ask you about a manuscript we bought," I said, forging ahead in spite of the usual big chill. "Connie Martino told me it's a self-help book by"—I tried not to choke on that accursed name—"Tara Messer."

"Wrong. The book isn't self-help. It's lifestyle. If you're going to rely on hearsay, at least get your categories straight, would you?"

See what I mean? "Sorry. A lifestyle book by Tara Messer. Is there anything you can tell me about it?"

"Julie acquired it." Julie Farrell was our editor in chief. "She thinks the author will be the next Martha Stewart, minus the baggage."

Tara had so much baggage, she needed a U-Haul to schlepp it around. "But we're not talking about actual Martha Stewarty domestic subjects, are we?" I couldn't picture my old pal serving up advice on cooking or gardening or raising chickens to produce genetically engineered powder blue eggs. She barely knew how to make ice cubes.

"Not really. The book is more about how women can create a beautiful environment by living beautifully. Inside."

"Inside what?"

"*Inside.* You know, in our hearts and minds and souls. Apparently, Tara Messer leads this perfect life, and in the book she explains how she does it."

I knew how Tara did it, and it had nothing to do with having a *soul*. It had to do with being born into a rich family and by having people, especially your best friend, be your doormat and by marrying the best friend's fiancé, whose family was even richer than your own. "So, did Julie shell out a nice advance?"

"More than nice. Mid–six figures."

I might have actually groaned here, such was the pain I felt.

"The author hosts a radio show that's very possibly going into syndication," said Betsy. "Julie's hoping her audience will follow her to bookstores once she breaks out."

Tara never broke out. Nope, not a single zit all through high school. And wouldn't you know her stupid little radio show was about to lead her to even greater glory? That was so Tara right there.

"You'll be the point person on this one, Amy, because we're going to do big publicity—national TV, a multicity tour, feature stories in newspapers and women's magazines. I expect you to do it all."

What I felt like doing at that moment was rolling over and dying. It seemed a viable alternative to being forced to work with Tara, to being forced to *promote* Tara, but I quickly reminded myself that dying was a rather extreme method of avoidance. I also considered quitting my job on the spot, but I ruled that out as being both impulsive and reckless. No, I decided, I would discreetly look for and get another job in publicity, with a rival publishing house, and then leave L and T before Tara's book came out. If we had only just acquired it, it would probably be a year before it found its way into the schedule, and I'd be long gone by then.

"The other piece of news about the book," said Betsy, "is that the author has delivered a really clean manuscript and we're crashing it out early instead of waiting the usual eternity for it to make it through the pipeline."

So much for my escape plan. "What's the rush? It's not as if we're talking about a headline maker here."

"Colman House has a similar book on their list, and we want to get ours out first. We're planning to publish in six months."

"Six months?" I'd told Tara I was getting married in six months. Now, I'd not only have to deal with her right away,

I'd have to find a fiancé right away. Maybe dying wasn't as extreme as I thought.

Betsy went on to discuss the technicalities involved in publishing Tara's tome ahead of schedule, while I was stuck in panic mode.

"Amy?" she said, snapping her fingers in front of my face. "What's the matter with you? I'm talking to you and you're not paying attention."

Damn right I wasn't paying attention. At that particular moment, I was trying to formulate the excuse I would use to bail out of having to work on the book, but I couldn't come up with one. Why didn't I simply admit to Betsy that I'd known Tara for years, that she and I were barely on speaking terms, and that it would be impossible for me to sing her praises to the media? Because the last publicity director who went that route got her ass fired. According to Connie, my predecessor, a woman named Francine, tried to opt out of working on a cookbook by a famous French chef. "I'm a vegan," Francine told Betsy. "I refuse to promote any food that has a face." Betsy's response? "You're a publicist. You don't have to eat it. You just have to sell it. But since you can't, I'll find someone who can."

So I couldn't take a hard line if I wanted to keep my job. Instead, I tried this milder approach: "To be honest, Betsy, I'm not a big fan of the whole 'Life would be better if only I took more bubble baths' genre."

Her lip curled. "Then you'd better become one, or get your paycheck someplace else."

"Right. I only meant—"

"Hear this loud and clear: Tara Messer has written a book that has the potential to sell a shitload of copies. So I don't want you delegating it to someone in your department. I don't want you farming it out to a freelancer. I don't want you turning up your nose at it because it's not going to win a Pulitzer. I want you to get the author as much publicity as humanly possible. In other words, Amy, you've got a choice: Either join the unemployed or go out there and give this your best shot."

My best shot? That settled it. I would shoot myself.

• • •

No, of course, I wasn't going to commit suicide. I wasn't going to call Marianne, my old shrink, and make an emergency appointment with her, either, although I contemplated it. Ultimately, it seemed that running back to her reeked of failure—hers and mine. I didn't want to be one of those patients who spends years in therapy analyzing and exposing and expressing but then winds up being too dense to put any of it to use. And I didn't want her to be one of those therapists who spends years in training at the Ackerman Institute in New York or the Menninger Clinic in Kansas, or wherever therapists go to become therapists, only to have the patient regress. Besides, I already knew what she'd say if I went back and sat on her cracked leather sofa: "Concentrate on your own life, Amy, not on what Tara has or doesn't have. Let go of the past. Stay *centered*."

So I vowed to solve my Tara Problem myself. As I saw it, there were essentially two parts to the problem. There was the professional issue, where I would have to work alongside her on the book, and there was the personal issue, where I would have to deal with my lie about being engaged. Regarding the professional issue, I decided that with courage and determination and a decent supply of Xanax, I could get through the publicity campaign for the book. Regarding the personal issue, I decided that by pretending I'd never told Tara I was engaged and hoping she'd forgotten all about it, I could get away with having said it in the first place.

To attack the professional issue, I asked Julie Farrell's assistant on Friday for a copy of Tara's manuscript, which was bundled in a large envelope, together with a press kit on Tara herself. I took the package home and read its contents over the weekend.

She's still the girl who won Best Looking in high school, I mused as I examined an eight-by-ten glossy of thirty-year-old Tara.

I was in bed that Saturday morning, propped up against a couple of pillows, a mug of coffee on my night table, the manuscript pages fanned out across the sheets.

Yep, she's still the Golden Girl, I marveled, observing Tara's face, clothes, pose, whatever I could glean from that photo. It was true that I had just seen her in the flesh on the street, but I hadn't really allowed myself to get a good, unmitigated look at her that day. I'd been too caught up in the surprise of seeing her, too caught up in the memory of her with Stuart, the confusion of having once been her devoted friend, the feeling of being thrust back into my role as second fiddle. I knew she'd looked great that day, but until I studied her photo, I hadn't realized how great.

Why great? What made her a standout? Why had she won Best Looking in high school, and how had she managed to keep the image going as an adult?

Well, it wasn't just that she was blond, because when we met in third grade, her golden hair had already begun to turn brown. It was *how* she'd brought it back around to golden, because the process reflected her flair and sophistication and ability to charm. Unlike the rest of us amateur-hour teens with our lemon juice and peroxide concoctions and our do-it-yourself home kits, Tara had consulted a professional at sixteen. She'd done her research by scouring all the fashion magazines, sought out the best colorist in New York, and, after pestering her mother for permission, ultimately won her over and got both the permission and the money to pay for the appointment. From then on, she was blond in that archetypal California blond way (long, straight locks streaked with thin, magical threads of strawberry and banana and copper and platinum, tresses that look like the work of a constant and benevolent sun). There's nothing worse than a blonde with no shine, and Tara shone.

And she didn't simply *have* the hair; she used it as a prop. She shook her head a lot, which required that she reach up and finger-brush away the strands that fell into her eyes. She appeared to perspire heavily, which required that she lift her hair with both hands so she could air out the back of her neck. She was athletic, which required that she reconfigure her hair to suit each level of difficulty—a ponytail with barrettes for tennis, a French braid with a bow for volleyball, a half-up and half-down do for cheerleading. She parted it on the side—on either side—as well as in the middle, and sometimes pulled it straight back. She had the sort of even-featured face that allowed for such flexibility. Even-featured—yeah, right. An understatement.

Tara's face could accurately be described as heart-shaped, and everything was exactly where it was supposed to be on it—hazel eyes, slightly upturned nose, generous but not distracting mouth, assertive chin with a hint of a cleft.

Her figure was always enviable, even back when I was still trying to shed my baby fat. She had thin hips, a reasonable bust, a flat stomach, and a graceful neck. And she had long legs, as I've already indicated, but there was trouble with those legs, which is to say they were the source of her single physical imperfection: Tara Messer was knock-kneed! Not obscenely, but enough to notice. I smiled when I remembered that this flaw existed and that not even the ever-glib, ever-persuasive, ever-magnetic Tara could talk her way out of it. Yep, she was knock-kneed and self-conscious about it, and as much as it pains me to admit this, I was ecstatic the day I first detected it, because I actually believed it might level the playing field.

What else made Tara such a hit in life? She had style—the right clothes and accessories for every occasion. For example, she was on top of trends well before I even knew they *were* trends, and she could always pull them off, even the outrageous ones. She could go with a hippie, bohemian look one day and do a debutante-with-pearls look the next, while I was still preoccupied with whether hemlines were heading up or down.

But the main reason she was so popular, at least when we were kids, was that she had energy, and I'm not talking about some New Agey type of flow. I mean she had bounce, stamina, liveliness. She was one of those people who initiated, stirred the pot, was never afraid of taking a risk. She was fun to be around back then—the silly, mischievous, giggle-till-you-drop kind of fun. "Let's call boys and hang up," she'd suggest. Or: "Let's take the train into New York and not tell our parents." Or: "Let's go skinny-dipping." My conflict in those days was that she made me feel special by virtue of the affection she showed me, but at the same time she made me feel inferior by virtue of the affection everyone showed her.

I sighed as I flashed back yet again to the scene with her and Stuart in the bedroom. The ache was still there, but even more fresh was the bafflement. What I continued to wonder was this: Why does someone who has it all want what you have instead?

4

Tara's manuscript was entitled *Simply Beautiful*, and I should never have read it on an empty stomach. It was a book that oozed with warmed-over, recycled ideas belonging to both well-known sages on the subject of inner beauty—like the Dalai Lama, Deepak Chopra, and, it goes without saying, Oprah—and to well-known sages on the subject of outer beauty—like makeup artist Bobbi Brown and that pioneer of pulchritude, Cher. There were tips on how to feel beautiful when you're paying bills (put some Enya on the stereo and an arrangement of flowers on your desk and wear a "happy color" like yellow), how to feel beautiful when you've got the blahs (go out and buy yourself a trinket such as a seashell, a letter opener, or a spanking new toothbrush), and, of course, how to feel beautiful while taking a bath (sprinkle fresh lemon juice in the bathwater, along with, perhaps, some Shalimar, use a terry-cloth face mitt and some delicious lavendar soap, and give yourself at least an hour in order to have a truly restorative soak). There were suggestions on coating the mouthpiece of your telephone with vanilla, making up your shopping list with a fountain pen instead of a standard-issue Bic, and studying up on your constellations and then going for a stargazing walk when the moon is full. No kidding. Most painful for me was the long discussion of how Tara herself practiced the art of living beautifully with her simply beautiful husband, Stuart. She explained how she kept him enchanted by writing him flirtatious little notes and leaving them where he least expected them; by applying a few drops of orange-blossom oil on the special ring she fitted atop the lightbulbs in the lamps in their bedroom; and by—get this—reading him poetry before they fell asleep at night. Oh, and she recommended that we women invest in a pair of lacy black stockings and a garter belt.

What I found amazing was that the old Tara, the wild and crazy party girl turned sedate surburban princess, seemed to have reinvented herself yet again. She was still self-involved, as well as enterprising, it was plain to see, but with a sort of "feng shui meets the Happy Hooker" approach. What killed me was that she was going to make money off the crap she was peddling. What also killed me was that I was going to help her make money off it. She'd be a shoo-in for talk shows and women's magazines and newspaper features, and by the time I was done publicizing her, she'd be a best-selling author. A best-selling author who was married to the man I was supposed to have married. You can understand why I was so grossed-out about all this, right?

I went to work on Monday, knowing I'd have to bite the bullet, call Tara and arrange a meeting. Since we were publishing *Simply Beautiful* in only six months, there was no time to waste when it came to formulating a publicity campaign. After a conversation with Betsy, during which we discussed the budget for the book, I sketched out a plan, which she endorsed in her own special way. "This looks good on paper," she said, "but it's pie in the sky unless you get results." Yeah, so *you* can take the bow, I thought to myself.

When I got back to my office, my assistant, Scott Poland, a gay man in his twenties, told me I'd had a phone call.

"Do we know a Tara Messer?" he asked. Scott was very proprietary with his "we" this and "we" that, and I found it extremely touching. He made me feel as if he and I were in the wacky world of promoting authors together, as opposed to me being the one who did the heavy lifting and him being the one who watched me do it, which was the reality. I don't mean to suggest that he was lazy, but, unlike the other three members of my department, he was more interested in schmoozing than working. He was a championship-caliber gossip, someone who knew everything—from who was taking whose job to who was sleeping with whose boss. He had the ear-to-the-ground radar that I lacked, and I had the skill and experience that he lacked, so between the two of us, we made a damn good publicity director.

"Tara called?" I said. Couldn't she at least have let me be the one to call her first?

"Yeah. A few minutes ago," said Scott. "Who is she? Oh, wait." He nodded, stroked his goatee. "She's the author Julie Farrell just signed up. I heard about the book last week."

"Of course you did." If a bird farted in Estonia, Scott heard about it. "We'll be doing a big campaign for the book, so Tara was probably calling to set up a meeting, God help me."

"*God help me?* What's this?" Scott cocked his head at me. He was adorable, with spiky sandy hair, bright blue eyes, and a tall, thin body. Like me, he wasn't in a romantic relationship or even dating anybody. The difference was that he hadn't bragged to anybody that he was. "I detect a note of resentment, Amy. We're not wild about this Tara person, are we?"

"Nope," I admitted. No point in trying to hide anything from Scott. "She and I were best friends growing up, but we had a falling-out a few years ago."

"About?"

"Guess."

"A guy."

"A cliché, I know."

"She was your best friend and she stole your guy and we hate her now?"

"We do. Or maybe we just hate what she did. Either way, we're not looking forward to working on her book, but we're going to do it anyway because we're professionals."

He considered this for a second. "You're the professional,

honey. Say the word and you'll be in charge of working on her book and I'll be in charge of sabotaging your efforts."

I shook my head. "If the book doesn't sell, everybody here will blame me. So we'll do our best with it. Both of us."

"Your choice. Just one question."

"What?"

"How does someone not on a daytime soap opera come to have the name Tara?"

"Her parents were watching *Gone With the Wind* the night she was conceived."

"Sweet, but why didn't they name her Scarlett, or Melanie, or—what was the Butterfly McQueen character?—Prissy?"

I laughed for the first time in days. "Oh, she's definitely not a Prissy. Her parents named her after the house because it represented security, and Tara is the most secure woman you'll ever meet."

"Are we talking about a diva?"

"No, not a diva. Just a prom queen. An ambitious prom queen, who always gets what she's after."

"Call her immediately," said Scott, passing me the Post-it note with Tara's number on it. "I must see this treasure for myself."

I closed the door to my office, took a few deep breaths and called Tara at her nouveau Tara in Westchester. A woman answered.

"Ms. Messer's office."

Ms. Messer's office? Give me a break. Tara was a local radio host, not the CEO of an international corporation, and her "office" was probably a guest room. Assuming the person on the other end of the phone was her secretary, what did this secretary do? Pay her Neiman Marcus bills? With Enya playing on the stereo? How simply beautiful.

"Is Tara there, please?" I said. "This is Amy Sherman, returning her call."

"Oh, right. I'll see if she's free. Would you hold?"

Hold this, I thought, wondering if Tara was busy soaking in a tub of Shalimar or perhaps leaving a flirtatious little note in one of Stuart's jockstraps. Or, since it was nearly noon, perhaps he had dashed home from work for a matinee and now they were soaking together in the tub of Shalimar.

After a minute or so, Tara picked up. "Amy. Hi, hi, hi."

"You sound rushed," I said, aware that my speech was sort of deadpan. I suppose I was trying to hold my emotions in check. "Did I catch you at a bad time?"

"No, not at all. I'm just so glad you called me back. I wasn't sure you would."

"Of course I called you back," I said. "We're going to be working together, Tara. I must say I was surprised when I heard you'd written a book and that L and T would be publishing it. You didn't mention it when we ran into each other on the street."

"I know, but I thought it would be better if you didn't hear about it from me. Look, Amy, the last thing I want to do is force myself on you. Not after what happened between us."

I had no interest in rehashing what had happened between us. More to the point, I didn't believe for a second that the last thing she wanted to do was force herself on me. She must have jumped for joy when she found out I was in charge of publicity at the publishing house that had acquired her book. Now she had a brand-new way to make me feel like her slave.

"Why don't we put the past behind us and concentrate on *Simply Beautiful*," I said, a declaration that Marianne would have applauded. "I've read the manuscript and—"

"Did you like it?" she asked, breathless with the possibility of being fawned over.

"It's very commercial," I said, avoiding the question. "I think it will sell extremely well. We're living in a precarious world, Tara—a time of genuine uncertainty, a time when women are yearning to get in touch with their, uh, inner beauty." Vomit. Vomit. Vomit. "The climate couldn't be better for a book like yours."

"I'm so glad," she said. "Now, what can I do to help the cause? I'm up for anything."

Up for anything. Yes, I remember that about you, I

thought, replaying the night that Tara was supposed to sleep over at my house and invited half the school to stop by. My parents were in Arizona, looking at condos (they moved there a few years later, due to my mother's asthma), and since Tara and I had reached the ripe old age of sixteen, they figured we could take care of ourselves. Imagine their surprise when they got home and found the house destroyed. Well, not destroyed, but not the way they'd left it. Tara was the one who spread the word that there'd be a party and I was the one who was grounded for a month. Typical. She had this uncanny knack for stirring up trouble and leaving me to pick up the pieces. Even after I explained to my parents that it was she who'd broken their rules, it was I who'd been punished. She'd just bat her eyelashes, flip her golden hair, say the right thing, and then—presto—you couldn't stay mad at her.

Only I did stay mad at her, I thought, pulling myself back to the present. I'd stayed mad at her for nearly four years, since the second I walked in on her and Stuart. It wasn't a lifetime, but it was probably a record.

5

Tara and I agreed that we should meet to discuss her book. We just couldn't agree on where to meet. I suggested my office. She suggested her house. I suggested Julie Farrell's office. She suggested her house. I suggested a restaurant—any restaurant. She suggested her house.

"You're the public-relations expert, Amy, and I wouldn't dream of trying to tell you how to do your job," she said, "but if you're going to be pitching me to the media as someone who's written a book about a simply beautiful lifestyle, shouldn't you come up here and see *my* simply beautiful lifestyle? I could show you the whole enchilada and then you'd have a genuine understanding of the simply beautiful idiom."

Of the simply beautiful idiot, too, I thought, wondering how Tara had conned L and T into buying the book in the first place.

She did have a point about my going up to see her house, however. As much as I hated to admit it and as much as I had no desire to set foot inside the love nest she and Stuart shared, it was true that I'd get a better handle on her whole enchilada if I witnessed it for myself.

"Okay, Tara," I said. "I'll drive up."

"Fabulous," she said. "I'll have Michelle make us lunch."

"Michelle?"

"Yes, my cook."

Her cook. Please. "I don't eat peppers," I said, just to be annoying. "Or anything with curry in it."

"I already know that, Amy," she said. "We were best friends once, remember? You don't eat peppers, curry, or hearts of palm. I have it all written down in my Hostess Diary."

"Your what?"

"My Hostess Diary. It's in the book. In order to be a simply beautiful hostess, you have to note the foods your guests like and dislike, so you don't offend them or, God forbid, make them sick."

Tara offended me and made me sick, but a job was a job.

I told Connie I was having lunch chez Tara, and she suggested I take along a little arsenic and force it down Tara's simply beautiful throat. I told Scott, too, and he suggested I tape our conversation so that he wouldn't miss a single simply beautiful word. But it was my mother's reaction to the forthcoming lunch that floored me. When she called from Arizona that night for her weekly check-in and I explained that Tara and I had not only spoken after our four-year estrangement but made a date, she was actually happy about it.

"I'm delighted that you girls are friends again," she said, then cupped her hand over the phone and yelled at my father to turn down the TV.

"We're not friends again," I said emphatically. "We're stuck with each other because of her book. But why would you be delighted in any case? Tara married Stuart, the man who was supposed to be *my* husband and *your* son-in-law. Has that little detail slipped your mind, Mom?"

"Of course, it hasn't," she said. "I was as heartbroken as you were when it happened. Your father and I were paying for the wedding, don't forget. We lost our deposit on the flowers and the DJ, although the people at the Elm Creek Inn let us off the hook."

"Okay, so you lost money on the deal. But how about your

disappointment, your anger at Tara for what she did? How
can you want me to be friendly with her now?"

"Oh, honey, honey." She sighed. "You know how angry
we were, but what's done is done and we can't change it.
What I'm saying is that you and Tara were like sisters once
upon a time. You were joined at the hip. You loved each
other. I remember that part, too."

Well, she was right that Tara and I had been inseparable.
Since I was an only child and my parents both worked, I was
desperate for company, and Tara more than filled the bill
with her golden looks and golden personality. My house was
always so quiet, except when she breezed in to liven things
up. It wasn't very attractive, either—a fifties ranch on a
postage-stamp piece of property, a house that lacked the ele-
gance and graciousness of the Messers' colonial across
town. It was in their house that I'd longed to live. Tara had
three siblings—an older brother and two younger sisters—
so their place was raucous and entertaining and bustling
with activity. I felt lucky to be included in their family out-
ings and grateful that Tara had picked me as her bosom
buddy, but that didn't mean that now I had to forgive and forget the not so swell aspects of our friendship, did it?

The much-dreaded lunch date was the following Tuesday.
With Scott holding down the fort at work, I made the half-
hour hop up to the town of Mamaroneck in lower Westchester County. During the drive, I reminded myself over and
over that Tara was just another author, not someone I cared
about, and that I owed her my professional expertise, nothing more. She'll never suck me in again, I vowed as I exited
off the Hutchinson River Parkway. I'll promote her book to
the best of my ability, but that's it.

Tara and Stuart, it turned out, lived in a grand Tudor-style
manor house on three sumptuously landscaped acres over-
looking Long Island Sound. I'm talking megaexpensive real
estate here, with the taxes to match. As I pulled into the cir-
cular driveway, I realized that I was openmouthed. It wasn't

as if I'd never seen such opulence or even that I was awed by big houses in general. I'd outgrown my childhood fascination with the way people with money lived. It was the way these particular people with money lived that got to me. I guess it hadn't dawned on me just how rich Stuart was.

His full name was Stuart Lasher, and he, along with his father and brother, owned Lasher's Meats & Eats, a small chain of gourmet food stores with three outlets in the tristate area. Yes, of course, I knew he had money. As I've indicated, my engagement ring was worth enough to the diamond merchant who bought it from me to pay for my three years in therapy with Marianne. But until I drove up to his new digs and actually observed the grandeur, I suppose it hadn't registered. I mean, Lasher's Meats & Eats wasn't exactly Wal-Mart. But what did I know? Maybe family businesses that sold ten different kinds of mushrooms were worth a fortune.

"Oh, Amy! Here you are," said Tara, who swung open the front door the instant after I rang the bell. Before I could stop her, she drew me into a hug—not one of those air-kissy affairs where you don't even brush up against the other person, but a *hug*. Imagine my surprise! When we'd had our chance meeting on the street, we hadn't so much as shaken hands! It was one of the oddest moments of my life, partly because her arms were draped around my shoulders, while my arms were dangling at my sides, and partly because she smelled of apples. Ah, yes, I thought, recalling the section of *Simply Beautiful* where Tara advised us to simmer apple cider on the stove with some cinnamon, cloves, and tangerines, and then lean into the aromatic vapor, so our hair, our skin, and our clothes would take on the scent of home and hearth and—gag—honesty.

"Hi, Tara," I said, extricating myself. "Nice to see you." See her? I couldn't miss her. Her Blondeness was a vision in the bright red sweater she wore with black jeans. I assumed she had chosen red because, as she asserted in her book, it's the essential color when you want others to view you as a woman of action. What was even scarier than her little apho-

risms was the fact that, the Hostess Diary aside, I had actually committed them to memory.

"Come in, come in," she said, ushering me inside the
house, the interior of which was straight out of *Architectural
Digest*. For someone who was preaching simplicity, there
was a lot of complicated decorating going on in there—from
the array of lushly upholstered chairs and sofas in the living
room, to the impeccably restored antique pieces in the dining room, to the wainscoted glass cabinets, the granite coun-
tertops, and the requisite super-duper appliances in the
kitchen/family room, to the buttery leather furniture in the
wood-paneled library, where, by the way, there was a crack-
ling fire in the fireplace, even though it was a balmy sixty-
eight degrees outside. "Let's sit in the sunroom," she said,
just when I thought we'd run out of rooms.

"Oh, let's," I said as she kept leading me through the
house and I kept trying not to stare at the silver-framed pho-
tos of her and Stuart that were virtually everywhere. There
was a picture of them on a beach, sipping drinks with little
umbrellas in them. There was a picture of them kissing in
front of some castle in Scotland. There was a picture of them
at the entrance to their own little castle in Mamaroneck (Stuart was carrying Tara over the threshold). And there was a
picture—the one I was both looking forward to and hoping
to avoid—of them feeding each other cake at their wedding.
I felt a stab of jealousy, then reminded myself that I didn't
love Stuart and didn't want to be his wife, no matter how
much money he raked in.

Tara and I sat together on linen-cushioned rattan chairs in
the sunroom, a glass-enclosed, tile-floored solarium that was
ablaze with color, thanks to the profusion of flowers in
pretty pottery vases. I commented that the tulips, in particular, were lovely.

"Fresh flowers are an essential part of the *Simply Beautiful* message," she said, running her fingers through her still-
stupefyingly great hair. "They provide nourishment for our
homes. They're a simple way to bring beauty into our lives."

"Sort of like using multicolored paper clips instead of the plain old silver ones?"

"Wow, Amy. I'm so glad that my paper clip anecdote in chapter eleven resonated with you. And I'm impressed that you actually read the whole book."

"That's what I do, Tara. I read the books I'm assigned to promote, yours included."

She smiled, flashing me the teeth that had been through braces and retainers and all the paraphernalia mine had. We'd gone to the same draconian orthodontist as teenagers. I couldn't help remembering the day when I yawned in math class and one of those awful rubber bands flew out of my mouth and landed on the desk of Chuck Curley, the captain of the varsity football team. I was mortified, naturally, but Tara thought it was a riot. To prove it, she yanked one of her own rubber bands out of her mouth and flicked it onto Chuck's desk. Everyone thought she was the coolest girl on the planet for doing that, and I was no exception. What I didn't realize then was that she did it not to support me, but to steal the attention. And now here she was, grabbing the limelight again, only this time as some sort of spiritualist author/lady of the manor.

"Getting back to flowers," she said, "I advocate that people should budget for them, the way they budget for food. Buying just one hyacinth or iris or black-eyed Susan and setting it on a table where you see it day in and day out can make the difference between feeling beautiful and feeling blah."

Blah. Now there was an adjective I could certainly throw at the editor of the *New York Times Book Review* without embarrassment. "Why don't you tell me how you came to write your book," I said, pulling out my legal pad and a pen. "What inspired you to write it?"

"I wrote it at the urging of friends and family and, of course, Stuart," she said. I only flinched slightly at the mention of his name. "They all kept telling me that I have a knack for making every day fun and special, whether it's the way I dress, or apply my makeup, or arrange a platter of strawberries. I'm not much of a chef, as you probably re-

member, Amy, but I do know how food should look—how
lots of things should look, I guess. So I decided to jot down
my own personal guide for living beautifully, and it evolved
into this book. My goal is to lift women up, to speak to their
souls."

As I nodded and made notes, trying not to roll my eyes,
she went on about the simple beauty of butter sizzling musi-
cally in a frying pan; of a scented candle flickering in a darkened room; of a particular shade of lipstick showing up at a
cosmetics counter after being out of stock. At a certain
point, I nearly wilted from having my soul uplifted. Tara
mistook my fatigue for hunger.

"Let's see if Michelle, my cook, has our lunch ready," she
said, bouncing up from the chair.

Her "cook" did have our lunch ready, only she was actually her "part-time housekeeper."

"Michelle comes in four days a week to clean," Tara explained, "but she makes the most marvelous poached salmon
for me whenever I have guests. Other entrées too, of course."

Of course. "It's delicious," I said, barely tasting the fish,
or the sprigs of dill that adorned it, or the dash of mint that
floated in my iced tea. I was dying to eat a candy bar—anything that wasn't garnished.

We continued to discuss the book over lunch. While I was
bored stiff, I was relieved, too—relieved that Tara hadn't
once asked about my engagement. It occurred to me, as I
chuckled silently, that I needn't have worried about having
to fess up about the Lie. She was far too self-involved to remember I'd even mentioned a fiancé. Besides, why would
she care about my romantic life when she had Stu boy? According to her, they were as deliriously happy as two narcis-
sists could be. Yes, in between her riffs on the profound
pleasures to be discovered in rainbows and kittens and
freshly laundered sheets, she wedged in a soliloquy about
how loving Stuart was, how sensitive to her needs, how enthusiastic about her career, and how eager he was to have a
baby and watch the little tyke grow up and assume his or her
place at Lasher's Meats & Eats.

At two o'clock, I'd had enough, and I announced that I had to drive back to the office.

"Is it because I've been talking about Stuart?" she asked. "I guess I shouldn't have brought him up."

"Stuart's your husband," I said, rising from my chair. "You've written about him in the book. He's a major part of your life. I can't ignore his existence, as much as I'd prefer to."

She smiled. "He and I wondered how you would feel coming here today. We thought you might be upset, but you seem okay with everything. Tell the truth. This hasn't been so bad with just the two of us chatting away like old times, right?"

Cardinal rule in publishing: *Never* tell an author the truth. "It's been fine," I said. "But I really do have to leave. I have other books to work on."

"Of course," she said. I walked toward the front door. She trailed after me. "It's just that we haven't talked about you, Amy. Now that we're friends again, I was hoping you'd share a little bit about your life. How are your parents?"

We were not friends again, and why did she think we were? Because I was being polite? I was just doing my job, for God's sake! "My parents are alive and well, thanks."

"They're still in Arizona?"

"Yep." I didn't ask about her parents or Stuart's. I had to get out of there before she peppered me with more questions. We were standing at her door. I had one foot *out* the door, actually. "Listen, I appreciate the lunch and the tour of the house. It was very helpful. I have some good solid background information now, so I can sit down and turn out an effective press release. I'll be in touch when there's copy for you to look over."

I headed for my car, my escape a tantalizing few seconds away.

"Wait!" she called out. "You didn't tell me a single thing about your man."

Damn! Damn! Damn! So she hadn't forgotten. In a split second, having made the decision to feign ignorance, I said, "What man?"

She giggled. "Boy, you *are* into your job. I'm talking about your man, your honey, your fiancé."

Quick. New strategy. "He's great," I said, ducking inside my car. "A really, really great guy. Successful, handsome, everything I could ever want, and, most important, the only man I've ever loved." I had to slip in that last one, just so she'd get it that I wasn't all broken up about losing Stuart.

"Well, you deserve him, because you're a wonderful person," she said, causing me to feel guilty all of a sudden. "And he's a lucky, lucky guy to have you. Oh wow. I just remembered that you two are getting married in six months, which is around the same time that my book comes out. Promise me you won't be on your honeymoon the day I'm making my national television debut on *The View,* okay?"

Scrap the guilt. She was thinking only of herself, as usual. "Actually, I *could* be on my honeymoon the day you're on *The View,*" I said, digging myself a deeper hole but feeling a nice little buzz at the thought of giving her the jitters. "But I'm sure there won't be a problem. My assistant is more than capable of taking you to all your appearances."

"How about the wedding ceremony? Are you having big, small, formal, casual, what?"

I was about to toss out an answer—any answer—when it occurred to me that Tara would probably repeat whatever I said to Julie Farrell, her editor, who, of course, would know nothing about my impending marriage and start asking questions of her own. "As a matter of fact, my fiancé and I have been keeping a very low profile," I explained. "We haven't told anyone at Lowry and Trammell that we're even a couple. We're planning to have a small, very intimate wedding and then tell everyone, so I'd appreciate it if you'd keep all this to yourself for now."

"Oh. Gosh. I'm incredibly flattered that you confided in me, that you trusted me, because it confirms that we're friends again." Wrong. "I won't breathe a word, I swear, but why the hush-hush? Is it because your fiancé works at Lowry and Trammell, too, and they have a policy against interoffice romances?"

"Something like that," I said. "Thanks for understanding. Well, gotta go." I closed the car door, inserted my key in the ignition, and was ready to roll.

"Obviously, I've never worked in the corporate world the way you have," she said while I started the car. "But I don't think it's fair the way they try to regulate people's personal lives. It must be horrible to have to carry on a relationship in secret."

"I bet it wasn't so horrible for you and Stuart," I blurted out before I could stop myself. Well, what did she expect? She had just given me an opening as big as her ego.

"Sorry. What did you say?" she asked, unable to hear me over the engine noise—or pretending she couldn't.

"Never mind," I said as I stepped on the gas and waved bye-bye.

6

When Tara called my office bright and early the next morning, I told Scott to tell her I was in a meeting. When she called again around noon, I told him to tell her I was on my way to lunch. When she called again later in the afternoon, I told him to tell her I was dead.

"She wants to speak to you, Amy, and she's not going to be deterred," said Scott. "I can feel her determination coursing through the phone lines."

"She can wait," I said. "I spent hours with her yesterday. There's nothing more about her book that I need to hear right now."

"She says she's not calling about the book. She says it's a personal matter." He sniffed. "Apparently, you didn't explain to her that there aren't any personal matters you don't share with me."

There was one, and I couldn't share it with Scott. Telling him about my supposed engagement would be like advertising on the Internet.

"She claims it's urgent, too," he added.

"All right, I'll call her," I said as Scott continued to hover. "*After* you've given me a little privacy."

He sniffed again and left my office.

I called Tara, whose urgent private matter involved inviting me and my fiancé to dinner.

"I thought it would be fun for both of you," she said. "Well, fun for Stuart and me, too, of course, but, more to the point, it'll be an opportunity for you and your fiancé to socialize openly instead of having to sneak around. I still can't get over that L and T has such a silly rule about coworkers not being allowed to date, because I always figured publishers to be so, you know, *liberal*. It must be incredibly frustrating that you two can't be seen in public at the precise time in your relationship when you should be out there proclaiming your love to all the world."

Sheesh. What had I done now? "It *is* frustrating that he and I have to stay undercover, so to speak," I said, "but we're both so busy with work that we just try to grab moments alone whenever we can. And speaking of work, I've got to rush into another—"

"Which is why I thought I'd give you a reprieve from all that," she persisted. "You two can drive up and have dinner with us at the house without fear of getting caught. Nobody will bother you here—except the occasional deer frolicking amid our specimen plantings."

You'll bother me, I was dying to say, but I couldn't risk offending an author and infuriating Betsy. Instead, I said, "Thanks for thinking of us, but we can't come for dinner. Things are too hectic at work."

"Oh." She paused, as if regrouping for another go-round, which didn't surprise me. This was the woman who never took no for an answer, because she never had to. "Okay, I get it now," she said. "It isn't about work at all, is it? It's about Stuart."

"Stuart?"

"Yes. After coming here yesterday and seeing what a happy life he and I have carved out for ourselves, you went home depressed about what might have been. But look, I don't blame you at all—not for being depressed and not for being envious. It's only natural. You were in love with Stuart. You were going to marry Stuart. Stuart's an amazing

man. Maybe you still care for him and you're down on yourself for not being able to hold on to him and you're worried
that bringing your fiancé up here to meet him would only
cause you to second-guess yourself. That's it, isn't it, Amy?
That you're just not over Stuart in spite of your efforts to
move on with your life?"

Well, I was so angry, I could hardly speak. She was accusing me of being depressed? Envious? Still hot for her
husband? Talk about patronizing! Talk about insufferable! It
wasn't bad enough that I'd had to sit in her sunroom and listen to her lecture me on ways to reduce water retention?
Now I had to listen to her feel sorry for me because I
wasn't—how had she put it?—"able to hold on to him." I
wanted to tell her to take a flying leap! But I had to keep my
mouth shut, had to keep my cool, or risk losing my job. I
had to put a pin in my fury, or sublimate it, or perhaps
rechannel it.

Yes, rechannel it, I thought. That's what I'll do. I'll show
both of those bozos that I'm not someone to be pitied—but
I'll do it by embracing them, not by rebuffing them.

"I've changed my mind. My fiancé and I *will* come for
dinner," I said to Tara, aware that I was about to go from
garden-variety liar to budding sociopath. Judge me if you
must, but I'd had enough of her bullshit and felt like slinging
a little of my own.

"You will?" she said.

"Yes," I said. "We'll come in the very near future, but I'll
have to get back to you with the date."

Not to mention the name of the date.

I was upset about my conversation with Tara and desperate
for a good long unburdening in front of the compassionate
yet costly Marianne. I was looking for support, as well as
sound, objective advice, but, as I've said, I didn't want to
crawl back to her like a kid who flunks a grade and has to repeat it. And so I did the next best thing: I twisted Connie's
arm into coming over after work. Usually, she rushed home
to Murray each night, but when I told her I'd accepted Tara's

invitation on behalf of me and my fiancé, she agreed that I was needier than Murray was.

I lived in a two-bedroom, two-bath condo on the tenth floor of a twenty-story building that was relatively new, and well maintained, and in a desirable part of the city. The apartment had hardwood floors, high ceilings, and a balcony, and I'd furnished it with a combination of Pier 1 items, flea market finds, and relics from my college dorm. It had a style I'd call "calculated funky," and until I'd visited Tara at her palace, I'd felt really good about it. But now that she'd raised the bar by reinserting herself in my life, I wasn't sure how I felt about anything.

"Just call her and say you can't make it after all," Connie suggested as she gnawed on what was left of the chicken leg I'd cooked on my George Foreman grill. She was a little wisp of a thing, as I've described, but she could pack it away.

"If I did, she'd only keep bugging me about it." I sighed. "This is the problem with lies. They multiply, like some scary bacteria."

"So what are you gonna do?"

"The only thing I can do. I have to find a guy to pretend to be my fiancé. As a favor. For one night."

She surrendered the leg, wiped her hands and mouth with her napkin, and took a sip of white wine. "You do realize that the pickings are slim if we're talking about a guy at L and T."

"What choice do I have? Tara's convinced that my heartthrob is someone I work with, so we might as well start there."

"We?"

"Yeah. You're going to help me think of someone."

Several seconds of silence went by. Connie didn't so much as clear her throat.

"Well?" I said.

"I'm thinking," she said, "and coming up empty."

"Think harder."

More silence. "Most of the guys are married," she said finally. "Their wives aren't gonna let them play kissy face with you at some author's house."

"I know."

"What about Scott?"

"My Scott?"

"Yeah. He's cute and gay and not seeing anybody. I bet he'd do it."

I shook my head. "He can't keep a secret to save his life. He'd blab about this to anyone who'd listen, including Celebetsy's assistant, who'd tell Julie's assistant, who'd tell Julie, who'd tell Tara. Keep thinking."

"What about Eddie Glickman?"

"Yech," I said, picturing our VP of sales. "He's not my type."

"I didn't think the guy had to be your 'type.' I thought he just had to be willing to play your fiancé for a night."

"True, but Eddie is overweight, obnoxious, and smells bad."

"Like I said, you don't have to give birth to his love child."

"Connie, the whole idea is to show Tara up, to impress her, to prove to her and to Stuart that I'm over them both. I can't do that with a fiancé who's a total turnoff. I need someone who's bright, articulate, funny, and great-looking—someone who'll make Tara and Stuart go, 'Wow. Amy sure has landed on her feet after what we put her through.'"

"In case you haven't noticed, we don't have any single men at L and T who are bright, articulate, funny, and great-looking. Oh, wait. There's Michael Ollin in Business Affairs, but he's an accountant, so I can't vouch for the 'funny.'"

"Let's put him on the list." I scribbled his name on the pad I'd brought to the table.

"What about Alex Cashman?" She was referring to our science fiction and fantasy editor. He and I had dated briefly. It was going pretty well until I admitted to him that I'd fallen asleep during the first *Lord of the Rings* movie. He dropped me so fast, I didn't know what hit me.

"I doubt he'd do it," I said. "Who else?"

"Can't think of anyone else."

"What about agents and authors? I didn't tell Tara my fiancé was on L and T's payroll, exactly. I just told her he and I worked together and that we weren't supposed to fraternize."

"Can't think of any agents you'd go for. And forget my mystery writers. They're a strange breed, which isn't all that surprising, considering that they spend their days plotting murders. What about your contacts in the media? Isn't there some book reviewer you can coax into doing this?"

"Never," I said. "Book reviewers are the most difficult people on the face of the earth. Look at how hard it is to get them to like a book. They sneer at every—"

I was interrupted by the ringing of Connie's cell phone. It was Murray calling. He was hungry, he said. Connie told him to look in the freezer for the lasagna. He said he saw the lasagna but didn't know how to defrost it. In the microwave, she told him. "I don't know how to use it," he told her.

"Gotta go home," she said after giving him step-by-step instructions. "Murray's lonely."

"Speaking of Murray," I said, "does he have any artist friends who'd pose as my fiancé for a night? They'd get a free meal out of it."

She laughed. "Murray's artist friends don't have clean clothes, don't wear shoes, don't even use utensils when they eat. I wouldn't invite them to dinner at a zoo."

"That bad?"

She nodded.

"Oh, Connie. Can't you stay for dessert?" I said, trying to tempt her with the chocolate cake in the refrigerator.

"Thanks anyway," she said, "but I'd better head home if I wanna make sure Murray doesn't nuke the whole place. The last time he tried to use the microwave, he forgot to put the food in it."

As I walked her to the elevator and hugged her good night, I thought how lucky she was. She didn't have to pretend to have a man who loved her. She had a real one. He wasn't rich and he couldn't operate your basic kitchen appliance and his passion, other than her, was painting black squiggles on blue canvases, but he was faithful and true, which, given my experience with the opposite sex, was saying something.

7

I went to work the next morning dressed to kill—or, rather, to attract the attention of hunky Michael Ollin in Business Affairs. Since I didn't know him very well and didn't have a lot of time to get to know him, I thought some slinky attire was in order. Normally circumspect in terms of my appearance, I threw on a clingy black dress, strappy black heels, and a little more makeup than usual.

"Hi, Michael. How're you doing?" I said after sashaying into his office. As a pretext for the visit, I was carrying a file containing the expenses an author had incurred on his book tour. This author had a drinking problem and expected us to pay his triple-digit liquor bills.

"I'm super," said Michael, who was tall, dark, and handsome. Oh, and he was tan, and it wasn't even summer yet. He was dressed nicely, too—expensive suit and tie, pinstriped shirt, wing-tipped shoes. I wasn't crazy about the gargantuan Rolex and the equally gargantuan gold bracelet, but even more off-putting than his jewelry was his cologne. Not only was it overpowering in its woodiness and muskiness but he applied it with a very heavy hand. In other words, his office needed to be fumigated.

"I was hoping to talk to you about some author expenses," I said as I imagined asking him to pretend to be engaged to me. I also imagined telling him he'd have to wash the cologne off his face, not to mention have his entire wardrobe dry-cleaned, before I could even think of putting him in the same room with Tara.

"Sure. Have a seat, Amy. You're looking mighty fine today, by the way. Migh-ty fine. And I don't mind telling you it's nice to see a woman dress like a woman for a change. This place isn't exactly a magnet for bodilicious females."

Okay, so this wasn't going to work. There had to be other men inhabiting the offices of L and T—men who'd be up for helping out a coworker but wouldn't use words like *bodilicious*.

But just to be absolutely certain that I wasn't jumping to conclusions or being too judgmental, I hung in a little longer. After we chatted about the alcoholic author, I asked Michael if he was enjoying the warm spring weather.

"You bet," he said. "I've been going to the Hamptons on weekends. You should come out to our place sometime, Amy. We've got plenty of room."

"Who's 'we'?"

"My girlfriend and I."

His girlfriend? He was flirting with me even though he was seeing somebody else? Living with somebody else?

"Why the look?" he said. "My lady's very sweet. She gives me my space."

"Are you saying she lets you—"

"Be with other women? She doesn't *let* me. I just do what I want, figuring what she doesn't know won't hurt her. Our Hamptons place has a very private guest room, so if you come out there, I could arrange for us to have lots of time alone together."

I just stared at him.

"Are you shocked?" he said.

"Of course I'm shocked," I replied.

"Why? Because I'm an accountant and accountants are supposed to be square?"

"No. Because you're a human being and human beings are supposed to be trustworthy."

God, what a creep. It was thanks to men like him that therapists like Marianne had thriving practices.

Fine, so he's not the one, I thought, calming myself, remembering that I just needed a guy for one night. I mean, how hard could it be to find him?

Even though he'd dumped me for not seeing the merits of *The Lord of the Rings,* I decided to try Alex Cashman, the science fiction editor, thinking maybe he'd mellowed toward me. He was interesting-looking in an unconventional way—curly brown hair, beard, mustache, suspenders, bow tie, sneakers even when it snowed—and very smart. Smart enough to impress Tara, I figured.

"Hey, Alex," I said after knocking on his office door. "Mind if I come in?"

He smiled. "Why should I mind?"

Oh good, I thought. Maybe he really has forgotten that he was mad at me about the Hobbit thing.

I entered his office and sat down. "I've been thinking about you lately," I said brazenly, since I didn't have time to waste. I had to skip the foreplay and find out if the guy was on or off the list. "I was just wondering how you're doing."

"That's funny, because I've been thinking about you, too," he said, playing with his mustache, which didn't have handlebars but did curve upward at each end.

"Oh," I said. "I'm glad." His answer bolstered my confidence and spurred me on. "What I've been thinking, Alex, is that we had a good thing going for a while there, you and I."

"We did," he agreed. "And I might as well confess that I feel like a pompous ass the way I acted toward you. People don't have to have the same taste in movies or books or any form of art in order to be compatible as a couple. I see that now."

"Really? I feel that way, too." Boy, this was going better than expected. So what if Alex went to *Star Trek* conventions and spoke in alienspeak when surrounded by like-minded individuals and collected rubbery toy monsters and accessorized his apartment with them? He was bright and presentable, and he'd really liked me once. Maybe he would really

like me again—enough to do me a favor and be my fiancé
for a night. "As a matter of fact, that's why I'm here," I went
on, "because I was hoping we could pick up where we left
off and resume our friendship." I looked down at the floor,
shy suddenly.

He reached across his desk and took my hand. "You're
the best, Amy. You always have been."

I looked up again. "Great. Then let's have dinner, so I can
talk to you about something. How's tonight, for example?
I'll cook for you at my place."

He released my hand and moved his across the desktop,
then lifted the picture frame that was resting there and pulled
it toward him. "I can't have dinner and I can't pick up where
we left off," he said, then showed me the photo in the frame.
It was of a woman in a ballet tutu, and she was in the midst
of a rather athletic leap. "Her name's Claudia. She's a prin-
cipal dancer with the New York City Ballet, and we've been
going out for three months. She didn't like *Lord of the Rings*
any more than you did, but I asked her to marry me last
night, and she accepted. That's why I was thinking about
you, Amy. She made me realize what a jerk I was with you."

Swell. So I'd found one who was ready and willing to be
a fiancé, just not mine. Timing is everything, isn't it?

I wished Alex well and went to the ladies' room, where I
sat on the toilet and pondered my situation. I didn't have a
next move—*that* was my situation. There was no one left on
the short list of prospective fiancés except Eddie Glickman,
the loud and obnoxious and bad-smelling vice president of
sales, and he wasn't really on the list, since I'd vetoed him.
But maybe I'd been too hasty.

I freshened my lipstick and ran a comb through my hair,
then marched off to Eddie's office. He was on the phone,
sucking up to some buyer at Barnes & Noble or Borders.
"Yeah, yeah, you are sooo right about that book," he was
saying, loudly enough for everyone in the city to hear him.
"You're a genius with covers, Cynthia. You didn't like the
big black gun with the smoke coming out of it, so we ditched
the artwork and used a samurai sword instead. That's right,

we listened to you, so now let's see you double your order for the chain, huh?" He laughed, then spotted me in his doorway and motioned me inside. "Yeah, I'll talk to you. Give my best to your better half, huh? Your puppy dog, too." He laughed again and hung up.

"Hi, Eddie," I said. I'm not even going to tell you how foul his BO was. After my description of Michael's cologne, you'll think I've got odor issues.

"Amy. What's up?" he said. While he waited for my answer, he grabbed the bag of Cheez Doodles on his desk, reached in for a handful, ate them, reached in for more, ate them, then licked the orange dust off his fingers, all the while showing me more than I ever wanted to see of his tongue.

"I was just wondering how the Georgette Peterson novel is selling," I said, for lack of a better conversation starter.

"It's not," he replied, then grabbed the can of Coke on his desk and slurped some soda. A trickle of brown liquid escaped from underneath his double chin and dripped down his neck and onto his shirt.

Yep, my first instinct was right about Eddie Glickman. He was a decent guy, but not the one I wanted Tara and Stuart to drool over. He did enough drooling of his own.

"I don't think this scheme of mine is going to work," I told Connie later that day, after sticking my head in her office before running to a meeting with Celebetsy.

"You're giving up after one day?" she said.

I shrugged. "I checked out every guy on the premises, and none of them fits the bill."

"I wish I could help, but I've got an author coming in. He should be here any minute."

"Who?"

"Tony Stiles."

I groaned. "I think I'll make myself scarce."

"He's not so bad, Amy. He's kind of a charmer, once you get past the gruff exterior."

"Believe me, there's a gruff interior, too. Every time he does publicity, he gives the interviewers fits with his one-

word answers and his 'I'm above all this' attitude. It's like
pulling teeth to get him to grace the *Today* show with his
presence on publication day—a booking most authors would
be thrilled about. Does he think he's Hemingway or something? He's a mystery writer, not some ultraliterary novelist,
and his characters are con artists, hit men, and other nut
jobs, not exactly the upper crust of society. Anyhow, he
needs to get over himself and his aversion to the media, and
stop taking his 'oeuvre' so seriously. He's like the Sean Penn
of writers."

"Maybe, but he makes a lot of money for us, so we have
to treat him like a movie star."

"*You* treat him like a movie star. I'm off to my meeting
with Celebetsy."

I was backing out of Connie's door just as Tony Stiles was
backing in, and we inadvertently head-butted each other.

"Hey!" I said, whirling around to face him just as he was
whirling around to face me.

"Hey yourself," he said, rubbing the back of his neck.
"Would it be too much to ask that you watch where you're
going?"

"No," I said, "but I didn't bang into you on purpose. I may
be clumsy, but I don't actually try to injure our authors."

"I'm sure nobody meant to hurt anybody," said Connie.
"Now, why don't you two make nice for a change."

I smiled sweetly as I shook Tony's hand, and as I did, I
had to admit that there was something movie starish about
him. He certainly had the bad-boy looks of a Sean Penn—
wavy dark hair, bushy dark eyebrows that hung over pierc-
ingly blue eyes, a slightly crooked nose, a pouty, thin-lipped
mouth, and a boxer's body, muscular but compact—and he
was the right age for a brooding leading man: mid-thirties. If
only he didn't have such a chip on his shoulder, I thought.
His books were a lot of fun, with their cast of entertaining
rascals, as well as their lovable hero, Joe West, a burned-out
cop, and his feisty yet devoted wife, Lucy. Well, maybe Connie was right and there was more to him than I realized.

"So, what's the hurry today, Amy Sherman, queen of

flacks?" he said with a smirk, tiny lines crinkling around those blue eyes. "Is there a publicity emergency going on somewhere? Do you need an author for an appearance at a Tupperware party? Or are we talking about a bigger, more prestigious booking—like a segment on the Home Shopping Network?"

On second thought, Tony Stiles didn't have a chip on his shoulder. He had a bug up his ass. But as I stood there close to him, so close that I could see glints of red in the strands of hair that curled around his ears, I found myself wondering if he ever dropped the wise-guy routine and, if so, what it would be like to be around him when he did. He was never without a girlfriend, rumor had it, so he had to be capable of at least some tenderness. Just none I'd ever witnessed.

"Actually, Tony, I'm about to pitch you to the Food Network," I said on my way out the door, my voice as perky as a publicist's should be. "They're doing a segment on what to do with beef that's extremely tough and hard to swallow. I think you'd be perfect."

8

H ave you pitched *Simply Beautiful* to the network morning shows yet?" asked Betsy, standing over me. As I felt her minty breath on the back of my neck (she was always popping Tic Tacs), I wondered why she bothered to have an office. She spent most of her time in mine.

"I've made preliminary calls," I said. "There's been interest, but no commitments. It's too early."

"It's never too early," she said. "You're supposed to create a buzz."

Buzz off. "We're not publishing the book for six months."

"Five and a half," she said. "Look, I want Tara Messer on national television, because that's what's going to bump up sales. I don't care what you have to do to make it happen. Just make sure it does. Got it?"

As she strutted into the hall, I wondered why she wasn't on Zoloft or something. Surely there was medication for people who caused other people to be depressed.

"Is it safe to come in?" asked Scott, peeking his head in the door. It was six o'clock, time to pack up and go home. I was drained from attempting to befriend my single male colleagues and was itching to climb into bed and pull the covers over my head.

"Sure," I said wearily. "What's up?"

"Hot bulletin," he said with the self-satisfied look he always assumed whenever he was about to spread potentially malicious gossip. "Betsy had lunch with the publicity director at Hartley and Hitchcock yesterday."

"Oh my God. Where'd you hear that?"

"From an assistant over there. I hate to sound paranoid, but do you think she wants to replace us?"

"It's possible. Or maybe she's just keeping her options open, in case I let a memo go out with a typo in it."

"She's such a diva. Just know that I'm your loyal servant. If I hear anything else, I won't tell anyone but you."

I smiled. "Thanks. I appreciate that."

I was about to turn off the lights, when my phone rang. Scott picked it up, then put the caller on hold.

"Guess who?" he said.

"I'm too tired to guess."

"It's Tara Firma."

I cringed. "What does she want this time?"

"She didn't say, but for two people who didn't speak to each other for four years, you and she are pretty chummy now."

"She's pretty chummy. I'm just trying to stay on Betsy's good side. Well, on her less bad side, I mean."

"At the risk of sticking my two cents in, maybe Tara's really sorry for what she did to you. Maybe she's reaching out, hoping you'll forgive her and be her best friend again."

"Maybe she is sorry, but we won't be best friends again, because her definition of friendship is different from mine. Mine is that people do things for each other. Tara's is that people do things for her; more specifically, that I do things for her."

"We're awfully cynical, aren't we?"

"We are, but we might as well see what's on her mind."

I picked up the phone. "Hi, Tara. How are you?" Dumb question. She was always great.

"I'm great," she said. "I hope I didn't catch you at a bad time."

"Actually, I was just heading out."

"Oh. Then I'll make it quick. I was calling for two reasons. The first is, I was checking to see if you'd talked to your fiancé about coming here for dinner."

"Not yet," I said, "but soon, I promise." Obviously, she wasn't going to give up on her dream of a fun-filled foursome, which made me feel even more pressure to produce the fiancé than I'd already felt. "What's the other reason you called?"

"Well, I was looking ahead to the weekend and realized that Stuart and I are both out of books. The weather's supposed to be fabulous, so we'll probably sit by the pool and be lazy. Which means we'll be up for some page-turners. Since you're in publishing, I thought maybe you could pop a couple of hot reads in the mail to us. By next day FedEx, if possible."

I was right. Her definition of friendship was me doing things for her. Nothing had changed. She had always treated me like her personal publicist, and now L and T was paying me to be her personal publicist. Boy, was I dying to tell her to shove it—not to mention go out and *buy* some damn books, since she and Stuart weren't exactly hurting for cash—but I kept my cool. The truth is, sending out freebies was a courtesy we extended frequently to our authors. "What sort of 'hot reads' are you interested in, Tara?" I asked with a sigh.

"I'd love to read the Georgette Peterson novel you just published."

"No problem. I've got a few review copies here in my office."

"Wonderful. Now let's see what Stuart wants to read. Hang on." She put her hand over the mouthpiece, but I could still hear her call out to him. "Stuart, honey? What do you feel like reading this weekend? I've got Amy on the phone, and she said she'll overnight us a couple of their books." I felt my muscles tighten as I pictured Stuart—my Stuart, who was now her Stuart—puttering around their Tudor mansion. Perhaps he was leaning up against their granite kitchen counter, sipping a tall glass of iced tea into which Cook had deposited a sprig of mint. Or perhaps he was in the cathedral-ceilinged living room, lighting one of Tara's favorite scented candles and gazing out at the water through their custom-made double-height windows. Or perhaps he was just sitting in a chair in their master bedroom, letting his toenails dry. In *Simply Beautiful,* Tara maintained that giving your man a pedicure is a surefire way to promote intimacy. "What did you say, hon? I can't hear you over the music." Or perhaps he was playing the violin. In the chapter devoted to her simply beautiful life with Stuart, she mentioned that he'd taken up the instrument recently and enjoyed serenading her when he got home from work. "Oh, sweetie, what a good idea. I'll ask Amy if she's got any." Tara came back on the phone. "Stuart says you guys publish Tony Stiles."

I rolled my eyes, reminded of my literal run-in with Tony only an hour earlier. "We did publish his last three books," I said, wishing we hadn't. "He doesn't have a new one coming out for almost a year, though, so I'll have to send you something else."

"Too bad. We're both passionate about him and his Joe West series. Stuart thinks he's the best mystery writer around, and I . . ." She paused before lowering her voice to a "just between us girls" little whisper. "Well, I'm absolutely in love with him. He's so sexy, with those blue eyes of his and that mean old growl of a voice. When his last mystery came out, he did a signing at our local bookstore and—I swear to God, Amy—I had all I could do not to rush over and throw myself at him."

I blinked a lot as she said this. Given my own experience with the notoriously difficult Tony (bookstore signings were the only publicity he did without giving me an argument, because they were relatively low-key affairs and allowed him to interact directly with readers and didn't require him to "shovel the shit on television," as he so delicately put it), I was amused by Tara's ardor for him.

"It is so amazing that you get to work with Tony Stiles," she went on, as if this discovery were on a par with, say, the fact that the earth is round. "You are the luckiest woman alive and I am sooo envious of you."

Wait, wait, wait. Just hold on a second, I thought, my mind doing cartwheels suddenly. Tara is envious of *me*? Because I know Tony? Because she wants to jump Tony's bones? Because Stuart thinks he's the best mystery writer around?

Well, this was all very interesting and quite a surprise, and as Tara continued to speak breathlessly about Tony's suspenseful plots and his endearing characters and his self-effacing charm (apparently, she'd seen the *Today* show interview where he'd answered Katie Couric exclusively in monosyllables, and she'd interpreted his monstrous attitude as *shyness*), I wondered, Is Tony Stiles the key to my payback scheme? If Tara is envious of me because I work with Tony, won't she be even more envious of me because I sleep with Tony? Because I love Tony and Tony loves me? Because I'm engaged to Tony and planning to marry him in six months (sorry, five and a half months)? And how about that cad Stuart? Won't he be unbelievably impressed (and maybe a little peeved) that I've found someone to marry who is even more successful than he is? Won't that whip up his competitive juices?

Okay, so Tony wasn't the most likely man to do this sort of a favor for me, given that he was such a purist and probably had a general policy against pretending to be someone he wasn't. But he was single and an L and T author and we did work together whenever he had a new book published, so it wouldn't be that big a stretch to tell Tara that our professional association required us to keep our relationship a secret. Yes indeed, he was the ideal guy for the job, our mutual antipathy notwithstanding.

The next morning, I bounded into Connie's office to share my brainstorm and to get her reaction to it. Just as I walked in, she was applying her lipstick—the shade of black-brown

I call "dog lips" because it is, in fact, the color of dog lips. Connie was such a good sport, she didn't even mind that I went "Wuff wuff" at her whenever she put it on.

"It turns out that Stuart is a fan of Tony Stiles and—this is the best part—Tara has an enormous crush on him. So I was thinking, What if I convinced him to be my fiancé for the night of her dinner?"

"Who?"

"Tony Stiles."

Connie laughed so hard that one of the teased and sprayed hairs on her head actually moved. "Why in the world would he do that?" She laughed some more.

"Well, he's single, the last I heard."

"Very single. He dates a lot of women but never gets involved. He's a total commitment phobe, and I doubt he'll ever get married."

"Who cares? All I want him to do is pretend to be engaged to me for a few hours."

"I'll say it again: Why in the world would he do that? He hates you."

"He actually told you that?"

"Not in so many words, but it's kind of obvious, isn't it?"

"Yes, but maybe he just hates what I stand for, hates the image of me as a corruptor of authors, a person who forces them to be sellouts, someone who represents the corporate mentality, whatever. Never mind that all my evil deeds have helped him get to number one on the *New York Times* bestseller list."

"Sowhaddayousuggesting?"

"What?"

"I said, What are you suggesting? That you present yourself to him in a whole new light so he'll like you better?"

"Exactly. Oh Connie, he really would be the perfect guy for this. You should have heard the way Tara squealed when she said his name. She'd absolutely die if I walked into her house with him as the man who popped the question. It would be the first time in the history of our relationship that she'd envy me. I'd have the upper hand for once. I wouldn't feel like the poor stepsister. It would be such sweet revenge for me, after the way she hurt me, after the way she betrayed me. Can't you see how much I need to do this one tiny thing?"

"Well, yeah, sure. But, as I said, Tony's not wild about you."

"I'm going to change that. I'm going to get him to like me—just enough so that he'll agree to play my fiancé."

"How?"

"By showing him how much we have in common."

"Do you two have anything in common?"

"Not at the moment. But we will if you'd just feed me a few personal details about him, his likes and dislikes, his habits, his passions—the little particulars that'll help me bond with him."

Connie looked skeptical. "I tell you the 'little particulars' and all of a sudden you'll be his soul mate?"

"Look, I know Tony's one of your most important authors and you're very protective of him. But wouldn't you be happier if the two of us got along? If we became pals instead of barking at each other all the time?"

"No question. But I don't like the idea of you exploiting him."

"I wouldn't be exploiting him at all. I'd be asking him to do me a favor. Besides, he's a big boy. He can take care of himself. And maybe with all the dating he does, he'd actually relish the idea of having a female buddy, someone who's not the least bit interested in him romantically."

She sighed. "If you're asking for my permission to try to seduce Tony—"

"Not seduce, Connie. Befriend. That's all, I swear."

"Okay, if you're asking my permission to try to *befriend* Tony, be my guest. But if you do anything—and I mean anything—to provoke him into leaving this publishing company, I'll break your legs."

"I understand, Connie. I do. I'll quit my job before I let him move to another house. But in the meantime, how about giving me those choice little morsels of information I mentioned, the background stuff that'll help put me in his good graces?"

She thought for a minute, then provided me with a few tidbits: Tony adored hockey, especially the New York Rangers; he was very knowledgeable about wine; he was a collector of sports cars, new and vintage; and he suffered from chronic neck pain due to all the hours he spent at the computer. And speaking of his work, he was obsessive when it came to researching his novels, doing whatever it took to develop his characters and make them seem authentic. And, despite his cocky attitude, he was hypersensitive to negative reviews.

No, Connie's intelligence report on Tony wasn't the stuff of CIA files, but it was a place to start.

9

Once back in my office, I called Tony. I knew he never picked up his phone while he was writing, so I left a message on his answering machine and hoped for a response by the end of the day. At five o'clock, Scott waltzed in with good news.

"It's our favorite author on the line," he said with an eye roll. "And I don't mean Tara the Terrible. I mean Tony the Terrible, as in Tony Stiles."

"Oh," I said eagerly. "Thanks, Scott."

He gave me a look. "What's this? We're happy to hear from him all of a sudden? Talk about a diva!"

"You think everybody's a diva," I said. "Now, let me have my conversation with him, okay?"

"Go ahead." He continued to stand there, arms crossed against his chest.

"Alone, Scott. I don't mean to throw you out, but I have business to discuss with Tony, and I can't do it if you launch into one of your imitations of him and crack me up." Scott was a wicked mimic. He did impressions of all of our authors, but his Tony Stiles impression was the best. He'd narrow his eyes and arrange his mouth into a smirk and say something wonderfully acerbic having to do with the burdens of money and fame.

"As you wish," he said, flashing me that very face as he closed the door on his way out.

I took a deep breath, got serious, and picked up the phone. "Tony?" I said sweetly. "It's Amy Sherman. How are you?"

"You just saw me yesterday. How did I look?" God, he was a chore. "I assume you're calling to apologize."

"You think *I'm* the one who should—" Okay, stop right there, I coached myself. This is not about what a pain in the ass Tony Stiles is. This is about what a kick in the ass it'll be when Tara thinks he's your fiancé. "Yes, that's exactly why I'm calling, Tony—to apologize. I wasn't watching where I was going when I backed out of Connie's office, and I'm really sorry. You once told me you have neck problems from all the hours you spend at the computer, so I hope our collision didn't make them worse."

"I don't remember telling you about my neck problems," he said. "Or if I did, I don't remember noticing that you gave a crap."

"Of course I give a crap." That didn't come out right. "What I mean is that I *care*."

"Come on, Amy. I'm just 'product' as far as you're concerned. As long as I turn out a book every year and show up for my interviews with a smiley face on and make as much money for your company as Grisham makes for his, you wouldn't care if my head exploded."

"That's not true," I said with as much earnestness as I could muster. "You're a person, not a product, and you're important to this company, not because of the money you make for us, but because you're a member of the L and T family." Okay, so I was laying it on pretty thick, but people in corporate America really say things like that. "What's more, I've got a herniated disk in my neck, so you're talking to someone who understands neck problems."

"Mine's herniated, too. Which disks of yours are affected?"

Which of my disks? I was clueless on this subject, since my neck was just fine, but I knew that "floppy disks" would not be the correct answer.

"I've got C-five/C-six degeneration," he volunteered.

"Same here," I said gratefully. "Who knew we'd have something in common?"

"Who knew." He sounded underwhelmed. "So why are you really calling? I've got a feeling you want me to appear at some garden club luncheon. Or are you trying to work up the courage to ask me to be a centerfold in *Playgirl?*"

"Oh Tony, you have such a great sense of humor." I laughed a little too giddily, because I sensed that Connie was on target: This guy hated me. Still, I was far from giving up. "Actually, I do want a favor from you."

"Thought so."

"I want to invite you to dinner at my apartment. Monday night, eight o'clock. I know it's kind of short notice, but I'd love it if you could make it."

"Ah. A command performance. Are any other trained seals coming, or am I the only author being pressed into service? This is one of those soirees where I mix and mingle with all your number crunchers and their spouses, isn't it?"

"For starters, my apartment isn't big enough for a party with all our number crunchers and their spouses. For another, you're the only author I've invited. And thirdly, it's not a business dinner. It occurred to me this morning that after three books together, it's high time we got to know each other. One-on-one. In a quiet setting."

"Interesting. What's the catch?"

"No catch. Well, except the catch of the day. I was thinking about barbecuing some fish on my George Foreman grill."

A reluctant chuckle. "What I meant was, why the suckup? I'm not in the middle of a contract negotiation with L and T. I'm perfectly happy with Connie as my editor. I don't have any plans to move to another publisher. So why is the publicity director romancing me?"

Because I have to stick it to the woman who used to be my best friend, and you're going to help me do it. "Because I'd like to get to know you better, as I said. More accurately, I'd like to get along with you better. You and I haven't had the smoothest working relationship, and I want to change that, pure and simple. So come Monday night, Tony. It'll be fun, you'll see. Please come."

"On one condition."

"That I don't talk business?"

"No, that you don't grill fish. Real men don't eat fish."

"Oh? And what do real men eat?"

"I was kidding. Fish will be just fine." Well? He was always so sarcastic, it wasn't easy to separate the kidding from the not kidding. "Now, why don't you tell me where you live, so I don't have to wander the streets calling your name."

"Then you'll come?"

"Sure I'll come. Far be it from me to turn down an invitation from a beautiful woman with a hidden agenda."

Well, he was right about the hidden agenda. But beautiful? He thought I was beautiful? Tara was the beautiful one. Everybody knew that. No matter how much satisfaction I hoped to derive from being able to play her for the fool this time, she'd always be the beautiful one and I'd always be the runner-up. Tony would realize that the instant I introduced him to her.

I gave him my address and confirmed the time of our "date."

"Got it," he said. "Now, what should I bring? My mother taught me that it's not polite to show up empty-handed."

Remembering that he was a wine expert, I suggested he bring a bottle. "You might go with either a Chardonnay that's not too buttery or austere, or you might consider a Pinot Noir that's been well aged in oak. Both are intensely versatile and will marry well with the flavors of the fish." I was a complete zero when it came to wine, but we'd published a book by a woman who owned a vineyard in California, so I'd had to learn the lingo. That's the thing about being the publicity director at a publishing house: You have to know a little about a lot.

"I had no idea you were into wine," said Tony, as if he had suddenly gained respect for me. "You're just full of surprises, aren't you, Amy?"

You have no clue, I thought, then wished him a nice evening.

I spent the weekend preparing for the big seduction. Sorry, the big *befriendment*. I cleaned the apartment. I did all my food shopping and prep work. I got my hair trimmed and blow-dried, and had a manicure. I even swallowed my pride (and disdain) and followed the advice in Tara's book about buying a bunch of scented candles and placing them strategically around the apartment.

As it turned out, the candles came in handy. About ten minutes before Tony was due to arrive Monday night, there was a complete and total power failure in my building, caused by an explosion at the Con Ed substation that serviced my neighborhood. I panicked. How would I feed him if I couldn't use my stove or oven, not to mention my George Foreman grill? How would I put him in a simply beautiful mood if I couldn't use my stereo and my new Enya CD? How would he even make it up to my apartment if he couldn't use the elevator?

Damn. He wasn't gonna show up. I just knew it. He'd hear about the power outage on the radio and turn right around and go back to his place. And then what was I supposed to do?

I was pacing, wondering if he'd come, not come, call, something, when the doorbell rang.

"Would you believe I just walked up ten flights of stairs in total darkness?" he said as he stood there in my hall in his snug-fitting black sweater and blue jeans, his face drenched with sweat. He was in great physical shape, as I've already indicated, but he was out of breath and steadying himself against the wall.

"I was sure you'd cancel," I said.

"Why?" he said between gulps of air. "Even when you booked me on the five A.M. farm report on that TV station in Kentucky, I didn't cancel."

"No, you didn't." He was ornery about appearing on talk shows to promote his novels, but he was right: He wasn't a canceler like some of the authors I worked with. He could have used his cell phone to call me from the lobby when he saw that the electricity was out, could have blown the dinner off and gone home, but instead he'd schlepped up all those stairs. A good omen, I thought.

And I have to say that there was something almost sweet about his state of disarray—the sweating, the windedness, the damp lock of hair that fell across his forehead. It put a dent in his tough-guy, "I'm a best-selling mystery writer" persona and made him seem vulnerable for a change.

"Come in," I said, taking his arm. "I lighted some candles, so there shouldn't be any more collisions between us."

He half-smiled, which also gave me hope for the evening. He didn't smile very often, at least not around me.

"I brought a 1987 Carneros Reserve Pinot Noir," he said, handing me the bottle he'd lugged up the stairs. "It was nicely chilled when I left my place, but it was so hot in that stairwell, it'll probably turn to vinegar any second."

"Then we'd better drink it right away," I said. "It'll be the perfect accompaniment to the meal, which was supposed to be grilled swordfish with sautéed spinach and roasted potatoes but will now be Brie and crackers." I shrugged. "I'm so sorry about this, Tony. I had planned what I'd hoped would be a delicious dinner for you."

"Hey, this isn't your fault," he said, nodding up at the useless ceiling fixture in my kitchen. "There are some things even you can't control."

"Oh, so you think I like to control things?" I asked as I opened the wine by candlelight. The cinnamon the candle was giving off was making me hungry for all the food we wouldn't be able to eat.

"Control is your middle name," he said. "In the three years we've worked together, I've never seen you leave anything to chance."

"Sometimes leaving things to chance isn't a good idea." Like when you assume it's safe to run out to the dentist while your fiancé is sleeping, only to come home early and find him in bed with your maid of honor.

He cocked his head, then narrowed his blue eyes at me. "All I know is that there's a reason you invited me here tonight. I just haven't figured out what it is yet."

I smiled and poured us each some wine. "I already told you: I wanted us to get to know each other better. So how about relaxing and enjoying my company?" I held up my glass. "In fact, let's make it official with a toast: to getting to know each other better."

Tony looked skeptical, but he clinked his glass with mine. "To getting to know each other better," he echoed as the candle flickered and went out, leaving us both in the dark.

10

"ere. Take my hand, Tony, and I'll lead you back into my living room," I said, afraid he might crash into something in my pitch-black apartment and then bark at me. "The cheese and crackers are already out there, so all we have to bring is our wine."

"I research my books by prowling around crime scenes. I think I can navigate my way out of this kitchen," he said, taking my hand nevertheless. It did not escape me that his grip was firm, his hand meaty and warm, and that making physical contact with him in a nonbusiness context did not feel as awkward or unpleasant as I'd expected.

Once in the living room, where there were candles galore, thanks to dear Tara and her "simply beautiful idiom," we let go of each other and sat on my sofa, which was upholstered in a nubby beige fabric and accented with too many toss pillows.

"Do you mind if I move these?" asked Tony, referring to the pillows. "They're nice, but they don't leave space for an actual person."

"I'll do it," I said, tossing the pillows onto the carpet. I'd never really liked them, but they'd been part of the display at Pier 1, and I'd bought the whole package off the floor. Still, leave it to him to complain about them.

"So how long have you lived here?" he asked, once we

had settled into our respective corners at opposite ends of the sofa.

"Four years," I said. Ever since I'd moved out of Stuart's and started my life all over again. "It's very comfortable, and the location is convenient to everything." I paused for a minute, recalling one of the tidbits Connie had slipped me about Tony, and decided that this was the perfect moment to dazzle him with my supposed knowledge of his favorite hobbies, to make him think we were astonishingly in sync. I'd done my homework. Now it was time to put it to use. "What's especially lucky is that I'm only minutes from Madison Square Garden for Ranger games."

He swallowed his sip of wine and blinked at me. "You're a hockey fan?"

I nodded, straight-faced, as if to say, Of course. Isn't everyone?

"I wouldn't have guessed that about you," he said. "Most women find the sport too violent or too fast-moving or too— I don't know—unglamorous."

"I think hockey is full of drama, passion, and precision," I said, parroting some commentator. "I'm not crazy about the fighting, it's true, but I love the fast pace. And who needs glamour? Hockey players aren't high-priced crybabies like other types of athletes, and that makes them endearing, as opposed to glamorous. They're sort of blue-collar in their work ethic. They get creamed out there on the ice, skate into the trainer's room for a few stitches, and then come right back out and score a goal. And the Rangers! Well, I live and die by that team. Ever since I was a child, I've been a huge fan, because my father told me all about the glory days of Gilbert, Ratelle, and Hadfield. The 'goal-a-game line,' they were called. I myself remember the Rangers' great battles against the Islanders in the early eighties. But I have to say that when we finally won the Cup in '94 after the fifty-four-year drought, it was one of the most exciting moments of my life. Seeing Wayne Gretzky in a Rangers uniform a few years later was icing on the cake." I giggled, tried to look

embarrassed. God, I was good. A natural liar. "Sorry to ram-
ble on about this, but I'm such a fan."

"Don't you dare apologize," said Tony, his blue eyes shin-
ing with a newfound admiration for me. And speaking of his
eyes, I had to hand it to the guy: He really was great-looking
when he wasn't scowling. Yes, the blue eyes were hard to be
blasé about. But his mouth had an appeal of its own. There
was a boyish quality about it, maybe because his two front
teeth stuck out just a little and hung up on his bottom lip, and
the result was kind of sexy. Well, I mean, if you liked grown
men with overbites. "I'm a Rangers fan, too. I'm just sort of
amazed, because I've never met a woman who's as obsessed
with the team as I am."

"How is that possible?" Boy, this is going well, I thought,
giving myself a silent pat on the back for reading all those
long, boring articles from *Sports Illustrated*'s archives.

"It just is. So who's your favorite Ranger?" he asked as he
spread some Brie on a cracker, took a bite, and drank more
wine. He did these things gracefully for a man so sturdily
built, with none of the bull-in-a-china-shop obliviousness
you often see in men as muscular. I hadn't noticed that about
him before—that he moved as smoothly as he wrote.

"That's a tough one," I said, "because I've had lots of fa-
vorites over the years: Ron Duguay, Phil Esposito, John
Davidson, Mark Messier, Eric Lindros." I felt like a complete fraud as I spit out the names of these men. They might
as well have been pole-vaulters, for all I knew.

"Yeah. They were all terrific." Tony went on to tell me
about the first time he saw a game at the Garden when he
was a kid, and as he related the story and as I pretended to
listen, my mind drifted off to Tara and Stuart's grand estate,
the setting for my even grander plan. I nearly salivated as I
imagined Tony and me sitting at their antique Louis the
something table for twelve in their banquet-size dining
room. I imagined all four of us munching on pheasant or elk,
or whatever poor wild animal was now in food fashion,
while an army of uniformed servers, hired especially for the

occasion, attended to our every need. I imagined us dipping
the tips of our sauce-stained hands into finger bowls between
courses. (Tara devoted a whole paragraph to finger bowls in
Simply Beautiful, even though no normal person our age
used them, not in this century anyway.) I imagined Stuart
peppering Tony with questions about his books and Tara
peppering me with questions about my engagement. I imagined her staring at me with her tongue hanging out, her
beautiful face contorted with envy, her gorgeous blond locks
limp with regret, her magnetic personality blunted by her
shock at my ability to rebound from her treachery. Most tan-
talizingly, I imagined her turning to Stuart, after Tony and I
had left their manse and gone back to the city, and thinking
that her happiness with him couldn't begin to compare with
the intellectually stimulating, financially rewarding, sexually satisfying, and, above all, profoundly unbreakable bond
she suspected I shared with Tony. Yeah, I enjoyed that notion
immensely.

After hockey, Tony and I moved on to sports cars, another area Connie had suggested I cover. He mentioned that
he'd driven up to my apartment from his loft in SoHo instead of taking a cab, and I asked what kind of car he owned.

He chuckled. "You name it, I own it. Cars are my one real
weakness, other than women." As you can see, he had
started to loosen up a little. "I've been pretty conservative
with all the money I've made from the books, except when it
comes to cars. I can't help indulging myself."

He explained that not only did he spend a fortune on cars
but that he paid handsomely to house them in a private
garage in lower Manhattan.

"So which one did you drive tonight?" I said, feigning
massive interest.

"The Ferrari."

I pretended to go orgasmic. "Oh God. You don't have the
three fifty Spider, do you?" Connie had tipped me off to this
factoid.

"Yeah. You know the model?" He appeared stunned by
my apparent psychic powers.

"Know it? I dream about it," I said with the sigh of a lovesick teenager.

"No kidding," he said, actually grinning. "That's quite a coincidence. You're a Ranger fan. I'm a Ranger fan. You like Ferraris. I like Ferraris. We must have been separated at birth."

It was my turn to grin. "Incredible what two people can learn about each other over a nice bottle of wine, isn't it?"

"Absolutely. So what is it about the Spider that speaks to you? Those twelve cylinders under the hood?"

"You got it." He was making this so easy that I almost felt sorry for him. All it took was a quick flip through *Road & Track* magazine, and I had him thinking I was a gearhead.

"I can't believe that you know about this stuff," he marveled. "I'll be honest with you. I never expected to have a single thing in common with you."

"Well, I had a feeling we'd hit it off. I sensed that all the friction between us was strictly about the promotion of your books, not about who we are as people." Whatever that meant.

"Then you're more perceptive than I am." He drained his glass and reached for the bottle to pour himself more. "So tell me, since we're becoming such buddies, is there a man in your life? Someone to take you to Ranger games, for instance?"

"Not anymore," I said. "I was engaged once, but it didn't work out."

"Sorry. Was the breakup awful?"

"Yes. It *was* awful, and I thought I'd never get over it, but it's all behind me now." Sure it was.

"I've never been engaged. Or married, for that matter."

"Why not?"

"The usual reason. I haven't met the right woman."

"Oh, come on, Tony. We both know you date zillions of women. Surely, there's been a 'right woman' in there somewhere."

He laughed again. He really was mellow now—so mellow, I began to worry that he'd fall asleep at some point. He'd consumed most of the wine, without any real food to absorb it, and I noticed that his words were beginning to slur and that his eyelids were droopy. "First of all, I don't date zillions of women. Billions, maybe." Another laugh. "No, seriously, my reputation as a sheikh with a harem is greatly exaggerated. Do I enjoy women? Yes. Do I shy away from involvement? Yes."

"Because?"

He shrugged. "A couple of reasons. For one thing, my father's been married three times—and that's not counting my mother, his first wife. He isn't the best role model when it comes to stable, committed relationships, obviously, so I guess I just steer clear of them. Plus, dear old Dad has to pay alimony to all four exes. I never want to find myself in his position, financially speaking."

"I'm sure you don't," I said, thinking it couldn't have been easy for Tony to have grown up amid such chaos, never mind all those stepmothers. "What's the other reason you haven't found the right woman? You said there were two."

"Yeah. The second thing is that I think women are only interested in the idea of me."

I laughed. "The idea of you?"

"Hang on. I didn't mean that to sound arrogant. I only meant that they have this image of me, and the reality never lives up to that image."

"What's the image?" Other than of a grouchy, moody, high-maintenance author, which, of course, was my image of him. Most of the time anyway.

"They think I lead the same kind of exciting and dangerous life as Joe West, my intrepid hero; that I'm this thrill cowboy or something. They're disappointed when they find out I spend most of each day at a computer."

"But you do go the extra mile to research your books," I pointed out, remembering what Connie had told me. "You've interviewed hit men and hookers and all sorts of rough trade to make your characters authentic. Why wouldn't a woman find that exciting? Even a little dangerous?"

"Because I don't tell them about it. I don't reveal my sources and I don't discuss the specifics of my research—

ever. It's confidential. That's the only way I get access to
these people. You understand that, because you're in the
publishing business, but most of the women I've met don't.
So they imagine that they're going out with Joe West, badass
burned-out cop, and instead they get Tony Stiles, badass
computer geek." He paused, put down his wineglass.
"Speaking of sitting at the computer," he said after a noisy
yawn, "I won't be much good tomorrow if I don't go home
and get to bed. It's a school night."

I glanced at my watch. It was only 9:30. "But it's early,
Tony. You just got here." He couldn't leave yet. I wouldn't
let him. We hadn't established enough of a friendship for me
to lay my little favor on him. "Stay a little longer, huh? Tell
me more about yourself, more about your background, for
instance."

"You wrote my bio. What can I possibly tell you that you
don't already know?"

"Plenty. Yes, I know the basics—that your full name is
Hamilton Stiles and you were born in London and your parents moved to New York when you were two."

"See?"

"How about brothers and sisters?"

"I'm an only child. Well, except for various half siblings."

"I'm an only child, too, so that's another thing we have in
common. Did you like being the only kid in the house?"

"Not at all. I used to camp out at my friends' houses, the
ones who had big broods, and pretend I was just another one
of the kids. There was something wonderful about the 'nor-
mality' of their situation. Or at least that's how I imagined it
then."

I smiled wistfully, remembering all the afternoons I'd
spent at Tara's wishing I were a member of the Messer household so that I might catch a whiff of her self-confidence.

Tony and I continued to chat about his family and mine.
He ended up staying another hour before rising from the
sofa and announcing that it was time for him to go.

"I feel terrible about reneging on dinner," I said as I
walked him to the door.

"You didn't renege," he said.

"Sure I did. I called you up and invited you over for a meal, Tony, not for some wine and cheese. I didn't make good on my invitation."

"Not true. You said you wanted us to get to know each other better, and that's what we've done. I have a whole new picture of you after tonight. A much clearer picture."

Not as clear as you think. "Same here," I said. "You're pretty easy to talk to when you're not biting my head off."

He smiled, and I found myself noticing his mouth again. Not because of what he was saying, but because of how expressive it was. "Is that what I do? Bite your head off?"

"Usually."

"Then I'll watch myself from now on."

He leaned over and kissed me on the cheek. It was just a quick peck, nothing with any heat behind it, but I was ecstatic about the display of affection—from a strictly goal-specific point of view, you understand. Perhaps I had won him over enough to ask him to help me out with Tara.

I was about to bring up the subject, when the power came back on, as if by a stroke of magic. The apartment lighted up and the kitchen appliances hummed, and I looked at Tony and shrugged. "Some timing, huh?"

"At least I don't have to walk down ten flights of stairs to the lobby," he said. "I wasn't looking forward to that."

He turned to go, but I couldn't let him leave. Not without hitting him with the favor.

"Wait," I said, tapping him on the shoulder. Actually, it was more than a tap. I sort of pulled on his sweater.

He turned back around. "What?"

"Well, I was just—" Come on, Amy. Spit it out, I urged myself. Suck it up and ask the guy already. "There's something else I'd like to say to you."

"Actually, there's something else I'd like to say to you, too."

"Oh? Then why don't you go first."

"Okay." He looked me straight in the eye, but his gaze was warm, not the usual chilly glare. "When you first invited

me for dinner tonight, I confess that I thought you had an ulterior motive."

"An ulterior motive?"

"Yeah. Call me a conspiracy theorist, but I was convinced
that you were out to wine and dine me so I'd do something
for you in return."

Oh God. Was I that transparent? "Do something for me in
return?" I laughed and waved him off, as if to suggest that
the very idea was absurd and that I was not completely
flipped out by his insinuation, which, of course, I was. "Like
what?"

"Like get me to appear at some function that I don't want
to appear at. You know how I hate being trotted out like a
show dog, just for the sake of impressing complete strangers.
I thought maybe your dinner was about softening me up so
I'd agree to do it."

Swell. So he hated being trotted out. So he thought I was
softening him up in order to impress complete strangers. So
he was right on all counts, and now there was no way I could
ask him what I desperately needed to ask him.

"But I see I was wrong," he continued, because I was too
dumbstruck to speak. "There was no hidden agenda, and I
appreciate that, Amy. Very much."

I nodded, trying to mask my frustration. I almost had
him. I know I did.

"Now, your turn," he offered. "What was it you wanted to
say to me?"

How the hell am I supposed to pay back Tara if you won't
cooperate? *That's* what I want to say to you, you jerk. "Just
that I hope to see you again soon," I said instead.

"Right. I'll pop my head in your office the next time I
meet with Connie," said Tony, who took his sexy but ultimately useless self away from my door and disappeared
down the hall to the elevator.

11

"Sohedoeshateyou," said Connie the following morning. She had dashed into my office before a meeting, dying to find out how my evening with Tony went.

"What?"

"I said, So he does hate you."

"No. We got along fine, and I think he likes me better than he did before he came over. But I decided that he's not the right guy for this assignment."

"This 'assignment.' Listen to how you talk, Amy. Maybe that power failure last night was a wake-up call, telling you to turn out the lights on your plan to pay Tara back. When you first told me what she did to you, I wanted to pay her back, too. But now? I dunno. Maybe you should just get over it and move on."

"*Get over it?* Connie, would you get over it if you walked into your bedroom and found me doing the nasty with Murray?"

She bared her teeth. "I'd kill you. Either that or I'd hire someone else to do it."

"See? You have the same need for revenge that I do. It's only natural. The only difference between us is that I knew and trusted Tara much longer than you've known and trusted me, which makes what she did to me even more disgusting. Plus, my impulses aren't as violent as yours. I don't want to kill her. I want to humiliate her, the way she humiliated me. Originally, I felt cornered when I ran into her on the street, so I stretched the truth a little. But now that she's one of our authors, I have to keep the lie going. And if I'm going to keep it going, I might as well make it a winner, which means producing a fiancé who will drive her crazy with envy."

She nodded. "I hear you. It's sick, but I hear you."

"So I've got to go back to the drawing board and think of other men to approach—men who aren't necessarily associated with L and T."

"What about trying one of those professional matchmaking services?"

"Too expensive. I want to humiliate Tara, but not if it means bankrupting myself."

"An Internet dating site?"

"Too risky. I could end up with a nutcase."

"A blind date set up by your mother?"

"Never again. The last guy she fixed me up with was the son of one of her friends from Arizona, and he was a clown."

"Why? Because he didn't call you again?"

"No, because he was a *clown*. Like in a circus. He showed up for our date in costume, for God's sake. I need a guy who will impress Tara, not honk his big red nose at her."

"I'm out of ideas, Amy. Besides, I've gotta run. Lemme-knowhowitgoes."

"What?"

"I said, Lemme know how it goes."

Since my lunch date bailed on me, I decided to use the time by grinding out a press release on Tara's book. I was in the process of describing one of her keys to a simply beautiful life—"According to the author, it's important to maintain a positive attitude, even when you break a nail, or misplace your keys, or, God forbid, find yourself at the supermarket without your shopping list"—when my phone rang. Scott was out for lunch, so I picked up the phone myself.

"Publicity," I said, grateful for the distraction.

"It's Tony Stiles," said the male voice.

I sat up straighter in my chair. "Tony. Hi." I was surprised to hear from him in the middle of his writing day, but then I realized he was probably taking his own lunch break and calling to thank me for the nondinner last night.

"Hi," he said, sounding rushed, tense. "I'm here with a dealer."

A dealer? As we'd discussed at my apartment, he was a stickler when it came to researching his mysteries, which usually meant going undercover and hanging out with lowlifes, but was he actually in the midst of interviewing a drug lord? Had he gotten himself into serious trouble this time? Did he need my help?

"I need your help," he confirmed.

I couldn't figure out why he was calling me instead of the police, but I would do whatever he asked. "Of course I'll help. Where are you?"

"With the dealer," he repeated, then exhaled loudly, as if he might be at wit's end. "I'm standing here with the guy right now."

"Okay, but what can I do? Should I send someone?"

"Send someone? Hell no."

"But you said you needed my help."

"I do. I'm about to buy a '65 Ferrari from a guy who specializes in antique and classic cars, and I need you to talk me out of it. You're the only one I could think of who might understand the temptation."

I relaxed. Sort of. "So you're about to shell out big money?"

"If I'm not careful. The object of my affection is the two seventy-five GTB. Short nose. Three carb. Open shaft. Red exterior, tan interior. It's in pristine condition, just gorgeous. What do you think?"

"What do I—Well, I think you have to go for it. We're not talking about a car. We're talking about a work of art." Sounded good to me.

"I knew you'd understand," he said excitedly. "I'll have to sell one of the others—maybe the '72 Maserati four-point-nine-liter SS coupe."

"Yeah, I'd sell that one," I agreed. Just as long as he held on to one of his chariots long enough to whisk us up to Tara's place in style. Yes, he was back in the running for the position of decoy fiancé, as far as I was concerned. His phone call was a sign.

"Thanks, Amy. I'll catch you later." *Click.*

Or maybe not a sign after all.

That night, I was home watching the Jim Carrey movie *Liar Liar* and sympathizing with the main character when the phone rang.

"Hi. It's Tony Stiles."

I hit the mute button on the TV. "Hello again," I said, wondering what it was this time. Maybe he was thinking about buying a vintage Winnebago and wanted my opinion on that.

"I was wondering if you'd like to go out," he said.

"Go out?" I was stunned.

"I don't mean right now, because you've probably got company. I mean whenever you're free."

Whoa. Talk about changing his tune. For three years, the man couldn't stand the sight of me. Now, after a little wine and some cheese and crackers at my apartment, he wanted to *go out*? Had my boning up on the New York Rangers been even more effective than I could have predicted? "So you want us to get together, Tony?"

"I know, I know. You're thinking, Why should I spend time with a guy who only twenty-four hours ago admitted he doesn't trust women?"

"It's a fair question."

"All I can tell you is that you're very easy to be with. You have no illusions about what I do for a living. You don't have some unrealistic expectation about me. I don't have to explain myself to you, because you understand writers."

"I see," I said. Well, this was an amazing turn of events. Tony Stiles was actually making a case for why we should become buddies. Was this too perfect or what? And to think I had already crossed him off the list.

"And then there's the fact that we have so much in common," he continued. "Hockey, wine, cars, and who knows what else. We're compatible, you and I."

"We are," I said, my hopes mounting. Yes, we were about to become friends—good, old-fashioned "We can tell each other everything" friends. The next time I saw him, I would definitely ask him to play my fiancé and he would definitely oblige, because friends help each other out.

"Of course, it doesn't hurt that there's chemistry between us."

Huh?

"Chemistry, electricity, heat," he mused. "Whatever you want to call it, it's there."

What in the world was he talking about? Friends don't have chemistry. Friends have movie dates and meals together and heart-to-heart talks.

"Come on, Amy. You know there's chemistry. What do you think all our fighting's been about?"

"I thought it was about my eagerness to promote your books and your unwillingness to promote your books."

"That's part of it. But the other part is that you and I have been hot for each other ever since we met three years ago."

"*What?*" My face flooded. I was so flustered, I could hardly speak. I had never given Tony Stiles the slightest indication that I had anything but a grudging respect for his literary accomplishments. Was he confusing my aggressive efforts to publicize his books with some sort of attraction to him? What a joke! If he only knew how mercilessly and often Scott and I made fun of him! Okay, okay. So he did have a few appealing physical characteristics. But the notion of my harboring a long-simmering passion for him was so ridiculous, I couldn't even finish my sentence. And as for his attraction to me, well, if he'd had one, he'd sure kept it to himself.

"Look, I didn't realize it either until I left your place last night," he said, "but, like it or not, there's chemistry on both sides. Chemistry and compatibility." He laughed. "Although I suppose it could turn out that we're a disaster in the bedroom."

Now I was really speechless. For some reason (probably because seeing Tara again had completely distorted my ability to think like a rational person), I had imagined reeling Tony in as my fake fiancé but hadn't counted on our having a relationship that was anything other than platonic. I'd certainly never considered the necessity of sleeping with him in order to one-up Tara. Even I wasn't that desperate.

"Hey, I'm kidding, Amy. About the bedroom stuff. Well, unless you beg me otherwise." Another laugh. "We can take it slowly, if that's what you want. Should we have dinner tomorrow night and find out where it leads?"

So Tony had taken the bait, and with an urgency I could hardly have anticipated. My plan had worked. I was on the verge of getting him to help me make a fool of Tara the way she'd made a fool of me. He was about to become the person who would bring me justice, sweet justice.

Then why were my hands so clammy? Because I was feeling guilty about pretending to be able to tell the difference between a '65 Ferrari and a Ford Taurus? Because I didn't know zilch about zinfandel? Because I wasn't the person Tony thought I was? Or was it because of this new wrinkle, this sex thing? I mean, yes, he was cute and not a complete jerk after all, as I've already admitted, but this game of mine was supposed to be about Tara and me, not about *some man* and me. What's more, I'd promised Connie I was not out to seduce her precious author, only to become his chum. And furthermore, why would I get involved, sexually or emotionally (they are the same to me; I am not one of those women who can sleep with a man without becoming attached to him), with a certified commitment phobe, a notorious bachelor who was probably only bringing up our supposed chemistry as a come-on?

I wouldn't. Not a chance. I had no interest in Tony Stiles other than to produce him at Tara's doorstep. Showing up with him would shut her up and put her in her place and give me enormous satisfaction, after which he and I could go back to hating each other, for all I cared.

"I'd love to have dinner," I said simply.

"Great. I'll make a reservation someplace, and I promise it'll have a wine list worthy of your sophisticated palate. You can regale me with more of your favorite moments in Rangers history and tell me what you think of the '79 Ferrari that was also on the showroom floor today. It was the five twelve BB in fly yellow with a black interior. You've seen the one, right?"

"Sure."

"Thought so. I'll call you tomorrow and we'll firm up dinner. Night." He hung up.

I hung up, too, then sank back onto the sofa like a deadweight. Who knew that lying would turn out to be so exhausting?

12

I had expected Tony to choose one of the ultrahip, ultra-trendy restaurants in his SoHo neighborhood—a place with sleek decor and dismissive young waiters and pulsating techno music in the background. Instead, he picked a traditional steak joint with exposed brick, crusty old waiters who'd worked there forever, and Frank Sinatra music in the background.

"This place is my home away from home," he said when he greeted me at the table, which was clearly the best one in the house, because it was cozy and private and tucked away in a corner. Since Tony was a regular as well as a celebrity, he was obviously given preferential treatment. He looked as if he'd given himself preferential treatment, too. His usually wayward waves of hair were neatly combed off his forehead. He was freshly shaved, as opposed to sporting the scruffy shadow he'd sported at my apartment. And he was dressed not in his customary blue jeans, but in a pair of nicely pressed khakis. The fact that he'd cleaned up for me, that he'd wanted to make himself appealing to me, caused me to flush with ambivalence. I was oddly flattered that he was eager to please me, but I had no intention of letting myself feel anything in return, since that certainly wasn't the point of the exercise.

"I took the liberty of ordering us something to drink," he

added, nodding at the two glasses of wine that had already been delivered to our table. "It's a 1985 Jordan Cabernet Sauvignon. I thought its velvety character would highlight the richness of the beef we'll be having."

"Right you are," I said, lifting my glass, swirling the wine around so vigorously that I almost spilled it, then sniffing the Cabernet and pronouncing its bouquet "delightfully impertinent."

He smiled, shaking his head.

"What?" I said, hoping I hadn't given away my ignorance. Perhaps red wine wasn't supposed to be called "delightfully" anything, least of all "impertinent."

"Just this. Us. Sitting here together on a Saturday night. A week ago, I couldn't have imagined it. But now? Well, I have to confess, I've been looking forward to it all day."

"Me, too." I *had* been looking forward to it. The sooner I got Tony to say he'd go with me to Tara's as my fiancé, the sooner I could move on with my life.

"You seem so much more open than you do in the office," he went on. "So much more approachable."

"I've always been approachable, Tony. You've always been the one with the attitude. Toward me and my job anyway."

"Maybe so, but you do understand why I've had the attitude, don't you?"

"Not really. If I were an author, I'd want my publisher to do everything humanly possible to gain exposure for my books."

"I do want that—except for the self-promotion. Some of us aren't salesmen. Some of us would rather leave the selling part to someone else. I, for one, don't feel comfortable showing up on morning television and shoving my latest book down people's throats. It makes me feel like I'm going door-to-door selling vacuum cleaners."

"But you're not selling vacuum cleaners. You're selling something that gives people pleasure. Your mysteries are terrific entertainment. They're very suspenseful, but they're also funny and fast-moving and full of smart observations about society and popular culture." I wasn't being insincere when it came to his books. They really were a joy to read, as well as to publicize. He was the one who'd always made the job a torturous experience.

"I appreciate the pep talk, but writers are insecure creatures. We never think anything we do is good."

"Come on, Tony. I've never figured you for the modest type."

"I'm not modest when it comes to anything else but my work. Look, let me try to explain what it's like to be in my shoes. You write a novel. You labor over it day in and day out. It's your baby. You care about it as if it has a life of its own. And then at some point, no matter how many times you've gone over the manuscript, no matter how many times you've made revisions, no matter how many times you wish you could chuck it and start over again, you let it go. You take it to Kinko's and have it copied, then send it off to your publisher. And then, months later, it's shipped to bookstores all over the country. Everyone expects you to get out there and promote it, to tell the world how amazing it is, but you're conflicted, because deep down you think the book might be total crap. That's the problem, Amy. You're supposed to sell it, but you think it's crap, or you're not sure if it's crap, or you're sure it's crap but you don't want anyone else to find out it's crap."

My, my. I was seeing a new side to Tony. I'd always attributed his reluctance to promote his books to his belief that he was better than other authors, less desperate for a sale than the rest, too high-and-mighty to promote them. "So this feeling that you might be perpetrating fraud on the consumer—that you're forcing them to buy books that might be crap—hasn't gone away, even though every installment in the Joe West series has made national best-seller lists?"

"Nope. With each new book, the imposter syndrome kicks right back in. All I have to do is read a bad review and I want to crawl in a hole and stay there."

I suddenly remembered another of Connie's tidbits about Tony: He was extremely sensitive to negative reviews of his books. "If the reviews bother you so much, then don't read them," I said. "I can tell Scott not to send you the ones we get from our clipping service."

He shook his head. "I have to read them. It's a compulsion. What really riles me is that they pick me apart and yet they treat Carl Hiaasen and Elmore Leonard and Robert Parker like gods."

Boy, he really was fragile on the subject. "They treat you like a god, too. If memory serves, you haven't had a bad review in the three years we've published you."

"Oh yeah? On the last book, *Publishers Weekly* creamed me."

"Creamed you? I don't think so."

"They did, I swear. Here's what they said: 'Another well-crafted whodunit with a truckload of engaging characters, Stiles's latest is bound for best-seller lists. Joe West embarks on a new escapade both zesty and riveting. Only his relationship with his ever-patient wife, Lucy, remains woefully underdeveloped.' "

I smiled, amused that he recalled portions of the year-old review word for word. "That's not a bad review, Tony. That's a great review with one tiny quibble."

"Well, the *New York Times* had the same quibble. 'Rollicking,' they called the book, then slammed my Lucy character as being 'one-dimensional, almost cartoonish.' Even *People* magazine beat me up about poor Lucy, saying her scenes with Joe 'fail to dazzle, given the flat, uninspired dialogue between them.' "

"The books sell like crazy," I said. "What do you care what some cranky reviewers write?"

"I care. I know I shouldn't, but I do."

"Okay, so you don't like to promote your books on television. And you don't like to read reviews, although you can't help yourself. Is there any aspect of the process that you do like?" I said.

"The promotion process?"

"No. The writing process."

"I love the writing process. Being a novelist is the hardest job I've ever had, but I love coming up with and then solving the mysteries, love revisiting and developing Joe West, love stringing a few decent sentences together. And I love dealing one-on-one with readers once the books are published. It's pretty miraculous to hear I've given them a good ride."

"Okay."

"Okay what?"

"I see the light now."

"You do?"

"Yes. I used to think you were too full of yourself to get out there and do publicity. Now I realize that you're not full enough of yourself to get out there and do publicity."

He laughed. "So I'm off the hook for the *Today* show when the next one is published?"

"No. You're doing the show, Tony, just like you always do. The only difference is that now I'll understand why you won't be happy about it."

We sipped our wine, munched on the sourdough bread the waiter brought to the table, and listened to the day's specials, which were steak, steak, and more steak.

"I think I'll have the steak," I said when it was time to order. "The filet. Medium."

Tony ordered the same. We continued to chat amiably and, I might add, more intimately, sharing information about our parents, our paths to our current careers, our favorite movies—all the things people talk about when they're getting to know each other.

"And who are your friends?" he asked once our food had been served and he had just told me about the week he'd spent with an old college pal.

"My friends?" God, this is fantastic, I thought. He's just given me the perfect opening for asking him to help me out with Tara.

"Yeah. Do you have a best friend? Someone you'll call as soon as you get home tonight? Someone who knows every single one of your secrets?"

His tone was lighthearted, teasing, and why not? He had no idea how loaded the subject was for me, how fraught with raw emotions.

"I had a best friend," I said. "When she and I were teenagers, we used to call each other the very instant we got home from a date, even if we went on the date together, as a foursome, and had only just left each other. Of course, she did most of the talking and I did most of the listening, but it seemed to me then as if there couldn't be two closer girl-friends in this world."

"I can't picture you as the passive one," he said. "You sure as hell aren't passive anymore."

"No. But back then, I would sit in my bedroom with the phone nestled in my neck and the cord wound around my finger, and hang on her every word. She would come up with clever nicknames for boys and create drama where I saw none and describe in fabulous detail what so-and-so said about this and that. Her take on whatever we did was always so different from mine, so much more interesting than mine, because her vantage point was that of the most popular girl in school."

He smiled. "Now I'm supposed to believe you were a wallflower? I can't picture that, either."

"Not a wallflower, no. But she was definitely the queen bee and I was the one who smoothed things over whenever she'd sting somebody."

"So whatever happened to her?" asked Tony. "You referred to her in the past tense."

"Whatever happened to her? She stung me," I said. "And there was nobody to smooth it over."

"Ouch. Sounds like there's a story lurking. Want to tell me?"

Yes, I want to tell you and I'm going to tell you, I pledged. I'm going to tell you not only because I planned the whole evening around telling you but also because you're not the prima donna author I always thought you were. You're actually pretty damn appealing and not a bad listener—and who would have guessed it?

I was enjoying myself, I realized as I sat there looking at Tony, at the impossibly blue eyes and the full head of wavy dark hair and the nose that did a little zigzag and rescued him from being too pretty. Not that I was about to let this new positive opinion of him distract me from my mission. It would just make spending time with him at Tara's less onerous, I figured.

"While you decide whether you're going to unburden yourself about your former best friend, let me tell you the story of a boy I grew up with," he said, and went on to share the tale of a kid who'd been his best friend until they were on opposing teams in Little League. It was a charming anecdote and he recounted it well, being the professional spinner of tales that he was, and I found myself thoroughly caught up in it. I also had a thought, unoriginal and hardly earth-shaking though it was: This is what people are—the sum total of our stories, our little histories, our life experiences, which pile up and shape us. There was something about this idea—that I, for example, wouldn't be the person I was without having had Tara in my past, for better or worse—that touched me, made me soften toward her, if only for a split second.

"So, back to you and your friend," said Tony. "What went wrong between you two, and how did you resolve it?"

I put down my knife and fork. I was poised to explain about Tara and me, then slide right into my pitch. I felt fairly certain that after he heard my sorry saga, he would agree to pose as my fiancé for one night, even though he hated to be put on display, as he'd told me over and over. He would do it because we'd made a connection. He would see my dilemma, excuse my lie, and help me out. Yes.

"What happened between my friend and me was that I was supposed to get married four years ago and she was supposed to be my maid of honor at the wedding, but then—"

Before I could even get to the part where I walked in on Tara and Stuart playing rodeo in our bedroom, the waiter rushed up to the table, leaned into Tony, and said in a hoarse whisper that was loud enough for me to eavesdrop, "Sorry to butt in, but she's here lookin' for you, Mr. Stiles."

Tony seemed—what?—alarmed by the interruption? Not exactly. Irritated? Yes. "Where is she?" he said to the waiter.

"Outside. I spotted her trying to come in and I stopped her. I said you were busy with another lady."

"What did she do?"

"Cried. Carried on. Eventually, she beat it. You're okay, Mr. Stiles. She's gone now. I took care of everything."

Tony reached into his pocket and handed the waiter some money. "Thanks, Bruno. I appreciate your trouble."

"No problem, Mr. Stiles."

When we were alone again, I quickly asked what all the intrigue was about.

"You don't want to know, trust me," he said with a weary sigh.

"Of course I want to know," I said, taking a bite of my steak. "I'm dying of curiosity."

"Okay, but remember: You asked."

"I'll remember."

"Well, there's a woman I used to go out with."

"Aha. And you broke her heart, right?"

"If she has a heart."

"Sounds like the split was ugly. How long were you together?"

"Not long. Three months maybe."

"Three months. Is that your usual cutoff?" According to Marianne, men who shied away from commitment rarely made it past the three-month mark.

"I don't have a *cutoff*," he said. "But I did tell this woman we were over, and she hasn't been willing to face it. She's been hanging around, waiting for me at all my haunts, trying to worm her way back into my life, and it's driving me nuts. Nothing like this has ever happened to me before, so I don't know how to handle it."

"You mean that all your casualties don't hound you after you dump them?" I said wryly.

"Hey. Be nice. The bottom line is that she wasn't the right woman for me, any more than I was the right man for her, and I tried to point that out to her in the gentlest terms," he said. "It's not my fault that she refuses to move on."

"Are we talking about an actual stalker here?"

"No. We're talking about a pest. She knows we never had a future together. She's just used to having her way."

"Oh, a spoiled one?"

"Not spoiled. But definitely bossy."

"Was it her bossiness that prompted the breakup?"

He shook his head. "It was her lying."

A piece of steak suddenly got stuck in my throat. Or maybe it only felt that way. "Her lying?" I said after swallowing hard.

"Yeah. She played me. Not only did she lie about a very key aspect of her life but she actually asked me to participate in her lie, to compound it by lying right along with her. Can you believe that?"

Well, duh, I could believe it. I'd been on the verge of *doing* it before that waiter appeared out of nowhere and ruined everything.

My God, I thought as Tony continued to rail against the woman. If she hadn't shown up at the restaurant, I would have asked him to participate in my own lie, and he would have been as furious at me as he was at her, not to mention highly unsympathetic to my situation. So now what was I supposed to do? How could I possibly follow through with my plan? I couldn't.

"I'm the last person to apply for sainthood," he went on, clearly fired up, "but she was bad news. For her to lie to me—and I'm talking about a whopper here—and then beg me to help her keep the lie going still pisses me off."

"I can see that," I said.

Well, I lost my appetite then. My resolve, too. For the rest of the meal, I sort of sat there in a daze, wishing I could be the Elizabeth Montgomery character on the old TV sitcom *Bewitched*, just twitch my nose and make Tara and all the problems she was causing disappear. I was totally distracted until Tony took hold of my hand. The affectionate nature of the gesture caught me off guard and nearly made me jump.

"You okay?" he asked. "I think I lost you during my rant."

"I'm fine," I said, wondering when he'd let go. Not that I

minded him holding my hand, exactly. In fact, my stomach started doing little flips as his fingers wedged between mine.

"Good. Then let's get back to you. Before Bruno came over, you were about to tell me what happened to your best friend."

"Right. But now that I think about it, it's really not that great a story."

"Why not let me be the judge?"

"No, really, Tony. I'd rather talk about this meal. It was delicious." What else was I going to talk about now that the very reason for the dinner had evaporated?

"Glad you enjoyed it. Any dessert?"

"Thanks, but I'm done." That's how I felt—done. I could no longer ask Tony what I'd come there to ask him, which meant that I didn't have a fiancé to drag up to Tara's. I was out of options, out of luck. Yeah, I was done. Cooked. Burned.

After he released my hand and paid the check, he told me how much fun he was having and how he didn't want the evening to end. To illustrate the point, he invited me back to his place for coffee. "I could put you in a taxi now, or I could put you in a taxi later," he teased.

Well, I was not about to have actual sex with Tony Stiles, as I've indicated, nor would I roll around on his bed fully clothed or make out with him on his sofa or even stare adoringly at him over coffee. Why bother? Yes, I found him much more attractive than I used to—we've established that, okay?—but why get involved? He was adverse to commitment as well as adverse to liars, so what good was he to me, and vice versa?

"I'm a little tired tonight, so I think I'll take that taxi now," I said, trying to seem apologetic.

"But we'll see each other again soon?" he said, looking as if he really had changed his mind about me, as if his image of me as a woman with a hidden agenda had been replaced by his image of me as someone with whom he did indeed have chemistry and was compatible.

"Of course we will," I said.

"How about next Friday night?"

Boy, he wasn't kidding about wanting to spend more time with me. But, to reiterate, there was no reason for us to get together again. No purpose whatsoever. We had no future as a couple. Zippo.

"Amy, do you want to go out Friday night?" he repeated.

"Sure," I said.

13

On Monday morning, Celebetsy planted herself in my office and grilled me.

"I want an update on the *Simply Beautiful* campaign," she said in response to my question about whether she'd had a nice weekend.

"I've written the release, and I'm about to finish up the other materials for the press kit," I said. "Since we aren't doing galleys, I'm sending everything out with bound manuscripts."

"Just make sure there's national TV coverage as well as reviews, or I'll be very disappointed," she threatened for what was probably the tenth time. "Have you called the *Today* show again?"

"No, but I will," I said.

"And the other shows?"

"I'll call them, too."

"You do realize that we have to keep the author happy—or, more specifically, you have to keep the author happy—so she'll sell us her next book."

I nearly blew breakfast. "Her next book?"

"Of course. If this one sells, we want to sign her for another one. I think we've got a franchise here if you don't screw it up."

"I have no intention of screwing it up." Well, I had a fantasy of screwing it up—a really great fantasy, where Tara would be homeless and Betsy would be jobless and I would be living it up in Bora Bora.

"I know you met with her at her house recently, but have you made up your media list yet?"

I had already given her my media list and she had already approved it. "My mailing list is all set," I said. "First, I'll be sending materials to magazine editors with long lead times. We'll wait for finished books to send to radio and—"

"Get the author to help you with the radio stuff," she ordered, interrupting me. "She has her own show, so she must know a lot of people in that industry."

"*I* know a lot of people in that industry, Betsy. I talk to them every day." Did she think I sat at my desk meditating?

"Even so, I want you to call the author and get her advice. She might have friends we should target. She might have enemies we should avoid, too."

Yeah, you're looking at one, I thought as she strutted out of my office without so much as a backward glance. Such a cool customer, that Celebetsy. How did her husband put up with her? That's what we all wondered after each encounter with her. She had zero warmth, except when she needed to ingratiate herself with someone she perceived to be important, and could be downright nasty on occasion. Do people like her even realize how mean they are?

I was contemplating all this when Scott stuck his head in to say that Tara was on the phone.

"Does she have us on speed dial or what?" he said, referring to the fact that she had been bombarding us with calls.

"It's okay," I replied. "I was about to call her anyway. Betsy threatened to whip me if I didn't."

"Betsy." He sucked in his cheeks and pouted—his dead-on imitation of her. "Just remember, I'm on your side no matter what."

I thanked him, then picked up the phone. "Hi, Tara. Did you get the books I sent you?"

"Yes, and they really came in handy."

"Why?"

"Stuart and I ended up flying to Bermuda for the weekend

instead of staying home, and they were perfect for airplane reading."

For the next several minutes, I was forced to listen to her crow about how Lasher's Meats & Eats had a corporate jet, as well as a client with a compound in Bermuda, and how the two of them flew to the island and spent two and a half fan-*tas*tic days there.

"It makes all the difference when you don't have to go commercial," she said. "I'm getting to the point where I can't even deal with first class."

Wait until your book tour, I thought, picturing Princess Tara having to fly to twenty cities in twenty days—in coach.

"So how was your weekend, Amy?" she asked when she had finished her travelogue.

"Fan*tas*tic," I said, throwing her simply beautiful word back in her face, then changing the subject before she could ask me any personal questions.

We went over my mailing list of magazine editors, chatted about the press release I'd written, discussed other aspects of the publicity campaign. I was almost off the hook, when she said, "Now, we really have to set a date for our dinner, so I can finally meet that elusive man of yours."

Damn. "I can't set a date yet," I said. "My fiancé's busy, as I've explained."

"Stuart's busy, too, but he makes time to eat, Amy."

"Right, but my fiancé travels a lot."

"He's around often enough for you two to plan your wedding. Why can't you bring him to dinner when he's in town?"

Okay, okay. You're wondering why I didn't just tell Tara to forget it, to leave me alone about it, to take her invitation and shove it. You're thinking, Gee, Amy, you're not a teenager anymore. You're a grown-up person with a grown-up job and a grown-up life, so why can't you stand up to your former best friend? Why do you regress whenever she's in the picture?

My answer is this: I couldn't help it. Not only was there the specter of Celebetsy and her edict to "keep the author happy" but the old pull Tara had over me was still in place, too. If you've never had a friend who's better at everything than you are, if you've never had a friend who coasts along while you struggle, if you've never had a friend who stole your guy right out from under your nose, then you probably won't understand why I kept wimping out. It's sad, I know, but Tara still had the ability to make me feel reduced, inferior, her subordinate. Of course, I'd made matters worse when I'd blurted out my big stupid lie.

"Tara, let me ask you something," I said. "Why is this dinner so important to you? If you and I hadn't run into each other on the street that day, we wouldn't even be in each other's lives. Our friendship was over at that point."

"Temporarily. I always knew we'd make peace."

"Yes, we have a relationship now, because of your book, and it's going along nicely, don't you think? So why not leave well enough alone and table the idea of meeting my fiancé?"

Silence.

"Tara?"

More silence, then gradually heavier breathing, followed by the sound of tears making their way down Tara's nose and throat. One sniff, then two, then several sniffs in a row. She was crying, just the way she'd cried after I walked in on her and Stuart, just the way she'd been crying when I met her on the playground in elementary school. Connie was right: She was a baby.

"I can't 'table it' because I care about you, Amy." Snort, sniff.

"That's lovely, Tara, but—"

"I want to show you that I'm here for you during your prewedding period. I want to be the maid of honor—figuratively speaking—that I failed to be when you were engaged to Stuart."

Ah, so that was it. She was intent on proving that she was capable of being in the presence of one of my fiancés without sleeping with him?

"I appreciate the sentiment, Tara. I do. But why don't you and I continue to rebuild our friendship slowly, without anybody else's involvement? No husbands and no fiancés. Just us."

"Without Stuart's involvement, you mean. You still care about him, is that it?"

"No, this is *not* about Stuart." Why did she keep saying that? "Look, let's just work together on your book and see what develops between us. My fiancé really is busy, so for the foreseeable future, you and I can—"

"Maybe there is no fiancé," she said, having stopped crying as abruptly as she'd started.

"Excuse me?"

"Well, Amy, I'm just beginning to wonder if he actually exists, since you're so tight-lipped about him. You've never even mentioned his name, for example."

Great. So now she suspected that I was scamming her? How humiliating was that?

"You never asked me his name," I said, stalling, hyperventilating, wishing I'd never opened my mouth that day on the street.

"Okay. Then what is it?"

"What's what?"

"His *name,* Amy."

Oh God. Now what? She had me up against the proverbial wall.

"Tara," I said, trying to sound distracted, "could I put you on hold for a second? Apparently, one of our authors has dropped by with some sort of a crisis."

"One of your authors? It wouldn't be Tony Stiles, would it?" She sounded seriously excited by the mere thought. "I'll die if you tell me he's right outside your office."

There it was again: the envy flowing in *my* direction for a change. And all because of Tony. Dear, sweet, "I hate liars" Tony.

"I'll only be a minute or two," I said hurriedly, then pushed the hold button before she could protest.

As I sat there staring at the phone, feeling hopelessly cornered, an idea descended on me. Not a sane idea, granted, but an idea that would not only appease Tara but impress her, an idea that would get her off my case about the engagement thing *and* let her know that I was no longer her poor pathetic handmaiden.

"Hi again. Sorry," I said when I came back on the line. "Crisis averted."

"Did it have to do with Tony Stiles after all?" she asked.

"No," I said. "But since you mentioned Tony, I might as well tell you the truth about him."

"Oooh, goodie. I love gossip. Is he going out with a famous actress or something?"

"No. He's going out with me."

She laughed. Laughed! "You?"

"Me. We're getting married, Tara. He's my fiancé, the one who's so busy."

She gasped. She sputtered. She said she couldn't believe it. She demanded to know why I hadn't told her before.

"It's a secret because of the L and T connection," I said, "and because Tony's in the public eye. He's dead set against any publicity leaks about us. He's adamant about keeping his private life private."

"I still can't get over this."

"Yes, it's wonderful, isn't it? But back to what I was saying . . . No one—and I mean no one—knows about us. I'm only telling you because . . . well, because we used to be such close friends."

"Oh my God," she said. "You and Tony Stiles."

"Right. But it's a *secret,*" I repeated.

"And you told me because of our friendship," she said. "I'm so, so touched by that."

"Touched but discreet, got it?"

"Absolutely. You can trust me, really. You two will come for dinner, and neither Stuart nor I will breathe a word to a living soul."

"Not even to him."

"To Stuart?"

"No, to Tony."

"I don't understand."

This was the sticky part, the part that made me feel even

more sheepish than I already felt. I was going to make Tara swear not to mention my impending nuptials in front of Tony, so that he wouldn't know that I'd brought him to dinner under false pretenses, wouldn't know that I'd trotted him out, put him on display, done the very thing he despised. Well, come on, he'd left me no choice, not after his speech about the woman who'd asked him to participate in her lie and then gotten herself dumped. Besides, my deception would only last one night—maybe three hours, max.

"You can't let Tony find out I told you that we're getting married, Tara. As I said, he's extremely touchy about people knowing the details of his personal life, and he'd be very upset if he thought I'd filled you in. So we'll come for dinner under one condition."

"That I don't let on that I know."

"Exactly. Not a single syllable about our engagement."

"I hear you. Now, pull out your calendar," she said excitedly.

I pretended to flip through the pages of my supposedly booked-solid social calendar. "What luck. We have an opening this coming Friday," I said, since I actually had plans with Tony for that night.

"Then Friday it is," she said. "Oh, won't this be fun? It'll be just like old times, double-dating the way we used to."

It'll be nothing like old times, I thought, not nearly as guilt-ridden as I should have been.

14

Tony called midweek to confirm our date for Friday night, at which point I told him there had been a slight change in plans.

"I hope you don't mind," I said, "but I accepted a dinner invitation for both of us."

"Oh, please no," he groaned. "Not one of those unbearable L and T command performances."

"Not exactly. One of our authors, Tara Messer, who also happens to be a woman I grew up with, invited me for dinner on Friday night. L and T is publishing her book in a few months, and Betsy Kirby—you know, our marketing director?—has been insisting that I give her the royal treatment. Anyhow, when Tara invited me for dinner, I told her I had a date, and she said, 'Bring him along.' So will you go with me, Tony? I promise we won't stay long."

He grumbled about how he'd been hoping to take me to a movie, but after surprisingly little begging on my part, he said he'd go.

"Thanks, Tony," I said, more than a little relieved, as well as flattered by how quickly he'd agreed, how keen he seemed to keep our date at any cost. "It won't be so bad. Tara and her husband live in Mamaroneck, on Long Island Sound. If nothing else, you'll enjoy the setting."

"My idea of a 'setting' is the two of us alone somewhere, not making small talk with a couple of strangers."

Yeah, he was keen all right, as if he'd done a complete 180 about me. Or maybe he was just between girlfriends and I was his conquest du jour. "We'll be alone at some point. We'll drive up to Westchester and be back in the city before you know it. Zip zip."

"Zip zip, huh?"

"Yes. You'll see. I'll earn brownie points with the author—and get Betsy off my case—and then we'll leave. It'll be painless."

I avoided Connie that whole week. Every time she'd ask me how my attempts to befriend Tony were coming along, I'd say fine and dash off to some supposedly pressing business. I couldn't tell her I was tricking him, that I was taking him to Tara's as my fiancé without bothering to ask his permission. She'd flip out on me. Besides, there was no reason to upset her. It was just one dopey dinner—a few hours of chitchat and then I'd be home free. Tara would be put in her place, and Tony would never know he'd been duped. End of story.

"Wow. You look incredible," he said when he picked me up Friday night.

"Do I?" I said, pleased by his reaction, although I hadn't spent hours getting dressed so that *he* would think I looked incredible. It was Tara I needed to look incredible for. And yes, that was twisted, but while women may dress to turn a guy on, it's other women we dress to impress, particularly women we can't stand. Go figure.

For this particular occasion, my goal was to project the image of an extremely successful career woman who had also managed to snare a handsome, wealthy, highly sought-after celebrity bachelor author as my fiancé—a woman who was radiantly happy because she had it all, in other words. Since a cold front was forecast to move through the tristate area during the evening, bringing heavy rain and wind along with it, I'd chosen a black gabardine pantsuit, a creamy

caramel-colored silk blouse, and black leather boots, plus
floating sea pearls on a champagne-gold chain around my
neck. My hair had gone a little wild, given the humidity, but
all in all, I felt good about what I saw in the mirror and was
psyched to show myself—well, myself with Tony—off.

He helped me into the passenger seat of the Ferrari,
which was so low to the ground I figured I'd need a forklift
to get me out of it, and away we went. Tony, by the way,
looked pretty incredible himself in his black slacks and
charcoal gray sweater. Not that I was affected by his appearance one way or the other, except from a purely detached
perspective. (Okay, I was affected by his appearance—he
looked utterly hot, and part of me was sorry he and I were
never going to be a real couple.) It was Tara who would fawn
over him, while I would just stand back and watch.

During the ride up to Mamaroneck, it started to rain and
the roads began to get slick. It felt as if we were on a race-
track instead of the Hutchinson River Parkway, and I found
myself ramming my foot down on some imaginary brake
pedal every time we'd pass another car.

"Everything okay?" asked Tony. "I assumed you'd be
comfortable in the Ferrari, since you're so familiar with it."

Yeah, I was about as familiar with it as I was with a 747.
"Everything's great," I said. "One of my boots is too tight,
that's all." Actually, he was driving rather conservatively in
the increasingly wet conditions, and I appreciated that he
wasn't one of those macho maniacs who values speed over
safety. I was just nervous about the evening, I realized as we
approached Tara's exit off the highway. Nervous and excited
about finally giving my old pal her comeuppance.

The rain came down harder as we continued to head east,
and although we made jokes about April showers, the
weather really had turned ugly.

"Here it is," I said, advising Tony that Tara's house was at
the very end of the private road we'd just reached.

"Thank God," he said. "Nobody should be out in this
mess."

The private road forked into two driveways, one of which

was Tara's. It was a long, winding, heavily landscaped driveway, and at the foot of it sat a NO TRESPASSING! sign that she
had hand-painted in yellow, her "happy color." The ground
was quite flooded already, and Tony wasn't thrilled about the
way the Ferrari was getting splattered with mud.

"Okay, we made it," I said when he finally shut off the engine in front of the house.

He glanced out the car window and laughed. "Your author
has a little money, I see."

"You're referring to her castle."

"Yeah. Does she have a big family?"

"Nope. Just her husband, Stuart Lasher, as in Lasher's
Meats & Eats. Business must be booming."

"Even so, did they really need the turret? I wasn't aware
Mamaroneck was at war."

"If you think the turret's a little over-the-top, wait until
you meet Tara."

Huddled under an umbrella, we hurried up the walkway,
where the lady of the manor herself was waiting to usher us
inside.

"Come in, come in, come in," she said. "You must be
soaked."

She, of course, was not soaked, unless you counted the
Shalimar; from the smell of her, she must have hosed herself
down with it, and her clothes, too. Speaking of which, while
I was dressed for success in my pert little black pantsuit, she
was dressed for excess. She was wearing what looked to me
like an evening gown but was probably just the latest in designer hostess attire—an ankle-length kelly green frock
made of some exquisitely delicate fabric that rustled when
she moved even an inch. The color was gorgeous against her
creamy skin and long golden hair, and the outfit was so
much more stylish and sophisticated than mine that I felt as
diminished as I always did when I was around her. In other
words, she looked so great, I wanted to choke her.

"Amy," she said, pulling me into a hug, although not as
tightly as she had the last time I'd visited. Possibly, she was
afraid I'd crush the fabric or drool on it. "I'm so glad you're

here. I thought you might cancel when you heard the weather report."

"No, we braved the rain and now we're—"

"And this must be *Tony,*" she said breathlessly, practically shoving me out of the way so she was free to extend her perfectly manicured hand to him. "I'm Tara Messer, and it's such a pleasure to meet you. My husband and I are huge fans of your books."

"Thanks, Tara. I appreciate that," he said with a smile. I could tell he was thinking what a babe she was, which made me want to lift up her green dress, say "Peekaboo," and show him her knock-knees. "And thanks for letting me tag along on your business dinner with Amy."

"Business dinner?" she said, then winked at me in such a ridiculous, exaggerated way that Tony couldn't possibly have missed it. "We can talk a little business if you insist, but there's a subject I bet you'd *much* rather discuss tonight. So once I've served you a drink and a nibble, I want *all* the delicious details, you two."

He shot me a truly puzzled look, but I was so caught off guard by her inability to keep her trap shut that I could only shrug helplessly in response.

"What's this I hear about a nibble?" said a male voice from down the hall.

Stuart. It was Stuart. My faithless Stuart. I hadn't seen him since the bedroom fiasco, hadn't laid eyes on him since I'd watched in horror as Tara climbed off his limp—

"Here comes my husband," she said to Tony. "He's your second-biggest fan." She giggled. "Sorry. Your third-biggest. Amy's your second, of course."

"Tara's referring to the fact that I'm always promoting you," I explained, giving her the evil eye. "I'm tireless when it comes to championing my authors, Tony. You know that." What was with her anyway? She wasn't acting like someone who intended to play by my rules.

I was about to take her aside and read her the riot act, when I heard Stuart marching toward us. I stood up straighter, stuck my boobs out, moistened my lips. It was an involuntary reflex. Yes, I still hated the guy, but I felt the need to impress him, too—to show him what a fool he'd been to let me slip through his slimy fingers.

"Hello, everybody," he said when he finally appeared in his version of host attire: a Brooks Brothers suit. He always wore Brooks Brothers suits, no matter how informal the occasion, except for the last time I'd seen him, when, of course, he'd been wearing his birthday suit.

At thirty-five, he was thinner than he was when we were together (Tara must have put him on a strenuous diet and exercise program), but still tall—six three or so—with excellent, almost ramrod-straight posture. His wiry dark hair was thinner, too; the bald patch he used to obsess over had multiplied, and now there were three or four areas where you could actually catch some scalp. He had a prominent nose, a slightly recessive chin, and large brown eyes. Oh, and he had a long neck. I used to think it gave him an air of authority, but now I thought it gave him the air of a giraffe. Yes, that's what he reminded me of—a preppy, nouveau-riche giraffe.

"Hi, Stuart," I said, taking the initiative and giving him a kiss on the cheek. I was trying to present myself as someone who was letting bygones be bygones, trying to affect the demeanor of a normal person, as opposed to a woman scorned.

"Amy." He grabbed my shoulders and held me away so he could get a good look at me. "Amy," he repeated, as if marveling at the fact that I had survived the loss of him. "It's great to see you. I was thrilled when Tara told me your news."

"My news?" I glared at her again. Hadn't she tipped him off? Didn't he know he was supposed to keep his trap shut, too?

"And you're Tony," he said, turning so they could shake hands. "I hope you realize what a lucky, lucky man you are."

"Oh, you mean because his books have sold so well," I said with a rather hysterical laugh. Would I have to police every word that came out of their mouths? If so, the evening was going to be interminable.

"I do feel lucky," said Tony. "But Amy's been a big part

of that luck. She's pushed me to do publicity even when I've resisted."

Stuart nodded knowingly, as if—what?—I'd pushed him to get engaged? Please. All I did was suggest that we either get married or break up, after it became clear that our relationship was losing its spark. He was the one who'd picked marriage.

"Tony and I often disagree on how to publicize his books," I said, attempting to establish that this was indeed a *business* dinner. "He's not big on self-promotion. But you, Tara, will be a natural on all the talk shows when your book comes out."

"Let's hope," she said. "Now, why don't you two come in and make yourselves comfortable. Tony?" She took his arm and waltzed him inside the house before I could stop her, before I could drag her into a corner and make her swear to lay off the subject of our engagement, before I could do anything at all to keep disaster at bay. Instead, I was stuck with Stuart.

"Amy," he said for the third time as he grinned at me. "You look fabulous."

"That's sweet of you," I said. "But if I do, it must be because I'm in love for the first time in my life." Well, I had to tweak him, didn't I?

He put his hand on my back as we began to trail after Tara and Tony. "I have to admit, I was really surprised when I heard about you and Tony Stiles. I never expected it. Not in a million years."

"Why? Did you expect me to enter a convent after you dumped me?" The nerve of the guy. I started to get steamed at him, then reminded myself that this was exactly what I wanted—for him to be awestruck by the caliber of fiancé I'd landed—and that I was the one manipulating him this time around.

"No, Amy. I didn't expect you to enter a convent or join a cult or swear off men forever," he said with a chuckle. "It's just that the guy you're marrying is my hero."

Yes. Okay. This was good. "He's my hero, too." I clasped

my hands together and sighed, as if overcome with hero
worship. "I never dreamed I could find a man like him—a
man of genuine integrity." Take that, you turd.

"I'm sure it doesn't hurt that he's made millions."

"I haven't checked his bank account lately, Stuart, but it's
true that he's very successful." God, had he always been so
materialistic? Had I never noticed? "Successful *and* passionate. If it were up to him, he'd scrap the engagement and
have us standing before a justice of the peace this very
minute. Unlike some people I know, he actually means it
when he says he wants to spend the rest of his life with me."

"Amy, Amy." Stuart slid his arm down my back, wrapped
it around my waist, and gave me a little squeeze. "I never
meant to hurt you. You know that, don't you?"

"What I know is that the past doesn't matter anymore."
Yeah, sure. "I've recovered from our breakup, as you can
see."

"You certainly have. I bet you're thinking that Tara and I
did you a favor by getting together. Look who you ended up
with instead of me: Tony Stiles, the best damn mystery
writer in America. I must seem like the booby prize to you
now, compared to him."

I smiled. He was getting the message all right, the loser.
"Well, you're not Tara's booby prize. She says you two are
deliriously happy."

"That's us, Mr. and Mrs. Deliriously Happy. But back to
you, Amy. You and Tony Stiles. I still can't believe that
you're tying the knot in a few months."

"Yes, but I hope Tara told you not to say anything about
the engagement in front of Tony. He doesn't like discussing
our romance with strangers. He doesn't think it's anyone
else's business."

"Strangers?" He scoffed. "Tara and I are hardly strangers,
hon."

He gave me another squeeze. Yech. And what was the
deal with the "hon"?

"You're strangers to Tony," I said, "so please play it cool

tonight and don't let on that you know about us. He's an extremely private person and reacts badly when—"

"Stuart?" Tara called out to him before I could emphasize how important it was that he button his lips. "Where are you, sweetheart? Tony and I are waiting for you to make everybody drinks, so we can take the chill off this damp and dreary night."

"Coming," he called back to her, hurrying us along toward the library, where Tara was chatting with Tony, batting her eyelashes at him, running her fingers through her gleaming golden locks so he couldn't help but be dazzled. At first, I felt stirrings of jealousy—he was mine!—but then I remembered that he wasn't mine, just a prop. I also remembered that I intended for her to fall all over him, hoping she would be so taken with him that she'd wish she could trade places with me.

"Oh, here you are, sweetheart," she said to Stuart. "Why don't you make the drinks while I run into the kitchen and assemble the hors d'oeuvres with Michelle?"

"I'll help you," I said quickly, hoping to get her alone so I could tell her to stop blabbing about the very thing she'd promised not to blab about.

"No, no, no," she said, shooing me away. "You're our guest, Amy. Stuart can help me. And our cook is here."

"There must be something I can do to lend a hand," I said pointedly, flashing her one of those awful winks she'd given me.

"I won't hear of it," she said. "Stuart? The ice bucket's in the kitchen. Come with me, sweetheart."

Before I could protest further, the two of them skipped off and busied themselves with hors d'oeuvring/bartending duties. Resolving to catch Tara at the very next opportunity, I sat next to Tony on the sofa.

"How are you holding up so far?" I whispered.

"Fine, but I'd rather be back in the city with you," he said. "Your author's a little too fond of herself for my taste."

So Tara hadn't dazzled him after all. "You noticed that, huh?"

He nodded. "And that book of hers sounds awful."

"It's beyond awful."

"And then there's this house." He rolled his eyes as he glanced around. "Ten thousand square feet feels like overkill for two people."

"Tara tends to overdo things. Take a look at all the orchids."

Tony stifled a laugh. "I know. When I asked her about them, she said—and I quote—'Orchids are the new sunflowers.'"

"That's Tara, always right on top of the trends. The other day, she announced that white is the new black, ottomans are the new coffee tables, and toile is the new leather."

"I don't know what the hell toile is."

"Don't feel bad. She probably doesn't, either."

He laughed again. "Yeah, she's definitely a strange one. When we were alone before, she asked me how our plans were coming along. I had no idea what she was talking about."

I tensed. "Our plans?"

"Yeah. Yours and mine. She started out by saying how L and T's policy was unfair but that she would keep our secret. What secret? Does this woman live in her own world or something?"

That did it. I was gonna kill her. The second she was alone in the kitchen, I would stab her with one of her fancy Henckel knives and watch her bleed to death all over her travertine floor. "Uh, well, she is sort of ditsy at times," I said. "But maybe she meant the secret of your success—of our success as a team. We did get your last book to the number-one spot on the *Times* best-seller list even though L and T decided not to do TV ads. That was probably the unfair policy she was referring to."

"Maybe. But why was she asking about *our* plans when it's *her* publicity campaign you came here to work out?"

Before I could tap-dance around that one, Tara returned.

"Time for those nibbles," she trilled as she floated into the room carrying a platter of canapés, each adorned with sprigs of this, dollops of that—seriously garnished, in other words. "And while we're on the subject of food," she added, beaming at Tony and me, "have you two decided on the menu for your big day?"

I tried not to flinch—tried to pretend I hadn't even heard the question—but it was obvious to me then that Tara couldn't control herself, even though I'd begged her to. What was also obvious was that it wasn't so much about her breaking her promise to me as it was about her needing to feed her own ego. She couldn't stand to be left out. She had to be the center of attention. It had always been that way with her, so what made me think she'd changed?

I suddenly flashed back to the sixth grade, when she had urged me to run for class president. I had resisted, thanked her for her support, but explained that I couldn't bear the idea of promoting myself (which was why I became a promoter of others when I grew up). "Oh come on, Amy, *please*?" she'd said, throwing her arms around me and folding me into a hug. "You're an *A* student and a hard worker and the kids respect you. Plus, running for president will be a good way for you to boost your self-esteem. Look, I'm your best friend. I wouldn't tell you to do something if I didn't believe it was the right thing for you. And with me behind you, you'll definitely win." I remember looking at her with such adoration. Sure, she could be full of herself—she honestly thought that she and her tremendous popularity could deliver the votes—but she was also my biggest champion, and I was endlessly flattered by the interest she took in me. I'd told her I'd think about running. A few days later, I was shocked to hear that Tara herself was running for class president. What was up with that? Had she deliberately set me up as her opponent, knowing she'd beat me by a landslide? Had she always intended to run but forgotten to inform me? Didn't best friends tell each other everything? So why had I been kept in the dark? When I'd confronted her, she'd turned on the charm and feigned no understanding of why I might be stung, or miffed, or, at the very least, confused. "Gosh, Amy, I never meant to hurt you," she'd said in what would become a familiar refrain over the years. "When you didn't decide right away if you were running, I figured

you weren't going to and that one of us should. You can understand that, right? I stepped in because you didn't want to.
That's all. But now that I'm running, I'd love it if you'd be
my campaign manager."

Why didn't I see it then? Or even after she stole Stuart?
Why didn't I see that, while I had my own weaknesses and
insecurities, Tara had problems of her own? She was toxic,
for God's sake! She couldn't keep her mouth shut about my
engagement to Tony after swearing she would, not because
she didn't care about me, but because she cared more about
being the star, being the one in charge, being the one stirring
the pot, even if that meant betraying me. It had happened before, over and over, and it was happening now. I had to get
out of there!

I checked my watch. Twenty minutes down. Only two
hours to go. I could make it through the evening. I would
make it through the evening. And once I did, I would never,
under any circumstances, trust Tara Messer again.

15

We haven't even thought about the menu for *Tony's publication party,*" I said with yet another glare in her direction. "We're not publishing his book until next year. It's your publication party we should be talking about, Tara, so let's get started. We should have the party here, I think. That way, all the media people and bookstore buyers and members of L and T's sales force will be able to observe your simply beautiful idiom firsthand."

"Oh," she said, sweeping her hair off the back of her neck. "What a wonderful idea."

Of course she thought it was wonderful. It was the same idea she'd thrown at me to convince me to come for lunch. "Yes, we should definitely have the party here, and it should be cocktails and a light supper, and you should come up with party favors for each guest—you know, the way you write about in the book?"

"Party favors! Yes! We'll do the favors and the gift baskets and the personalized poems—the whole enchilada," said Tara, who was easily distracted from the taboo subject, since the new subject revolved around her. I shouldn't have worried so much. The minute I started tossing around scenarios that placed her at center stage, she was putty in my hands. For a full half hour, she talked to me about herself while Stuart pumped Tony for a preview of the next Joe West mystery. Stuart was thrilled to have the chance to pepper his favorite author with questions about the books, and Tony was good-natured about explaining how he couldn't discuss the specifics of his research but that the crimes Joe West solved were based on real ones. Most important, nobody mentioned marriage.

Eventually, Tara departed for the kitchen so she could oversee the plating of the food by Michelle, her cook/housekeeper, who had probably been preparing the meal all day, in between cleaning chores.

We were assigned seats at the dining room table (yes, there were place cards, even though we were only four) and served our herbed game hens—perfectly plump little birds that were accompanied by a green salad and a very impressive-looking side dish involving chanterelle mushrooms in puff pastry. We all oohed and aahed and said everything smelled and tasted delicious, and just when I was about to return the conversation to the exciting things in store for *Simply Beautiful* and its author, there was a ferocious crack of thunder, which stunned everyone.

"This storm is turning out to be much worse than they predicted," said Stuart.

"Can you imagine having a wedding on a night like this?" said Tara.

"Why?" asked Tony. "Do you know someone who's getting married?"

She and Stuart thought that was hilarious, while I nearly spit out my mouthful of game hen.

"Someone's getting married all right," she said with another wink-wink smile at me. She turned to Stuart. "We'd better start thinking about a gift for the lovebirds, sweetheart."

"You're the creative one," he said. "You'll come up with something."

Tara turned back to Tony. "Are you registered?"

"You bet," he said. "I'm a lifelong Democrat."

She and Stuart laughed again. Ha-ha-ha. What a scream that Tony Stiles was.

"No, really, Tony," she said when she'd caught her breath. "Is there anything you can use?"

"Anything I can use?"

"Yes. In your home, for instance?"

"I can use a new fax machine. My old one just died."

"Tony, Tony." She blinked at him, as if he were such a kidder. "I meant—well, you know what I meant."

"Speaking of home," said Stuart, "have you been looking at apartments? Or are you staying where you are?"

"I love my place," said Tony. "I've got a loft in SoHo and it suits me just fine. Why would I move anywhere else?"

"SoHo's fine for now," said Tara, "but what about when you have kids? You'd have to send them to private school, wouldn't you?"

Tony glanced at me as if to say, Are these people weird or what? Either that or: Why are they acting as if we're getting married when we're only on our second date?

"Don't saddle him with kids before he's even taken the trip to the altar," Stuart chided Tara.

O-kay. That did it. I had been sitting there in silence, hoping the storm—the one outside and the one at the table— would blow over, but now I had to act fast in order to reroute the conversation once and for all. I had wanted to choke Tara, but the person I needed to choke at that moment was myself.

"Oh"—cough—"my"—cough—"God." I grunted, clutched my chest, coughed again as I pretended my throat was closing up. "I think a piece of meat is caught in my—"

As I pointed frantically at my windpipe in an effort to prove how dire the situation was, Tony leapt from his chair, stood me up like a rag doll, and grabbed me around the middle.

"Try not to panic, Amy," he said.

"Yes, don't panic," Tara chimed in. "Tony's going to Heimlich you."

"Be gentle," I said in short grunts, hoping he wouldn't crack one of my ribs. Yes, I wanted to pay back Tara, but not at the risk of injuring myself.

"I will," he said. "Just stay calm."

Tara and Stuart watched wide-eyed as Tony pressed his fists against my midsection. It only hurt a little, but the best part was that nobody in that room was thinking about anything except the morsel of herbed game hen that was allegedly threatening my life. I figured the drama I had created was good for at least another hour, what with the maneuver and my hair-raising brush with death, not to mention the concern everyone would show for my welfare and the need to have me rest quietly on a sofa in the aftermath.

As it turned out, my pseudodrama was trumped yet again by Tara. Well, not by Tara herself, but by a force of nature, which was the same thing.

After I told Tony that he could stop Heimliching me because I had successfully swallowed the piece of game hen and was out of danger, there was another clap of thunder, then a loud crash.

Tara and Stuart flew around the house, checking to see which priceless, ridiculously expensive, one-of-a-kind object might have fallen.

"The minute they come downstairs, we're leaving," I said to Tony. "I've accomplished everything I needed to here, so there's no reason to stay any longer."

"Ready when you are," he said. "But I'll tell you what: I have new respect for you after tonight, the way you have to deal with off-the-wall authors. Tara's even more high-maintenance than I am."

"You have no idea."

When our hosts reappeared, Tony and I announced that we were going home.

"I'm pretty exhausted from my choking episode," I said as the four of us stood in the threshold.

"And I'm not sure how bad the roads will be," Tony added. "We'll probably have to take it very slowly."

"We understand," said Stuart.

"Of course we do," said Tara.

Tony and I thanked them profusely for the dinner and the hospitality. There was much hugging and shaking of hands, and when Stuart wished Tony the best of luck, Tony thought he was talking about the drive back to the city, not the stroll down the aisle.

As for me, I was seriously relieved. I was getting out of there without anybody catching me in my lie. (Okay, lies.) I could spend the rest of my life replaying the look on Tara's face when I showed up with Tony Stiles as my fiancé. It was so worth all the aggravation.

"Let us walk you out to your car," offered Stuart. "I've got a golf umbrella that's bigger than the one you brought."

"Yes, we'll both walk you out," said Tara, "since the rain has let up for the moment."

I didn't object. I figured it would be icing on the cake when they saw Tony's trillion-dollar Ferrari.

My feelings of well-being were short-lived, however. When we all stepped outside, we gasped in horror when we saw that a huge tree had fallen during the storm—right smack across the driveway. No, Tony's car wasn't damaged, but the tree was completely blocking our escape route.

"We'll never get anyone over here to move it at this hour," said Stuart, who did indeed flip out when he spotted the Ferrari. I could tell he was dying to ask Tony how much he'd paid for it, how fast it went, and all the other things men want to know about cars that are essentially penis substitutes, but he held himself in check.

"You're right, sweetheart," said Tara. "That tree isn't going anywhere tonight, and neither are Amy and Tony."

"Excuse me?" I said.

"Well," she said, "you won't be able to get your car up the driveway."

"But you must have a handyman on staff," I said, feeling helpless, desperate, as sick as if I *had* choked on the game hen.

"A handyman can't move the tree, Amy," said Tony, who started to wipe the debris off his windshield, then gave up. "It'll take someone with a chain saw and maybe heavier equipment, and nobody's coming tonight. There must be hundreds of people needing help after this storm."

"I still don't see why we can't move the tree ourselves," I

said, my dread mounting. "I could lift one part and you could lift—"

"Amy," said Tony, "the tree weighs more than all of us put together."

"But I'll bet we can sort of drag it to the side of the—"

"It's settled!" Tara said. "You and Tony will spend the night; then we'll worry about the tree tomorrow. We'll start by having a lovely, lovely brunch. I've got eggs and Canadian bacon and some fan*tastic* French bread. We'll eat in the sunroom and drink Bloody Marys and talk some more. It'll be just like the grown-up slumber parties I write about in *Simply Beautiful,* where couples stay over at each other's houses instead of booking rooms at country inns. Remember that chapter, Amy?"

This isn't happening, I thought. This cannot be happening. I was so close to getting out of there, so close.

"Sure you'll stay with us," said Stuart, patting Tony on the back. "It'll be our pleasure to have a literary luminary sleeping under our roof. That's what the guest house is for."

The guest house. The too-precious-for-words little replica of the castle. It was just as opulently decorated as the main house, with its sitting room, minikitchen, and full bath. Oh, and it had a very romantic bedroom. That's right. One bedroom. With one bed in it. A bed that Tony and I would be sharing even though we were not engaged or going steady, and certainly not having sex.

"Tony has to get back to the city," I said, my voice sounding screechy and pained. "He has a strict writing schedule, which includes working on weekends. The only days he takes off are Christmas and his birthday. Right, Tony?"

"Right," he said, "but even if we arranged for a cab to meet us at the foot of the driveway and take us home tonight, I'd still have to come back during the week to get the car. That would use up more of my writing time than staying over."

"It just seems that if we call around—Tara, you must have contacts within the police, the fire department, a towing company, somebody—we can get the tree moved," I said. "Then there'd be no need for us to stay over."

"Don't be silly, Amy," she said, taking me by the elbow and escorting me back inside. "You won't be imposing, if that's what's bothering you."

What was bothering me was that I had lied, cheated, and choked my way through the evening and had managed to emerge unscathed. I had impressed Tara with the man I'd landed, and that should have been that. But that was never that when it came to her. Never.

16

Naturally, Tony didn't understand why I was so upset about us having to sleep over in the Lashers' guest house. While I was pacing frantically around its small living room, which was furnished with a love seat and two chairs and more flowers than a funeral parlor, he was sitting calmly. "Look," he said, "I want to get away from these people as much as you do, but it's not as if there's anything we can do about the tree falling in their driveway. We might as well just grin and bear it."

"You grin and *bare* it," I said as I continued to pace. "I overheard that exchange between you and Stuart, where he offered to lend you something to wear for the night and you told him you didn't need it because you sleep in the nude." Tara had given me a sheer black nightgown to wear to bed. I'd taken it only because I couldn't very well sleep in my clothes without looking rumpled the next morning—and because it was really fetching—but I assumed Tony would sleep in his underwear or a sheet or *something*.

"What's this? Is the fearless publicist to the stars afraid of a little male nudity?" he teased.

"Of course I'm not afraid." Well, I wasn't. I was merely caught off guard by the idea of spending the night with a naked author. Okay, with a naked Tony Stiles.

He laughed. "You're a nervous wreck, but you can relax.

I do sleep in the nude—when I'm alone. I was only busting Stuart's chops when I made that comment. He's such a pompous jerk, he probably sleeps in that Brooks Brothers suit."

"Actually, he sleeps in pajamas. Light blue pinstriped pajamas with his initials monogrammed on the sleeves."

Tony did a double take. "And how would you know that? It's not as if you've ever slept with him."

I sighed. There was no point in trying to keep the game going any longer. No point in trying to keep Tony in the dark about his unwitting role as my fiancé and my past history with Tara and Stuart. No point in trying to fool any of them. I wouldn't be able to. The tree in the driveway took care of that. There was no way I could spend another whole day lying to everybody and not get caught.

Yes, I might as well tell Tony the truth, I decided. He and I didn't have a future together, so what did I care if he hated my guts for being yet another woman in his life who had a hidden agenda? He was adverse to commitment. He'd admitted it. We might have had a fling. A torrid fling even. But then in three months, we'd have been in the same situation I'd been in countless times: He'd stop calling and I'd start wondering why, and eventually we'd have the "I don't think this is working out" conversation. Who needed it?

"Tony, there's something I have to tell you," I said wearily, sinking into the chair next to his.

"I already know what it is. Judging by your reaction to the mere thought of me in the buff, I'd say you're about to tell me you're not up for sex tonight."

I rolled my eyes. "It's not about sex. This will be hard for you to comprehend, but I can live without ever seeing your body up close and personal."

"Is that so?"

"Yes."

"Well, in case it *is* the sex thing that's got you so rattled, let me assure you that I'm perfectly capable of sleeping in the same bed with a woman and not ravishing her. I'll stay on my side and you'll stay on your side, and you won't even know we're in the same room. I'll make sure you get a good night's rest and then return you to the city tomorrow—with your virtue intact."

So he was saying he wasn't attracted to me now? After all that business about our chemistry and compatibility? Call me a hypocrite, but I would have preferred that he at least *try* to have sex with me.

But back to my first order of business. "I really do have something to tell you," I said. "No more kidding though, okay? It's serious."

"Fine. No more kidding. Talk."

"Will you promise you won't leave L and T because of what I'm about to say?"

"Leave L and T? Why would I do that?"

"Promise first."

"I promise, but I don't see—"

"Just listen." I cleared my throat. "For starters, here's how I know that Stuart sleeps in monogrammed pinstriped pj's: I was engaged to him."

"Engaged?" He blinked at me, his expression one of bemusement. "You were actually going to marry that twerp?"

"At a big fancy ceremony catered by the one and only Lasher's Meats & Eats."

"Wow. I can't picture the two of you together at all. He seems like such a lightweight, not to mention slippery."

"Slippery?"

"Yeah. You ask him a question and he answers by asking you a question. All night long, I tried to get him to tell me about his business, his hobbies, his house, his wife, something, and he was evasive every time, throwing the attention back onto me."

"Probably because you're his idol. He loves your books, Tony. Maybe he was starstruck."

"Or maybe he's got something to hide. I've interviewed plenty of crooks over the years, and they can be evasive that way. This is just instinct, but I wouldn't trust Stuart Lasher if you paid me."

I nodded ruefully. "I wish you'd tipped me off to that before I met him. You see, Tony, Stuart ended up dumping me for Tara. The two of them had been having an affair behind my back. I caught them in a compromising position a couple of weeks before the wedding."

His trademark smirk vanished. "What a hideous story. I'm so sorry."

"It gets worse. Tara was my best friend growing up—the one I mentioned to you at dinner the other night."

"The queen bee who stung you?"

"Yes." I explained about Tara then. About how I'd loved her as much as I'd resented her throughout our childhood and teenage years; how I'd needed to be around her as much as I'd needed to separate myself from her; how her beauty and popularity had made me feel inferior even though it had opened doors for me; how we'd continued to get together as young women, even as our interests took us in different directions; and how I'd asked her to be my maid of honor for old time's sake. "After I found out about her and Stuart, I severed my relationship with her and didn't expect to see her again. Then all of a sudden, her book turned up on L and T's fall list and it became my job to promote it."

Tony pulled his chair closer to mine, took my hands in his, and held them. "For you to have to hype her to the media, given what happened, sounds above and beyond the call of duty to me."

"To me, too, but there's more."

"Go on."

I recounted my chance meeting with Tara on the street. "I'd just spent three years in therapy and had finally managed to put her out of my mind," I said. "Then there she was, in the flesh, looking so damn perfect, and all my old insecurities came flooding back. The more she went on and on about her fabulous life with Stuart, the more my self-esteem took a dive. It was as if some old habit kicked in, some old reflex where I was instantly reduced by her presence."

"But you have so much more going for you than Tara does," said Tony. "Why would you feel reduced by someone so one-dimensional?"

I smiled, heartened that there actually existed a man who failed to be captivated by her. "History, I guess. Once I was standing on that street next to her with her gorgeous clothes and gorgeous hair and gorgeous everything, it didn't matter what I had accomplished in my life—how many jobs I'd gotten, or friends I'd made, or good deeds I'd done. It didn't even matter that it had been years since I'd viewed her with anything resembling respect. She's not fun or cool or interesting anymore, the way she seemed when we were kids. She's still beautiful, of course, but she's become almost a parody of herself—the cheerleader/prom queen who peaked in high school, never really evolving. And yet—and this is what's so crazy—all that mattered to me that day on the street was that she was Tara Messer and I was her second fiddle. I reverted right back to type."

"But she was the one who behaved badly, Amy. She was the one who should have felt reduced when you two met again."

"I know. Look, maybe this isn't a guy thing, so it's hard for you to understand. Maybe it's only women who get caught up in these kinds of emotions. All I can say is that when Tara asked me if I had a boyfriend, I felt this overpowering urge to tell her I did, even though I didn't. I had this compulsion to *show* her, Tony. To show her I was doing just fine in the romance department. Better than fine. And so— here's the bad part—I lied. I told her I not only had a boyfriend but that he and I were engaged and getting married in six months. It was a spontaneous remark, something I just blurted out without considering the consequences. I wanted her to walk away thinking to herself, Amy Sherman is so amazing. Even after what I put her through, she's found a way to have it all—a great career, a great apartment, and a great guy."

"Well, it may be a female thing more than a male thing, but I don't blame you for lying. I really don't."

"Right, but here's where you will blame me." I paused, imagining his face when I told him the rest. "Once Tara was back in my life, she kept asking about my 'fiancé' and I kept avoiding the issue. Then one day we were on the phone and she announced that you were her favorite author—hers and Stuart's. She started raving about you, Tony, and it dawned on me that the key to impressing—"

"Stop."

"Why?"

"Because I know what you're going to say. All through dinner, I kept wondering why they were making those references to weddings and kids and that sort of stuff. I thought maybe they were one of those pushy married couples who wants everyone else to be married, too. But now I get it. You told them we're engaged. Tara raved about me, and suddenly I was your candidate for fiancé. See that? I'm not as dumb as I look."

"You're hardly dumb, Tony. But are you okay about this?"

"Do I wish you'd told me what was going on beforehand? Yeah, I do."

"I couldn't tell you. Not after you made it clear how angry you are at that woman who came to the restaurant, the one who lied to you and tried to get you to participate in her lie. Remember how the waiter practically had to bar her from the door?"

"I remember." He shifted in his chair, his discomfort obvious at the mere mention of her. "But let's get back to you, to the dilemma you've created for yourself."

"It is a dilemma, and—Oh, Tony, I know you're such a straight shooter and it's not in your nature to pretend to be somebody you're not. But this is important to me. It shouldn't be, but it is. So please. Is there any way you would agree to play my fiancé? Just for a little while?"

He didn't answer right away. Instead, he looked at me with those piercing blue eyes, looked at me as if he couldn't decide whether I was a wacko or a woman who'd simply made a mess of things. "What do you mean by 'a little while'?"

"Well, at first I thought the charade would only have to last for tonight, or whenever we get out of here. But now I realize that it might have to go on for a few months, until Tara's book is published and she's out of my life for good.

What I'm saying is that I'll have to continue to see her after tomorrow, which means that we would have to continue to see her. As I've told you, Betsy Kirby has given me strict marching orders on *Simply Beautiful*: I'm supposed to keep the author happy or else, and socializing with her is part of the equation. You know how it is. I tried to socialize with you each time you had a new book out, but you always begged off."

"That's because your idea of socializing was dragging me to some L and T thing and selling me out to a bunch of number crunchers."

"Tony. Could you stop being a wiseass just for a second and tell me if you'll do it?"

He thought a minute. "If you'd asked me a few weeks ago, I probably would have turned you down."

"But now?" I said hopefully.

"Now I know you're a die-hard Rangers fan. Major difference."

Whoops. I'd forgotten about that particular lie of mine. About the wine and the sports cars, too. Minor details, all of them. No need to tell the truth about those, I figured. "So you'll go along with it? You'll say yes to our playing the part of an engaged couple? Keep in mind that it's not a forever type of commitment. Once Tara's out of the picture, you can throw yourself back into circulation."

He smiled, ran his gaze over me. I felt myself flush from the attention. "I guess it wouldn't be that hard to play a guy who's made a commitment to you."

My flush deepened and my heart did a little skip. So he did like me. Not that his liking me was crucial to the mission, but it was better than the alternative.

"I assume that in order to really inhabit our roles as an engaged couple, we'd have to spend a lot of time together," he went on, "and put on public displays of affection and learn to tolerate each other's annoying habits. Oh, and we'd have to see each other exclusively. No dating other people."

"That's what *commitment* means, Tony." And he was the wordsmith? "But as I said, it would only be temporary."

"And we'd have to fall into an actual routine—really behave as if we were getting married."

"Yes. Exactly."

He nodded vigorously. "It just might work. It just might be a good exercise."

"A good exercise?" That's an odd way to describe the situation, I thought, like I'm—what?—his Thighmaster? But I was so grateful for what appeared to be his cooperation that I could hardly quibble. Besides, he had just leaned toward me, arranged his face so close to mine that it was tough to concentrate on anything but how much I wanted him to kiss me.

Yeah, I did want him to kiss me. Partly because he was being so nice about everything and partly because I hadn't been kissed by a man in ages and partly (okay, mostly) because I liked him as much as he apparently liked me.

"Yes," he said. I could feel his breath on my skin. "This could be the perfect opportunity for me."

"Opportunity for you?" I said dreamily.

"For my books, I mean."

"I'm not following you."

"Oh, Amy, Amy. This could be just the ticket to solving my Lucy West problem."

I pulled away suddenly. So much for the kiss. "Lucy West? Your character?"

"Yeah. You know. Joe West's wife."

"Sure, but what does she have to do with you pretending to be my fiancé?"

"Everything," he said with growing excitement. "I've been getting trashed by reviewers, remember? They think Joe's marriage to Lucy has been weakly written, thinly developed, not up to the other elements of my books. They claim the relationship doesn't 'ring true.' Well, tell me I'm thin-skinned, but all the criticism has been driving me nuts and I've been trying to figure out what to do about it. Thanks to you, I've got my answer."

"Thanks to me?"

"You and this scheme of yours. If I pretend to be your fiancé for a few months, I can really research what it's like to

be in a committed relationship. You know me—it's all about
the research." He chuckled. "And once I've done my research, I'll be able to write about Lucy and Joe with more
authority, and the reviews will reflect that. Hey, this could be
great for both of us, right?"

"Right." So he wasn't helping me because he liked me.
He was helping me because he wanted better reviews. Well,
it didn't matter why he was helping me, just that he was.

"It'll be sort of a quid pro quo," he said. "I'll be your
project and you'll be my project."

"I suppose you could look at it like that."

"Sure, because you'll get what you need and so will I."

"Uh-huh."

"So now that we've worked all this out, we should get to
bed," he said, rising from the chair. "Speaking of which, do
you want the right side or the left?"

"Either one," I said blankly as I watched him wander off
into the other room. He was mumbling about how he wished
he'd brought his laptop, so he could type up some spur-of-
the-moment ideas for Joe and Lucy's bedtime rituals.

After he left and I'd had a chance to process the rather
surprising way that *my* plan had evolved into *his* plan, I
slipped on Tara's slinky black nightgown. The irony of the
situation didn't escape me. There I was, plotting to gain control over her for a change, when she'd found a way to dress
me in her clothes.

No, the joke's definitely on her, I reminded myself. She
probably thought Tony and I were in the guest house screwing our brains out, when in reality we were sleeping on opposite sides of the bed, because we were only kidding about
being engaged and because he was too busy researching his
book even to notice me in her slinky black nightgown.

Okay, so maybe the joke was on me, too.

17

ood morning, good morning, good morning!" said Tara as she waved us over to the breakfast table. It was 9:00 A.M. on Saturday. The sky was clear, the wind was calm, and she had just come back from her daily five-mile jog and was now bustling about the kitchen in a pink velour sweatsuit and matching running shoes. Her hair was in a ponytail and she wasn't wearing any makeup except for lip gloss. Despite the strenuous workout and the early hour, she looked fresh and perky enough to be on her way to cheerleading practice, and, once again, I wanted to smack her.

I, on the other hand, looked like hell. While Tony slept like a baby—well, a baby who snores—I spent the night trying to avoid bumping into him accidentally. He was a roller, which meant that he didn't stick to his side of the bed as promised. He rolled over to my side, he rolled back over to his, he rolled over to the middle, and then he lay there spread-eagle. He was all over the place, in other words, and I ended up exhausted. By 6:30, I gave up on sleep and crept out of bed, put my clothes back on, and started flipping through the issue of the *Robb Report* that Tara had placed ostentatiously on the night table. In case you're not familiar with the magazine, it celebrates the lifestyles of the super-rich. I was skipping over ads for yachts and jewelry and authentic British butlers when I came upon a photo of Stuart, of all people. He'd been interviewed for an article called "High-Style Birthday Parties," in which he described how, on the occasion of Tara's thirtieth birthday, he'd thrown her a million-dollar bash at their rented villa in Tuscany. It sounded like sort of an upscale toga party, and my head exploded as he described the lavishness of it. What I'm saying is that I slept badly and then awoke badly, so by the time I landed in Tara's kitchen, I had to force myself to rally in order to play the part of the dewy-eyed bride-to-be.

"Here's some fresh-squeezed orange juice," she said, handing Tony and me our glasses, both of which were rimmed with brown sugar, just as she advocated in *Simply Beautiful*.

"Thanks, Tara," said Tony. "And thanks for letting us sleep in the guest house last night." He leaned over and gave me a loud mushy kiss on the cheek. "It turned out to be a pretty romantic spot for us, didn't it, buttercup?"

Buttercup. Nice. No wonder the critics panned Joe's marriage to Lucy. Tony had a lot of work to do if he wanted to make that relationship ring true. "Oh Tony." I sighed, as if reliving some passionate X-rated moment. "Last night could have been a rehearsal for our honeymoon."

Tara averted her eyes, which I loved, because it suggested that my bliss was too much for her to take. "I'm glad you two have decided to abandon the reserved, hush-hush bit," she said, "and are letting everybody see how happy you are together."

"Not everybody," I cautioned. "We're still keeping our engagement under wraps, Tara. We're only sharing our news—our joy—with you and Stuart."

"Your secret is safe with us," she said. "Now, how about some breakfast? Michelle's not here, but I can whip something up for you guys. Stuart likes scrambled egg whites, since he's watching his cholesterol. What do you two usually eat for breakfast?"

Since I had never eaten breakfast with Tony, I could only speak for myself. But he had other ideas.

"Amy and I aren't really breakfast people," he said. "Just a cup of coffee and we're good to go. Right, buttercup?"

Okay, so I would talk to him about the buttercup. I would also talk to him about the fact that I drank tea, not coffee, and that I *was* a breakfast person and was starving.

We made it through the first fifteen minutes of chitchat, then were joined by Stuart, who had traded his Brooks Brothers suit for the same sweatsuit as Tara's, except that his was black.

"Good morning, everybody," he said to the room at large, then glanced at his idol. "Sleep okay, Tony?"

"Like a rock," he said, "once Amy and I had worn ourselves out in the bedroom."

This time, it was Stuart who averted his eyes, but only briefly. "Well, I just wanted to make sure our star author got his rest." He patted Tony on the back, as if they were two manly men with a knack for satisfying their women. "I'd hate to think that it was our tree falling in the driveway that gave you a case of writer's block."

"Not to worry, Stuart," said Tony. "I have a feeling this whole episode is actually going to stir my creative juices."

"Good. Good. Glad to help. I've called the tree people, by the way. They can't get to us until this afternoon because of all the other damage in the area, but they'll be here between three and five."

Swell. That was hours away.

"And since our garage is blocked, too," he went on, turning to Tara, "I'll be doing a little work at home today."

"Oh, do you really have to, sweetheart?" she said. "I was hoping you could spend the whole time with Amy and Tony and me."

"Me, too, but Mandy's coming over soon with some papers for me to look at."

"Mandy's his secretary," Tara explained.

"And then Walter's dropping by to go over the company's taxes."

"Walter's his accountant," she said.

"And then Bobby will be here to stretch me out."

"Bobby's his personal trainer," she said.

"And then there's my standing appointment with Chaya."

"Chaya's his massage therapist," she said. "She teaches yoga, too, but Stuart's not very Zen, so he sticks with the massage."

"I'm sorry about all the visitors," said Stuart, who didn't seem that sorry; instead, he seemed rather pleased with his own importance, "but they're previous commitments. I had no idea we'd be having guests today."

"Don't give it a thought, either of you," said Tony, who gazed at me adoringly. "Amy and I can keep ourselves occupied. We can always go back to *bed*."

I thought Tara's eyes would bug out of her head. "Uh, well, you're free to do whatever you like, but I'll be at your disposal today. We could sit and talk some more. I'm dying to hear how you two became a couple, for instance. I know you work together, but how did the romance blossom? I mean, which one of you was the pursuer?"

"He was," I said at the very instant that Tony said, "She was."

Tara laughed. "Come on. Get your stories straight."

"The truth is that I made the first move in that direction," said Tony. "And let me tell you, I had to get my courage up to do it."

"Your courage?" Tara said skeptically. "You don't strike me as the wimpy type, Tony."

"Are you kidding? I was totally intimidated by the idea of pursuing Amy. You probably don't realize this, Tara, but she's a legend in book-publishing circles. Authors would kill to have her as their publicist. She's considered the best in the business."

Yesss! Tony was playing his part magnificently. Tara seemed surprised to hear what a success I was. Even Stuart poked his head out of his newspaper for a minute and was viewing me with new respect.

"And then there were all the men she'd been linked with," Tony continued. "I'm talking about big guns—the CEO of a

Fortune 500 company, an Emmy award–winning television producer, the senator from a certain New England state. Powerful competition, right? The thought of asking her out on a date made me feel like an insecure high school boy."

Well, yeah, maybe he was going for too much, but I was lapping up every word, especially the high school reference. Even *I* thought I sounded like hot shit. And you should have seen Tara and Stuart. They were listening to Tony but staring at me, as if to try to reframe me in their minds from poor sweet Amy to Amy the siren.

"And, of course, there was her beauty," said Tony, reaching over to stroke my cheek. "I know you and she were friends when you were kids, Tara, so you probably witnessed the effect her looks had on people back then. She was the prettiest girl in town, right?"

That did it. The muscle to the left of Tara's mouth actually started to twitch. "She was always pretty, yes," she said in a voice that was extremely subdued.

"What amazed me," Tony went on, "is that a find like Amy had never been married. At first, I thought maybe she was only interested in her career—you know, the type that avoids commitment to focus on climbing the ladder. But then, when we finally got together, she told me she'd been engaged once. I asked her why she and her fiancé broke up, and she said that he dumped her for another woman right before the wedding. Can you believe it? I mean, what kind of an idiot would give up the chance to be her husband? He must have been deluded, to think he'd found someone better."

He was brilliant, absolutely brilliant. I'd always known what a good storyteller he was, but the scenario he'd just recounted was priceless. Tara was so stricken, she looked as if she'd caught a bad stomach virus. As for Stuart, he stuck his head back in his newspaper, the coward.

"Suffice it to say that Tony summoned up the nerve to ask me out and I accepted," I chimed in. "One date led to another, and it wasn't long before we were talking about marriage."

"You bet we were, buttercup," he said. "Now, how about giving me a big kiss to show me how much you love me?"

Before I knew what was happening, he pulled me up from my chair and planted a soulful, tongue-involved kiss on my lips. It was entirely for the benefit of our hosts, just part of the performance, so I couldn't very well push him away. I had to make the kiss look convincing, had to make our relationship look convincing, and so I kissed him back with everything I had. It was a head-spinning kiss that lasted whole seconds, and I nearly keeled over from the heat it was generating throughout my body.

Naturally, I told myself that the "heat" was only embarrassment over our public display of affection; that it had nothing whatsoever to do with any feelings I might be developing for Tony. Still, when he finally released me and my blood pressure returned to normal, I had to admit to myself that I didn't hate the experience and, should the need arise, I would certainly be willing to repeat it.

During the rest of the day, Stuart's retinue—the secretary, the accountant, the trainer, the masseuse—paraded through the house at their appointed hours, and we didn't see much of him once they arrived. Tony spent an hour or so washing the Ferrari and making sure it was ready for the trip back to New York. Which left Tara and me alone for a chunk of time, during which she sat me down and said she wanted to talk.

"If it's about the publicity for *Simply Beautiful,* we should probably wait until Monday, when I've got my notes in front of me," I said. "As a matter of fact, I think you should come into the office and meet Scott, my assistant, so he can be up to speed on everything we're doing."

"It's not about the book, Amy. It's about you and me."

"Oh?" So my act with Tony had gotten to her, made her give up the superficial nonsense and get down to emotional business.

"Yes. Ever since we were reunited, we've been tiptoeing around what happened with us, with our friendship."

"You mean Stuart, I assume. Because if you do, there's really nothing—"

"Please listen. I just want to say that I'm *very* grateful that you didn't tell Tony the whole story. You kept our names out of it, and we appreciate that. We'd hate it if he thought badly of us."

You didn't seem to mind that I thought badly of you. "I had no desire to poison him against you two. Why should I? As you can see, I've moved on with my life."

"I know, and I want to congratulate you for everything you've accomplished. I had no idea you were such an important person in the publishing field. And I had no idea you were in such demand socially. And then there's Tony." She put her hand over her heart and sighed. "He's fabulous, Amy. And he's crazy about you, obviously. But your greatest accomplishment, in my opinion, has been your ability to stay centered." Marianne would be thrilled to hear that one. "I'm in awe of the professional, courteous way you've handled our interactions regarding the book, given how stressful they must have been at first, and of how friendly and forgiving you've been with Stuart. You seem as if you really have put aside the hurt we caused you, and I'm just . . ." She paused. She was on the verge of tears—her standard operating procedure whenever she wanted my sympathy.

"Just what?" I said, loving this.

"Just amazed by your strength." She shed actual tears now—two of them—and they plopped down along her left cheek, as if her eye had sprung a leak. "You're an inspiration," she said, wiping them away with her French-manicured fingers. "I mean it. I'm so, so impressed by you."

Well, there they were—the words I'd been longing for, the words I'd gone to so much trouble to wring out of her mouth. She was awed by me as well as impressed by me, and I finally felt that justice had been served.

Of course, I also felt like an utter fraud. I had gotten Tara to acknowledge me as someone who not only measured up to her but surpassed her. Yes, judging by the "awe" and the "impressed" and the "inspiration," it sounded like she was the one with an inferiority complex for once. But I hadn't made it happen without resorting to tricking her. And so, right on the heels of the euphoria came the guilt, heavy guilt. I had lied, she had fallen for the lies, and suddenly there was a hollowness inside me that I hadn't anticipated.

"Sorry to go on like this," she said, bowing her head, as if she were truly reduced by my presence.

"No, I'm the one who's sorry," I said before I could stop myself.

She looked up. "What for?"

I stared into her face, the same beautiful face that was probably buried in Stuart's privates the day I walked in on them, and snapped back to reality. Nope. I wasn't sorry, or at least not that sorry.

"Amy? You were going to apologize for something."

"Just that I'm sorry Tony and I left the guest house in such a mess," I said. "I'd better go straighten it up."

18

Over the next two and a half months, I managed to stomach frequent encounters with Tara. I spoke to her on the phone, met with her in my office, and saw her with Stuart. With Tony and Stuart. As we counted down to both the publication of her book and the day that I would become Mrs. Hamilton Stiles in a civil ceremony attended by virtually none of our friends and family (that was our story and we were sticking to it), we were, on the face of it, a jolly foursome—two average couples who double-dated now and then. When it was Tony's and my turn to reciprocate for the dinner in Mamaroneck, we took Tara and Stuart to a Broadway show, for instance. Then they hosted us on their sailboat. Then we invited them to a movie screening. And so on.

The get-togethers were awkward for me, sure, but they were a win-win situation, too. They gave me the opportunity to keep sticking it to Tara about what an impressive person I was, and they gave Tony the opportunity to simulate the mind-set of a fiancé. Oh, and they also gave me a better shot at hanging on to my job, since Celebetsy had instructed me to suck up to Tara, and that's exactly what I was appearing to do.

The hardest part was getting on the phone every day and

trying to sell the media on Tara. Imagine my conflict. Imagine my consumption of Pepcid.

"She's *wonderful*," I kept enthusing to the producer at the *Today* show. "Not just gorgeous but also smart and articulate and perfect for your demographic in the eight o'clock hour." Oh, and by the way, she's a miserable excuse for a friend.

"She'll be a *terrific* guest," I told the *Good Morning America* producer. "You'll probably want to make her a regular contributor." As long as she doesn't try to upstage Diane Sawyer.

"She'll get along *great* with the other women," I told the producer of *The View*. Just don't introduce her to any of the men in their lives.

I made these calls, but nobody was biting. Well, except Celebetsy, who bit my head off when I explained that I'd succeeded in getting Tara some feature stories and radio interviews but no national TV appearances yet.

"Don't you realize that the clock is ticking?" she snarled at me at one of our meetings. "We need results and we need them now."

"I've gotten results," I said. "But the talk shows don't always commit until the last minute."

"Maybe if you put in more time at the office, you'd have more bookings to report."

"More time at the office?" I practically lived there.

"Yes. I noticed from your last expense account that you've been lunching a lot lately."

"The people I've been lunching with are the people I've been pitching about Tara," I said. "They're business lunches, Betsy."

"I'm just saying—and I hope I don't have to say it again—that I want *Simply Beautiful* on the best-seller list. Got it?"

How could I miss it?

"She was horrible to me," I whined to Connie an hour later. "She had a total hissy fit."

"Soundslikehormones."

"What?"

"I said, It sounds like hormones. Or maybe there's trouble at home. Maybe her husband's been screwing around and she caught him in the act, sort of like what happened to you."

"Yeah, maybe he got tired of waiting for her to thaw out. Whatever the reason, she's treating me worse than ever."

On the opposite side of the spectrum, Tony was treating me as if we really were headed down the aisle. He called every day to check in, ask me how I was, tell me what was new with him, talk about a doctor's appointment, a visit from the plumber, totally mundane stuff. I swear, if you were eavesdropping on our conversations, you'd think we'd been together for years. He also stopped by my apartment a few nights a week, so he could "step into the shoes of a man in a committed relationship."

One night, he showed up with a gallon of chicken soup when I was sick with a cold.

"You really don't have to do this, Tony," I said as he was reheating the soup. My nose was so stuffed that his name came out "Toady."

"What kind of a fiancé would I be if I didn't bring my buttercup some Jewish penicillin?" he said.

"A cruel, heartless fiancé," I said, kidding. "But seriously. I don't want you to catch my germs."

He paid no attention and continued to stir the pot on the stove. When it was hot enough, he spooned some into a bowl, sat me down, and ordered me to eat.

"What about you?" I said between sneezes. "Aren't you hungry?"

"I'll watch you polish off the soup, then get myself a pizza on my way back downtown."

"You don't have to watch me," I said, even though I was grateful for his company.

"I like watching you. Did that ever occur to you?"

"No."

He reached across the table and dabbed at my chin with a napkin. Apparently, I was leaking. "You like watching me, too," he said with a cocky smile. "I can tell."

"I have no idea what you're talking about."

"Sure you do. You just won't admit it."

I felt myself flush, because I did like watching him, observing him, being near him. The truth was, I'd gotten used to spending time with him, and I missed him when we were apart.

"You're blushing," he teased.

"No, I'm feverish," I said. "From my cold."

"Really? Then you must have had a cold when we were watching TV last week. I complimented you on your sweater and your face turned the same color it is now."

Embarrassed that he had read my mind, I slurped more soup.

He laughed. "It's okay, you know."

"What is?"

"That you're enjoying this . . . this . . . association of ours. I am, too."

I was about to answer but sneezed instead. "You should go, Tony, or I'll infect you. I'm probably contagious."

He smiled again, got up from his chair, and kissed the top of my head tenderly. "No 'probably' about it."

There was something about the way he said it, something about the way his voice got low and soft, that suggested a change in direction. Our eyes met, and for the first time since we'd begun our "association," I allowed myself the possibility that I had gotten to him—that he felt more for me than friendship. It had been clear enough that he'd gotten to me, even though I was using him to get back at Tara and he was using me to research his book. I didn't even mind that the times we were alone together were chaste meetings and that we saved our hot performances for when we were with Tara and Stuart. On those occasions, we held hands, gazed adoringly into each other's eyes, and exchanged sappy declarations of love while kissing. Yes, there was more kissing. More great kissing, I should add. What I discovered, over the course of those two and a half months, was that Tony was right when he'd insisted we had chemistry and were compatible. It had started as a game, but we meant something to each other. I knew we did.

Still, I was not about to become a casualty of his short attention span when it came to women. Enjoying each other's company was one thing. Falling in love was quite another. Besides, I had to keep my focus on the immediate challenge, which was not letting anyone except Connie in on the secret of our phony engagement. Especially my devoted assistant.

"Our new best pal Tony Stiles called again," said Scott when I returned from *lunching* one afternoon. He perched himself on the edge of my desk and did his Tony impression. "I think it's time we came clean about what's going on there."

"Nothing's going on," I said with a chuckle. "He and I are hashing out a campaign for his next book, that's all."

"Please." He shook his head. "This is me you're talking to, not some temp. His book isn't coming out for a year."

"Right, but it's never too early to start. You know that."

"What I know is that we've recently gone from wishing this guy would drop off the face of the earth to looking ecstatic when he calls."

"I don't look ecstatic."

"You do so."

"No, I don't, Scott. What I look is relieved that he and I aren't at each other's throats anymore. We've made a truce, so he's much easier to deal with these days."

"Whatever. On another subject, I heard that Rhonda in Sub Rights is sleeping with Michael Ollin in Business Affairs."

"Doesn't surprise me. That guy gets around."

"That's it? No questions? No gory details? Here I bring you my latest piece of gossip, because I'm your loyal servant, and all you can say is, 'Doesn't surprise me'?"

"Maybe I've got too much on my plate right now with Tara's book coming out in just over a month."

"Speaking of the diva, her husband called while you were out," said Scott, getting up to go.

"Stuart? Are you sure?" Now *that* was a surprise. He was

never the one who arranged our get-togethers; Tara was the social director. So why in the world would he be calling me? To ask for more free books? To reminisce about the good old days? To discuss peace in the Middle East? What?

"Yeah, I'm sure. And he said to give you his *private* number." Scott raised an eyebrow as he handed me a Post-it and left.

Only one way to find out what was up. I dialed his number.

"Stuart Lasher," he said.

"Oh, Stuart. It's Amy Sherman, returning your call. I didn't expect you to answer your own phone."

"I'm answering it because it's my private line," he said. "I only give it out to very special people."

"I'm honored," I said, trying not to let too much sarcasm creep into my voice. "So, what can I do for you?"

"What can you do?" He hesitated, then said, "Nothing. I was just wondering how you are."

Why would he be wondering how I was? He just saw me three nights ago, when the four of us met for dinner. "I'm fine, Stuart."

"That's good. Your parents okay?"

"They're fine, too."

"Good. Good. Work going well?"

"Sure." This was weird. Why the insipid questions?

"You and Tony doing all right?"

Ah. Could that be the reason for the call? Was he checking up on my relationship with Tony because he suspected it was bogus? Had Tara whispered something in his ear about us? Were they onto the fact that we were playing them? "Tony and I couldn't be happier," I replied with what I hoped was a dreamy lilt.

"You look happy. With him, I mean. It's nice to see that in a couple."

"Nice to see what?"

"The way his eyes light up when you walk in the room. The way you get all shy when he says your name. That stuff."

Now what was he talking about? Tony's eyes didn't light

up and I didn't get all shy. Not that I was aware of anyway. But more to the point, why did Stuart sound so wistful about Tony and me? If ever there was a happy couple, it was Stuart and Tara. He was married to a perfect woman (minus the knock-knees) and she was married to a wealthy man, and they led a simply beautiful life, didn't they?

"I remember how happy you and I were once upon a time, Amy."

"Not as happy as I thought we were," I said. How odd. What could possibly have provoked this trip down memory lane? Was he just feeling nostalgic? Or was it the fact that I'd won the seal of approval from the great Tony Stiles and was, therefore, more desirable all of a sudden?

"Oh, come on," he said. "We had plenty of good times back then. What I remember most is what a good listener you were; how you were always there when I needed a shoulder."

This was bizarre. Was he in some kind of trouble? Or was he looking for trouble by calling me and bringing up our past? "Stuart, I'm getting the feeling that you want something. Tell me what it is so we can both get back to work, okay?"

"Fine. You want me to tell you? I'll tell you." Silence.

"Well?"

He cleared his throat. "I was wondering if we could get together. Just the two of us."

I shifted in my chair. He was making me extremely uncomfortable. "Is it my shoulder you're interested in or, perhaps, some other body parts?"

He laughed. "That's something else I remember about you: your great sense of humor."

"Why do you want to be alone with me, Stuart?" I said. "Tara's your wife. Be alone with her."

"Are you so busy you can't spare an hour or two? For an old friend?"

"That depends on what the old friend has on his mind."

"You. I have you on my mind. I need to see you, okay?"

He *needed* to see me? "I have no idea where you're going

with this, but I'm engaged to Tony. I doubt very much if he'd be thrilled about this conversation."

"Tony doesn't have to know about this conversation. Neither does Tara. It's between us. Nobody else. Please say you'll meet me."

"Meet you?"

"Yes. It would mean a lot to me. You mean a lot to me."

Well, I was beyond surprised now. I was floored. His were the last words I expected to hear, after the way he'd tossed me aside for Tara. If I meant so much to him, why did he let her into our bed? If I meant so much to him, why did he call off the wedding? If I meant so much to him, why did he stand up at the altar and tell her he'd love her until death did one of them in?

"All I'm asking is that you consider—just consider—spending some quality time with me. I'll get a room at a hotel. Someplace nice. We'll order up, have a few drinks, a little bite, anything your heart desires."

"Stuart, let me get this straight. You want me to meet you in a hotel room?"

"A room. A suite. You name it."

"It's not the type of accommodations I'm worried about."

"Then what? The fact that I can't stop thinking about you?"

So he was interested in more than my shoulder? What kind of man was he? A man who had no qualms about cheating on his wife, apparently.

As I sat at my desk, still reeling from his phone call, I flashed back on the past few weeks, on the times when I'd been in his company in Tara and Tony's presence. Had he been coming on to me without my realizing it? Actually, now that I thought about it, there was the arm around my waist that lingered longer than necessary, the quick hello kiss that landed on my mouth instead of my cheek, and the amorous look—yes, it was rather amorous now that I really focused on it—whenever he thought no one else would notice. So this "I can't stop thinking about you" business wasn't totally out of the blue, I had to admit.

"I hope your silence doesn't mean you're rejecting me," he said.

Rejecting Stuart Lasher. Now there was a tempting idea. If I did meet him at the hotel, I could reject him, the way he'd rejected me. I could show up, get cozy with him, and then, just when he was feeling confident about me, tell him to fuck off. I wasn't a nasty person, but this was Stuart we were talking about. Giving him a taste of his own medicine would only be fair, wouldn't it?

Yes, the rejection angle definitely appealed to me. But there was another angle that appealed to me, too: the fact that I'd be having a clandestine date with Tara's husband. No, of course I wouldn't have sex with the jerk. Just meeting him in that hotel room, behind her back, was the point, because it would represent the ultimate one-upping of her. She'd had her secret assignations with him when he was mine. Why shouldn't I have my secret assignation with him when he was hers? It had a nice symmetry to it, didn't it? She'd never find out about it, but *I'd* know about it, and knowledge is power, right?

And it wasn't as if I was really engaged to Tony, so I wouldn't have anything to feel guilty about on that score. I hadn't made a real commitment to him, any more than he'd made a real commitment to me. We were just business partners in a way—two people doing each other a favor. Well, okay. Maybe we did have feelings for each other, but we hadn't expressed them, so they didn't count.

And then there was another thought that occurred to me—a motive for rendezvousing with Stuart that was much more compelling than either rejecting him or one-upping Tara. If I went to the hotel to meet him, I could find out what was really going on in that marriage of his. Tara had painted them as deliriously happy—two people who loved and respected and supported each other. But how could that be the case if he was hot to hit the sheets with me? There was definitely something wrong with this picture.

"Don't leave me hanging," said Stuart.

"Oh, you mean like you left me hanging two weeks before we were supposed to be married?"

"Let me make that up to you. Agree to meet me and I'll prove just how sorry I am."

He was sorry all right—a sorry excuse for a husband, just as he'd been a sorry excuse for a fiancé. "I'll have to think about it, Stuart. I can't give you an answer right now."

"I see," he said, "but please don't keep me waiting long. I'm begging you, hon."

He was begging me. The man who'd dumped me for my best friend was begging me.

I've got to tell you the truth: I was enjoying the plaintive tone in his voice as much as I was cringing from it. Judge me if you must, but there were a million times in the years since his betrayal that I had fantasized about this moment. I had imagined him calling me up and saying how he'd finally realized that I was the woman he wanted, not Tara, and then how I'd hang up on him in midsentence, squashing him like a bug. Now here he was, begging me. So I have to say, in the interest of full disclosure, that his proposition was vile, but not the worst thing that had ever happened to me. You can understand my ambivalence, can't you?

19

Tara called about an hour after Stuart did, which made me feel guilty, even though all I'd done was *talk* to him. She apologized for bothering me at the office, but said she just had to tell me that business at Lasher's Meats & Eats was so good that the two of them were planning to buy a second home, in Palm Beach. She went on and on about the merits of "the island," as she referred to it, and then entered into a debate with herself over whether a gated community was preferable to your run-of-the-mill beach-front estate with caretaker and state-of-the-art security. She added that she would be spending stretches of time at the house whenever her radio show was on hiatus but that Stuart would commute back and forth to New York on the corporate jet.

I found her latest riff on her simply beautiful life as dizzying as all the others, but I also wondered whether there was more behind the intent to buy a place in Florida—more behind Stuart's intent, I should say—than having another trophy. Clearly, with Tara out of the picture, he'd have more playtime.

I pondered the matter of their increasingly puzzling marriage while she prattled on about the gift she was running out to get for him.

"Remember how I write in the book about buying him little presents for no apparent reason and then slipping them inside his briefcase, or his dresser drawer, or under his pillow?" she said. "To keep the magic alive?"

"I remember." Some magic. She was slipping little gifts under his pillow and he was trying to make pillow talk with me.

"Well, I'm going to buy him a new leather date book," she said. "A small one that'll fit right in his jacket pocket. He's not a Palm Pilot sort of guy—he can't even figure out how to program the VCR—so he's got to write all his appointments down on paper. If he doesn't, he forgets where he's supposed to be." She sighed. "There are times when he literally rushes out of the house because he realizes at the last minute that he's missing a meeting."

Yeah, a meeting with one of his mistresses. Maybe I wasn't the only woman he was propositioning—in which case, Stuart was a very bad boy and deserved to be teased and then tossed.

When he called again the next day to ask if I'd made up my mind about the hotel room, I told him I had.

"Where and when?" I said, much to his delight.

He told me he'd reserve a room at the Plaza and that we should meet at noon the following Monday.

My curiosity piqued, I agreed. Besides, the lunch hour worked for me. I could tell Celebetsy that someone else was picking up the check this time, so her precious budget would remain intact.

"Will the room be registered under your name or a fake name?" I said, naïve in matters of sneaking off to trysts with married men.

"My own name. Why not?" he said.

"Because Tara might find out what you're doing," I replied.

He laughed. "Tara won't find out. She'll be too busy buying marbleized pencils, or tying ribbons around all our wine bottles, or writing in her journal about the wonder of newly fallen snow."

So he was making fun of her to me? It was one thing to

come on to an old flame, but to ridicule his wife's passions suggested that he didn't even love her and that their "deliriously happy" marriage was a total sham.

"But what if she does find out?" I persisted, the possibility unnerving me suddenly. Yes, I relished the opportunity to turn the tables on both of them as well as to find out what was really going on behind their picture-perfect smiles, but I didn't want to get caught with his pants down. My relationship with Tara was complicated enough. Not only would she accuse me of being vengeful and vindictive; she would also realize that my declarations of love for Tony were complete nonsense and she would think I was as sad a case as ever.

"Hey, trust me, hon," said Stuart. "She won't find out. I'm not going to tell her and you're not going to tell her, so what's to worry about?"

I did not run out to shop at Victoria's Secret in anticipation of my nooner with Stuart, although I did manage to find some panties in my drawer that were not ripped or faded or pulverized by the washing machine. As I've said, I wasn't intending to have sex with him, but arousing him and then rejecting him was still a viable option. And so I shaved my legs. That was the extent of my preparation for our rendezvous. Well, that and the skirt that was the size of a paper towel.

As per Stuart's instructions, when I got to the Plaza, I went straight to the registration desk, where I said I was a guest of Mr. Lasher and that I understood that a key to his room had been left for me.

"Yes, Ms. Oates. Of course we have your key," said the clerk as he handed it to me.

No. He didn't make a mistake. While Stuart had no problem using his name, I had a problem using mine. When he'd asked me what name he should give the hotel instead, I happened to be reading a review of a new Joyce Carol Oates novel, so there you are.

"I hope I'm not late for my *business* meeting," I told the clerk. Well, I couldn't let him think I was a hooker.

"You're not late," he said. "Mr. Lasher hasn't arrived yet,

but you're welcome to go on up to the room, Ms. Oates. Will
you be needing a bellman?"

Yeah, like I had luggage. "No thanks. I'm fine."

"Then enjoy," he said.

I smiled and headed for the elevator. As I ascended to the
fourteenth floor, I started to feel oddly naughty, sort of wan-
ton. I mean, I never did this sort of thing—taking off in the
middle of the workday to meet a man in a hotel room. Particularly a married man. Particularly a married man to
whom I'd once been engaged. I was fairly traditional when it
came to dating and sex, if you didn't count my unorthodox
relationship with Tony, so this was all new territory for me.
Tara was the one in high school who bordered on sluttiness,
while I obeyed my parents' curfews and didn't let boys go
too far and honestly thought I shouldn't sleep with anyone
unless I loved him. But now here I was, prancing down the
hall, twirling a room key in my hand, counting the minutes
until Stuart showed up.

I counted a lot of minutes, as it turned out. He was late.

To occupy myself, I perused the room. It was a lovely
room, by the way—the hotel's top-of-the-line guest room,
with a king-size bed and a separate sitting area and a swell
view of Central Park. The bathroom, too, was deluxe: two
fluffy terry-cloth robes, lots of fancy toiletries, shower built
for two, huge tub, the works. Stuart certainly hadn't scrimped.

I opened the minibar and took out a pint-size bottle of
Bailey's Irish Cream and a small bag of smoked almonds—
the almonds because I was getting hungry, the Bailey's because I was getting anxious. He was fifteen minutes late now
and giving me too much time to think about what I'd gotten
myself into.

I flipped on the flat-screen TV, channel-surfed, watched a
little CNN. Still no Stuart. I considered haranguing him on
his private line, but I figured he was already on his way and,
therefore, wouldn't be in his office to hear my harangue.

I went back into the bathroom. I opened the moisturizer
and applied some to my hands, turned on the hair dryer and
blew my hair around, slipped on the bathrobe over my

clothes and posed in front of the mirror. Tried to kill more time, in other words. Still no Stuart.

Okay, where are you, Stu boy? I finally get the chance to burn you and you burn me instead?

Feeling ever more frustrated, I did call his private line, got his voice mail, and hung up, deciding not to incriminate myself by leaving a message. I also pestered the front desk to make sure they hadn't sent Stuart to the wrong room, but they had the right room in the computer, just no Mr. Lasher to claim it.

Pissed off as well as ravenous, I went back to the minibar, foraged for more to eat, and settled for a couple of those cheese balls that come individually wrapped in wax.

This is silly, I thought, picturing the stack of papers on my desk. I should get back to the office and let Stuart pine for me on his own time.

Speaking of my office, it occurred to me that maybe he'd been detained, through no fault of his own, and left a message for me there instead of tracking me down at the hotel. But after checking in with Scott—he asked where I was and I said, "Having lunch with an old producer friend"—I discovered that there were no messages from Stuart, although there were several from Celebetsy.

I waited until two o'clock—yeah, two goddamn hours. By then, I had consumed the Bailey's, the almonds, the cheese, some trail mix, and a can of Sprite, and I felt sick. Sick that I had eaten all that junk. Sick that I had stooped so low that I had actually thought meeting Stuart in a hotel room was a good idea. Sick that I had allowed my obsession with Tara to turn me into a person I didn't recognize. In short, I was repulsed by myself.

I was also furious that I'd been stood up. How dare he lure me to the Plaza with talk of how much I meant to him and how I was such a good listener and how he really, really wanted to be alone with me. The man had begged me, remember? Did he have such little regard for other people—the hell with other people, for *me*—that he would blow me off like this? Not come? Not call? Not anything? Thank God

I hadn't married him when I'd had the chance! He couldn't be trusted even to appear at an appointed place at an appointed hour! He was the absolute pits!

I grabbed my purse, took a quick scan of the room to make sure I hadn't forgotten anything (the mere thought of the hotel housekeeper finding out that I'd been there was too mortifying to contemplate), and left, slamming the door behind me.

Once down in the lobby, I went to the front desk and handed the key to the clerk, who asked me if everything was "to my liking." The truth was, *I* wasn't to my liking, but that wasn't his problem.

I went back to the office. I did not return Betsy's ninety-seven calls. I did not make follow-up calls to media people. As a matter of fact, I was so angry, hurt, and humiliated by Stuart's no-show that I avoided everybody; I told Scott I wasn't feeling well and headed home early.

At about eight o'clock, I had hunkered down in my apartment—was in bed, under the covers, with all the lights off—when the doorman buzzed me to announce that I had company.

He wasn't specific, because he was Croatian and his English wasn't the best, but I knew who was there: Stuart. Who else? He had probably cooked up some lame story about how he'd gotten held up with a business thing earlier and didn't have a second to call me but that he had come to my apartment to ask for another chance. With flowers, I figured. Or, given that he was such a high roller these days, a diamond bauble, like the ones he gave his wife.

Well, bauble or no bauble, I'm not interested, I thought, and told the doorman I wasn't receiving visitors.

I trudged back to bed, about to get comfy, when there was a knock at my door.

I kicked off the blanket in disgust. Leave it to Stuart to dole out a big tip to the doorman so he could march himself up to my apartment without an invitation.

I was so mad, I didn't even bother to change out of my bathrobe or run a comb through my hair or plop on some makeup. Who cared what I looked like for that bastard? I didn't. Not anymore. Let Tara have him. Let them have each other. Good riddance to bad rubbish, as my grandmother used to say.

I pumped my fist as I realized that, for the first time since I'd walked in on the two of them in our bedroom four years before, I didn't care what either of them thought of me. I really didn't. Maybe Stuart's not showing up at the hotel was the last straw, the final indignity, the blow I needed to conquer my demons once and for all. Maybe it had been good for me to sit by myself in that room at the Plaza, swilling chocolate-flavored Irish whiskey and stuffing my face, to show me what a waste of energy it had been to try to compete with, stick it to, one-up, or pay back Tara. Maybe I saw how pathetic it was that I'd allowed myself to get hooked into her life again instead of living my own. Maybe I'd hit rock bottom with my Tara Messer addiction.

That's it, I thought as there was another, louder knock at the door. I've been liberated. No more toxic friendship with her. No more turning myself inside out for her or because of her. No, I had achieved my moment of clarity. She was never going to have power over me again.

I know what you're thinking: famous last words. And you'd be right, sort of. When I flung open the door, fully prepared to announce to Stuart that he should get the hell out of my sight and go back to his wife, where he belonged, I was stunned to find it was not Stuart after all, but three police officers.

"Amy Sherman?" said one of the cops while flashing his badge at me.

"Yes?" I said, clutching my robe to my chest.

"I'm Detective Rojas and this"—he nodded at the others—"is Detective Burnett and Detective Vincent. We need to ask you some questions."

"Oh, okay. So this must be about the guy in Seven G, right?" I said, referring to one of my neighbors. He'd gone a little postal a few days ago and whacked the washers and dryers in the laundry room.

"No, but we'd like to come in," said Detective Rojas.

"Why? I'm not in trouble, am I?" Yes, I had left work early, but Celebetsy wasn't crazy enough to sic the cops on me, was she?

"We'd just like to talk to you, Ms. Sherman," he said, and muscled past me into the living room, his buddies close by.

Now I was getting nervous. What could they possibly want to talk to me about?

"Tell us about your relationship with Stuart Lasher," said Rojas when we were all seated and after he had explained that he was with the NYPD but that the other two were from Mamaroneck.

My relationship? God, had they wired that hotel room? And if so, why? "He's married to a friend, that's all."

"When was the last time you saw him?" said Rojas.

"Let's see. Maybe a couple of weeks ago? He was with his wife and I was with a date, and we all had dinner together."

"But you were supposed to see Mr. Lasher at the Plaza earlier today, weren't you, Ms. Sherman? *Weren't you?*"

Yikes. So they knew about us? So they did wire the hotel room? So they overheard me talking to myself as I sat there waiting for him to put in an appearance?

"Yes, I was supposed to see him at the Plaza," I said, figuring I might as well come clean. I'd become a big fat liar, but even I drew the line at cops. "I had planned to meet him there at noon, but he never showed up."

"And you have no idea where he is?" said Burnett.

"No. Why?"

"Because he seems to have disappeared," he said.

I grabbed the arm of the chair. "Run that by me again?"

"Mr. Lasher is missing," he repeated. "We're just checking around, gathering information."

"Oh my God. You think he's dead, is that it?"

"It's possible."

I felt dizzy suddenly, as if I might go into some sort of swoon. Sure, I'd wished Stuart dead plenty of times after the way he'd betrayed me—he was a shit, after all—but I'd never really meant it. No, he couldn't be dead. Maybe he just went off to play golf and got lost driving home. Maybe he was on some highway somewhere without any way to communicate with the outside world. Maybe it was his cell phone battery that was dead, not him.

"Just curious," I said. "How did you guys know I was supposed to meet him today?"

"There was a notation in the address book that was found in his car," said Rojas. "He had written down your name and the date, place and time of your meeting. What can you tell us about that, Ms. Sherman?"

"Oh, well, the address book was a recent gift from his wife," I said. "She buys him these little—"

"Not interested in that part," he said rather sternly. "What can you tell us about the reason for your meeting with him? And don't bother pretending it had to do with the publicity campaign for his wife's book, because she didn't know anything about the meeting until we told her about it."

They'd told Tara about it? You see that? I couldn't get away with anything. Leave it to her to find out I was planning a rendezvous with Stuart, even though he and I had taken such pains to keep it a secret. Leave it to me to agree to a rendezvous with a man and then have that man go missing.

Tara must be ready to scratch my eyes out, I thought, trying to imagine her coping with Stuart's disappearance and the fact that he and I were, on the surface of it, "involved."

"Ms. Sherman, I asked you a question," said Rojas, bringing me back to the matter at hand.

"Right. You want to know why I was meeting Mr. Lasher at the Plaza," I said. "I'll tell you everything, but first let me process all this a second, would you? You've just given me very disturbing news, and I'm trying to compose myself. Does Mrs. Lasher have any idea what could have happened to her husband?"

"That's why we're here," said Rojas.

"What is?" I said.

"Mrs. Lasher," he said. "She thinks you killed her husband."

"Killed him? Me?" My eyes almost popped out of their

sockets. How could she accuse me of something so heinous? Even if she did assume I was fooling around with Stuart, how could she believe that I was capable of murder? And how could she blab to the cops that I was capable of murder? She had pulled some pretty rotten stunts over the years, but this was beyond rotten. This was—

"Weren't you engaged to him once upon a time, Ms. Sherman?"

"Yes, but—"

"And didn't he break up with you just before your wedding so he could be with Mrs. Lasher?"

"Yes, but—"

"And weren't you extremely bitter about it?"

"Yes, but—"

"And weren't you so bitter, in fact, that you didn't speak to either of them for several years?"

"Yes, but I went to therapy! I worked it out! I got centered!"

"Not according to Mrs. Lasher. She claims you said you wished her husband didn't exist."

I racked my brain. Had I ever said that? Had I? Okay, yes. I'd said a variation of that, when I went to their house for lunch the first time. But I hadn't meant anything by the remark! It was just a throwaway line!

"Now, why don't you tell us why you were meeting Mr. Lasher at the Plaza today," said Rojas, his voice turning soft and sympathetic, as if he hoped to soothe me into confessing to the ultimate crime of passion.

Oh, I told them what they wanted to know all right. More. And when I was finished, I wasn't the only one with the bull's-eye on my forehead. Yes, by the time I'd given them an earful about Tara—especially how she was supposed to be so happily married but must have known full well that her husband was hitting on other women—the back-stabbing Mrs. Lasher had some explaining to do of her own.

TARA

20

Poor Amy. Poor, poor Amy. That's what you're thinking as you contemplate her current predicament, isn't it? Of course it is. You're asking yourself, How could such a bright, caring, well-intentioned woman have gotten herself into trouble with the police? How is it possible that someone so kindhearted, so hardworking, so eager to please landed smack in the middle of something as tawdry as a love triangle involving a man who was missing and presumed dead?

I'll tell you how it's possible: Amy Sherman is not Mother Teresa, any more than I'm the Antichrist she'd have you believe I am. That's right: Contrary to what she's been handing you, beautiful blond prom queens are not, by definition, evil incarnate. We're decent human beings who have our own crosses to bear, so to speak. For example, the general public assumes we're stupid. What's more, women are always jealous of us. Worst of all, everybody sucks up to us, wants something from us, even though they don't like us very much and only pretend to. Take dear sweet Amy. She just got through telling you how she used to *adore* being my best friend as a kid, but she was secretly hating my guts! How two-faced is that?

Granted, she does have her pluses. She's skilled at her job and respected by her colleagues and she helps blind people across busy intersections. Oh, and she rescues tiny animals. When we were in elementary school, she was always rushing to the aid of birds. They would fall out of trees and she would feed them eyedroppers full of Gatorade and then build them little infirmaries out of shoe boxes and cotton balls. A regular Girl Scout, that Amy.

But listen up, people. She is not perfect. She doesn't wash her hair often enough, she has dreadful taste in clothes, and she's hopelessly clueless when it comes to accessories. I used to have to drag her to buy new handbags, for instance. If left to her own devices, she'd wear the same purse forever, with whatever outfit she had on her back, and it was frustrating, because she was a pretty girl. She's still a pretty girl. She's just so damn holier-than-thou, if you know what I mean. You heard her version of our story up to this point, and it's bullshit. Total bullshit. She wants you to buy into the idea that I'm this selfish, shallow, morally bankrupt bitch and that if it weren't for me, her life would be one big piece of cake.

Well, here's a bulletin for you: Her life is not my problem. Was she, in fact, my best friend at one time? Yes. Did I hang out with her on a daily basis when we were younger? Yes. Did I get a kick out of her worshipful attitude toward me? Even take advantage of it on occasion? Yes. But am I responsible for making her feel bad about herself? Not a chance. As a famous person once said (either Eleanor Roosevelt or Dr. Phil, I can't remember which), "No one can make you feel bad about yourself without your permission." If Amy feels "reduced" by me, as she relentlessly puts it in her version, then she's the one doing the reducing.

Have I been blameless in every case when it comes to Amy Sherman? Definitely not. I've made mistakes and I'm ashamed of them. But there are two sides to every story, and I'd appreciate it if you'd allow me to lay out mine. With your indulgence, I'd like to go back to the beginning, to the part where she was moaning about how I stole Stuart two weeks before their wedding. Once you've heard the saga from my

perspective, you might just change your attitude toward me.
So do I have your attention? Good.

"Can I buy you dinner, Tara?" Stuart said one evening after
Amy left us to run off to a fund-raiser for oppressed writers
in Swaziland or someplace like that. It was a little over four
years ago, just a few months before their wedding. I had accompanied the two of them to Bloomingdale's because Amy
wanted to show me the china they'd registered for. Actually,
she didn't want to show me the china. She wanted my "input" on the china. She was always gushing about how she
valued my opinion when it came to things like china and
crystal and stemware, not to mention skirts and slacks and
tops and jackets and shoes and lingerie and jewelry and makeup and—Well, as I've already said, her taste isn't great. The
point is, *she* was the one who pulled *me* in the night Stuart
invited me to dinner. I didn't insinuate myself in her little
prewedding crap. She initiated all of it—the maid of honor
thing, the getting to know her fiancé thing, the traipsing
around Manhattan, looking at the china thing. I was happy to
help, really, but I want to make it clear that I had a life of my
own and it didn't include sucking my thumb while I waited
for my old pal Amy to call. I was living and working in the
city, and I was hardly inactive socially. Yes, it's true that I
was between boyfriends, having just endured a wrenching
breakup with an actor on *Guiding Light*. It was also true that
I was tired of the dating merry-go-round. I wasn't getting
any younger. I wanted to find a man who was interested in
settling down and starting a family. So I suppose that's what
drew me to Stuart—the fact that he was interested in settling
down and starting a family, just not with me.

"Dinner?" I said. "Sure."

"Great. How about the Four Seasons?"

That was another thing that drew me to Stuart: He not
only had money, he enjoyed spending it. I admit, I like that
in a man. I also found him appealing physically. He was very
tall and on the slim side, with narrow wrists and long, ta-

pered fingers. But I liked his big brown eyes the most; they were eager, like a puppy's, full of frisky need.

We went to the restaurant and we were alone together for the first time since Amy'd introduced us. Stuart ordered champagne and we toasted his upcoming nuptials and he filled me in about Lasher's Meats & Eats—specifically, how he planned to take over the family's chain of gourmet food stores when his father retired.

"What about your brother?" I said. "Or isn't he as ambitious as you are?"

Stuart smiled. He seemed to appreciate that I was reading the situation correctly. "Jimmy takes after Dad. He's a walking cliché: 'Everything by the book'; 'The customer's always right'; 'Slow and steady wins the race.' You know the type."

"You're more of a fast mover, is that it?" I asked, engaging in what I assumed was harmless, if slightly flirtatious, banter.

"Let's just say I go after what I want," he replied, and then he summoned the waiter over and instructed him to tell us the specials.

Once our meal was served, we picked up the thread of What Stuart Wanted, which turned out to be not only the top position in the family business but all the perks that went with it. "I can't deny that I'm attracted to nice things," he said, then ran his brown eyes over me.

Wow, I thought. He's actually flirting with me, too. The guy's marrying Amy, but his cheeks are flushed and he's loosened his tie and he's giving me the Look.

It's probably just the champagne, I decided, and steered the conversation back to Lasher's Meats & Eats. There was discussion of the soaring prices of caviar, truffles, and everything organic. There was discussion of expanding the network of stores into other states. There was discussion of how hard it is to get and keep honest employees. And then, as I was about to ask whether Lasher's had considered selling fancy cookware to go along with all the fancy food, out popped another remark about me.

"Amy told me you were the most popular girl in school," said Stuart. "I can certainly see why, Tara."

"You can see why she told you, or you can see why I was popular?" I said, teasing him.

"Both," he replied. "I guess what I mean is that you're not only beautiful but you're easy to talk to."

"Thank you. But why do you sound so surprised?"

"Oh. Well, I guess it's just that Amy never described you that way."

"What way?"

"Easy to talk to. Accessible. Sympathetic. Intelligent."

My smile faded as he ticked off his adjectives, and I actually flinched on the last one. "How did Amy describe me, then?"

"I got the impression from her that you were sort of"—an embarrassed laugh—"taken with yourself and not wildly concerned about others and that your interests weren't particularly broad."

My eyes widened. "Amy said that?"

"Well, not in those exact words."

Stuart started to look genuinely uncomfortable now, and to compensate, he ordered us another bottle of champagne. We both drank it. Too quickly.

"So tell me more about what you think of me, versus what Amy has told you about me," I prodded, trying to keep my tone light but itching to dig further inside this little Pandora's box he'd dropped on the table.

"What I think of you is that you're beautiful and vivacious and charming. And really, really sexy." He was slurring his words. *Vivacious* came out *vicious*.

"Aw, shucks, Stuart. You're just flattering me." I feigned modesty, but I *was* the most popular girl in school, and guys had been having wet dreams about me since I was fourteen.

"No, I'm not just flattering you. If I weren't engaged to Amy"—he hiccuped—"I'd chase after you myself."

"That's sweet, but you are engaged to Amy," I reminded him.

He pouted. "You're hard to resist, Tara, and it wouldn't be

the worst thing if you and I got together for one night. One teeny-weeny night of *passion*." He made growling noises to give me a taste of what an animal he'd be, I guess. "Come on, hon. It would be my last hurrah as a single man."

"Stuart." I wagged a finger at him. "I'll say it again: You're engaged to Amy, and Amy's my best friend."

He shook his head. "Amy hasn't thought of you as her best friend in years."

"What did you say?"

He drained his glass of Dom Pérignon and poured himself another. "I probably shouldn't have opened my mouth. Never mind."

"Don't be silly. I'm a big girl. I can take whatever it is. Go ahead, Stuart. What did you mean when you said Amy doesn't think of me as her best friend anymore?"

He sighed. "She told me she only asked you to be her maid of honor for old time's sake, as a nostalgia sort of thing. She doesn't think you two have anything in common now, except your"—he hiccuped again—"history. Basically, she threw you a bone, Tara. She fulfilled her childhood obligation to you by sticking you in the wedding party. She doesn't plan to see you again after the big day, so if I were you, I'd forget about the 'best friends' bit and just go on with your life once the festivities are over."

He patted my hand, as if to console me, but I was too stung to feel his touch. I went numb, actually. Cold. Out of body.

Was he telling the truth? I asked myself. Had Amy really said all that to him? Or was he just a mean drunk, trying to put a wedge between us so he'd get me into bed? Maybe he messed with people's heads on a regular basis, for all I knew.

On the other hand, Amy had been sending me mixed signals since we'd gone our separate ways after college. One minute, she'd act as if she wanted to keep her distance; the next, she'd call me to ask if we could get together. One minute, she'd give me attitude about my interest in clothes and hair and makeup; the next, she'd plead with me to help her with her own. One minute, she'd put me on a pedestal; the next, she'd knock me off.

"I'm sorry if I spoke out of turn," he said. "It's just that you seem like such a straight shooter. I thought I should be straight with you about Amy. About you and Amy."

Yeah, Stuart was telling the truth, I realized as my stomach went sour. He had sensed her ambivalence toward me and articulated it pretty well, considering his inebriated state.

"Tara?" he said. "You okay?"

No, I was not okay. So Amy was throwing me a bone when she asked me to be her maid of honor, huh? Doing me a big fat favor by fulfilling her *obligation* to me?

And how about that nostalgia part? What was I, some sort of relic from her kiddie past? I was Tara Messer, the most popular girl in school. I wasn't anybody's obligation. And I certainly didn't need to walk down the aisle in that blue crepe fashion mistake she'd picked out for me to wear.

What an idiot I was even to think she wanted me by her side on the most important day of her life. And what a hypocrite she was to pretend we were best friends when we were nothing to each other anymore. Nothing!

I was so filled with anger and hurt, I wanted to smack somebody. But I wasn't a violent person. I was, however, a person who didn't sit there passively while others behaved badly toward me. Amy had made a fool of me, and I would pay her back.

"Tara?" Stuart jiggled my arm. "If it makes you feel any better, I think you're terrific and I'm glad you'll be in the wedding, even if Amy has her misgivings."

Her misgivings. I'd show her misgivings.

After another half hour or so of chitchat at the restaurant, I gave Stuart a rousing farewell to his bachelorhood. We staggered out of the Four Seasons, hopped in a cab, entered my apartment, and promptly had sex. Revenge sex. That's what it was for me anyway. Not that I didn't find Stuart attractive, as I've said, and he certainly seemed taken with me. My God, you should have heard him that night. "You're so beautiful. You're so passionate. You're so adventurous." (Amy did have a prudish streak.) "You're the kind of woman I've always dreamed about." When you're feeling unappreciated, it never hurts to have a man overwhelm you with compliments.

Look, I'm not proud of what I did, okay? I acted like a spoiled child, not to mention a slut, but I was wounded, and I struck back at the source of my wound. And I rationalized that what I did wouldn't have consequences. I knew that Stuart would never tell Amy what happened, and God knows I would never tell Amy what happened, so there was no point in making myself sick with guilt over it.

But then everything changed. The morning after our torrid fling, Stuart sent me a dozen white roses. And not the kind you pick up at the supermarket, wrapped in plastic. They were luscious roses that had already been clipped and arranged in a magnificent crystal vase (we're talking Baccarat; the guy was a spender, I'm telling you) and hand-delivered by a florist on the Upper East Side. The card that accompanied the flowers read: "Dear Tara. I remembered that you think the red ones are a cliché. Thank you for a night I'll never forget. I hope it was as special for you as it was for me."

At first, I didn't know what to make of the roses or Stuart's grandiose language. Special? Had our night together been special? To tell you the truth, the champagne had sort of clouded my memory of it.

A few hours later came another delivery: a chocolate layer cake from the Four Seasons. No kidding. The card read: "Dear Tara. At the restaurant last night, you mentioned that this was your favorite dessert. You were going to order it, but then we left in such a hurry that you never got to. Enjoy."

Well, flowers were one thing. A whole cake was another. I couldn't *not* call him to say thanks, could I?

"I need to see you," he said right after I told him I was appreciative of his gifts but that we had to cool it, given the fact that he was engaged.

"What do you mean?" I said, knowing exactly what he meant. I could hear the desire in his voice.

"Look, I know it's crazy," he said, "but I can't stop thinking about you. You're everything I've ever wanted in a woman."

"No, I'm not, Stuart. It just feels that way because I'm forbidden fruit."

"It feels that way because it's true."

"Then why are you marrying Amy?"

"I'm not so sure I can. Not anymore."

"Don't say that. It's not only inappropriate; it's probably just because you—"

"Please. I want to see you. Tonight. Let's find out if there's something between us before it's too late. I'll be there at six."

"I really don't—"

Click.

There was no use protesting, I discovered. Stuart Lasher was on a mission, a crusade, a campaign to win me over, and I was too dazzled by all the flattery, never mind flummoxed by the peculiar set of circumstances, to resist.

At six o'clock on the dot, he arrived at my apartment bearing another gift: a garnet choker.

"I remembered that you said your birthday is in January," he said as he draped it around my neck and fastened the clasp. "Garnet's your birthstone."

He remembered when my birthday was. He remembered that I liked chocolate cake. He remembered that I thought red roses were a cliché. The guy was on a mission, as I said.

We never left my apartment that night. We ordered up some dinner and talked. Well, Stuart did most of the talking. He said his relationship with Amy had deteriorated over the past several weeks and that they hadn't been getting along at all. He said that he'd been having second thoughts about the wedding even before he and I had, well, become intimate. He said he thought he loved me.

"Don't be ridiculous," I said. "You can't love someone after one night."

"Wanna bet?" he said, and kissed me before I could express myself further on the subject.

Yes, I let him kiss me that night, but nothing more. I told him I wasn't about to steal Amy's fiancé, no matter how angry I was at her about the maid of honor thing.

The next day, Stuart dropped by in the middle of the afternoon. He said he couldn't concentrate on work. He said he could only fantasize about touching me. Oh, and he brought me another trinket: a cashmere shell and matching cardigan.

"I guessed about the size," he said.

"You guessed correctly," I told him, delighted with his purchase. I'd admired exactly the same sweater set at Saks the very week before.

"I love you," he said. "So you might as well get used to it. I'm going to keep buying you clothes and jewelry and whatever else your heart desires to prove to you that I'm real. That we're real."

Clothes and jewelry and whatever else my heart desired. He drove a hard bargain, you know?

From then on, our romance took on a life of its own, as romances—especially clandestine romances—often do. Stuart courted me in a way I'd never been courted, and I fell for him. If that rendered me selfish, shallow, or morally bankrupt, so be it, but I just couldn't resist all the attention.

Behind Amy's back, he and I plunged into a full-fledged affair. We exchanged declarations of love, even as we asked ourselves if we had it in us to destroy Amy's happiness in order to pursue our own. We weighed the pros and cons of it all. We went right down to the wire, ultimately deciding two weeks before the wedding that we belonged together, however randomly and dishonestly our union began. I felt horrible about the deceit—I really did. Amy may have treated me shabbily, but she didn't deserve what Stuart and I were about to do to her. Nobody did.

He had planned to sit her down and deliver the news properly. He was going to tell her about us, that we'd fallen in love in spite of how much we both cared about her and that he hoped, in time, she would forgive us.

But then she walked in on us during that particularly spirited coupling—she was supposed to be at the dentist's, remember?—and there was nothing to be done in the way of damage control except to say we were sorry.

And I *was* sorry. So very sorry. I cried that day and I've cried since, and not just because I betrayed my best friend. As it turned out, I had a bigger problem—a problem I honestly didn't see coming. What I'm saying is that Amy isn't the only one who's had heartache. I may be a prom queen, but bad things happen to good-looking people, too.

21

We felt it would be in poor taste to have an elaborate wedding, given that Stuart had just pulled out of one, so we eloped. We flew to Hawaii, trotted over to the Health and Human Services Department in Honolulu, signed a form, swearing that we weren't related to each other, and became husband and wife. A quickie wedding, that's what we had. I felt a little cheated, after spending my entire girlhood picturing myself in some sensational gown with a full retinue of attendants, but Stuart had splurged on the premier suite at the palatial Royal Hawaiian Hotel on Waikiki Beach, so I snapped out of it.

We honeymooned there for a week, and most of the trip was heaven. Stuart couldn't do enough for me or to me (he was as randy as a frat boy). We ate. We screwed. We swam. We screwed. We snorkled. We screwed. You catch my drift.

We talked, too, of course. I was eager to get to know my new spouse, who, when you came right down to it, was practically a stranger. We shared our hopes and dreams for the future, which included buying a home in the suburbs—something extremely grand, befitting the big shot Stuart expected to become once his father retired and handed over the chairmanship of the company, and something extremely roomy, befitting the doting mother I expected to become once I gave birth to many precious, well-mannered children.

Yes, I loved the idea of moving out of his apartment and into larger quarters, and I intended to begin the house hunt as soon as we returned to New York. Aside from the ugly business with Amy, the future sounded fantastic to me—Stuart's promotion at Lasher's, the quality of life his important position would offer us, the numerous walk-in closets I would have, the whole enchilada.

There was just one tiny blemish on our otherwise blissful trip.

On our last night at the hotel, there was a luau on the beach, complete with mai tais and Hawaiian music, followed by an all-you-can-eat buffet consisting of mahi mahi and other dishes with two names. (I had joked to Stuart that I just wanted a hamburger hamburger.) Anyhow, after a hotel employee greeted each of us with a lei, I discovered that my new husband was cruising for a lay of his own. While I was waiting in line at the buffet, having gone back for a second helping of something called lau lau, I glanced back at our table and noticed that he was sitting there hitting on our waitress. She was a pretty young woman dressed in traditional native garb, and his hand was planted smack on her traditional native butt.

"What the hell were you doing?" I said when I returned to the table and the waitress had scurried away.

"Nothing," he said, taking another sip of his mai tai. He was sort of drunk, but then he'd been sort of drunk throughout the honeymoon. "She was a sweet kid, that's all."

"You're not supposed to fondle 'sweet kids' or any other female," I said.

"Oh, come on, hon. You're making too much of this. I was just being friendly, honest. Sorry if I upset you."

After a few more back-and-forths, I calmed down. But my antenna was up from then on. Stuart was a toucher, a groper, a "friendly" guy, I had now discovered. I wasn't crazy about this little quirk in his personality, but then, I should have anticipated it. He'd hit on me when he was supposed to be committed to Amy, hadn't he?

Back in New York, his parents threw a small reception for

us at their house in Westchester. It afforded me yet another glimpse of the man I'd married.

"Welcome to the family," said Benjamin Lasher, Stuart's sixty-five-year-old father, as he kissed me on the cheek. He wasn't as tall as Stuart or as upright in terms of posture, but they had the same elegant features. I liked him immediately upon meeting him, because he was supportive of me, even though I'd been thrust upon his family in such an abrupt way. It was Stuart who would never win his support, I would come to learn. Every time he looked at his oldest son, his disdain and disappointment were apparent.

"Yes, welcome, dear," said Jean, Stuart's mother, a painfully dull woman who did occasional charity work but mostly played canasta. "I hope you and Stuey will be very happy, in spite of the situation."

"The situation," as she never let me forget, was that I had not only stolen *Stuey* away from Amy, with whom she had bonded, but had robbed her of watching her boy say "I do," thanks to our elopement.

And then there was Jimmy, Stuart's brother, the one who was really in charge of Lasher's, it turned out. He was a decent guy, very conservative and prudent, just as Stuart had first described him to me. He was married to Peg, an unadorned, harried woman whose life revolved around carpooling her two kids in her SUV and organizing the household for Jimmy. It was clear after chatting with them that they both tolerated Stuart and his delusions of grandeur but regarded him as kind of a lovable jerk. They didn't have to take him seriously. They were secure in the knowledge that Dad would do the right thing when he was ready to retire, designating Jimmy, not Stuart, as the official chief executive. You see, they all understood what I didn't when I rushed off to marry my new husband—that he didn't have the brains, the talent, or the judgment to run anything.

After spending many Sundays looking at houses with Realtors, Stuart and I found one in Mamaroneck and moved in. (You've already heard about our "manse" from Amy, so I won't bother describing it.) I threw myself into the decorating of it. That took a year and provided a welcome distraction from not being able to get pregnant and wondering why.

Once the house was furnished and staffed and shown off at numerous parties, I rechanneled my energy into my search for a career. I'd worked briefly as a production assistant at WABC when I lived in Manhattan, so I decided to find a radio job in Westchester. I was hired by a small station that broadcast out of White Plains, and I worked again in production. My break came when the woman who hosted a half-hour show called "The Cosmetics Counter" became unhinged while going through an acrimonious divorce and had to quit. Knowing a thing or two about cosmetics myself, I asked if I could replace her, and the general manager said yes. I renamed the show "Simply Beautiful," and instead of focusing strictly on products that made women look beautiful, I expanded the discussion to include products that made women feel beautiful. The show was a hit, albeit on a local level, and was far more fun for me than spending my time in the stirrups of fertility specialists. About a year after we went on the air, there was talk from one of our sponsors about putting "Simply Beautiful" into syndication. A few months after that, I got the idea to spin the show off into a book.

I labored over *Simply Beautiful* as if it were the child I couldn't manage to coax into existence. Yes, it was about "fluffy" stuff like bubble baths and scented candles and foot massages, but I never claimed to have the intellectual gifts of, say, *Amy.* When we were teenagers, she was always the one with her nose in a novel, while I was more interested in *Cosmo.* Still, I knew what I knew, and I was sure there was a market for the kind of book I was writing.

Unfortunately, the threat of my becoming a success in both the radio world and the literary world sent Stuart into a funk. Like Amy, he fed off my popularity but also resented it. I had a knack, it seemed, for bringing out the worst in both of them.

His ambivalence toward me was exacerbated by his own professional failure. His father was constantly putting him down, and he was gradually and bitterly coming to the conclusion that Ben was going to turn over the reins of Lasher's to Jimmy, not him. He compensated for his shattered expectations by availing himself of the company's profits, ensuring the two of us a lavish lifestyle, no matter what his family thought of him. We traveled. We ate well. We treated ourselves to only the best. We were, from every vantage point except our own, a deliriously happy couple.

Oh, and then there was that one other hitch: the fact that the groping of the waitress in Hawaii wasn't an isolated incident, nor was it the extent of my husband's bad behavior. Stuart, I learned, wasn't merely a groper; he had a roving dick.

I don't know why I was so surprised. Weak men like him, men with a whiff of desperation coming off them, often get their jollies by fooling around. I guess I'd just hoped that grabbing a woman's ass wouldn't automatically lead to having actual sex with her, and I felt as if I'd been slapped when I found out I was wrong. It took a while for me to realize that it was mostly my vanity—my image of myself as someone more accustomed to being worshiped than cheated on—that had taken the hit.

Stuart's infidelity came to light as I was fishing around in his dresser drawer for his cummerbund—we were throwing a black-tie bash for his thirty-fifth birthday—and unearthed a breathless love note from his secretary.

"You've been sleeping with Cheryl?" I said, throwing the balled-up note in his face when he returned home that night. I was shaking with fury, even as I was aware that I'd rather he sleep with her than with me. I was no longer attracted to him physically and hadn't been for some time. You lose your respect for a guy, you lose your libido for him, too.

He went pale but denied the affair. "I haven't been sleeping with her. I've had a drink with her now and then, that's all."

"Oh, really? She seems to think you two are sleeping together. Let's see. How did she put it in her pathetic little letter? 'Stuart, darling. That last afternoon at the hotel when you stroked my—'"

"I don't have to listen to you mimic her. She's a nice girl. She doesn't act like I'm a loser, unlike *certain* people around here."

"I'm glad she's a nice girl, because she's going to need a new job starting tomorrow, and being 'nice' should help her find one."

"You expect me to fire her?"

"Yes. Do you think you're up to making that kind of executive move, or do we have to depend on Jimmy to take care of it for you?"

It was a low blow, I admit, but he deserved it.

From then on, we carried on in public as if we were madly in love, while in private we stayed out of each other's way. Why didn't I leave him the minute I knew the marriage was a dud? For one thing, I was the Golden Girl and had my reputation to maintain. People looked up to me, or they looked enviously at me, or they simply looked at me as someone who never failed, never had a problem, never had a pimple. I couldn't bear the thought of them thinking, Tara Messer must have lost her magic. For another thing, I couldn't bear the thought of Amy finding out that the man I'd stolen from her wasn't worth stealing. For a third thing, a publisher had bought my book, and Stuart figured prominently in it. I could forget about making the best-seller list if I admitted that its entire premise was based on a lie. (Look, my priorities weren't the greatest. If I had it all to do over again, of course I would dump him. But we all do what feels right at the time, and living a lie seemed like the best course of action then.)

A lie. Yes. That's what my marriage was. But I was determined to make the best of the situation. Nobody would guess what was really going on, especially not dear sweet Amy, although when I ran into her on the street, totally out of the blue, I had to give a pretty convincing performance to keep her in the dark.

I was standing on the corner of Fiftieth and Fifth that warm April day, thinking about whether or not to stop at Saks before driving home, when I spotted her. She was a mess, as usual—her hair was unwashed, her outfit an embarrassment—and my heart lurched. I wanted to rush over to her and throw my arms around her, apologize for what had happened, make it all right between us. Our childhood friendship came flooding back in big loopy Technicolor scenes—the sleepover dates at my house, the pranks in Mr. Halbert's history class, the marathon phone conversations, the postmortems after dates. But as the traffic light changed and she started to walk in my direction, I stiffened. Suddenly, all I could remember was how much she resented me.

"Amy," I said, approaching her. "It's been forever since I've seen you. How *are* you?" I did not reach out to touch her. Instead, I tossed my head back and flashed her a big phony smile.

"I'm great," she said, looking like the "Before" picture in one of those ads for makeovers.

"I'm happy to hear that," I said, and I was. "I thought about calling you, but I didn't even know where you lived."

She volunteered her address, described her apartment, and told me she had a job as publicity director at a publishing house.

"Oh," I said. "Which one?"

"Lowry and Trammell," she replied.

"Really?" I said. "That's an amazing coincidence, because—" I stopped myself. I couldn't bring myself to drop the bomb that her publisher was now my publisher and that, whether she liked it or not, she'd be forced to work with me. It felt too much like her wedding, when she'd been *obligated* to ask me to be her maid of honor. "So you're doing okay?"

"I'm doing more than okay," she said, her tone a mix of hostility and defensiveness. "What about you? I'll bet everything in your life is just perfect, right?"

See what I mean? There was no way I could come clean to someone with that snotty attitude. Is it a crime to have great hair and skin and nails? Is it a sin to have a terrific wardrobe? Is it the worst thing in the world to wear shoes that actually match your handbag? No. She was dishing out her holier-than-thou crap, and it was pissing me off. She wanted perfect? I'd give her perfect.

"My life is fantastic," I said. I told her about the house. I told her about my radio show. I told her about Stuart's job at Lasher's. And—this part was truly grotesque, because he and I hadn't so much as shared a kiss recently, unless it was for public consumption—I told her we were trying to get pregnant.

"Well, I wish you two the best with that," said Amy, even though her expression suggested just the opposite.

"Tell me about your love life," I said. I figured she must be involved with someone, given that it had been four years since her breakup with Stuart. God, if only she knew how lucky she was that I'd taken him off her hands. I'd saved her from him, and yet she hated me. It was almost laughable. "Are you seeing anybody?" I asked.

She didn't answer for a beat or two. "I, uh, I'm engaged," she said finally, and then smiled broadly. I think she had cream cheese wedged between her teeth.

"That's wonderful." Again, my bravado nearly fell away, and my instinct was to hug her. But I resisted it. "When's the wedding?"

"In six months. I'm very excited."

"I'll bet you are. Who's this special man?"

"Oh," she said, waving me off. "He's no one you know."

Why? Because I wasn't *literary* enough to know someone from her artsy-fartsy crowd? "Well, maybe we can have lunch one of these days and you can tell me all about him."

"We'll have to do that."

She gave me her number and I gave her mine, but she didn't want to have lunch or any other meal with me. She didn't need me anymore, just as she hadn't needed me at her wedding. She had new friends and a new man, and I was a relic from her past.

"Gotta go," she said. "Say hello to Stuart."

"I will," I said. "He'll be thrilled about your news." Yeah, like he'd ever be home long enough for me to tell him. He was probably out banging his latest secretary right that very minute.

I drove back to Mamaroneck in tears. I felt horribly

guilty about lying to Amy, but if I'd confided how crummy things had ended up, she would have stuck her tongue out at me and said, "What goes around comes around" or something equally sour grapesy.

No, I had to lie to preserve my dignity. The only question was, How long could I keep the lie going?

22

You'll never guess who I ran into today," I said as Stuart was making himself a vodka on the rocks. I had cornered him in the library, his inner sanctum in our house. He was always holed up in there, either making himself a drink or plotting some new get-rich-quick scheme with one of the endless string of hangers-on I declined to meet. I turned a deaf ear to his wheeling and dealing at Lasher's—I had no desire to involve myself in his family business other than to make sure our personal bills were paid—and assumed he was simply trying in vain to get the attention, never mind respect, of his father and brother.

"Who?" he said after taking his first sip. He did not offer me a drink, by the way. If we'd had company, he would have been waiting on me, slobbering over me, fawning over me, but when we were alone, he dropped the act.

"Amy."

He set the glass down. "Amy Sherman?"

"How many other Amys do we know?"

"Where'd you see her?"

"On the street in the city. It was quite a surprise, obviously. It's been—what?—four years?"

"Sounds about right. How is she?" he asked, his expression suggesting an interest in someone other than himself.

"Oh, you know. A walking 'Fashion Don't.' But otherwise she seemed to be doing fine. Better than fine. She's engaged."

His eyes widened, as if he couldn't believe that Amy had moved on.

I laughed. "Yes, Stuart. It looks like she's over you, hard as that may be for your ego to absorb. She said the wedding's in six months."

"Well, good for her. I really mean that. I wish her only the best."

"So do I, and I told her that."

"Who's the guy?"

"She didn't say. Probably some nice unassuming man. Amy always liked nice unassuming men. I think you were her only bastard."

"Let's dispense with the name-calling. Just for tonight."

"Oh, why not. Actually, there's more to the story. She told me she's publicity director at Lowry and Trammell, of all places. How's that for a coincidence?"

"So you two will be working together?"

"Looks that way. I'm okay with it if she is, although it would have been easier to deal with a stranger on the publicity. Now I'll have to keep up appearances."

He smirked. "That shouldn't be any trouble for you, hon. It's who you are."

I gave him my iciest stare and left the room.

The following week, my editor at L and T, Julie Farrell, called to tell me she'd announced her acquisition of *Simply Beautiful* at their editorial meeting and that the reception, particularly from the company's marketing director, was very positive.

"You'll be hearing from our head of publicity, Amy Sherman, to discuss the campaign for the book," she said. "Or you might want to call her and introduce yourself."

Introduce myself. To Amy Sherman. What an idea.

The truth was, I was nervous as I picked up the phone to call her. I wasn't looking forward to the edge in her voice when I broached the subject of how we would collaborate on the promotion of the book, given the bad blood between us. And then there was the inevitable condescension about *Simply Beautiful* itself. I had no doubt that she'd sneered at it when she was told about it, because it wasn't *War and Peace*. Well, tough shit if she didn't like it. She was stuck with it. Stuck with me, too. Julie Farrell had plunked down serious money for the book, and Amy would just have to hold her nose and promote it. Still, I had flashbacks of that now-famous dinner with Stuart, when he'd blurted out how she'd only picked me as her maid of honor out of a sense of obligation. Now she'd feel obligated to publicize my book, and I wasn't wild about that.

I dialed her number at the office, a knot in my stomach, but ended up with her assistant.

"Amy's in a meeting," he said. "May we return?"

We? I thought. How chummy. "Sure," I said, and left my business number.

A few hours later, *they* returned.

"Amy. Hi," I said, throwing myself into the part of the amazingly confident, fabulously charming, ever-the-epitome-of-wonderfulness Tara Messer. "I'm so glad you called me back. I wasn't sure you would."

"Of course I called you back," she said, her words polite but her tone snippy. "You're one of our authors now. I just wish you'd told me yourself when I ran into you. It was sort of odd having to hear it from someone at the company."

Oh, so I was in the doghouse yet again. God, she was sanctimonious. "Look, Amy. The last thing I want to do is force you to work on my book. If you're uncomfortable about it, maybe there's someone else at L and T who'd take over the *chore*."

"No, no. It's not a problem for me. In fact, I've read the manuscript and I think it's very commercial, Tara."

Which was her way of saying it was trash. She went on and on about why she thought the book would sell, but I could tell she thought it was beneath her. As I said, tough shit.

"I think we should have lunch," I said, forging ahead. "And I also think the best way for you to get a sense of the simply beautiful idiom is to come up to the house and see it for yourself, see how I apply it in my daily life."

"There's no need for me to go up there," she said. "I'm sure you could explain it to me here at L and T. We could meet in my office or Julie's office, or in our conference room. Whatever."

Clearly, she didn't want to lift a finger for *Simply Beautiful* or for me. "Let me ask you something. When you have a cookbook author, don't you usually sample the author's recipes before undertaking the publicity campaign, so you'll have a better idea what you're selling?"

"Yes."

"And when you have an author who's, say, a world-class athlete, don't you usually go and see him or her excel in the sport?"

Sigh. "Yes."

"Then I think it follows that you should come to my house and see my simply beautiful lifestyle, since that's what you'll be selling."

She didn't answer. She probably had her hand over the phone and was mouthing to her assistant about what a pain in the ass I was.

"I don't know, Tara. I'd have to check my schedule before commiting to going up there."

"So check your schedule. I'll hold on."

No, I wasn't being pushy. I just knew Amy, almost as well as I knew myself. When she wanted to do something, she jumped right in. When she didn't, she dragged her feet.

Like the episode in sixth grade. I'd urged her to run for class president, since she was a straight-*A* student and very up on current affairs. I'd thought it would be good for her to show herself off more, to step into the limelight and out of my shadow, to let everyone see what I saw, which was a girl who was smart and capable, and fun, too, once you got past the serious side. Well, she couldn't make a decision about whether to run, not for weeks. She kept stalling, said she felt awkward about going around bragging about herself and her accomplishments, said she wasn't 100 percent sold on the idea. Eventually, the deadline for declaring candidacy arrived, and she still hadn't made up her mind. Such a neurotic! I had to do something to keep the know-it-all kid with the buckteeth from winning, so I decided to run myself, figuring Amy could be my campaign manager. What was so horrible about that? You'd think I'd committed a crime, the way she treated me. No, she didn't yell and scream—she never just came right out and told you how she felt; she was much too passive-aggressive for that—but she did act chilly around me. And all because I'd been trying to help her, for Christ's sake. So now here she was, hedging about whether to drive to my house in Mamaroneck. It was a measly half hour away from her office, so what was the big deal? Once again, I was only trying to help her—in this case, to help her promote my book—but, as usual, she turned it around and made me out to be the villain.

"Let's settle this," I said. "Are you coming up or not?"

"Yes, yes. All right. We'll meet at your house so I can get a closer look at your *simply beautiful idiom.*"

She didn't even bother to disguise her contempt. "Good. I'll have Michelle make us lunch."

"Who's Michelle?"

"My cook." Michelle was actually my housekeeper, who happened to have a way with food. Thanks to Lasher's, I always had a refrigerator full of gourmet treats, and she was much more clever about throwing them together than I was. One of the tenets of *Simply Beautiful* was to let others perform tasks for you, especially if they were better at them than you were.

"Your cook, huh? Well, I don't eat peppers. Or anything with curry in it."

"I remember. You don't eat hearts of palm, either. You're also allergic to penicillin, afraid of spiders, and fluent in French. And you've seen the movie *Rebecca* a hundred times. Oh, and we used to be best friends. I remember that, too."

Silence. Like she couldn't even acknowledge that we'd been as close as sisters. Stuart or no Stuart, had she forgotten all the nights she slept over at my house? Had it slipped her mind how my family took her on trips with us? Was she in denial about the fact that back when I was the blond prom queen, with everybody vying for a spot in my social circle, she was the one I let in, trusted, and, yes, loved?

Obviously, the answer was that she didn't give a damn about me or what we had meant to each other. And so, as a result, I tried not to give a damn about her, either.

We finally agreed to have lunch the following week. I would have Michelle prepare us a lovely meal. I would make sure the house was a walking advertisement for the book. And I would see to it that Stuart wasn't around for the festivities. There was no way I would allow Amy even to suspect that he and I were a disaster, or that my life, as it turned out, wasn't simple or beautiful.

23

"Why can't I stick around and say hello?" asked Stuart as I shoved him out the door the morning of the lunch with Amy.

"Because it's a business meeting," I said. "My business. Do I sit in on your meetings with the people who sell you Belgian endive?"

"You're afraid I'll embarrass you, is that it?"

"You already do embarrass me, Stuart, but let's not get into that."

He stroked my cheek. "Someday, after I've taken over Lasher's and made more money than even you can spend, I won't embarrass you anymore."

I batted his hand away. "You could make more money than Bill Gates and you'd still embarrass me. You and your girlfriends. Or are you between women these days?"

"You're the only woman for me, hon, and you always will be." He laughed. "There. Wasn't that a good-enough performance for Amy? I think it sounded pretty damn heartfelt."

"You'd have to have an actual heart for it to sound heartfelt, Stuart. Now go."

He gave me a little wave and left, thank God. The minute he was out the door, I ran around the house like a crazy person, getting everything ready. Yes, I wanted to impress Amy, to show her that, unlike prom queens who plateau once they

move into adulthood, I had flourished over the years and was
improving with age. But mostly, I wanted to excite her about
the book, to display all my ideas in such an appealing way
that she would get right on the phone to her media contacts
and rave about them. I needed her—her professional expertise, that is—and I was determined to win her over. No more
hanging back. No more playing cat and mouse. I was going
to wage a full-out assault on her, dazzle the hell out of her,
make sure she promoted the book, regardless of our tangled
history.

When I heard her car pull into the driveway, I rushed outside and launched my charm offensive.

"Amy," I said, drawing her into a hug. The poor thing
didn't know what hit her. Yes, that was the ticket—strike before she could put up her defenses. "Thanks so much for
coming, especially considering your busy, busy schedule."

"No problem, Tara. L and T is really high on your book,
so we want to do whatever it takes to get it on the best-seller
list."

"That's terrific." I flashed her a big smile even as I was
thinking how badly she still dressed. Granted, the black suit
was more than appropriate—very neat and businesslike—
but the shoes! My God, did she buy them from the Salvation
Army? I wondered. They were these clunky black pumps
that were so scuffed, they looked as if she'd worn them
mountain climbing. And the handbag? Well, suffice it to say
that it was brown.

I escorted her inside the house and felt a twinge of pleasure as her eyes took it all in. And yet there was a moment—
when she glanced wistfully at my wedding photo—when I
wanted to slit my wrists from the guilt of it all.

"Let's sit in the sunroom," I said after I'd finished giving
her the tour.

"All the rooms are beautiful, Tara. You did a great job
with the decorating."

"Thanks. I used Norman Scott."

She looked at me blankly. I explained that Norman Scott

was the interior designer whose work was on the cover of the previous month's *Architectural Digest.*

"Stuart must be doing well," she said with a tiny tremble in her voice.

"He's doing fabulously, thanks. And he's so supportive of my book. Even with all his responsibilities running Lasher's—"

"He's running Lasher's now?"

"Practically. He and Jimmy." Okay, so Jimmy was running the place and Stuart pretended to. Amy didn't have to know that.

"Well, speaking of work, I'll have to speed this up a little if I'm going to get back to the office for my afternoon meeting." She pulled out a notepad and pen. "Why don't you tell me how you came up with the idea for the book, Tara."

I did my spiel about the radio show and how the book's theme sprang from it. "It struck me how women really need advice on how to feel beautiful, how to pamper themselves, how to live with a sense of peace as well as style."

She nodded and scribbled and appeared to be interested.

I went on to give her numerous examples of how I, personally, created a simply beautiful environment in my home. Actually, I probably gave her too many examples, because she had stopped writing at one point and was just staring at me. Had I overloaded her with information? Overwhelmed her with tips on bathing in lavender and color-coding one's paper clips and using finger bowls at dinner parties, even casual ones? Or was she just hungry?

"Let's see if our lunch is ready," I said, remembering what a good appetite she always had. When we were teenagers, it drove her nuts that I'd eat the same burgers and fries that she did and yet I wouldn't gain a pound, while she—Well, what can I say? She sort of went porky in eighth grade. It's all in the metabolism, I guess.

We continued to talk about the book over the poached salmon Michelle had made for lunch. Amy seemed to have revived. She actually complimented me on the meal and looked more relaxed than when she'd arrived.

"So Stuart really plays the violin and reads you poetry and lets you give him a pedicure?" she asked, picking the sprigs of dill off of her salmon and relegating them to the side of the plate. Apparently, she didn't appreciate the simple beauty of garnishes.

"Oh yes," I said. "He's an incredibly sensitive man underneath that Brooks Brothers suit. Very romantic. We're about as happy as two people could be."

"How nice," she said in a tone that made me think I'd gone a little overboard on the Stuart stuff, particularly since it was shortly thereafter that she announced that she had to leave.

"Is it because I hit a nerve?" I asked, genuinely sorry I'd spent so much time on him. I honestly didn't mean to rub salt in her wound, only to present my book in the best possible light. "Should I have kept my mouth shut about Stuart?"

"No. He's your husband. You devoted a whole chapter to him in the book. I can't ignore his existence, as much as I'd prefer to."

"I understand." I patted her hand. "You know, I wondered how this would go today. You and I. Here together. Just the two of us. It's been a long time coming. Too long. I've missed our little talks. I hope this will be a new beginning for us."

"A lovely sentiment," she said, yanking her hand out from under mine and rising from her chair, "but I really do have to get back to the city."

"Right." I tried to keep up with her as she walked briskly out of the room. "It just occurred to me, though, that we never got around to talking about you."

She stopped in her tracks, seemed disoriented momentarily (perhaps she was lost; my house must have been a maze to her, compared to her little apartment), but then recovered. "Next time," she said, and moved toward the foyer.

I trailed after her again as she headed out the front door. "But what about your special man?" I asked.

"What special man?" she said. By this point, she was inside her car and I was draped over her open window.

I smiled. "Hello? Did I get you so caught up in my book that you forgot about your fiancé? You told me about him when we met on the street, remember?"

"Oh, of course," she said with a shy giggle. "Silly me."

"Well, tell me about him. What's he like?"

"What's he like?" She paused. "Well, he's just the best. Not only exceptionally bright but gorgeous, too. Oh, and funny." She laughed, holding her sides, as if suddenly reminded of one of his jokes. "And he's so loving. So giving. So full of compassion and sensitivity. I'm ecstatic, as you can see."

Now I was the one looking wistful. Was she ever lucky to have found a guy like that. He sounded like Superman, for God's sake. A far cry from the Superjerk I was married to.

She stuck her key in the ignition. "Now, I've got to get going."

"But you haven't told me about the wedding. It's in just a few months, isn't it?"

"Yes, practically around the corner." She checked her watch. "Oops. I really do have to go."

"In a sec. Tell me what kind of event you're planning. Big? Small? Indoors? Outdoors? Come on, Amy. I need details."

"Details?" She looked confused, or was it conflicted?

"Is something wrong?" I asked.

"Not wrong, just a little tricky. I can't give you details because—Okay, here's the deal. My fiancé and I have been keeping a low profile. More than low, actually. Invisible. We haven't told a single person at L and T that we're seeing each other. So I'm asking you to keep our secret. Will you do that? Please?"

She was asking me to keep her secret. Wow. Apparently, I had done such a great job of warming her up toward me that she was trusting me with confidential personal information. Good work, Tara!

"I won't say a word," I assured her, then asked why the hush-hush. She explained that L and T had a policy against coworkers getting married or even dating. "In this day and age, they have a policy like that?"

"Yes," she said as she started the car. "It's hard to believe, but they do."

"Well," I said over the engine noise, trying to show solidarity with her and sympathy for her predicament, "it must be horrible to have to carry on a relationship in secret."

"I bet it wasn't so horrible for you and Stuart."

The minute the remark had slipped out, it was obvious from her eyes—they went wide with surprise—that she was taken aback by her own boldness and wished she'd shut up. As for me, I was stunned. She had been the picture of restraint all afternoon long, but now she had exposed her true colors. The woman still hated me. She still hated me for stealing Stuart and would go on hating me for the rest of our lives. And yet, if she was so "ecstatic" over this fiancé of hers, why was she clinging to her hatred of me? If he was so brilliant and funny and gorgeous, if he loved her and she loved him and they were getting married in six months, why was her anger still so vivid, so pervasive? Why hadn't she moved on even a little bit? When you're really, truly happy, you mellow out, don't you?

Or was it possible that I'd misheard her because of the noisy car? I think she needed a new muffler or something, for it was making a terrible racket.

"Sorry. I didn't catch that. What did you say?" I asked, practically shouting. Might as well give her the benefit of the doubt. A word here, a word there. It was possible that I'd misunderstood.

"I was just saying thanks again for the lunch," she shouted back, then stepped on the gas and floored it.

No, I heard her correctly the first time, I thought as I watched the gravel fly up. You don't tear out of someone's driveway unless you're in a big hurry to get away from them. So the question was, Why was she in such a big hurry to get away from me? Was it really because she still hated me for stealing Stuart? Or was it because her relationship with her fiancé wasn't quite as cozy as she made it out to be and she was afraid I'd figure that out?

24

"Can I talk to you a minute?" asked Jimmy Lasher. We had all gathered at his parents' house for dinner and had just finished dessert. Stuart was in the kitchen, probably grabbing the very sizable ass of the Lasher's maid, while the rest of the family had scattered. Now his brother was steering me into the den, clearly hoping to have a private conversation with me.

"Sure, Jimmy. What's up? You look upset."

"I'm not happy."

"Is this about Stuart?"

"What else?" He shrugged, as if my husband had brought him a lifetime of grief. "Look, Tara. I don't want to burden you with our business headaches, especially since your own career is on the upswing, but has Stuart mentioned any problems at work?"

"No. Why? What's going on?"

"Who knows what's going on inside that mind of his. I was hoping you'd be able to enlighten me."

"Not unless you give me more information, Jimmy."

"Okay. One of our employees met with me about a week ago and said Stuart had told him to mislabel a truckload of melons."

I squelched a laugh. Melons? He was looking as if someone had died, and we were talking about melons? "Mislabel them how?"

"By stickering them as organic when they're not."

"Why would Stuart ask this employee to do that?"

"To jack up the prices. We can charge the customer fifteen percent more for the organic stuff."

"But that's fraud, Jimmy. Stuart comes up with ludicrous ideas from time to time, but he's not a criminal."

"I know, and I'm not implying that he was cheating the company. I think he was just trying to prove his worth to us. If profits increased and he had something to do with the increase, he'd feel like he'd contributed. That's my guess anyway. What's yours? You live with him. Has he been acting differently? Is everything okay at home?"

I hesitated. Jimmy was no fool. He was aware of his brother's flaws. But he loved him, and I didn't want to disabuse him of that love. "Everything's fine at home," I said. "I agree with your theory about this. He must have wanted to puff himself up by adding to Lasher's bottom line."

Jimmy nodded. "Then we're probably talking about a one-time thing, as opposed to a pattern. No harm done."

"Good, but what about the employee who tipped you off about the melons?"

"I handled that. I gave him a nice raise and a pat on the back and had him sticker the melons the way they were supposed to be stickered. End of story."

"So you didn't read Stuart the riot act?"

"Not the riot act. It's touchy between us, Tara, because he's my big brother and I hate to show him up. I just told him to keep his hands clean, and he said he would."

I breathed a sigh of relief. "And I'll stick closer to him, Jimmy. Spend more time with him. We can't afford a scandal, any of us, so you can count on me to do my part."

He gave me a hug. "I was hoping you'd say that. Stuart won the lottery when he married you. I love Peg more than anything, but she's innocent, naïve, not real savvy in the ways of the world. You're different, Tara. You're a realist.

You cut right through the crap and see things as they are, then deal with them, accept them. I admire that. Especially now that Stuart's misbehavior has taken a potentially tricky turn. As you put it, we can't afford a scandal. It would kill business at Lasher's."

"Not to worry. I'm on top of it."

And I was. I followed Stuart around as if I were glued to him, treated him with civility, acted more like a wife than an adversary, kept an eye on him. When we took a quick trip to Bermuda, for example, we swam together and played tennis together and went shopping together, and while I'd be over-stating it if I said we enjoyed each other's company, we man-aged. I was so conscientious about my duties that I wasn't the least bit tempted by the hunky specimen who was taking care of the pool that weekend. He'd flirted with me—not an unusual occurrence when you look as good as I do—but I didn't even allow myself a single stolen kiss. I'd always been too careful to engage in any extramarital activities. Be-sides, I wasn't as promiscuous as Stuart, nor did I need the validation from other men, and so I figured I'd just bide my time over the coming years, just keep things going either un-til I did get a divorce or Stuart died. The point was, I was still young and I knew deep down that I wouldn't be stuck with him forever, so why not play the game and let the clock run out?

It was in this new spirit of partnership that I suggested we invite Amy and her fiancé for dinner. Stuart said he loved the idea.

Unfortunately, Amy was less enthusiastic. Our telephone conversations about the book were extremely cordial, but whenever I brought up the subject of the four of us having dinner, she demurred. Her excuses were always the same—that her fiancé was too busy and that she was paranoid about someone from L and T finding out about them—and she wouldn't commit to making a date. Typical Amy, dragging her feet when she didn't want to do something. What in-trigued me was why she didn't want to come for dinner with her fiancé. Even if she hated me, I was her author now, her prized author at that. Wasn't she supposed to court me, not avoid me?

"If I didn't know better, I'd think you didn't want me to meet him," I said after she rebuffed me yet again.

"He's busy," she said. "Extremely busy."

"Stuart's busy, too, but he makes time to eat. So come on. Bring him up here and I'll feed him. You'll see. It'll be fun. For once, you two won't have to sneak around. You can even hold hands at the dinner table." I laughed. She didn't.

"I'm just curious, Tara. Why do you care so much about meeting my fiancé?" she asked. "It's not as if you and I are best friends anymore."

Ouch. I don't know why her words stung like a son of a bitch. Of course things had changed between us. I wasn't stupid. But when she actually articulated her feelings, I was transported right back to the humiliation of Stuart telling me she'd only picked me as her maid of honor to humor me. *Because we weren't best friends anymore.*

And so, before I could stop myself, the tears welled up, the result of a sudden and spontaneous wave of hurt. Damn, I hated when that happened. I prided myself on my steely demeanor. I didn't cry a lot, but it always seemed to be Amy who caused it when I did.

"I wanted to have you and your fiancé to dinner so I could show you I'm here for you," I said, wiping my eyes. "I wasn't there for you when you were engaged to Stuart, but I'd like to try again with your new man."

"That's very sweet, Tara, but why don't we just continue to work on your book and leave the men out of it?"

"Leave the *men* out of it? So is this about you're not being comfortable seeing Stuart?" I said. "You still care about him, is that it?"

"No! It has nothing to do with Stuart. I don't still care about him, believe me. It's about my fiancé and how busy he is, as I've already told you."

I wasn't buying it. Either she was still pining for Stuart and wouldn't admit it or she was afraid I'd steal this fiancé the way I'd stolen the last one and that history would repeat itself. Yeah, that was probably it. Or maybe there was something about the fiancé that she was hiding—like he wasn't the stud muffin she claimed he was. Maybe he was a shrimpy little thing with bad skin and bad hair and she didn't think he was impressive enough to trot out in front of me. Or maybe this fiancé wasn't a he at all. Maybe he was a she and we were talking about a lesbian relationship. Too many maybes, so I kept fishing.

"You're sure the reason you can't come for dinner has to do with your fiancé and not Stuart?" I asked.

"For the hundredth time, yes, Tara."

"Well, then maybe the next question should be, *Is* there a fiancé?"

"What's that supposed to mean?"

"Just that I'm beginning to wonder if he exists, since you're so tight-lipped about him. You've never even mentioned his name. Or her name, for that matter."

"Her name? I don't—"

She suddenly cut herself off in midsentence, told me there was a crisis with an author, and put me on hold. My guess was that she was flustered and stalling, trying to decide whether to admit she was gay. After a few minutes, she came back on the line.

"Did this author crisis have anything to do with Tony Stiles?" I said, sort of as a taunt. Recently, she'd told me she handled his publicity and I'd gushed about him. He was Stuart's favorite mystery writer. Mine, too.

"No," she said, as evasive as before.

Didn't think so. Go on, Amy. Tell me the truth about your so-called fiancé, and let's move on. It's not as if I'm homophobic, for God's sake. So you'll bring *her* up for dinner instead of *him.* Who cares?

"But since you mentioned Tony," she went on after clearing her throat, "I might as well tell you the truth about him."

"Great. I love gossip. Is he going out with a famous actress or something?" Obviously, she was still ducking me about her fiancé, but she wasn't off the hook. Not yet.

"No. He's going out with me."

I laughed, more out of confusion than anything else. "You and—So you're like—what?—traveling together on one of his book tours?"

"Tony and I are getting married. He's my fiancé, Tara, the one who's always so busy."

I think I actually choked on my own spit. I certainly coughed, gasped, something. Tony Stiles, the best-selling and best-looking writer in America, was Amy Sherman's fiancé? I was blown away. Totally shocked. How had my old pal, smart and pretty and principled though she was, managed to snare a catch as big as that?

"I can't get over this," I said after several seconds. "Why didn't you tell me before?"

She explained about L and T not approving of employees dating authors and about Tony's almost pathological need for privacy.

"No one knows about us. I'm only telling you because, as I said, we used to be so close."

"I'm touched." Mostly, I was dying to meet Tony Stiles.

"And discreet? You really can't tell anyone."

"I won't, I won't. You two will come for dinner, and Stuart and I won't breathe a word to a soul."

"Not even to him."

"To Stuart?"

"No, to Tony."

"I don't understand, Amy."

"You can't let Tony find out I told you about our engagement. As I said, he's extremely private and he'd be very upset if he thought I'd blabbed about us to you or anybody else. So we'll come under one condition."

"That I don't act like I know."

"Exactly."

Well, it was weird. That's all I can say. What she was proposing was downright strange. She was engaged to a fabulous guy, but I was supposed to pretend that the two of them were just friends? Business associates? Author and publicist? I mean, I was the queen of game playing, but this was

outrageous even for me. Still, I was thrilled for her that she
and Tony Stiles were getting married, and I was more than
eager to meet him, so what the hell. Besides, I figured that
once they got to the house and had a drink, they'd loosen up
about the whole secrecy thing.

"You're on," I said. "Pull out your calendar and we'll
schedule this dinner."

She told me they were free that Friday night, so we made
a date. I would call Michelle and ask her to cook something
sensational. I would fill the house with flowers and candles
and music. I would wear a knockout dress with knockout accessories to match. All doable. The only challenge would be
to make sure that Stuart behaved. Amy's guy was rich, sexy,
and smart. My guy was rich, oversexed, and dumb. But more
problematic than Stuart being only one out of three was
whether he'd keep his dick in his pants. God forbid that he
should start hitting on Amy after a vodka or two and trash
my image. I needed her to view me as half of a deliriously
happy couple, both because of the book and because of our
past relationship. I was the prom queen and she was supposed to envy me. That's how it was and that's how it would
stay. Yes, it would have been preferable to throw out old pat-
terns and stop reverting to type, but I couldn't help myself.
What I didn't see was that in trying so hard to keep Amy sus-
pended in a state of worship, I was keeping myself sus-
pended in a state of bullshit—bullshit that could come back
to haunt me if I wasn't careful.

25

It was pouring the night Amy and Tony came for dinner, and my mood was just as foul as the weather. There I was, only an hour before they were supposed to arrive, absolutely at my wit's end. I had made the house beautiful. I had made myself beautiful. I had made the food beautiful. (Okay, so Michelle had made the food beautiful.) And yet where was Stuart? Not home. Not at the office. Not answering his cell phone. How was I going to present us as the couple of the century when I didn't even know where my goddamn husband was?

It was a mere fifteen minutes before the lovebirds were due to show up when Stuart finally breezed in, the cuffs of his suit pants wet from the rain.

"Where have you been?" I demanded. So much for our détente.

"Nice greeting, hon. Does this mean you missed me?" he said, straightening his tie.

"You promised me you'd be home in time to help me get everything ready."

He surveyed the living room. "Everything looks ready to me. The house is like a museum, as usual. Not a blooming orchid out of place."

"Are you going to tell me where you've been or not?" I had promised Jimmy I would keep an eye on Stuart, but the job had become increasingly more difficult recently. He was often out of the office and not picking up his cell. Short of having him tailed, it was impossible to stay on top of him twenty-four hours a day. I had a radio show to do and a forthcoming book to publicize, and I simply didn't have the time or the energy to be his keeper.

He smiled. "I was out paying for that thirtieth birthday party I threw for you in Tuscany. That's where I've been."

"What are you talking about? The party was almost a year ago."

"It was an expensive party. And if I know you, you'll be expecting something even grander for your thirty-fifth. I'd better start saving, huh?"

"Stuart, I'll try this again. Where have you been? You said you'd be home early."

He leaned over and gave me a dry peck on the cheek. "Don't worry your beautiful head about it or you'll get wrinkles. I wasn't with any women, if that's what you're thinking."

"Why? Did all their fathers lock them in their rooms tonight?"

"Oh, so now you're accusing me of fooling around with jailbait? That's beneath even you."

"Fine. So you weren't with any women. Where were you? Tell me fast, because Amy and Tony will be here any minute."

"I was with some businesspeople, okay?"

"Does Jimmy know these 'businesspeople'?"

"No, he doesn't, because I'm allowed to have my own contacts in the industry. Maybe you haven't heard, but Jimmy is not my boss."

"Actually, he is, Stuart. He's in charge of Lasher's and you work for him."

"With him, Tara. I work *with* my brother."

He said this in sort of a menacing tone, so I dropped the subject. I didn't want us to take on that look of a couple who'd been fighting. Not when Amy and Tony were about to walk in the door.

"See if you can work with *me* now," I said. "Be charming tonight. I'd like this dinner to go well."

"I'll be so charming, you'll thank your lucky stars I married you instead of Amy."

"Let's not get carried away. Just try not to do anything awful. Oh, and you might want to run upstairs and change your suit. Your pant legs are wet."

Before he could argue, I heard a car in the driveway. He went upstairs. I went to greet my guests.

Wow. Nice wheels, I thought as I caught a glimpse of the Ferrari. I also caught a glimpse of Tony opening an umbrella and helping Amy out of the car.

Yes, nice wheels and nice manners.

"Come in, come in, you two!" I called out to them. "You must be soaked."

Huddled together, they hurried up to the door and came inside.

"Amy," I said, giving her sort of an arm's length hug. No reason to get as wet as the rest of them. "I'm so glad you braved the elements and made the trip."

"I promised you we'd come, Tara. *I* don't renege on my promises."

God. That insufferable holier-than-thou bit again.

I turned to face Tony. He was even more striking looking than he was on television. His dark wavy hair was wavier, his hooded blue eyes bluer, his toned and sexy body sexier. I was momentarily flustered by his appeal, the way people often are around celebrities.

"And you must be Tony," I said, shaking his hand. "It's a pleasure to meet you. My husband and I are big fans."

"Well, shucks. Thanks for the kind words," he said with a naughty grin. "Oh, and thanks for letting me tag along on your business dinner with Amy."

"Business dinner?" I sneaked a peek at Amy and winked at her. Yeah, yeah. I was supposed to play along with her game, but she couldn't have been serious about it. Not when Tony had such a mischievous quality about him. Only an uptight jerk wouldn't want anybody to know he was in love, and my impression of Tony was that he was no uptight jerk. The truth was, he was the most attractive man I'd been around in ages. "We can talk business if you insist, but once I've served you and Amy a drink and a nibble, I'd rather move on to a much more entertaining subject."

Amy shot me the evil eye, but I completely ignored her. Talk about uptight. She wasn't dressed for a dinner party. She was dressed for jury duty.

We chatted for another minute or so, then Stuart made his appearance. He'd changed his suit, run a comb through his hair, and applied some cologne. I noticed that Amy stayed fairly calm in his presence, even though it was her first look at him in four years. He was positively beaming at the sight of her. He grabbed her and kissed her and said how great it was to see her, which was all well and good as long as he kept his fly zipped.

"This is wonderful," he said to her. "I was thrilled when Tara told me your news."

"My news?" asked Amy, glaring at me again.

"And you're Tony," he said, shaking Tony's hand. "I hope you realize how lucky you are. You've got yourself a real gem."

Amy jumped in and said something about her work on Tony's books, and he made a remark about what an excellent publicist she was. Fine, so they were sticking to the "We're just friends" subterfuge for the moment. I had every confidence that they'd let down their guard eventually.

I took Tony's arm and led him into the library. "So tell me," I said, "is it true what I've been reading about you?"

He laughed. "That depends on what you've been reading about me."

"Oh, just that you're a ferociously hard worker, that you research the crimes in your books by talking to actual criminals, and that you live and breathe Joe West."

"Guilty as charged."

"Well, whatever you do, don't stop, because the books are impossible to put down."

"I knew there was a reason I came here tonight." He held my gaze. "Flattery and dinner, too. An irresistible combination."

"Plus, you get to spend time with Amy," I added. "Outside of your usual environment, I mean."

"Right. Normally, we see each other in the city."

"Yes, but I meant that you don't normally socialize with other couples."

"Not unless she drags me to one of those L and T parties with the sales reps and their spouses. That's not my idea of a good time, let me tell you."

"Well, here's hoping tonight will make up for all that. You and Amy can just relax and enjoy. Stuart and I have been sworn to secrecy."

"Secrecy?"

I pressed my finger to my lips. "Shhhh. Mum's the word." I invited him to have a seat, then called out to Stuart. "Where are you, sweetheart? Tony and I are waiting for you to make everybody drinks."

"Here I am, hon." He entered the room with his arm around Amy. I considered myself fortunate that it was only her waist he was fondling.

"You take the drink orders while I rustle up the hors d'oeuvres," I said. "The ice bucket's in the kitchen, so come with me, sweetheart. I'm sure these two can occupy themselves while we're gone."

I winked at Amy again before disappearing with Stuart.

"She landed a prize all right," I whispered to him while Michelle was in the butler's pantry, putting the finishing touches on the canapés. "Tony Stiles is to die for."

"Yeah, well try to keep those panties of yours dry. He belongs to her."

"That's what I love about you, Stuart. You have such a gentlemanly way of putting things. But speaking of panties, I'd leave Amy's on if I were you. Tony probably has contacts in the underworld, so you don't want to make him mad."

He grabbed the ice bucket, then my ass, and went back into the library.

I followed a few minutes later with the tray of hors d'oeuvres. "Here are those nibbles," I said, passing them around.

"Which reminds me, Amy. Have you planned the menu for the big day?"

She reacted to my question by nearly spilling her white wine. What was her problem anyway?

"We haven't planned the menu for Tony's publication party," she said, "because it's so far off in the future."

Okay, so she was still doing her number. It was becoming tiresome, in my opinion, and totally unnecessary. Tony seemed perfectly comfortable being with us. So why not discuss their engagement? She wouldn't let me, that's why. Every time I brought it up, she changed the subject and focused the attention on me, on my book. In other words, I kept having to do my own number, kept having to pretend that my marriage to Stuart was bliss, that we were the happiest couple ever, that ours was a life to be envied. There were moments when even I wanted to throw up from myself. But I'd worked hard on *Simply Beautiful,* and there was no way in hell that Amy Sanctimonious Sherman was going to blow my cover.

After an hour or so, I served dinner. Amy continued to ask Stuart and me questions about our house, our families, our travel plans. It was torture, because I was dying to shift the conversation back to her and Tony. At some point, when she finally shut up for a second, I said, "Can you imagine having a wedding on a night like this?"

She practically choked. No, now that I think about it, she did choke. She had taken a bite of Michelle's game hen and started gagging and gasping and clutching her throat. Tony leapt to her side, wrapped his arms around her, and performed the Heimlich maneuver. Naturally, I felt terrible—I had my issues with Amy, but I didn't want to be responsible for her death—and offered to call 911. But Tony must have known what he was doing, because she recovered in record time.

Unfortunately, the drama wasn't over. The storm that was raging outside produced a loud clap of thunder, which produced an even louder crash. Stuart and I bolted up from the table to check the other rooms—it sounded as if something had fallen—but nothing was amiss. When we returned to the dining room, Amy and Tony were on their feet.

"I hope you don't mind, Tara," she said, "but I'm pretty exhausted from my choking episode. I think we're going to head back to the city a little earlier than we'd planned."

"The roads are bound to be slippery," Tony added. "We'll have to take it slowly."

Stuart and I said we understood—frankly, I was relieved to be done with my charade, relieved that I wouldn't have to make nice to my husband for a single second more—and we walked them outside with our umbrellas.

To our dismay, the loud crack we'd heard earlier hadn't been a figment of our imagination. A tree had fallen across the driveway, blocking Tony's car.

"Can you call someone to move the tree?" asked Amy, looking pained.

"Not at this time of night and not in this storm," said Stuart.

"But surely we can get it out of their way so they can leave," I said, feeling a little pained myself. It had just dawned on me that if Amy and Tony couldn't go back to the city, they'd be forced to spend the night with us, and I wouldn't be off the hook so fast after all.

"That tree isn't going anywhere, and neither are we," said Tony. "Not unless there's a chain saw handy."

"Is there?" Amy and I asked simultaneously.

Stuart and Tony laughed at our duet.

"Is there a chain saw handy? No," said Stuart. "But we do have some fabulous old port, so I suggest we go back in the house, where it's dry and warm, and have ourselves a nightcap. Then you two will sleep over in our guest house. Right, hon?" He nudged me. "*Hon?*"

"Yes. Right. The guest house," I said.

"We can't," said Amy. "I mean, we don't want to be any trouble."

"No trouble at all," I said. "You'll get a good night's rest and then we'll feed you a lovely breakfast tomorrow and you can hit the road as soon as the driveway's clear."

Stuart put his arm around my shoulder. "My wife has that guest house decorated just like a honeymoon cottage. It'll be our pleasure to have you stay in it."

Our pleasure. Yeah, sure. I didn't know what Amy was looking so peeved about—she was about to spend the night at what amounted to a first-class B and B, for God's sake— but I had a valid reason to be disgusted. I had already expended more than enough energy performing for her benefit, and now, thanks to the stupid tree, I'd have to keep the act going. What's more, while she was going off to snuggle up with a brilliant, sensitive man, I'd be stuck with a guy who had the brains, not to mention the sensitivity, of a shoe. Like that was fair?

As everybody trudged back inside, I decided that I would buy a chain saw the next time I was at Home Depot. Who knew they were such useful little gadgets?

26

The rain stopped during the night, thank God. So I went for an early-morning jog to clear my head before having to deal with Amy. And it was a good thing I did, because she and Tony were mighty hard to take all of a sudden. They must have decided to lift their veil of secrecy once they were alone together in my romantic little guest house. They came prancing into the kitchen like teenagers in heat, instead of pretending to be business colleagues, and it was revolting. He was calling her "buttercup" and she was fluttering her eyelashes at him, and they never stopped touching each other. Imagine how I felt. Yes, of course I was happy for her—especially since her happiness took the onus off of what Stuart and I had done to her—but my husband never called me "buttercup" or any other term of endearment except when we were putting on a show. And he never, ever looked at me with the kind of unadulterated affection that Tony obviously had for her.

But the absolute worst, in terms of my feeling envious of her and sorry for myself, was when Tony made his big speech about what a Wonder Woman she was.

"I'm dying to hear how you two became a couple," I'd said innocently enough while the four of us hung around the kitchen, waiting for the tree people to come. Well, I was curious about them. Amy had her attributes, as I've admitted, but it was still a shocker that she'd hooked as big a fish as Tony Stiles.

"I was the one who pursued her," he said. "And I had to get my courage up to do it."

And then he went on and on about how intimidated he was by Amy. Yeah, Amy. The one who had always been intimidated by me. He said she was a legend in the book business. He said she was linked with lots of rich and powerful men. He said she was beautiful and suggested that it must have been difficult for me to grow up around the prettiest girl in town. What a nightmare, right? I mean, was I supposed to just sit there when he said that about her, knowing that it had been the other way around with us? Sit there and smile even though *I'd* been the prettiest girl in town?

Oh, and then he really laid a winner on me, on Stuart and me. He was all worked up about how he'd fallen in love with Amy and asked her to marry him and how it was only after he proposed that she confided that she'd been engaged once before.

"She told me her fiancé dumped her for another woman right before the wedding. Can you believe it?" he said. "The guy must have been deluded to think he'd found someone better."

I was so mortified, I couldn't even look at Stuart. And I sure as hell wasn't making eye contact with good old Amy.

Fortunately, the doorbell rang before Tony could continue his homage to his bride-to-be.

"I'll get it," I said, eager to leave the room.

"No, I'll get it," said Stuart, blocking my path. "It's just Mandy with some papers for me to sign."

I stiffened but tried not to show it. Mandy was Stuart's latest secretary/squeeze. Or so I assumed. She was always calling, always hovering. And now a home visit? I was not amused.

"Why is she coming here?" I asked, willing myself to appear chipper.

"Because our driveway's blocked, remember?" said Stuart. "I can't go to the office, so she's delivering the papers to me here." He apologized to our guests for having to run, then ran—probably straight into Mandy's exuberant breasts.

I offered to make Amy and Tony breakfast, but they declined, preferring to go back to the guest house. Meanwhile, Mandy came and went. Stuart emerged from the library looking like a man in lust.

"For God's sake, at least try to act married," I hissed. "Amy will notice if you don't."

"What if she does notice?" he taunted. "She's always been the understanding type."

"If you so much as whisper the truth about us, I'll make sure Jimmy gets an earful about you and Mandy."

"A threat. How sweet. Well, I'd love to chat some more, but Walter's coming over. Since he bores you to death, you might as well take off."

Walter was Lasher's chief bookkeeper, or maybe he was their accountant—I could never remember which. "My, you have your whole entourage dropping by today."

"Hey, I'm the boss. If I can't go to them, they come to me."

"I hate to break this to you yet again, Stuart sweetie, but you're not the boss of Lasher's. Your bro is. Bye-bye."

I left him to wait for Walter and occupied myself in the bedroom. About a half hour later, I discovered I'd left my cell phone downstairs and went to get it. As I passed by the library, I saw that the door was slightly ajar. Mildly curious to know if Walter had arrived or if "Walter" was really just another woman having a fling with my husband, I stopped to listen. When I heard men's voices, I was satisfied that Stuart really was conducting business. Relieved that Amy and Tony wouldn't stumble on him in a compromising position and find out our marriage was a joke, I turned to go.

And then I caught something that kept me glued right where I stood.

It was the other man's voice—the man who was supposed to be Walter but couldn't have been, I realized. I'd met Walter Stein two or three times, either when I was over at Lasher's headquarters or attending some corporate function, and he had an unmistakable New York accent. The man in our library at that moment was no New Yorker. He sounded Slavic or Russian. Definitely foreign.

I pressed my ear to the door.

"I give you finest," said the man. "You never gonna do better."

"Well, the price is certainly right," said Stuart with a chuckle.

There was a noise from in there. A zipper opening or closing? A suitcase being locked or unlocked? I couldn't tell, despite straining to hear.

"Pure gold," said the man. "And I bring more whenever you need."

I tensed as I asked myself what could be going on? *The finest? Pure gold? More whenever Stuart needed?* What the hell were they talking about?

As they moved toward the door and Stuart escorted the man outside, I peeked around the wall and got a glimpse of him. He had slicked-back brown hair, a roly-poly body and a mustache, and he was wearing jeans and a Mets baseball jersey. He looked harmless enough, but he was not Walter Stein, that was for sure.

As Stuart came back inside, I scurried into the kitchen, where I tried to make sense of their snippets of conversation.

The mention of gold made me wonder if Stuart was buying one of his girlfriends some jewelry from a wholesaler. He wasn't buying the trinket as a surprise for me, I'll tell you that, because he knew better. (For one thing, it wasn't my birthday or our anniversary. For another, I didn't wear jewelry unless it came from Tiffany or was a reasonable facsimile.)

But then there was the word *need* that struck me as interesting. The man had promised he'd bring more of whatever it was whenever Stuart *needed* it. That implied drugs, didn't it?

Oh God, I thought. As if I don't have enough to handle, my husband's an addict, his craving so out of control that the tree in the driveway forced him to sneak his dealer in and out of his own house, right under my nose.

And yet Stuart had never seemed stoned, high, or impaired. What's more, while he loved to spend money (one of the few traits I enjoyed about him), he loved to spend it ostentatiously, overtly, so that his spending could be seen and appreciated by others. Drugs were a private, solitary affair, which didn't suit Stuart at all. What good was buying them if they couldn't be shown off in some glossy magazine?

Still, what else could the two of them have been discussing? It was definitely a deal of some sort and it definitely involved Stuart's surreptitious purchase of "the finest." Yes, it had to be drugs. And if it had to be drugs, the public perception of my simply beautiful marriage was more imperiled than ever.

I was about to confront Stuart, when Bobby, his personal trainer, rang the bell.

"Don't answer that," I said as he went for the door. "We have to talk."

"Can't," said Stuart. "I called Bobby this morning and told him I needed stretching out. Now he's here."

You need stretching out all right, I thought. On a rack.

"Bobby can wait," I said. "I want to know who was in the library with you before. I heard a man, and he didn't sound like Walter."

He smiled. "It's not polite to eavesdrop, hon. Didn't anyone ever teach you that?"

"Look, Stuart. I don't know what you've gotten yourself into this time, but I'm not about to let you—"

I was stopped in midsentence by the unfortunately timed appearance of our houseguests. Yes, there they were, the lovebirds, Amy and her best-selling mystery writer, arm in arm, with big smiles on their faces, their cheeks flushed from what I assumed was their latest romp in my sack.

"We didn't mean to interrupt," said Amy. "We were just wondering if there's been any news from the tree people."

"But if there hasn't," said Tony, "we'll just keep busying ourselves, won't we, buttercup?" He planted a soulful wet one on her lips.

"You're not interrupting," I said brightly. "Stuart and I were just going over some household matters. And now his trainer is here."

"Right," said Stuart. "See you guys later."

Stuart went off with Bobby, leaving me to play the gracious hostess.

"Well," I said, "since my better half is in such demand today, I'm afraid it's just the three of us now."

"Minus one," said Tony. "I think I'll go outside to check the car. All that falling debris might have caused some damage."

After he left, there was an awkward silence between Amy and me. And then, at precisely the same time, we both started talking about *Simply Beautiful* in a desperate attempt to fill the dead air, I guess.

"Why don't we sit down," I said when I couldn't listen to another word about my perfect life.

"Sure." She followed me into the sunroom, where we sat on opposite ends of the sofa. "Thanks for letting us stay over, by the way," she added. "Tony and I really appreciate it. Spending the night in your guest house has been like having a preview of our honeymoon."

"That's nice. Look, Amy. I'm the one who should be thanking you."

"Me? Why?"

"For not telling Tony the whole story about your broken engagement to Stuart. You kept our names out of it, and that was a classy thing to do."

"Oh, don't think twice about it. I had no interest in poisoning him against either of you. Why should I? As you can see, I've moved on with my life."

"I can see, and I'm so impressed by everything you've accomplished. The power career. The power boyfriends. And now, of course, Tony."

She glanced down at her feet. "Yes, I finally have it all, just like you."

Just like me. Ha. If only she knew the truth, I thought. If only I could bring myself to tell her the truth. It would be so liberating not to have to pretend with someone. But how could I tell *her*, of all people, what a sad marriage I really had? Why would she show me an ounce of sympathy?

No. I could never tell her, and the reality of how isolated I was and how much I needed a best friend brought tears to my eyes. I always seemed to cry around her, best friend or not.

"What's the matter?" she asked. "Everything's great with you and Stuart, isn't it?"

"Of course it's great," I said. "These are tears of joy, because I'm thrilled for you, for all your success." I wiped my eyes, tried to regroup. "Sorry to lose it like that. I don't know what came over me."

"No, I'm sorry," she said softly.

"What for?"

She didn't answer at first. She just stared at me, as if she were suddenly flashing back to her own memories. And from the way her brows furrowed, I assumed they weren't pleasant ones.

"Amy? You were going to apologize for something."

Silence.

"Amy?"

"Oh. Right. Just that I'm sorry Tony and I left the guest house in such a mess. I'd better go straighten up."

Before I could tell her to leave it for the housekeeper, she jumped up from her chair and rushed out of the room. Odd behavior, wasn't it, but who was I to criticize?

27

For the next two and a half months, Stuart and I saw Amy and Tony socially. Or professionally. I couldn't tell which. From my standpoint, it was professional. I needed to keep her excited about the book so that she'd do everything she could to promote it. She was the one who insisted on making every get-together a foursome. My hunch was that, while she'd certainly gotten over Stuart (and who wouldn't have, given the choice between him and Tony Stiles), it gave her a kick to flaunt her new fiancé in front of her old one. As for Stuart, he'd rarely mentioned Amy until she reappeared in our lives. Now, he was constantly asking about her—when would we see her again, how was I getting along with her, did I really think she and Tony were well matched. It was pretty sickening, actually, because he'd had his chance with her and blown it, so why the sudden interest?

"I like Amy," he said when I posed the question one day. We were on a flight back to New York from Palm Beach. We'd been looking at houses with a real estate agent. Stuart thought we should have a second home in Florida, and I wasn't about to object, but we hadn't found anything we wanted to buy. "As a matter of fact, I've always liked Amy."

"Liked Amy? You were in love with her," I pointed out.

"Yes, but I married you, hon," he said.

"You know, I've always wondered: If you'd married Amy

instead of me, do you think you'd be cheating on her the way you're cheating on me?"

He patted my hand, then motioned for the flight attendant, asked for a Bloody Mary, and opened the newspaper. Clearly, he was not planning to answer me.

After our trip, I noticed that Stuart seemed sort of distracted, preoccupied, even jumpy. I asked him about it, but he shrugged it off, told me I had too much time on my hands. In a way, I did. My radio show was on hiatus, and there was no real work to be done on the book until closer to publication. Still, Stuart's twitchy behavior was hard to miss. When he was in his womanizing phase, at least he was sort of happy-go-lucky, but now he was anxious, somber.

Apparently, I wasn't the only one who observed the change in him, because Jimmy Lasher took me aside at a family gathering.

"Stuart's been avoiding me," he said. "He's not showing up for meetings, doesn't take my calls, won't even give me two seconds tonight. What's going on?"

"I don't know, but something's weighing on him. He hasn't been himself since we got back from Florida."

"Which reminds me: I know my brother's never met a dollar he couldn't spend, but how does he get off affording a house in Florida? Tell me to butt out if you want, but did you make a killing on that book of yours?"

I smiled. "Not a killing, just a really nice advance for a first-time author. Why do you ask? Obviously, Stuart can afford the house without help from me. Business at Lasher's is booming."

Jimmy's jaw dropped. "Is that what he's been telling you?"

"Well, not in so many words. It's just that he's always got plenty of money, so I assumed—"

"See, here's what's bothering me, Tara. Business at Lasher's isn't booming. The economy's in a slump, in case you haven't been reading the papers. Sure, the high-end customers are still buying, and they're our core customers, but we've had a drop-off in terms of the rest. We're a gourmet foods retailer at a time when most of the country is shopping at Costco and the other discounters."

"I had no idea. I guess I should have been paying more attention. It's just that Stuart always acts as if everything's fine with the company. Better than fine. And, as I said, he's got more money than ever."

Jimmy's eyes narrowed and his expression darkened. "Wonder where he's getting it, then."

"Okay, this may be totally irrevelent and nothing to worry about, but a man came to our house to see Stuart a few weeks ago and it sounded like they were making a deal."

"Who was he?"

"I don't know. It was the day after the big rainstorm. Our driveway was blocked and we had houseguests, so I was too frazzled to pin Stuart down. I just remember that he told me he had a meeting with Walter Stein, but the man he met with instead was some character in a baseball jersey, and he barely spoke English."

"Weird. Anything else?"

"I overheard them talking. The guy was definitely selling Stuart something at a bargain price and promised there was more where that came from. Oh, and he mentioned the word *gold.*"

"So it was jewelry?"

"I thought it might be drugs."

Jimmy shook his head. "Stuart's no angel, but he's no druggie, either."

"Could he be selling drugs instead of using them, Jimmy? Is it possible that the money he's been spending like water is drug money?"

He put his head in his hands. "I hate this. I hate having to police my own brother. But I'll have to confront him. Actually, I think we both should confront him. If we double-team him, maybe we can get answers."

"Whatever you want to do."

Jimmy and I waited until the family party broke up, then cornered Stuart in their parents' front yard.

"You two are totally out of line," he said after we brought up the subject of drugs. He was indignant, defensive, told us we were crazy.

"Then who was the man who came to the house, Stuart?" I said. "The one with the foreign accent."

He laughed. "Is that what all this is about? His name is Sergei and he's a friend of mine—kind of a hanger-on, but a nice guy. He used to work at the Westport store."

"I don't remember anybody named Sergei in the Westport store," said Jimmy.

"You're much too important to notice every lowly employee, Jimmy. You're the boss, running the show. Isn't that what everybody keeps telling me?"

"Stop it, Stuart. Tara and I are concerned about you."

"Tara wouldn't care if I dropped dead this minute, as long as her bills are paid."

"That's not true," I said. Well, not quite. "So let's quit being melodramatic and get back to Sergei. He's a friend?"

"He's a friend, yes. I'm allowed to have my own friends, aren't I? Or have you both decided to regulate who I see and what I do and when I do it?"

"If he's a friend, then why did you pretend Walter Stein was coming to see you that day?" I asked. "Why didn't you introduce me to this Sergei?"

"I didn't think he was your type, hon. Not dressed in the designer duds you like everybody to be wearing when they walk through our front door. And we had houseguests, if you recall. What would Amy think if she found out your husband socializes with a man who used to run our produce department but is now peddling gold chains out of a suitcase?"

"You mean he does sell jewelry?" I said.

"Not your sort of jewelry, but some women wear it," he replied. "Sergei's got a wife and kids to support, so I help him out and buy a few things whenever he comes around. What's the big deal?"

I was dying to ask who the recipients of this magnificent jewelry were, but I didn't want to inflame the situation by bringing up Mandy and the others.

"By the way, when you mentioned Amy before, did you mean Amy Sherman?" asked Jimmy.

"The very same," said Stuart. "She's handling the publicity for Tara's book and we've been seeing a lot of her lately."

The conversation veered off at that point, so that Jimmy and Stuart could reminisce about how special Amy was. Nauseating.

In the end, Jimmy and I were semisatisfied that Stuart had really befriended some former Lasher's employee named Sergei and that he wasn't involved in anything illegal. As for where he was coming up with the money for a house in Florida, his answer for that was less reassuring.

"That's what banks are for," he said. "They keep lending and I keep spending."

"Not very smart," said Jimmy. "Eventually, those loans come back to bite you and you end up losing your shirt."

"Yeah, well, you may be the steady one, baby brother, but I'm the creative one," said Stuart. "I have no intention of losing anything. Right, hon?"

As he looked at me, I felt my stomach turn. Leave it to my lame husband to gamble with our money and risk not only our security but our image. Oh, go ahead and call me shallow. Maybe I am. But I had worked my ass off building my simply beautiful concept, and even Amy, the world's greatest promoter, wouldn't be able to salvage it if my house went into foreclosure.

As Stuart stood there talking to Jimmy, I cursed myself for getting involved with him in the first place. He was such a loser. Why hadn't I recognized that? What could I have been thinking when I got mixed up with him and stayed mixed up with him? And how was I going to untangle myself?

During a night of tossing and turning, I came up with a plan. At about 4:00 A.M., I decided that as soon as the book was published, which would be another month or so, and I made it through the interviews and the store signings and all the other activities Amy scheduled for me, I would divorce Stuart. Yes, I would wait until *Simply Beautiful*'s sales were at their peak and then cut the guy loose. I knew I should have done it a long time ago, but it wasn't too late. I was still young. I could find a new man, the way Amy had found Tony. I could salvage some measure of dignity.

Yes, there were bound to be people who'd label me an imposter after the way I'd gushed over Stuart in the book, but they'd get over it. What's more, I would help them get over it by launching the second phase of my plan: I would write another book.

It would be a best-selling sequel about what happens when prom queens outgrow their crowns. It would be about ditching the image, about living for yourself instead of having to be other people's Ideal, about trying to develop honest friendships with other women, as opposed to isolating yourself in a bubble of perfection. It would be about possibilities.

So you see, despite Stuart's infidelities, his debts, and his failures as both a husband and a man, I was feeling very upbeat the next morning. He had already left the house by the time I got up and dressed, so I didn't even have to lay eyes on him. To celebrate my forthcoming freedom, I took a drive. I had no destination, no list of errands, no agenda. I just hit the road.

The weather was warm and sunny, so I put the convertible's top down and made my way up the Boston Post Road, heading into Connecticut. I stopped at the beach and took a long walk in the sand, then went to a hot dog stand and ate the kind of food I usually avoided. I stopped at a funky little store and bought myself a needlepoint pillow adorned with the words *Of course you can do it.* I felt free. I had a handle on things. I only had to get through the book's publication; then I would leave Stuart before whatever hole he was digging for himself sucked me in, too.

It was nearly 3:30 by the time I finally headed home. When I pulled into my driveway, I wasn't expecting to find the police car, naturally, but there it was, parked right in front of my door—a bummer after an otherwise fantastic day.

My first thought was that we'd been robbed, that maybe the burglar alarm had gone off and the police had come to check things out, the way they always did. But as I approached one of the officers and he said, "Mrs. Lasher, we'd like to talk to you," I knew I was in for more serious business than stolen silverware.

"What's wrong?" I asked.

He introduced himself as Detective Burnett. The other one's name was Detective Vincent. "Why don't we go inside first," Detective Burnett suggested.

I unlocked the door. We all went in. I offered them a beverage—ever the hostess.

"It's about your husband," said Burnett once we were seated in the living room.

Oh God, I thought. The fool has gotten himself arrested. Was he stickering unorganic melons again? Engaging in lewd acts with minors? Doing drugs, in spite of his denials to Jimmy and me? What?

"Where is he?" I asked, feeling my body tense. I was not going to let him wreck my plan. I needed him to stay out of trouble just until the book was published; then he'd be on his own and could do whatever the hell he wanted.

"We were hoping you could tell us," he said. "He isn't home?"

"No. At least I assume he isn't. I just got home myself."

"Mind if we look around the house?"

"Go ahead."

I took both of them on the tour. No Stuart.

"And you haven't heard from him?" asked Vincent when we were back in the living room.

"No."

"And you have no idea where he might be?"

"No! Now would you please tell me why you're asking?"

"Well, his car was in some kind of an accident," said Burnett. "It was found in an alley in back of Lasher's headquarters, and it was banged up pretty bad. The windshield was smashed and the seat was cut up."

I blinked. "Cut up?"

"Like with a knife or some other sharp object. There was blood on the seat, too, Mrs. Lasher. We'd like to do a DNA test to determine if it's Mr. Lasher's."

Okay, I hated Stuart. We know that. But blood? His blood? How unpleasant.

"We checked area hospitals, but your husband hasn't been admitted anywhere," said Vincent. "And we interviewed his coworkers at the office, but no one's seen him since this morning. He seems to have disappeared."

I relaxed slightly. "He disappears all the time. Nothing earth-shattering about that."

"Maybe not. And we don't want to jump to conclusions. Normally when we find an abandoned car, we have it towed and that's that. But given the condition of your husband's car and the possibility of foul play—"

"Foul play?"

"The blood on the seat, Mrs. Lasher."

"The only lead we have is this," said Vincent, holding up the black leather date book I'd bought Stuart the week before. "It was on the floor of the car, under the driver's seat."

Suddenly, the reality of the situation hit me, and I felt as if someone had punched me in the stomach. These cops weren't kidding around, I realized. They thought something gruesome had happened to Stuart. It was all over their faces.

"You think he's dead, don't you?" I said. "You think someone dragged him out of the car, killed him, and left him someplace."

"It does look suspicious," said Burnett. "But we have no proof of a homicide. Until we find a body, we're only speculating about—"

"Right," I said. "No body. No murder. Just a disappearance. Maybe Stuart had a problem with the car—engine trouble or a flat tire—and while he was off renting another one, some mischievous kids broke the windshield and slashed the seat. That kind of thing happens all the time, doesn't it? As a matter of fact, I'll bet he took the rental car and drove straight to a business meeting and simply forgot to tell his secretary. He's probably at the meeting as we speak."

Vincent flipped through the date book. "There's no business meeting entered for this afternoon. Just his meeting at the Plaza Hotel at noon."

"There. You see?" I said. "Maybe the noon meeting ran long. Did you check with the hotel to see if he's still there?"

"Yeah. He's not," said Vincent.

"How about the person he was meeting? Did you check with him?"

Vincent cast Burnett a look.

"What?" I said.

"The person he was meeting at noon was a *her,*" he said. "Mr. Lasher, uh, reserved them a room."

I knew it. Stuart hadn't been murdered. He'd been having sex, for God's sake, and the cops were too polite just to come right out and tell me. I mean, how much humiliation was I supposed to take?

"So which woman was he meeting?" I asked impatiently. "Mandy something or other?"

"No. Amy something or other," he said. "The date book just mentions an Amy. Does the name ring a bell?"

Amy? Poor sweet "I'm not your best friend anymore" Amy? Well, dingdong, I thought. Ding-fucking-dong.

I sank back into the chair, heavy with this latest revelation. So she was having an affair with Stuart. Imagine that. And after all the years I'd spent feeling guilty over what I'd done to her. After all her declarations about how she'd moved on with her life! The woman was not only sleeping with her old flame but cheating on her new flame. At least when I slept with Stuart, back when he was hers, I was unattached!

"Yes, the name Amy Sherman rings a bell," I said. "If something happened to my husband, she should be your prime suspect."

"If you give us her address, we'll pay her a visit this evening," said Burnett. "But in the meantime, maybe you could tell us everything you know about her."

"With pleasure," I said, practically licking my lips.

AMY

28

Y ou were sleeping with Stuart Lasher?" Tony demanded as we stood in my kitchen. "Behind my back?"

"Behind your back?" I said. "This may come as a news bulletin, *buttercup,* but you and I aren't engaged. We've been faking it, remember?"

"And doing a pretty good job of it, too," he said. "That is, until you cheated on me."

"I didn't cheat on you, Tony! Stop saying that!" Boy, I hadn't expected this reaction when I'd called him in a panic and told him I'd been interrogated by the police. He'd come right over to my apartment that night, which I appreciated, but what I didn't appreciate was all the badgering.

"Hey. I'm teasing you about sleeping with the guy," he said, his voice assuming its more customary wiseass tone. "I know you can't stand him any more than I can."

"Oh, so that performance you just gave was only *mock* indignation?"

"Not entirely. You're still gonna have to explain to me why you were meeting him at the Plaza. Fiancé or no fiancé, I never figured you'd do something like that."

"Fine. I'll explain. I went there to satisfy my curiosity. He called me out of the blue and said he wanted to be alone with me. I wondered why."

"Because you're a beautiful woman and he was hot to get you into bed, that's why."

"Maybe he was and maybe he wasn't. I couldn't tell from his phone call. But I also wondered how I would feel about being alone with him after what happened four years ago. There was something tempting about being the one to reject him this time around."

"Okay. You were hurt by him once. I can understand that."

"And then there was the issue of his marriage to Tara. I wondered why he was calling me if the marriage was as rock solid as they made it out to be. I was dying to find out if there was a chink in her armor. I couldn't help myself."

"That part I don't understand. Your obsession with her is off-the-charts nuts."

"Was, Tony, *was*. That's what I realized when Stuart didn't show up at the Plaza today. I'm over my need to prove myself to her or pay her back. I'm done with all that. Finished. Cured."

"I'm not buying it."

"Buy it, because it's true. After I sat there waiting in that hotel room for over two hours, I promised myself I'd never be humiliated by either of those two again. Of course, the cops at my door added a new wrinkle to the situation. She actually had the nerve to—"

"Hang on. Before we get into serious police business, I need a drink. Do you have any red wine open?"

"I think there's some Cabernet in the refrigerator."

He looked at me as if I had six heads. "Cabernet in the refrigerator?"

Damn. In the hubbub over Stuart, I'd forgotten that I was supposed to be a wine connoisseur, and wine connoisseurs don't stick Cabernet in the fridge. I was caught. It just wasn't my day, I guess.

"I don't know a thing about wine," I said sheepishly. "I only pretended to, because I had to get you to like me enough to play my fiancé."

His eyes widened. "You mean your entertaining speeches about noble bouquets and velvety textures were—"

"Bullshit. Yes. I don't know anything about hockey, either. New York Rangers. Forest rangers. They're all the same to me."

"I don't believe this. I'm really shocked."

"I'm sorry."

"I suppose your passion for Ferraris was part of the ruse, too? No real interest in the three fifty Spider with the twelve cylinders under the hood?"

I lowered my eyes, too ashamed to meet his. "No real interest," I said.

"Good. Because there *is* no three fifty Spider with twelve cylinders," he said. "The car has eight cylinders and they're not under the hood. They're mounted in the middle, behind the seats."

I picked my head up. "What?"

"You heard me. I made that stuff up about the car—to test you. I had a feeling you were pulling something that night you invited me to your apartment for dinner, and I was right."

"Tony!"

"Well? That's what you get for playing games with a smart guy like me."

I smiled in spite of myself. So he'd known all along. And my games hadn't deterred him from helping me, standing by me, being there at my apartment in my hour of need. "I really am sorry. I shouldn't have lied. It's just that when Tara started raving about you, I thought I'd wage a campaign to win you over. Connie told me you were into—"

"Connie was in on this?"

"Only because I begged her. I told her I needed you to pose as my fiancé, and while she didn't love the idea, she agreed to aid and abet."

"So you pretended to like the things I like in order to—what?—convince me that we had a lot in common?"

"Exactly."

"Then here's the question: Is there anything at all about you that's real?"

"I—Of course there is."

"Name one."

"That's easy. What's real is how much I've enjoyed these past few months with you. I've become very fond of you, Tony."

"*Fond* of me?" He smirked.

"Yes. We're pals, aren't we? Partners? You've been doing me a favor and I've been doing you a favor. That's all it's been for you, too, right? An arrangement that was practical for both of us?" Sure, I was fishing. What else was I supposed to do?

"'An arrangement'?" he repeated, his blue eyes drilling me.

"Well, yes. You've been my fiancé and I've been your research project."

"Give me a break. You know it's been more than that for me."

"Do I? If memory serves, you only decided to play my fiancé to get a better handle on what it felt like to be in a committed relationship, so you could flesh out Joe and Lucy's marriage and make converts out of the reviewers who've been tough on you."

"That was a big factor at first."

"At first?"

"Yeah. Once we started spending time together, I just wanted to be with you."

"Oh." So there *had* been a change in direction. I had sensed it but couldn't let myself believe it.

"That's all you have to say? 'Oh'?" He moved closer to me.

"I, well, what's your point?" I said, feeling my face flush now that he was nose-to-nose with me.

"My point is that I've been playing your fiancé not so that I could research Joe and Lucy's marriage, but so that I could keep doing this."

He leaned over and kissed me. It was another one of those knockout kisses that made my insides melt, only there was no audience this time, no one to perform for, and the fact that Tara and Stuart weren't around to observe it gave it an exquisite sense of intimacy.

"So you haven't just been using me as a writing aid?" I teased when I came up for air.

He smiled. "No, although I think the love scenes in my books are ripe for some tweaking."

He kissed me again, longer this time, and with his body pressing against mine. Whatever defenses I'd been putting up, whatever reservations I'd had about getting involved with him, whatever reasons I'd given myself for keeping my distance, all faded away in that moment. After the shock of Stuart's disappearance and Tara's accusations, life was suddenly too short not to let myself succumb to Tony Stiles's considerable charms.

"I, um, really do need to talk to you about what happened to Stuart when you have a chance," I sputtered as he slid his lips down the side of my neck and his hands down the sides of my thighs. "Those detectives showed up at my door out of nowhere tonight. I don't have any idea who's coming next."

"I do," said a very aroused Tony as he took my hand and led me into the bedroom.

"So you really don't like the Rangers," he mused as we lay in each other's arms on my bed, our faces rosy with the afterglow.

"I don't know the Rangers," I said. "I could like them, I guess. I'm sure they're nice people."

He laughed. "You'll learn to like them, just the way you learned to like me. It wasn't all that long ago that you couldn't stand the sight of me, don't forget."

I ran my bare foot along the inside of his leg. "The sight of you was never the problem, Tony, believe me."

"Then it must have been my personality you weren't wild about."

"Well, you were pretty difficult to work with," I said as he was tracing little circles around my belly button with the tip of his finger.

"I wasn't difficult. I was 'my own man,' as they say."

"No, you were difficult."

He laughed. "Well, I've mellowed. Now I just want to be your go-to guy."

"My go-to guy, huh? The one I can count on no matter what?"

"That's the general idea."

"Then tell me what I'm supposed to do about this Stuart mess. Tara ratted me out to the cops."

"What did you expect? She thought you were screwing her husband. She must have been furious at you and felt like striking back, and I can't say I blame her. Look, we don't even know if he's dead. We only know that he's missing. Either way, you were probably at work when they found his car this morning. Chances are, you have an alibi. She can't hurt you."

I smiled. "You're right. She can't hurt me. Not anymore. But if he is dead, I think she's the one who did it. I think she found out he was meeting me and got so mad that she killed him."

"You don't think that and you know it. She was your friend for a very long time and, regardless of what's gone down between you, you care about her."

"I do not."

"Yes, you do. You wouldn't try so hard to impress her if you didn't care about her."

"You're wrong. I hope she fries for his murder."

"Amy."

"Fine, no frying. I'll settle for a stoning in the public square."

"She didn't kill him, because he's not dead. Call it instinct, but that's what I think."

"Okay, then where is he?"

"Don't have a clue."

"Well, you're my go-to guy now. Plus, you're the best mystery writer in America. If anyone can solve this puzzle, it's you."

He rolled over onto me. "Why don't we just leave it to the police to sort out? Or not?"

"What do you mean 'or not'?"

"Right now, all they've got is an abandoned car. They're probably figuring that Stuart's alive and well and left town without telling anybody—to hide from creditors, to be with another woman, whatever. Their investigation has got to be very low-level at this point, because people vanish every day, usually of their own volition."

"Okay, but I'm still not crazy about being under suspicion. What'll it take for the police investigation to go from being low-level to high-level?"

"Time. The longer Stuart stays missing, the more heat you and Tara will feel from the cops."

"Swell."

"Not to worry. He'll resurface. You'll see. Meanwhile, I'd much rather concentrate on our new and improved relationship."

"Oh, you mean our pretend-free relationship?"

"That's the one. For instance, I could pretend that I don't want to make love to you again now, but I'm not going to."

I laughed. "You can't pretend about that. Your anatomy is giving you away."

He lowered his head and kissed me, and there was nothing inauthentic about what happened next.

29

There wasn't a single item in the newspapers about Stuart. According to Tony, it was a nonstory from a crime reporter's perspective. As he'd already explained to me, Stuart could have just taken a trip without telling anybody. And it wasn't as if he was famous and readers were clamoring to follow his every move. He was just the lesser of the two sons of a man who owned some gourmet food stores. His whereabouts weren't news.

Still, the fact that he was missing put me in an extremely awkward position. I was supposed to be forging ahead with the publicity for *Simply Beautiful,* which was due to hit bookstores in only four weeks. The entire campaign was predicated not only on what a perfect life Tara led but by what a happy marriage she had. I had arranged a multicity tour for her, to be kicked off with a publication party—not at her house, because it was too far for the media types to travel, but at Julie Farrell's Park Avenue apartment. What's more, while I'd struck out with the three network morning shows, which had passed on *Simply Beautiful* because the subject was too soft (this from the same people who frequently do segments like "The Latest in Hosiery"), I'd managed to convince the producer at *Today's Woman,* a hot new afternoon show, to have their anchorwoman, Barbara Biggs, tape an interview with Tara at the party. Even Celebetsy was impressed by that booking, although, according to Connie, she took full credit for it, claiming that I got it only because she was a personal friend of Barbara Biggs's. Like that was possible. Betsy didn't have any personal friends.

"What should I do about the publicity?" I asked Tony one night. "I'm the only one at L and T who knows there's anything wrong up in Mamaroneck. Apparently, Tara hasn't even hinted to Julie that Stuart is AWOL."

"You have to call her," he said.

"Julie?"

"No, Tara. Or better yet, go see her."

"Are you serious? She thinks I was having an affair with her husband. She'll try to set me on fire with one of her stupid candles."

"Then tell her you weren't having an affair with Stuart. Clear the air for once, Amy. You two have unfinished business, so finish it; then you can figure out what to do about the book. She may want to cancel all the publicity because of what's going on."

"Tara? Cancel the publicity?" I laughed. "She's never met a spotlight she wasn't dying to shine on herself."

"Then you're a perfect match," he said. "You've never met a spotlight you weren't dying to shine on an author."

He had a point. So, in the interests of doing my job and satisfying my curiosity about what had happened to Stuart, I drove up to Tara's the following Saturday, knowing she was always home after her morning jog. I thought it best not to call first, figuring she'd slam down the phone when she heard my voice. Better to surprise her.

I rang the bell and waited, telling myself it wasn't a mistake to have come unannounced.

She opened the door. As I'd anticipated, she was in her sweatsuit, her blond hair in a ponytail, her complexion dewy from her morning exercise. She was as beautiful as ever, but it was safe to say she was not happy to see me.

"Whore," she said.

"Look who's talking," I replied.

"I wasn't engaged when I slept with Stuart four years ago," she said.

"No, but *I* was engaged when you slept with Stuart four years ago. To *him.*"

We both took a second to breathe.

"I wasn't having an affair with him, Tara," I said, hoping she'd let me in the house eventually.

"A likely story. The police showed me his date book. Your little tryst with him was right there in his own handwriting."

"He asked me to meet him," I said. "It was the first time he'd ever done that, I swear."

"And you went. He called and you just couldn't restrain yourself."

"Only because he sounded desperate."

"Yeah, desperate to get you into bed."

"That's what Tony said."

"Tony was right. God, you were always so naïve."

"And you were always so vain, as if nobody but you could ever attract a man. Well, memo to you: Stuart liked me; he liked me before you seduced him and he liked me after."

"Please. He liked everything with a vagina. If you think you were the only woman he invited to the Plaza, you're delusional. That place was his home away from home. I'm surprised they had time to change the sheets between visits."

"Interesting. So he *was* fooling around on you. And you let us all think that you two were the picture of wedded bliss."

She looked away, as if she hadn't meant to drop the tidbit that Stuart cheated on her regularly. But she had just confirmed what I'd suspected—that she'd been lying to me, to everyone, about the state of her marriage. Suddenly, my own lie loomed even larger. I couldn't very well fault her for inventing a life when I'd been guilty of the same offense.

"Could I come inside, Tara? We need to talk."

"About what? You want to know if I killed him? If his screwing around drove me to commit murder?"

I didn't answer right away.

"Oh, give me a break," she said. "If you think I did it, you've been reading too many of lover boy's mysteries."

"Actually, he's one of the reasons I'd like to come inside," I said.

"Stuart?"

"No. Tony."

"Spare me the details about your goddamn wedding, would you? I've got my own problems."

"There is no wedding, Tara."

"Really? Don't tell me this one dumped you, too?"

I flinched but hung on. "Tony and I were never engaged. We only pretended to be."

She arched a perfectly plucked eyebrow. "Now what are you talking about?"

"Tony isn't my fiancé. We were putting on an act for you and Stuart. I lied to you about him, Tara, but I'll explain why if you let me come in."

"So come in already."

She opened the door wider and waved me inside. I escorted myself into the sunroom, the scene of our other chats, and sat down.

She followed me there and sat, too. "I'd offer you a beverage but, considering how I feel about you right now, I'd probably throw it at you."

"I'm not thirsty. Listen, this insanity started when I ran into you on the street all those months ago. When I saw you that day, I thought I was over you, over what you and Stuart did to me. I'd been in therapy. I was content with my job and my friends and my single life. Sure, I hoped I'd find a man, but I was okay with not having one. Then you turned up on that corner, and I was totally unprepared. I mean, there you were with your gorgeous clothes and shoes and matching handbag, and—"

"It's called knowing how to shop, Amy. You make it sound like curing cancer."

"I'm paying you a compliment, Tara. I'm saying that you looked beautiful and I was as intimidated by you as ever. In my head, I was instantly your second fiddle again. My body may have been on that corner, but my mind was back in elementary school. Back in high school. Back in Stuart's bedroom. It was traumatic."

"Too bad your shrink didn't give you one of those panic necklaces."

"Shut up and let me finish. I was standing on the street, feeling crappy about myself, and you started telling me about you and Stuart, about this house and your radio show and his promotion at Lasher's, about how *fantastic* your life was. It was really hard for me to take. By the time you asked me about myself—especially about whether I had a boyfriend—I felt as if I'd accomplished nothing. So I lied. I said I was engaged. I just wanted to show you, to prove to you that I'd done okay for myself, that I was right up there with the prom queen. I figured I'd never see you again after that, so what was the big deal?"

"And then you found out about the book." She shook her head. "You must have shit."

"I did. And it only got worse. You kept calling and insisting I bring my fiancé here for dinner."

"And you kept telling me he was 'too busy.'"

"Right, until you insinuated that I might be bluffing about being engaged, remember? During one conversation, you said, 'Maybe there is no fiancé.'"

"Well, I was beginning to wonder."

"So I went running around the office, looking for a guy who'd play my fiancé for the night. Talk about panicking. I only picked Tony because you said he was your favorite author. Yours and Stuart's. I thought, Now this guy would impress them, make them respect me, maybe even make them envy me. I convinced him to do it, Tara. And it wasn't easy, because he and I didn't get along."

She permitted herself a smile. "I find that hard to believe. You look like you're mad about each other."

I smiled, too. "We are now, but we weren't then."

"This is incredible. You dragged Tony Stiles up here to play a role?"

"Yes. I told him it was just for one night. And then the

tree fell in your driveway and we had to sleep in your guest house."

She nodded. "So that's when you two clicked—when you were stuck in the same bed."

"Nope. We didn't admit our feelings for each other until recently. I don't know where the relationship will lead, because Tony's not one for commitments, but we're taking it day by day. What I'm trying to say is that I lied about him and I'm ashamed of myself. I should have told you the truth months ago instead of keeping up the charade. I'm sorry."

She nodded again. "It's funny that you were intimidated by me. I used to wish I could trade places with you when we were kids."

"You wanted to be me?"

"Sure. You were nice and smart and everybody liked you."

"Tara, they adored you."

"No. They were afraid of me. They sucked up to me. They held me at a distance. You were someone they could relate to, and I envied you."

"I had no idea you felt that way."

"Nobody did."

"Well, since you're letting your hair down, do you want to tell me the truth about Stuart?" I said. "About what was really going on between you?"

She got up from her chair, paced a little, then sat back down. "Only if you'll give me your shrink's number when I'm done."

"I promise."

She let out a long, tortured sigh. "I don't even know where to begin."

"How about telling me when your marriage fell apart?"

She laughed ruefully. "Like on our honeymoon."

"But I thought—"

"Forget what you thought. Here's the truth. Everything went to hell when you asked me to be your maid of honor and I was dumb enough to say yes."

"Why did saying yes make you dumb?"

"Because you didn't really want me in your wedding. You just asked me out of obligation."

"Obligation? It's true that we weren't spending as much time together as we used to, but we'd been best friends for most of our lives. I thought that should count for something."

"So you threw me a bone, introduced me to Stuart, figured you'd put me in the wedding party, then never see me again."

"Where'd you get that idea? It never occurred to me that we wouldn't see each other again."

"Stuart told me. The night you left us for some publishing dinner. He took me to the Four Seasons, and after a lot of champagne, he came right out and said you thought I was shallow and superficial and in love with myself and that as soon as the wedding was over, we'd be history."

I couldn't believe what I was hearing. "He had no right to talk to you that way. He didn't know anything about our friendship. Why in the world would he cause trouble like that?"

"Well, he did want to sleep with me. The guy was a cheater even then."

"Wait. So you slept with him that night? Your affair started the night I left you two alone?"

"You got it. I was hurt by what he said. I mean, how demeaning was it that you put me in your wedding as a pat on the head for being your childhood pal but that, basically, you couldn't stand me? I wanted to pay you back, so I took your fiancé up on his proposition and slept with him that night. It was supposed to be a one-night stand and you'd never be the wiser."

"I can understand why you were hurt, but you could have talked to me about it instead of having sex with the man I was about to marry."

"Oh, like you were always so honest with me? Please. Honesty has never been an option with us. Obviously."

"Okay, so you slept with Stuart one night. How did that lead to marriage? He wasn't that good in bed, if you want honesty."

"No, he wasn't. But he courted me as I'd never been courted before. He told me you two were having problems, then bombarded me with gifts. Before I knew it, I had fallen for him. Or so I thought."

"Well, he and I *were* having problems. He wasn't wrong about that."

"Even so, I don't know how I let myself get involved with him. You ended up with a broken heart. I felt awful about it for a very long time. I still feel awful."

"Okay, so you feel awful. But you're leaving something out, aren't you? What went wrong in your marriage? It certainly started off with a bang."

"Ha-ha." She heaved another anguished sigh, only this one was accompanied by tears. "Six days into our honeymoon, I caught him flirting with a waitress. I figured it was harmless. Then we got home and I found out I had married the womanizer of the year. He slept with his secretaries, for God's sake. One after the other. We only stayed together because we were both too paralyzed and self-loathing to do anything else."

"I don't know what to say."

She wiped her eyes with the back of her hand. "And then came the book. I'd written it and included this big phony valentine to him. My plan was to get through the publicity somehow and divorce him once the hype died. How could I have predicted that it was Stuart who would die?"

"You're not sure he's dead, are you?"

"No. He could be living it up in Tahiti, for all I know. His brother, Jimmy, and I are trying to piece things together—quietly. Stuart was having problems at work, and we think his disappearance could be connected somehow. But we don't want a scandal. Business at Lasher's is bad enough."

So even the part about Stuart's illustrious career was a lie. I tried to take everything in, absorb all the new information, but mostly what nagged at me was how so sad it was that Tara and I couldn't have been there for each other through all our trials. Or, more accurately, that we couldn't have been honest enough with each other to avoid the trials in the first place. Wasn't that what best friends were supposed to be? Honest? At the very least? Had we clung to our respective types as prom queen and second fiddle so strenuously that we'd turned into childhood buddies who never grew up? Such a waste.

"I'd like to lend a hand with the Stuart situation," I said, "and we need to figure out how to deal with the book promotion. But mainly, I want us to start over, Tara."

"Start over?"

"Well, start fresh. We can't go back, can't undo the hurt we've caused, but we can take another crack at our relationship. I'd much rather have you as a friend than an enemy."

She smiled through her tears. "Same here. By the way, have you ever noticed how I cry with you? I never cry around other people."

I stood up, went over to her, and hugged her. "No more crying," I said. "No more lying, either."

She was about to say something, but the doorbell rang.

"Do you have to get that?" I asked.

"Yes. Michelle's off today."

"Then I'll come with you."

We left the sunroom and walked in lockstep to the front door. Normally, whenever we were side by side, I felt dwarfed by her, diminished, but on this day, despite the height differential, I felt her equal.

She opened the door to find four men of varying shapes and sizes.

"Mrs. Lasher?" said one of them, the guy with the paunch and the Mets jersey. He had a nice, jolly smile.

"Yes?" said Tara.

"We came to talk to your husband," he said, pronouncing the *h* in *husband* with lots of phlegm behind it. With a Russian accent, in other words.

"Stuart isn't here," she said. "But you're Sergei, aren't you? I remember when you stopped by to meet with him."

"Correct," he said with a little bow.

"You were selling him gold," she said.

He seemed surprised. "He tell you what I sell him?"

"Yes," said Tara. "But I don't know where he is, Sergei. He's, uh, traveling."

"Then you must find him and tell him I look for him," he said, and the sentiment was echoed in a choruslike way by his companions.

"I'll tell him," she said. "But I really don't know when that'll be."

He smiled again, wider this time. "I don't like to scare you," he said, "but please find him fast or you have serious consequence."

Tara looked at me for help. I didn't know what to do, because the guy's demeanor seemed so friendly and yet his words sounded so menacing, and I was confused. Or was he the one who was confused?

"Maybe you didn't understand Mrs. Lasher because of the language barrier," I said, trying to keep the mood light. "She doesn't know where her husband is at the moment."

He bowed at the waist, just as he'd done before. "Who are you and what's it your business?"

I squared my shoulders and stuck out my chin. "I'm her best friend."

He nodded. "Then you have serious consequence, too."

Before I could think of a snappy comeback, he stepped closer, apologized for having to disturb us on a lovely Saturday, then issued a final warning, the gist of which was this: If he didn't hear from Stuart soon, we'd be sorry.

I've got to tell you: After a morning of apologies, neither of us had the energy to be sorry for anything else.

30

O kay, Tara. Who the hell is this Sergei character?" I asked when the coast was clear and we were back in the sunroom.

"He's some guy who used to work at Lasher's. I think Stuart said he was in the produce department at the Westport store."

"So what's he all upset about? Did Stuart fire him? Are we talking about a disgruntled employee?"

She shook her head. "Supposedly, he's in the jewelry business now. He came here once to sell Stuart some gold chains. It was the morning after you and Tony slept in the guest house, in fact."

"He's in the jewelry business? Then why wasn't he wearing any?"

"Jewelry?"

"Yeah. Usually, people who sell it wear it, because they get it at cost. I didn't see so much as a pinkie ring on either Sergei or his buddies."

"Truthfully, I never bought the gold chains story. When I overheard them in the library that day and Sergei used the words 'pure gold' to describe what he was selling, I thought it might be drugs. Jimmy and I even confronted Stuart about it, but he never gave us a straight answer."

"I think you should call Jimmy and tell him what just happened."

"Good idea."

She got up to call her brother-in-law, while I sat there counting my blessings that I hadn't become a Lasher—that Tara had married Stuart and saved me the headache. Still, I had vowed to be her best friend yet again and, according to Sergei, that meant that her serious consequence was now my serious consequence.

"Jimmy was on another line, but Peg will have him call me right back," she said, returning to the room.

"Meanwhile, I've been thinking about Sergei's visit. Now that you've got this guy coming to your house and making threats, you can't sit back and wait out Stuart's disappearance anymore, Tara. Besides, Tony said the cops could turn up the heat on us the longer he's missing."

"On us?"

"Yeah. Because you're the scorned wife who hated him and I'm the jilted fiancée who hated him. If he doesn't show his face around here soon, they'll decide that there was foul play and we'll be at the top of their list of suspects."

"Lovely."

"We have to find out what happened to him. And we have to do it right away."

Before she could answer, the phone rang. It was Jimmy. She told him about Sergei, then listened. And as she did, her normally rosy complexion turned pale.

"What did he say?" I asked when she hung up.

"He checked with Lasher's Human Resources person, and guess what? Nobody named Sergei ever worked for them. Not in the Westport store. Not in any of the stores. So Stuart was lying to us. Such a piece of work, my husband."

"Does Jimmy have any idea who Sergei is or how Stuart might have met him?"

"None. And he's afraid to involve the police because, as I mentioned, he doesn't want to stir them up and create a circus atmosphere at Lasher's. And then there's my book. I can't let my asshole husband wreck sales."

She twirled the ends of her golden locks around her index finger and looked hopeless.

"Okay," I said, trying to be upbeat. "First things first. Regarding Stuart's disappearance and how Sergei may or may not have anything to do with it, I think we should bring in a professional."

"I already told you. We don't want a scandal. No police."

"Forget the police. I meant Tony."

She allowed herself a half smile. "Your fiancé for hire?"

"Why not? He's a mystery writer. He spends his days dreaming up murder plots and then solving them. Not only that; he's got amazing contacts in law enforcement, on the street, you name it. I'll bet he can figure out who Sergei is and why he's so interested in finding Stuart. Maybe he can even find Stuart himself."

"Part of me doesn't want him to find Stuart. It's been a pleasure without him around. If the past few days are any indication, my life will be fantastic after I divorce him—if he's still alive for me to divorce, that is."

"You do have to find him, and if anyone can help, it's Tony. I know he can. So what do you say? Should we twist his arm?"

"You're the one who manages to get him to do things he wouldn't otherwise do, aren't you? I'll leave this in your capable hands. Speaking of which, how can we ensure that this mess won't affect *Simply Beautiful*?"

"You haven't told Julie Farrell about Stuart, right?"

"Not a word."

"So as far as she's concerned, you two are the blissfully happy couple you wrote about."

"Yes."

"Well, then there are a couple of options. Either you tell her what's going on and see if she wants to postpone publication or you don't tell her what's going on but we cancel the publicity campaign."

"Actually, there's a third option," she said. "I don't tell

her what's going on and we follow through with the publicity campaign as planned. That's my pick."

So I was right. Tara couldn't resist the spotlight. "The third option will be tricky. We've only got a month until your launch party at Julie's apartment. If Stuart doesn't turn up in one piece in time to stand by your side at that party, it's going to be hard to explain to the media why your adoring, poetry-writing, violin-playing, simply beautiful husband isn't there."

"You just said Tony's the best at all this stuff, that he would find Stuart, dead or alive."

"He *is* the best, but we've only got four weeks to—"

"You also said you and he are very close now," she added, interrupting me. "And you have me to thank for that. If I hadn't been so persistent about inviting your 'fiancé' here for dinner, you might never have become—let's see, what are you two, exactly?"

"We're not engaged, if that's what you're hinting at. We're just enjoying each other's company for now."

"Which is another way of saying you're in love."

"In love? Come on. He has the worst track record when it comes to women. He's had girlfriend after girlfriend, without putting a ring on any of their fingers. I care about him, sure, but there's no point in being in love with him."

"Amy Sherman. You and I have a long history together. I know you better than anybody. You may have fooled me with the fake fiancé thing, but you're not fooling me about your feelings for Tony. You love that guy, whatever his track record is. I can see it on your face. And who can blame you? He's smart and adorable and rich. The whole enchilada."

"Getting back to finding Stuart," I said. "I'll ask Tony if he'll take time off from his writing to investigate. But as for the publicity for the book, we'll have to—"

"Carry on as if Stuart hasn't gone anywhere."

"What? Oh, Tara. I'm the last person to pull back from a publicity campaign, but Betsy Kirby, my pain-in-the-ass boss, breathes down my neck and doesn't let me get away with anything. And then there's Scott, my assistant. Keeping him out of my business is always a challenge. So how in the world could I execute an effective campaign while pretending that Stuart hasn't disappeared?"

"Hey, we've both been doing plenty of pretending lately. This shouldn't be a stretch for either of us."

"True, but, practically speaking, what am I supposed to say when the media wants to interview you and Stuart together?"

"That he's away on business."

"How about if it's a radio show that wants to do a call-in interview with him?"

"Say he's *far* away on business and there's no cell-phone signal where he is."

"Okay, but magazines like *People* are going to want a photo of you two sipping champagne in the bathtub. What do I tell them? That Stuart can't do the tub thing because he's traveling the outer reaches of the globe in search of the most virginal olive oil?"

"Works for me."

That night, I waited until after Tony and I had made love and he was, literally, putty in my hands before I related what had happened at Tara's and asked him if he'd investigate Stuart's disappearance.

"You realize you're asking me to put aside my novel," he said. "Trying to find a missing person is a full-time proposition."

"I know. But you're our only hope." I nibbled his earlobe for extra emphasis.

"Connie won't want me to stop writing," he said. "She's got a tight deadline."

"*I've* got a tight deadline, Tony. Tara's book party is in precisely three weeks, four days, and twenty-two hours. I can hear the clock ticking in my sleep. If Stuart isn't there, the book is toast and so's my job. Hell, if he isn't there, Tara and I could be toast. You said it yourself. The longer he's gone, the more attention the police will give the investigation. You don't want to see me in handcuffs, do you?"

He smiled. "I'd love to see you in handcuffs," he said as I

continued to nibble. "Actually, I might have a pair in the closet. Should I get 'em?"

"Another time. Listen, don't worry about Connie. I'll handle her."

"Even so, there's no guarantee that I can be the hero here," he said, starting to become aroused again.

"You're my hero no matter what," I said, abandoning his earlobe so I could nibble farther south, down the side of his neck.

"That's very sweet, buttercup, and I'd like to pitch in, but—"

"And then there's the fact that Sergei included me in his threat," I said, climbing on top of him when I realized how quickly he'd risen to the occasion. "You wouldn't want any harm to come to me, would you? Not when we've only just discovered how much we mean to each other?"

He kissed me hard on my mouth and rolled me over. We indulged in some pretty hot kissing for a minute or two.

"I've got a question for you," he said at the first opportunity.

"What?" I said, breathless and longing for more.

"Do you ever stop pitching? Or am I doomed to be your poor browbeaten author who always gets talked into doing what he doesn't want to do?"

"Oh, I think you're doing exactly what you want to do," I whispered, resting my case.

31

"You want Tony to what?" said Connie after I popped my head into her office, confided in her about Stuart, and told her I'd asked her star writer to stop writing. Little did I know that Julie Farrell had just lectured her about the importance of getting her manuscripts to the production department earlier, so my timing wasn't great.

"We're only talking about three weeks," I said. "Tara and I need him to find out what happened to Stuart—*before* her publication party."

"Tara and you? Don'ttellmeyou'refriendsagain?"

"What?"

"I said, Don't tell me you're friends again?"

I nodded. "I know what you're thinking—that she's manipulating me, just like the old days. But I volunteered this time. Besides, we've both made mistakes, and she's really in a bind now and I can't *not* help her. Which is why Tony has to take a break from working on his book. He's a professional crime solver. You've said so yourself."

"Look, I'm not his keeper. He's a grown man and he can do what he wants. But if that book is late and we have to bump it back in the schedule, it's your ass on the line, not mine."

"Enough said."

"Good. So what's with you and Tony on the personal side?"

"On the personal side?"

"Yeah. Now that you two spent all those months together, pretending to be engaged, you've fallen for him, right?"

"What do you mean by 'fallen for him'?"

"You know damn well what I mean. Do you love the guy or not?"

"I—" First Tara. Now Connie. Couldn't I just enjoy Tony without defining our relationship? Okay, so the truth was, I wasn't ready to let myself love him. Not before I knew how he felt about me. "I like him a lot" was how I answered the question.

"It would be very helpful if you could tell me about Stuart's specific duties at Lasher's," said Tony. He and Tara and I had gone to Lasher's headquarters that night for a meeting with Jimmy, figuring he was the best place to start. At first, it was awkward between us—between Jimmy and me, that is. After all, I hadn't seen him since I first got engaged to Stuart. But I'd always liked Jimmy and bore him no ill will, so we quickly moved to the matter at hand.

"It pains me to say this about my own brother," he began, "but Stuart had no patience, no follow-through when it came to business." He stopped, caught himself. "I can't believe I'm talking about him in the past tense. He could be alive, right?"

"Of course he could," said Tara, patting him on the hand.

"What I'm trying to say," he continued, "is that Stuart is drawn to shortcuts, and his shortcuts usually result in trouble for the company." He related the episode about the mislabeling of melons.

"Was there any trouble at the time of his disappearance?" asked Tony.

"Only that profits in general have been down," said Jimmy, "and yet Stuart continued to live like a king. His personal debts were mounting and he was feeling pressure from his creditors."

"Interesting," said Tony as he scribbled in a small note-book. "Getting back to his job—what, exactly, is his role at the company?"

"For the past year, he's been in charge of our imported delicacies. He came to me a while ago and asked if he could handle caviar, truffles, and the like."

"Not a huge part of your inventory, I'm guessing."

"No, except that it's gotten more complicated recently, particularly the caviar. After the Soviet Union collapsed, the whole industry went crazy. Their government used to control the harvesting of the sturgeon, as well as the exporting of the caviar, but now the poachers and smugglers run the show, and the sturgeon's practically endangered. So Stuart's been spending time finding legal sources to keep up with our customer demand."

"Legal sources?" asked Tony.

"Legal as of 1998," said Jimmy. "That was the year the U.S. government put strict guidelines in effect to control the exporting of the good stuff."

"When you say 'the good stuff,' you mean beluga?" asked Tara.

"Yeah," he said. "The real Russian beluga from the Caspian Sea. Caviar lovers call it 'black gold.'"

She and I looked at each other.

"Black *gold?*" we said in unison.

Jimmy nodded. "Why the reaction?"

"Because the mysterious Sergei, the one Stuart claimed used to work in Lasher's Westport store, but who didn't, came to our house to sell Stuart 'pure gold,'" said Tara. "We thought he was selling jewelry or even drugs, remember, Jimmy? Well, it must have been caviar. They were probably talking about *black* gold."

"A good possibility," said Tony. "Sergei could be one of those sources you mentioned, Jimmy. But not a legal source."

"If he's a smuggler, he's taking big chances in this country," said Jimmy. "The new guidelines make it tough on them. The federal Fish and Wildlife Service requires permits at every port. They even take samples from shipments and use DNA testing on them."

"Yes, but Stuart was so secretive about him, so it would make sense that he's a smuggler," said Tara. "I just don't know why he showed up at my door and threatened me. It's not as if I had anything to do with the business."

"Maybe Stuart owes him money," said Tony. "Maybe he wasn't paid for the last shipment because Stuart's financial situation is worse than anybody thought."

"The question is, Why would Stuart have to pay him at all?" said Jimmy. "If Sergei's been selling Lasher's caviar, the money would come out of the company's pocket, not my brother's."

"Not if they had a side deal," said Tony.

"A side deal? That would mean Stuart's been ripping off his own family." Jimmy shook his head at the grim possibility.

"Tell you what," said Tony. "I've got a pal who's got a pal who works in Fish and Wildlife. I'll do some checking around and see what I can find out. Meanwhile, Jimmy, if you'd give me a couple of invoices from the caviar company Stuart's been buying from, I could run them by the feds. Maybe the company will turn out to be a totally reputable distributor and we can take our search for Stuart in another direction."

The next morning, Scott breezed into my office. "Guess who Betsy had lunch with the other day?"

"I don't know, Scott." I have more important things on my mind than Celebetsy's eating partners.

"Guess."

"Tell me. I'm really busy." I was just about to return a call from Barbara Biggs, the host of *Today's Woman*. She'd left word on my voice mail that she wanted to confirm the details of the segment she was taping at the party and had made specific mention of Stuart's participation. I was going to have to do some serious tap dancing.

"Patty Beecham, publicity director at Forster Books.

Sounds like everybody in town has been interviewing to be
your replacement."

He stood there beaming. It occurred to me at that moment
that he was more interested in snaring a good piece of gossip
than being my "loyal servant." Or maybe he actually wanted
me replaced and wasn't as loyal as he pretended. Either way, I
didn't have time for his nonsense. There was work to be done.

"We're not going to comment?" he said, pouting.

"We're not, no. Could you close the door on your way out?"

Looking extremely miffed, he started to walk out, only to
have Celebetsy walk in. My lucky day.

"I want to talk to you," she said, tapping her Manolo
Blahniks on my floor, arms crossed over her chest.

"Is there something I can do for you, Betsy?" I asked
wearily.

"Yes. Your job," she barked. "I had lunch with Ginny Sie-
gal at *Lifestyle Weekly* yesterday and she said you put her off
about interviewing Tara Messer and her husband. I'd like an
explanation, because I was under the impression that you
were hired to try to *get* publicity for our authors."

She had me there. It was true that I'd pitched Ginny about
an interview with Tara, and the conversation had gone well
until she said, "And I think it would be fun to get the husband's take." Well, what was I supposed to do? The husband
wasn't around to offer his "take" or anything else.

"I'm waiting until publication," I told Betsy. "If we give
the magazine the interview now, we can't be sure they'll
hold it until books are in the stores."

"Oh. Well, don't wait too long, Amy. These editors hold
grudges if they think you're ducking them."

She turned and strutted out of my office. Talk about
grudges. Lately, she seemed to have one against me, and I
couldn't for the life of me figure out why.

Two days later, Tony's contact put him together with an inspector at Fish and Wildlife. Tony showed him a couple of
the invoices Jimmy had let him borrow. They were from a
company called Caspian Classics.

"According to the inspector, there is no Caspian Classics," he reported when I met him at his loft after work. "It's a bogus company with a PO Box in Brooklyn. Definitely not on the government's list of approved importers."

"Oh God. Where does that leave Stuart?" I said.

"In really big trouble. Instinct tells me that he's the brains—or lack thereof—behind Caspian Classics and that Sergei's got a smuggling operation that feeds into it. The two of them have probably been billing Lasher's for top-dollar beluga, then taking a huge chunk of change for themselves."

"But how?" I asked. "I still don't get it." I knew Stuart was a jerk, but I had no idea he'd turn out to be a crooked jerk.

"Jimmy said Stuart has a habit of going for the shortcuts and that these shortcuts inevitably lead to trouble, right?"

"Right."

"He also said Stuart's finances were stretched thin, so your ex-fiancé was probably looking to make fast money. A lot of it. From what the federal guy told me, bootlegged caviar can deliver fast money."

"How?"

"Easy. Legally imported beluga sells for fifteen hundred a pound. Smugglers—and we could be talking about the Russian Mafia here—sell the same stuff for as little as ten dollars a pound. So let's say Stuart set up this phony company and Sergei smuggled in the caviar. Then Stuart invoiced Lasher's for the full amount, took his cut, and gave Sergei his—in cash."

"Unless he missed a payment or two and didn't give Sergei his cut. That would explain the threats." I sighed. "It'll break Jimmy's heart if Stuart's been stealing from Lasher's. His parents will be devastated, too."

"Which is why we're not going to broadcast this theory of mine until we have proof. No point in getting everybody all upset."

"Sounds like you already have proof. The inspector said Caspian Classics is a bogus company."

"Yeah, but we need proof that it's Stuart's bogus company."

"How will you get that?"

He smiled. "We crime writers have our ways."

32

It was Tara who provided the proof—or at least helped to provide it. Tony asked her to go to Lasher's and get one of the canceled checks they'd paid to Caspian Classics so he could see where the check had been deposited. Sure enough, it had gone into a bank in Brooklyn—into the Northeast Bank of Brooklyn, to be specific.

"Okay, so now we know exactly where Lasher's money went," Tony said when the three of us had assembled at his loft. "The next step is to tie the account to Stuart."

"You want me to go to this bank and demand that they open their records?" Tara asked. "I'm his next of kin. I could do it, couldn't I?"

Tony shook his head. "Not if your name isn't on the account. I've got another idea."

"Which is?" I said.

"After all the books I've written about Joe West, I've managed to make a few friends at the NYPD," he said. "I'll just call in a favor."

"No way. The whole point of imposing on you, Tony, is to avoid bringing in the police," said Tara. "We have to keep Stuart's disappearance quiet."

"I said I was calling in a favor, didn't I? The favor is that whatever this friend does will be strictly off the record."

"Yes, but—"

I interrupted before Tara could protest further. "Tony knows what he's talking about. I trust him completely."

And I did. Despite his reputation as a love-'em-and-leave-'em type, he had proven how dependable and steadfast he could be. He had promised to stick by me as my supposed fiancé and he'd done it. Then, once the the charade was over, we'd grown even closer. And now that Stuart had vanished, he was giving up his precious writing time in order to help us find him. That was enough to merit my trust, wasn't it?

Tony's buddy, a cop with twenty years on the force, went with him to the bank in Brooklyn, told the manager he was investigating a missing person's case, and, after a little flashing of his badge and a lot of vague references to a search warrant, asked to see the file on the Caspian Classics account. Lo and behold, the account holder was Stuart. Even more startling was the fact that he had two other accounts at the bank: one in the name of a company called Truffles Magnifique; the other, a company called New Life Organic. Still more startling was that all three accounts had been closed on the day before his abandoned car was discovered in the alley.

Tony and I took the information to Jimmy and Tara for another after-hours meeting at Lasher's.

"But Truffles Magnifique was supposed to operate out of Provence, not Brooklyn," said an understandably devastated, not to mention bewildered, Jimmy.

"I hate to break this to you," said Tony, "but, according to what we uncovered at the bank, the truffles themselves didn't even come from France. Lasher's has been selling the cheaper Chinese variety. Stuart's been running a scam with some guy named Ho."

Jimmy was speechless. But Tara wasn't. "So this Ho could show up at my house next, demanding his money? Wasn't Sergei enough to give me a heart attack?"

"Actually, you could be getting a visit from someone named Miguel, too," said Tony.

"Who the hell is he?" wailed Tara.

"He's the Sergei/Ho equivalent at New Life Organic. It seems that Stuart was importing garden-variety produce from Mexico, selling it to Lasher's as organic, and paying Miguel a substantial cut of the profits."

Jimmy pounded his fist on his desk. "You're telling me my brother set up three dummy companies so he could funnel money out of his own?"

"He never thought of Lasher's as *his* company," said Tara. "He resented that you were the one running it, Jimmy. This was probably his twisted way of proving himself to you, to all of us."

"And then his overspending caught up with him," I mused. "He probably stiffed Sergei, Ho, and Miguel, cashed out what was left of the money in the accounts, and took off before they all came after him."

"Right. I'm guessing he trashed his car, sprinkled a few drops of his own blood on the seat, and abandoned it in the alley to make it look like a homicide," Tony said. "But guys like Sergei and the others are too smart to buy that scenario."

"Then he is alive?" asked Jimmy, as if he wasn't sure whether that was good news or not.

"Probably alive and living in the lap of luxury somewhere," said Tony.

"He's not holed up in a shack, eating peanut butter and jelly sandwiches," said Tara. "He likes the good life too much for that."

"God, how am I going to tell my folks?" said Jimmy. "They were aware of Stuart's problems, but they'll be brokenhearted about this."

"You're not going to tell them," said Tara. "Not yet anyway. For now, you're going to keep selling your customers caviar and truffles and organic produce—from reputable distributors—and they'll never be the wiser. And my book will come out and *Today's Woman* will cover the publication party, and nobody will be the wiser there, either."

"*If* we can find Stuart and drag him back here for the party," I said. "I can only keep pretending he's out of town for so long. He's got to put in an appearance at the party or it'll look bad. The media will make a stink about it and your credibility will be as pitiful as the book's sales."

"Before you start worrying about book sales," said Tony, "there's one other problem you should be aware of. You and Amy."

Tara and I sat at attention.

"My cop friend tipped me off that the detectives who were first assigned to Stuart's case are finally stepping up their investigation."

"Oh great," I said. "Are they going to lock us up or something?"

"No. But they'll be digging into your whereabouts on the day Stuart went missing."

"That does it," said Tara. "We've got to find that lousy husband of mine and we've got to find him fast." She looked pleadingly at Tony. "How do we even start to search for him?"

"The first thing for you to do is check around the house, Tara. Go through every drawer, every piece of paper, everything he touched. Hunt for clues. Then do the same at Lasher's. Talk to the people who worked with him on a daily basis. He had a secretary, right?"

"Please," said Tara, rolling her eyes. "He had all his secretaries, in a manner of speaking."

Jimmy gave her a look.

"Come on, Jimmy," she said. "Let's not play games anymore. You know as well as I do that your brother slept around. Mandy, the latest one, even made house calls."

"Yeah, I know all about Stuart's flings," he said. "I've always known about them. But you can forget about wringing information out of Mandy."

"Why?" asked Tara. "Did Stuart swear her to secrecy?"

"I have no idea," he said. "I only meant that she's not at Lasher's anymore. She quit last week."

"She quit?" Tony said.

"She lost her boss," Jimmy reminded us. "We offered to reassign her to someone else, but she told Human Resources she wanted to leave to pursue other interests."

"Could one of those interests be Stuart?" I asked. "Is it possible that if we find Mandy, we find him?"

"Exactly what I was thinking," said Tony.

• • •

Jimmy instructed his Human Resources person to give Tara Mandy's home phone number and address. She called Stuart's former assistant but got no answer. Not her voice mail. Not a roommate. Nothing. When she drove to White Plains to try to confront Mandy face-to-face, she didn't fare much better. There was nobody home at the condo. What there was, however, was a neighbor. Tara asked the woman if she'd seen Mandy recently, and she said Mandy had moved away. When Tara asked where, the woman said she didn't know. Then, just as Tara was walking to her car, the woman shouted, "Wherever she did go, it's gotta be someplace warm, because she gave me all her winter clothes."

"No doubt about it. He went to Florida and she went there to join him," said Tara after Tony and I arrived at her house that night to brainstorm what to do next.

"What makes you so sure?" he asked.

"Amy, remember when I told you that he and I were down in Palm Beach looking at houses with a Realtor?"

"I do," I said. "You'd decided you needed a second castle."

"He was the one who'd decided. And now I'm willing to bet that the trip was his cover," she said. "He was probably looking at houses for himself and Mandy, so they could hide out together."

"They don't call the state of Florida 'debtor's heaven' for nothing," said Tony. "People who file for bankruptcy, for example, buy property there so the government can't seize their assets. It's very possible that Stuart put his money into a house, just like O.J."

"And Mandy could be there, keeping him company," said Tara.

"Do you still have the name of the Realtor you dealt with?" Tony asked.

"Yes," she said. "His address, too."

"Good," said Tony. "We're going to pay him a surprise visit."

"Hey, this is great," I said. "The search is moving faster

than I expected. There's only one problem: I can't go to Florida now. Betsy is on me every minute about *Simply Beautiful*, never mind all the other books I've got on my plate. For me to just take off would be suicidal."

"Of course it would," said Tara, looking entirely too cheerful all of a sudden. "Tony and I will go by ourselves. My radio show's on hiatus, and he's been kind enough to interrupt his writing for the moment, so we have more free time than you do, Amy."

"We know you have a lot of work to do," he said sympathetically. "We'll have to manage without you, that's all."

I couldn't speak. I opened my mouth, but nothing came out. Yes, Tara and I had made up. Yes, we'd cleared the air about our respective gripes. Yes, we'd pledged to move forward with our friendship, to stop reverting to our childhood behaviors, to approach the future with a spirit of cooperation, maturity, and—here was the biggie—honesty. We were going to give up all the lying and posturing and backstabbing and trust each other. That's what we'd said.

But now I wasn't so sure about any of it. I mean, how could I let her fly off to Palm Beach with Tony? My Tony. The Tony who was not only her favorite author and a certified stud muffin but the person who was poised to rescue her. Talk about a turn-on. The Tony who'd been incredibly attentive to me but who also had a tendency to jump from female to female. The Tony I loved—yeah, loved. Why not say it? I'd probably been in love with him since the beginning. But now I was supposed to send him on a trip with the same woman who'd stolen the first and only man who'd ever wanted to marry me? It was a ghastly idea. Completely unacceptable.

"Amy? Are you okay with Tony and me going to Florida without you?" she said, sounding all sweet and innocent but looking trampy in her nearly up-to-the-crotch red miniskirt.

No, I wasn't okay with it, but what was I supposed to do? It was either stay behind in New York and do my job or chaperone the two of them in Florida and risk Betsy's wrath.

"Sure I am," I said, even as it dawned on me that I was

now stuck playing second fiddle to Tara yet again. "The important thing is finding Stuart, getting the police off our backs, and making sure your book is launched properly."

She squished me into a hug. "Oh, I knew you'd understand."

"That's what best friends do," I said, forcing my face into a big stupid smile.

33

I couldn't bring myself to tag along with them to the airport. That's how messed up I was about their trip. Tony asked me to come, so he and I could have one last goodbye before he boarded the plane, but I begged off, claiming I had a meeting with an author. I mean, did I really have to watch her walk through the security checkpoints with him? Watch her take his arm as they trotted down to the gate? Watch them cuddle up next to each other in their first-class seats, sip their drinks, eat their meal, do the dopey airline magazine crossword puzzle together, hold hands during pockets of turbulence—

Okay, so I was getting carried away.

"Hey, if my spending even five minutes alone with Tara upsets you, tell me and we'll figure something else out," he said as we lay in bed the morning of their flight.

"I've got a demanding job with an equally demanding boss," I said. "I can't just take off whenever I feel like it."

"I didn't ask if you could go. I asked if you wanted me to stay." He kissed me. "Look, I'm not a complete jerk. I know you must have mixed feelings about the trip, even though you begged me to help Tara find Stuart and even though you and she have mended fences. So if you've changed your mind, tell me now."

I did want him to help Tara find Stuart and I had mended

fences with her. It was just the history that was bothering me. Just me being insecure. "I'm fine with it," I said. "If you both think Stuart might be in Florida, then that's where you should go."

"You're a good sport, you know?" he said. "I'm more impressed with you every day."

"You are?"

"Damn right. Most women wouldn't be so generous, so self-confident. But you—"

He stopped, smiled, kissed me again.

"You just keep growing on me," he said, finishing the thought.

"I'm glad," I told him. I certainly didn't feel generous or self-confident at that moment, never mind a good sport, but I wasn't about to talk him out of his opinion.

"It's true," he said. "I haven't been very clever about relationships—no bulletin there. I've made bad choices when it comes to the women I've been involved with. But spending time with you has given me a whole different perspective on what it means to commit, on what it means to value and respect a woman. My point is that you can trust me, Amy. You can trust me here in New York, down in Palm Beach, wherever I am and with whom."

I stared into those soulful blue eyes of his, searched them, studied his face. He'd always been incredible-looking, but who knew he'd turn out to be so caring? Still, his reassurances aside, picturing him alone with Tara made me sick.

"Can I really trust you?" I asked softly.

"Let me show you," he said, gathering me in his arms and kissing me until I almost believed him.

They left for Palm Beach later that morning and checked in at the Breakers after they landed. I was a nervous wreck, imagining them changing their plans the minute I was out of sight and deciding to stay together instead of in separate rooms. Paranoid, that's what I was. Paranoid and stuck in the past. I felt only marginally better after Tony called me at the office to say they'd arrived safely and I fished for the specifics of their sleeping arrangements.

"Why don't you knock on Tara's door so I can talk to her, too," I said.

"That would take too long," he said. "Her room's way down the hall."

Thank God for small favors, I thought.

He went on to tell me that their first plan of attack in the search for Stuart was to go and see the real estate agent who'd shown Tara and Stuart houses.

"Do you really think this person will lead you to him?" I asked.

"It's worth a shot," he said.

While my "go-to guy" was running around a glamorous and sultry resort with the glamorous and sultry woman who'd stolen my fiancé, I spent the day trying to coax various media types to cover her publication party, which was a mere two weeks away.

"I'm definitely coming," said the reporter from *New York* magazine, who, after a zillion pitches on my part, had agreed to do a feature on *Simply Beautiful*.

"That's great," I said.

"And I'm bringing a photographer," she said. "I want to shoot the author."

"Same here," I said.

"What?"

"I meant that I want you to take a photo of Tara," I said.

"Right. I'd like to get a few quotes from her husband, too," she added. "And maybe a shot of them together."

"No problem," I said. "I'm sure he'll be there."

"I would think so, given that he serenades her with a violin." She laughed. "Tell the truth, Amy. Are they for real?"

"Why don't you decide when you meet them?" Notice I didn't say "if." I said "when." I had faith that Tony would find Stuart and drag him back for the party. Unless, of course, he got distracted by a certain best friend of mine.

. . .

He called again after I got home.

"I'm checking in," he said.

"You don't have to do that," I told him.

"Sure I do," he said. "Besides, I have information."

"Already? You've only been there a few hours."

"It's not good information."

"Oh. The Realtor didn't know anything?"

"He knew plenty. He just wasn't talking. He remembered Tara, remembered showing her and Stuart houses. But when she asked him if Stuart had come back to buy a house, he clammed up. He wondered why Tara didn't know where her own husband was, said he didn't want to get in the middle of a domestic dispute, and told us to take the matter up with a lawyer if this was a fight over assets."

"So now what?"

"Now I call Jimmy and tell him what I just told you. Then dinner and a bottle of decent wine, I hope."

I felt my heart drop a few feet. "Oh, you and Tara are going out?"

"Actually, we're ordering from room service," he said. "She's tired and wants to kick back."

Kick back. That's what I would do if I were down there. I would kick her back. "So you're eating in your room?"

"Yeah. We've got to strategize for tomorrow. Basically, I think the next step should be to check recent issues of the local paper for real estate transactions. All closings have to be listed by law. If Stuart bought a house in the area, it'll be right there in print—the purchase price and, more important, his name and his new address."

"I'll keep my fingers crossed."

"Thanks. How was your day? Everything okay up there?"

"I miss you, but otherwise I'm fine."

"I miss you, too. I wish we could—"

There was a knock at his door. I could hear it through the phone.

"Hang on a sec, okay?" said Tony. "It's Tara."

I sat there with the phone pressed against my ear, strain-

ing to catch her voice, trying to detect even a hint of flirta-
tiousness in it. But mostly, I just detected that she was hungry.

"She wants to say hi to you," said Tony when he came
back on the line.

"Put her on," I said.

Tara took the phone and told me how beautiful the hotel
was and how fantastic the weather was and how it was a
shame I couldn't be there to enjoy it.

"Well, you're not there for vacation," I reminded her.

"I realize that," she said. "I only meant that if you have to
hunt for your rat-bastard husband, this isn't a bad place to
do it."

"Sorry your real estate agent wasn't much help," I said.
"Maybe tomorrow will bring better news."

She yawned. "I hope so. Meanwhile, I intend to get a little drunk, have something to eat, and go to bed."

Get a little drunk. Swell. Remember what happened the
last time she got a little drunk with one of my men?

I gulped back the lump in my throat and wished her luck
tomorrow.

"Don't you want to say good-bye to Tony?" she asked as
I was about to hang up.

No, I didn't want to say good-bye to Tony. That was the
problem. I wanted to hold on to him forever. "Just tell him
I'll talk to him soon," I said.

The next morning, I was in the office bright and early so I
could make more calls about Tara's party and fudge my way
around the Stuart issue yet again. After about my tenth call,
I congratulated myself on being perfectly suited to public re-
lations. Other than politics, what other occupation actually
rewards lying? My job was all about fudging—spinning,
slanting, hedging, exaggerating, what have you. Not lying,
exactly, but manipulating the truth a little. Yes, I was good at
this stuff. Everybody I spoke to bought every word.

Tony reported in around four o'clock that afternoon. I
did not ask him how dinner went. I did not ask him what

time Tara went back to her room after dinner. I did not ask
him whether she did go back to her room after dinner. Instead, I said, "How did it go with your search through the local papers?"

"The good news is that the real estate market is booming
down here," he said. "The bad news is that none of the property owners was listed under the name Stuart Lasher or S.
Lasher or even one of his phony companies."

"Sorry. Do you think you're on a wild-goose chase?"
Which was another way of asking if he was giving up and
coming home.

"Not necessarily. I have a really strong hunch he's in the
area. We'll keep going until it's pointless."

"How's Tara?"

"Okay now."

"Now?"

He let out a long sigh. "She was really bummed last
night. I think all of it finally hit her—how miserable she's
been in her marriage, how difficult it's been to keep up the
happy front, how clueless she was about Stuart's business
activities. She had one glass of wine too many and totally
unraveled."

I sat up straighter in my chair. I think I also stopped
breathing. "So you had to comfort her?"

"I don't know how much help I was, but, yeah, I tried to
be supportive. I mean, the woman was sobbing."

"She always was a crier."

"What'd you say?"

"I said, She always was a trooper. I guess it was only natural that she'd break down eventually."

"I guess."

"Hopefully, she'll feel better now that she's gotten everything off her chest." And a perky chest it was, especially
when she wore those underwire push-up bras of hers.

"Hopefully," he agreed. "She was so wobbly by the time
she finished dinner that I had to walk her back to her room.
And then once we got there, she kind of pitched forward and
passed out right in my arms."

Okay, now *I* was about to pass out. Well? You try contemplating the scene he just described—the two of them staggering down the hall to her lair, then falling all over each other. "So you're saying she got so drunk or overcome with emotion or whatever that she was unconscious?"

"Just about. I literally had to put her in bed."

That did it. I was officially and undeniably crazed with jealousy. And don't tell me you wouldn't have felt the same way under the circumstances or that my imagination was playing tricks on me. It was Tara we were talking about. Tara hitting on my guy. The only thing that kept me from hopping on a plane and breaking her neck was this particular guy. Tony had made that nice speech before he left about how I should trust him, about how he valued me and respected me and felt committed to me. I was right to trust him. He would fend off her advances. He wasn't Stuart. I could take heart in that, couldn't I?

34

I awoke feeling a little better about things, but the day quickly went sour. First, there was the surprise visit at my apartment from the detectives who'd questioned me the last time. Apparently, they really were taking a renewed interest in the case. They wondered if I'd heard from Stuart. They wondered if I'd like to change my story about the day he disappeared. They wondered where his wife had gone, because they wanted to talk to her, too.

"She's in Florida, getting a tan," I said.

"Where in Florida?" one of them asked.

"Palm Beach. At the Breakers."

Okay, so you're thinking I was a skunk to lead them right to her. But they were bound to find out where she was. Cops have their ways, don't they? Plus, it wasn't as if she'd killed Stuart, so she didn't have anything to worry about. The detectives would be a nuisance, that's all. A distraction. A couple of guys to take her mind off *mine*.

The sourness continued after I got to the office. I sat there making call after call, trying to persuade more media people how awesome Tara was, even as I pictured her throwing herself at Tony, pleading with him not to resist her, and ultimately forcing him to cave in to temptation so they could screw their brains out. Like I said, I was not coping well.

Then came a fitting end to the day. I had misplaced the

list of bookstores where Tara was supposed to appear on her publicity tour, and I was hoping Celebetsy would let me make a copy of hers.

She wasn't in her office when I showed up, so I asked her assistant if she could find the file for me.

"I'm kind of busy," she said. "Just go on in and take a look. Betsy's in a meeting, so you've got the place all to yourself."

I didn't think Celebetsy would want me poking around in there, since she was so tight-assed about everything, but it was her own assistant who'd given me the go-ahead, so what the hell.

I was picking through the stack of files on her desk when I noticed a photo that was buried underneath all the papers. It was probably her husband, I decided. A normal woman would put his picture in a nice frame and display it, but Betsy? Leave it to her to hide it, the nutcase.

Curious to find out what the mystery man looked like, I slipped the black-and-white glossy out from under the files. I nearly had a heart attack when I saw that it wasn't her husband in the picture, but Tony! It was the jacket photo from his last book for us, and I wouldn't have gotten so hysterical about it except that he had written Betsy a love note on it! Well, not a love note, exactly, but he did write, "Let the good times keep rolling, sexy lady," and then signed it with X's and O's! Why would he have given her the photo (he hadn't so much as given me an autographed book) and why would she have kept it? And what "good times" was he talking about anyway?

"Looking for something?"

I turned when I heard the familiar imperious voice, and there she was, standing in the doorway, her hands on her little hips, her face contorted with anger and maybe a little embarrassment, too.

"Betsy," I said, sliding the photo back onto her desk. "I misplaced the list of bookstores that Tara is—"

"So now you know," she said, cutting me off, kicking her door closed with the heel of her shoe, and stepping inside. "I'm glad you know."

"Know what?" I asked, feeling as if all the air had been sucked out of the room.

"That I had an affair with Tony before he started seeing you," she said. "A very passionate affair."

"You what?" I said, incredulous. "I thought you were married."

"I am, but my husband's never around. He travels a lot."

"So the affair happened while your husband was out of town?"

"Yes, but it wasn't just an affair. It was a relationship. Tony and I were having a fabulous time together; then all of a sudden he broke up with me. He's a commitment-phobic freak, in case you haven't noticed."

"How could Tony feel committed to you if you're committed to your husband?" I said.

"He didn't know I had a husband then," she said. "I didn't tell him until Alex—that's my husband's name—came home. Our affair was a big secret. We were completely under the radar. No one had a clue that we were going out, not even your nosy assistant."

I tried to listen to what she was telling me, but the idea of her with Tony was truly repulsive. Had he really been seeing her? Romantically? No wonder I'd hated him back then. Her rotten disposition had probably rubbed off on him. "If you two were so hot for each other, how come he broke it off, commitment-phobic or not?"

"Because I finally told him I was married. He went ballistic, called me a liar, accused me of roping him into a sordid love triangle. I begged him not to shut me out, but he wouldn't listen. I even followed him around like some pathetic stalker."

A stalker. So Betsy was the woman who'd come to the restaurant in SoHo, the woman Tony had tipped the waiter to get rid of.

"He wouldn't reconsider, wouldn't take me back," she went on. "And I wouldn't accept it. I couldn't accept it. Not when he'd been so crazy about me. And he *was* crazy about me, Amy. *Me*." She pounded on her bony chest for emphasis. "I demanded to know why he wouldn't give me another chance. I promised him I'd divorce my husband and never lie to him again about anything. I was willing to do whatever it took. But do you know what he said?"

"What?" I asked.

"He said he couldn't see me anymore because he was engaged to you."

Great. No wonder she'd been treating me like shit. "But we weren't really engaged," I managed, still reeling. "It was sort of a prank."

"I didn't know that at first, so I backed off. I really believed you and Tony were tying the knot, because he was very convincing. He said, 'I'm marrying Amy, so that proves I've moved on. I suggest you move on, too.'"

"But how did you find out our engagement wasn't real?" I asked.

"Scott," she said.

I did a double take. "Scott?"

"He's the company snitch, isn't he?" she said. "He was sleeping with Julie Farrell's assistant, who is now sleeping with mine, which is how the news made its way to me."

"I don't understand. Scott would never—"

"Oh, grow up. Scott's a gossip queen. He'll sell you out in a minute if the tidbit is juicy enough."

"But how did he find out about Tony and me?"

She shrugged. "I think he was sniffing around your office one day—sort of the way you're sniffing around mine now—and overheard you and Tony laughing about how you were only pretending to be engaged. Naturally, he passed the morsel on. When I heard about it, I was furious. I confronted Tony, and he admitted that he'd agreed to the whole engagement 'prank' just to blow me off."

"He said that?" I was floored.

"You bet. He wanted me to get the message that he and I were through, and *that's* the reason he signed off on your insane idea."

"No. That's not how it was," I said. "Tony pretended to be engaged to me to help me impress this friend of mine. Oh,

and to research his next book. And then, once we spent a lot
of time together, we realized we really cared about each
other."

She laughed. "Tony cares about Tony, period. He uses
women. He turns on the charm, then moves on to someone
else. Without a single second of remorse, by the way."

"That's not true," I said, feeling the tears well up. "It's
different with us. He and I have a genuine connection."

"Really?" she said with a sneer. "Then why didn't he tell
you about me?"

"Actually, he did tell me about you," I said. "He told me
there was a woman who'd lied to him and that he was finished with her."

"But he didn't tell you that the woman was your own
boss, did he?"

"No."

"And he sure as hell didn't tell you that he used your supposed engagement to make me believe he and I were over—
not to help you with your friend and not to research his
book. All that was bullshit. Got it now?"

I couldn't answer her. I was too busy trying to figure out
how Tony had the nerve to keep his affair with Betsy a secret
from me, how he could let me complain about having to
work for her and never even hint that she was more than a
business acquaintance to him. Was it because I meant nothing to him? Was I just another one of his conquests, someone to be toyed with and then dumped? Were all his
middle-of-the-night declarations total crap?

Oh God, I thought, suddenly picturing him ordering up
another cozy room-service dinner with Tara. If he couldn't
be trusted to tell me about Betsy, how could he be trusted to
spend even a minute alone with the prom queen? Especially
in her currently oh-so-vulnerable condition?

I had to get out of there.

"Going to lick your wounds?" asked Betsy.

"Actually, I'm going to find Tony." I elbowed my way
past her. "Just so you know, I'll be away from the office for a
few days."

"Oh no you won't," she said. "You've got Tara Messer's party in less than two weeks. You're staying right here and—"

I silenced her with a finger in her face. "I said I'll be away for a few days. If you so much as raise an eyebrow about it, I'll tell everybody at the company that you committed adultery with our most important author."

Before she could respond, I walked out of her office. Without a word, I went back to my own, grabbed my purse and my briefcase, and marched over to Scott's cubicle.

"You're so fired," I said.

"Good imitation of Betsy," he said with a laugh.

"You're still fired," I said.

"Uh-oh. So we're—what?—in a cranky mood?"

"*We* aren't anything. *You're* clearing out your stuff and finding another job."

"Look, I don't know what's going on with you, Amy, but I—"

"What's going on is that Betsy told me you've been spreading little tales about me and Tony Stiles, the problem with that being that I need an assistant who can keep his mouth shut. So I'll be asking Human Resources to start interviewing for your replacement. In the meantime, I'm leaving town for a few days and I'll ask Connie Martino's assistant to answer my phones until I get back. Any more questions?"

"I—"

"That's what I thought."

I left the building, hailed a taxi, went back to my apartment, and booked myself a plane ticket to Palm Beach. There was a late flight out of La Guardia and I would be on it. When I landed, I intended to head straight for the Breakers. It would be around bedtime then—the perfect opportunity to see for myself what my go-to guy was really up to.

35

When I arrived at the Breakers, I marched straight to Tony's room and knocked on his door. No answer. I tried a couple of more times. Same deal.

Assuming he must be with Tara, I stomped down the hall and banged on her door. No answer.

Either they were out, having a late supper, or they were in, having each other.

I stood there in the hall, trying to decide what to do next. I was angry, hurt, and really, really hungry. The "meal" on the flight had consisted of a granola bar and an orange.

I figured I might as well satisfy my appetite as well as summon my strength by going back downstairs, getting a table in the hotel's main dining room, and eating something. I needed fortification for what was ahead.

"Table for one," I told the maître d' as I surveyed the other diners. They were all decked out in designer resort wear, while I was still in my straight-from-the-office business suit. The least of my problems, right?

As I was being led to my table, which was in the back, next to the kitchen (where they usually put women eating alone), guess who I spotted at a secluded table for two by the window, drinking champagne and canoodling? You got it. Tara was throwing back her head and laughing at something wonderfully witty Tony must have said, and he was leaning forward to take a bite of whatever goody she had on her plate. Sharing laughs? Sharing food? Was that not proof of their treachery?

After telling the maître d' that I'd be taking a detour, I stormed over to the happy couple.

"Well, isn't this an instant replay," I said, my voice quivering but tinged with sarcasm.

Tony and Tara looked up. I had caught them by complete surprise, obviously.

"What I meant by that," I went on before either of them could get a word in, "was that when you seduced Stuart, Tara, it was a night just like this one. I wasn't around. You ordered champagne. One thing led to another. Well, you remember."

She started to speak—apparently, she'd had enough champagne to make her speech slur—but Tony stopped her. He got up from his chair and tried to hug me. I pulled away.

"Okay. No hug. What's wrong?" he asked. "Something must be, or you wouldn't have come all the way to Florida."

"You're sitting here with her, guzzling champagne, and you're asking me what's wrong?" I said. "But hey. I don't want to intrude. You two are celebrating. How romantic. I guess my only question would be, When's the wedding?"

"Amy, what the hell are you talking about?" he said. "Yeah, Tara and I were celebrating, but not for any romantic reason."

"So you say." I glanced from him to Tara and back again. I noticed that there was an almost empty bottle of Dom Pérignon in a nearby ice bucket and a gooey chocolate soufflé on a plate between them—with two spoons. Plus, she was decorated with a bright pink hibiscus in her shimmering blond hair. Wasn't that festive?

Now it was her turn to stand. She was wobbly, and she hung on to the table for support. "Amy, you're making a mistake here. A big one."

"You're telling me. I left you two alone, just like I left you and Stuart alone four years ago. Fool me once, shame on you. Fool me twice, you're an incredible bitch."

"What did you just call me?"

"The same thing I should have called you after I found out about you and Stu boy."

"But I didn't do anything this time," she said. "Look, why don't we get the waiter to bring another chair and we can all sit and talk."

"No. Why don't you take your slutty ass out of this dining room and let me sit and talk to Tony."

Her eyes blazed. "Watch it, honey. Someone got you all stirred up, but I'm not in the mood to be your scapegoat."

"No? Then what are you in the mood for, *honey*? A roll in the sack with your stud muffin here?"

"Amy, keep your voice down," said Tony. The other people in the restaurant were craning their necks to see what all the commotion was about, but I couldn't have cared less.

"I'll get to you later, Tony. First, I want Tara to go back to her room and start packing."

She shook her head. "Quit ordering me around. I'm not going anywhere."

"Why? Because you think Tony will commit to you? He doesn't commit to anybody. He hits, then runs. Actually, now that I think about it, you two are a perfect match. You're both sluts."

"That's enough," said Tara, although it came out more like "Thassnuff."

Before I could anticipate her next move, she grabbed her spoon, scooped up a decent-sized portion of their soufflé, and flung it at me as if she were wielding a slingshot. Her aim was excellent; the dessert landed smack in my right eye.

I was so stunned that all I could think to do was retaliate in kind. After wiping my eye with my finger and licking it— it tasted pretty damn good, I have to tell you—I reached down with my bare hand, picked up the rest of the soufflé, and dumped it on top of her golden head.

"You maniac," she shouted. "I just washed my hair."

"You're the maniac," I said. "A nymphomaniac."

"Excuse me, but you're the one who barged in here acting crazy," she said, bumping me this time.

"Yeah, but you're the one who started the food fight," I retorted, bumping her back.

"Maybe I should forget the food," she said, and went for the champagne bottle.

Tony held her arm before she could either sock me or soak me, while I hurled a few verbal shots at her. At some point, the maître d' hurried over and demanded that all three of us leave the dining room immediately.

"I'm not budging," I said.

"Neither am I," said Tara.

"Oh, we're budging all right," said Tony. "We have no choice, thanks to you two. Not the sort of publicity you want for your authors, is it, Amy?"

"I guess not," I admitted. "Let's take this to your room."

"Good idea." He steered Tara and me into the elevator and kept us apart as we rode up seven floors.

"Now," he said when we were safely inside his room. "Will everybody please behave, or should I call for reinforcements?"

I didn't answer. I was too exhausted. Tara didn't answer, either. She was too preoccupied with the chocolate remnants that were stuck in her hair.

"What provoked all this?" Tony asked me.

"You mean, aside from her?" I nodded at Tara.

"Yeah. Why are you in Palm Beach? You said you were fine with letting us try to find Stuart without you."

"I came because of Betsy," I said.

"Betsy?" he said.

"Yeah. You know. Betsy Kirby, my boss. The one you slept with but then failed to mention."

Tara stopped playing with her hair and glared at him. "You slept with Amy's boss?"

"That's not all," I said. "He tried to get rid of her by telling her we were engaged. What's more, he never let me in on his little game."

"Can't anyone in this room ever tell the truth?" asked Tara. "I mean, really. We're all guilty."

"I'll tell the truth right now," Tony said to me. "I'm sorry about Betsy. I should have confided in you about her. But she was a miserable chapter in my life, and I wasn't thrilled about reliving it."

"How miserable?" I asked.

"She was married. I didn't know. It was messy."

"Life is messy," I said. "That's no excuse for keeping me in the dark. I work for the woman, for God's sake."

"Amy's right," said Tara. "If you love her, you have to be honest with her."

"If he loves me?" I said. "You're drunker than I thought."

"He does love you," she said. "Before you crashed our dinner, he was waxing poetic about it."

"Is that so?" I said, challenging him.

"It is. I've loved you since the night you invited me to your apartment and made me cheese and crackers by candlelight."

"A likely story."

"A true story."

"Then what about Betsy?"

"She was a fling. When I found out she was married, I ended it."

"That still doesn't explain why you didn't tell me about this so-called fling."

"I didn't tell you because you already thought I was a womanizing creep. If you knew I'd been with her, would you ever have taken my feelings for you seriously? Would you ever have believed that I love you?"

"If you love me, why were you celebrating with Tara to-night instead of trying to find Stuart?" I asked.

"We did find Stuart," he said. "That's why we were cele-brating."

"Or at least we think we found him," said Tara. "We'll know more tomorrow, hopefully."

I stared at them. "You're not kidding?"

"No," said Tony. "We caught a break today. We figured it wouldn't hurt to order a bottle of champagne to reward our-selves for a job well done."

"So you weren't—"

He shook his head.

"And Tara wasn't—"

She shook her head.

"So there was no reason at all for me to—"

They both shook their heads.

I lowered mine. I had acted like a huge jerk, and I was so ashamed. Yes, Tara and I had shared a tangled past. And yes, Betsy's revelation about Tony had flipped me out. Maybe lots of people would have lost it under those circumstances, but I still felt awful.

"Would anybody mind if I dug a hole and crawled in it?" I said.

Tara sighed. "You and I have been going at each other for so long in one way or another. Don't you think we should give it a rest? For real this time?"

I nodded sheepishly.

"And how about me?" asked Tony. "Can I get in on this goodwill?"

I leapt up and threw my arms around his neck.

"That's better," he said, then kissed me hard on the mouth.

"Okay, you two," said Tara. "I think I'll slip out before things get steamy."

I pulled away from Tony. "Oh no you don't," I said to her. "You can't leave until I've heard all about Stuart. Is he here in Palm Beach? Did you actually see him? Is he coming back to New York?"

Tony smiled at Tara. "Do you want to tell her or should I?"

36

Even after searching the local newspapers for listings of real estate closings and failing to find one for Stuart, Tony didn't give up.

"Instinct told me he cleaned out the bank account in Brooklyn, then came down here with the money and put it into a house," he said as he and Tara began their chronicle of the day's events. "So I decided to comb the papers again, since all transactions are printed up by law."

"And he means dozens and dozens of newspapers," she added.

"We spread them all out on the floor and took another look," he said. "It was Tara who nailed him."

"Nailed Stuart? How?" I asked.

"I found his house," she said.

"So it *was* listed in his name?" I asked.

"No," she said. "It was listed in Mandy's."

"Mandy? As in his secretary?"

"That's the girl. But I couldn't remember her last name. So I called Human Resources at Lasher's to make sure she was 'our' Mandy."

"They confirmed that her last name was the same as the one in the *Palm Beach Post*," said Tony. "It's Koplitz, by the way. Can't be too many Mandy Koplitzes out there, right?"

"This is amazing," I said. "So Stuart's using her as a front?"

"Bingo," said Tony. "The abandoned car with the blood on the seat was a decoy. He's here and he's camping out with her."

"Have you paid a visit to the lovebirds yet?" I asked.

"No," he said. "We drove over to the address in the paper, but nobody was home. We figured we'd try again in the morning."

"Then I got here just in time," I said. "I wouldn't have missed this for the world. Does Jimmy know?"

Tara nodded. "He wants the whole mess kept quiet as much as I do. His poor parents are totally in the dark, and he's worried about their health if they find out what Stuart's done."

Tara went on to describe the house where her husband and his secretary were holed up—she dubbed it "a monstrosity," which probably meant that it was even grander than their castle in Mamaroneck—and then Tony suggested we all call it a night.

"We've got a big day ahead," he said. "I think we should rest up."

"I agree. Get some sleep, you two," Tara said on her way out the door, then added with a wink, "Or at least a little sleep."

When Tony and I were alone, I reminded him that I'd reserved my own room at the hotel.

"You won't be needing it," he said, enveloping me in his arms. "What you need is quality time with me."

"I do," I said. "For starters, I have to apologize for that awful scene downstairs in the dining room. I jumped to conclusions, based on the past. I acted like a lunatic."

"You acted like a woman who's been hurt before," he said. "It can't have been easy to find out about Betsy and me, especially at the same time that I was down here alone with Tara."

"I know, but I'm still sorry. I should have had more faith in you."

"Apology accepted. I should have told you about Betsy, and I'm sorry about that. But the truth is, it's hard to talk about old relationships with the person you're trying to win over. I didn't want to turn you off or turn you away, or just plain piss you off. So I took the path of least resistance and kept quiet about her. Forgive me?"

"I already have."

He smiled. "Then how about we move on?"

"I'd like that, although I do have one little topic to revisit. In the restaurant before, somewhere between the catfight with Tara and my tirade over Betsy, I seem to remember that you said you loved me. I'd like to hear more about that."

He smiled. "You want to hear about how I love you?" He brushed his lips across my cheek. "I love you with these." Then he tightened his arms around me. "And I love you with these." Then he took my hand and pressed it against his chest, over his heart. "But most of all, I love you with this."

"Do you?"

"Without a doubt." He kissed me. "Which is another way of saying that I'll never run off with somebody else the way Stuart did, and history will not repeat itself. I'm yours, body and soul, if you want me."

"If I want you? I've wanted you for longer than I could admit to myself. I—"

"What?"

Damn. I was going to tell him. I had every intention of telling him. But when it came down to actually spitting out the "I love you," I froze.

He drew me to him. "There's no need to say it," he whispered. "Not until you're ready. I know how you feel, and that's good enough."

I nodded, feeling for the very first time as if I'd been the one to walk off with the prize, as if I'd been crowned prom queen.

No, scratch that. What I felt—what I truly experienced at that moment—was that I'd finally outgrown the prom queen fantasy and, instead, was grateful to be exactly who I was.

• • •

The three of us piled into the rental car at nine o'clock the next morning, bound for an address north of the hotel.

"Leave it to Stuart to land in a pricey neighborhood like this," said Tara as we drove past mansion after mansion.

"Everybody probably thinks he's a man of mystery," I said, "the type people assume is in the CIA or something."

"He wouldn't be the first one," said Tony. "South Florida is full of shady characters trying to reinvent themselves."

"Well, he can reinvent himself all he wants," said Tara, "*after* he fulfills his obligations to me, which means showing up at my book party and getting Sergei off my back."

"Then there's Ho and Miguel," I said. "They're liable to show up at your door one of these days."

"Don't remind me," she said. "I don't know which of these people I'm dreading more—and that includes the police."

Oops. I'd forgotten all about my chat with the detectives. I filled Tara and Tony in on the questions they'd asked me and admitted that I'd tipped them off about Palm Beach.

"So they're coming to get me now?" she asked.

"Not to worry," said Tony. "Both of you will be in the clear as soon as we prove that Stuart's alive."

"Then drive faster," she said.

"Don't have to. We're here," said Tony as he pulled up in front of a tidy but unappealing one-story stucco house of fifties vintage—definitely the least expensive house on the block.

"It's not exactly a monstrosity, but it's not what I expected," I said.

"It's a teardown," said Tara. "Stuart will make a fortune on land value alone."

Tony shut off the engine. "Are you sure you're ready for this, Tara?"

"Ready to walk in and see him with another woman?" She laughed ruefully. "Amy had to walk in and see him with me once upon a time. I guess it's my turn."

"We'll be right here with you," I reassured her. "Let's go.

The sooner we confront him, the sooner we can tell the cops to close the case."

We got out of the car, walked up to the front door, and rang the bell. After a few seconds, a woman appeared. She was in her late twenties and not especially attractive. Her nose was too long, her mouth was too wide, and her figure was on the chunky side. And then there was the wad of gum. Some sort of lime green gum. My jaws ached watching her chew it. Yes, despite the miniskirt and the tight halter top, she was not the femme fatale I'd pictured, but she had to have other charms or she wouldn't have been able to seduce Stuart. On the other hand, maybe it didn't take much to seduce Stuart.

"Hello, Mandy," said Tara in the voice she always used when she wanted to cut someone dead.

"Mrs. Lasher?" Mandy was taken aback by the appearance of her boyfriend's wife, obviously. "What, um, are you doing here?"

"You know exactly why I'm here," said Tara. "Now, get out of my way."

Tara gave Mandy a little shove and marched into the house, with Tony and me trailing after her. Once we were all standing in the living room, which was cramped even without the moving cartons, Tara said, "Okay. Where is he?"

"Where's who?" asked Mandy.

"Cut the crap and tell me where Stuart is," she said. "Or should I give myself the tour?"

Mandy seemed genuinely confused. "I don't get this," she said. "I thought he was dead."

"Yeah, right," said Tara.

"I did. I swear," she said. "First they found his car. Then I was called into a meeting at Lasher's and told I'd have to work for someone else. I left the company because I didn't want another boss."

"You left the company because your boss set you up in this house," said Tony.

"Huh?" she said articulately.

"Stuart bought the house and put it in your name," I said. "We know everything, Mandy."

"You're wrong," she said. "You're all wrong. This is my house now."

Tara snorted. "Is that what Stuart told you?"

"No. That's what my lawyer told me. Well, my aunt's lawyer."

"Your aunt?" asked Tony.

"Yeah," said Mandy. "This was her house. She died and left it to me, since I was her closest relative. I decided I might as well move in, since I didn't have a job up north anymore."

"So you're saying that Stuart didn't pay for the house and turn it over to you for legal reasons?" Tara persisted. "Or simply to keep his whereabouts a secret?"

"Why do you keep asking me about your husband, Mrs. Lasher?"

"Because you've been having an affair with him, for God's sake."

"I have not." Mandy thought a second. "Well, okay. There was just that once, the night of the company Christmas party."

"Maybe we should search the house and get it over with," I said.

"Go ahead," said Mandy. "All you're going to find are my aunt's clothes and stuff. I'm packing them up and donating them to Goodwill."

"I think we'll have a look just the same," said Tony.

The three of us went through every corner of the house, checking for evidence of Stuart's presence but finding none. All we saw were closets full of women's clothes, just as Mandy had said we would.

"Do you suppose she's telling the truth?" I asked.

"Stranger things have happened," said Tony. "It'll be easy enough to find out if the aunt lived and died here. I can check with the medical examiner's office."

"Great, but let's say Mandy is telling the truth," Tara proposed. "Let's say she's not Stuart's partner in crime and doesn't have any idea where he is. What do we do then?"

"Come up with plan B," said Tony. "If you're really a fan of my novels, Tara, you know that the solution to the mystery is usually in a place where you least expect it."

37

We left Mandy and took a drive to Worth Avenue for a late breakfast and a conversation about what our next move should be. Tara suggested we go back to New York and try harder to retrace Stuart's steps during the days before he disappeared. I agreed with her, thinking there must be clues we'd overlooked. But Tony held fast to his hunch that Stuart was in Florida and insisted we stay for another day or two.

"There's a reason he wanted you two to fly down here to look at houses," he said to Tara. "My guess is that he was scoping out the territory so he'd be ready when it was time to make his getaway."

"Then why isn't he with Mandy?" I asked.

"And how will we find him now that he isn't with her?" Tara added.

"Just give this one more day," he said. "I have nothing to go on except my gut, but I've spent my whole adult life writing about criminals and I know how they think. Stuart's here somewhere, trust me."

Tara and I deferred to Tony and said we'd do whatever he thought best.

We finished our breakfast, left the restaurant, and strolled down Worth Avenue en route to our car. As we were passing

by antique shops, art gallerys, and one clothing designer after another, Tony bent down to tie his shoelace. Since we had
stopped walking momentarily, Tara and I peered into the
store window in front of us. The shop sold gourmet foods,
and the display in the window captured our attention. A
beautiful table had been set with place mats and napkins and
silver and crystal, with a dozen or so imported products laid
out decoratively among them. There was some pâté, some
cheese, some fruit, and a baguette. There were also several
one-ounce jars of caviar, six mother-of-pearl caviar spoons,
and a bottle of vodka in an ice bucket.

"I know we just ate breakfast," I said, "but my mouth's
watering."

"Same here," said Tara.

"What are we looking at?" asked Tony, now upright.

I pointed to the display in the window.

He pressed his nose against the glass. And then, without a
word, he hurried inside the store.

"I guess he's hungry, too," said Tara as we followed him.

Tony had more on his mind than food, it turned out. He
walked right up to the display, reached in, grabbed one of
the jars of caviar, and examined it.

"Well, what do you know," he said. "My hunch was right
on the money after all."

"Your hunch about Stuart?" I said.

"Here," he said, holding the jar in front of our eyes. "See
for yourselves."

Upon closer inspection, the jar bore the label of Stuart's
bogus company, Caspian Classics.

"I don't believe it," said Tara, shaking her head. "He's
selling his bootlegged stuff down here?"

"Unless this is some bizarre coincidence," said Tony.
"Let's have a chat with the manager."

Gerald Franks was a portly man who spoke with an affected faux-British accent. He not only managed the shop
but owned it, and had for years.

"We just started carrying Caspian Classics," he said after

Tony introduced himself as Harvey Kraus and began his inquiry. "Black gold has been getting ridiculously expensive, but the gentleman who distributes this brand gives me a break on the price."

"Interesting," said Tony. "Any idea where we could find him?"

"Not if you're trying to compete with me, Mr. Kraus," he said with a chuckle. "I don't need anyone cutting into my business."

"I'm not local competition," said Tony. "I've got a couple of stores in the Chicago area, so I'd like to talk to your man about selling Caspian Classics in my part of the country."

"Oh. Well then, have at him," said Gerald, who dug around in his desk for Stuart's card, then handed it to Tony.

"He doesn't give his address," said Tony. "Only a pager number."

"I know, but it's the best way to reach Mr. Dunsmore," said Gerald.

"Mr. Dunsmore?" said Tara, squelching a laugh.

"Yes," replied Gerald. "Ronald Dunsmore. He's a very cordial fellow."

Tony thanked Gerald for the time and the information, and Gerald wished Tony luck with his stores in Chicago. And then off we went.

"No wonder Sergei's pissed," I said when we were back out on the street. "Not only did Stuart stop paying him, he elbowed him out of their deal altogether."

"Cordial my ass," muttered Tara.

"What now, Tony?" I asked. "Without an address on the card, we've got nowhere to go."

"I'll call the pager number," he said.

"And tell him you're here to hunt him down?" said Tara. "I don't think that'll go over well."

"I'm not here to hunt him down," he said with a smile. "Harvey Kraus is here to do business with him. Or weren't you listening to what I told Gerald?"

He dialed the pager number, then punched in his cell number after the voice-mail prompt. The three of us huddled together while we waited for him to call back. When Tony's phone bleated out the *William Tell* Overture, we practically jumped.

"Harvey Kraus," said Tony, altering his voice so Stuart wouldn't recognize it. He was trying to sound midwestern, but there was still a touch of New York in his speech. "Oh, yes, Mr. Dunsmore. Thanks for getting back to me so quickly. Gerald Franks gave me your card. I've got a couple of shops like his in Chicago and I'm looking to better my margin on caviar. He said you were the man to talk to. . . . Yes. . . . Uh-huh. . . . Is that right?"

Tara and I were dying of curiosity, since we could hear only one side of the conversation.

"That'd be great," Tony went on. "I'm in town for another day or so. I could meet with you today, sure. I'm staying at the Breakers. Why don't we say lunch at one o'clock? I'll make the reservation in my name. . . . No, it's Kraus, not Cross. Harvey Kraus. . . . Right. Bye."

Tony hung up and grinned. "We've got him—at least for the moment."

"This is huge," said Tara. "You proved he's here. And now that he's on the hook, all we have to do is reel him in."

"I think I should reel him in," said Tony. "You two stay out of it."

"Not a chance," said Tara. "I want to see the look on that jerk's face when he realizes I'm on to him."

"Me, too," I said. "I've been waiting a long time to watch him squirm."

At 12:50, the three of us sat down at Harvey Kraus's table for four and waited. We were all wearing wide-brimmed hats and sunglasses so that Stu boy wouldn't recognize us right off the bat and bolt. We looked like tacky tourists, but that was sort of the point.

We were giddy with anticipation as we traded possible scenarios of what he would do and say when he realized we'd found him. In fact, we were having a good laugh when I noticed that two men were approaching our table.

"Oh my God. It's the detectives who interviewed me yesterday," I said. "I can't believe they actually followed us here."

Sure enough, the same two cops to whom I'd blabbed about the Breakers came right over and announced that they wanted to question Tara in connection with her husband's disappearance.

"I'm not guilty," she said. "And neither is Amy."

"If you give us a few minutes, we'll prove it," I said.

The cops looked dubious, so Tony took over. He explained that Stuart was very much alive; that his car had merely been in an accident and he'd been too careless to report it; that he'd flown to Palm Beach without telling his friends and family; and that he was, in fact, due to arrive at the hotel shortly. "You can question him yourselves," he said. "Do whatever you need to do to close the case. But let us have some private time with him first. Or, rather, let these two long-suffering ladies have some private time with him." He winked at the detectives, then added in a whisper, "There was a love triangle, and they need to sort it out. You understand."

The detectives nodded at Tony in that manly way men have when the subject of sex comes up, then said they'd be waiting outside the restaurant to interview Stuart when we were done with him.

"Wow. Good job," I said to Tony as the cops walked out and Stuart walked in. "And not a moment too soon."

At one o'clock on the nose, he appeared. And he was not the Stuart of old, with the preppy suit and the preppy hair. The new Stuart had gone tropical. He was in a Hawaiian shirt, khakis, and sandals, and he'd dyed his hair a color that was meant to be blond but was an unfortunate orange instead.

He stood at the maître d's station, where he must have said he was meeting a Mr. Kraus, and was immediately escorted to our table. (Lucky for us, there was a change of shift from the night before, so the maître d' on duty was not the one who'd thrown us out.) We kept our heads down and our glasses on while he walked toward us. It was only after he slid into the empty seat next to Tony and said, "Mr. Kraus? I'm Ronald Dunsmore" that we removed our hats and glasses, as if in a perfectly choreographed dance, and shouted, "Surprise!"

At first, Stuart seemed too stunned to register a reaction of any kind. He just sat there, his eyes moving from Tara to me to Tony and back. But after a beat or two, he made a move to flee.

Tony was too fast for him. He grabbed Stuart's hand, stepped on one of his feet, and held him right where he was, only knocking the saltshaker off the table—a far cry from the commotion we'd caused the night before.

"You might as well stay," said Tony, "because there are two cops at the door who are even more eager to talk to you than we are."

Stuart froze at the mention of police. "Fine. I'll stay," he said. "How did you find me?"

"Your fish eggs smelled," said Tony. "We just followed the scent."

"I don't know what you're talking about," he said.

"Caspian Classics. Truffles Magnifique. New Life Organic," said Tara, ticking off his crooked ventures. "They're what we're talking about. I'm sure Sergei, Ho, and Miguel want to talk to you about them, too."

"Who?" asked Stuart.

"We know everything," said Tony. "So does Jimmy. How could you steal from your own family?"

"Not that it's any of your business—and that goes for all three of you—but my family's been stealing from me for years. I was the rightful heir. I was the one who should have run Lasher's. Instead, Jimmy got the job and I was the second fiddle. How fair was that?"

The second fiddle. There it was again. The pesky syndrome that had dogged me. Only this time, it was Stuart who was suffering from it. Had that been our common bond when we were together—our mutual insecurity about being the "also ran"? Not exactly a sound basis for a relationship, was it?

"You would have run Lasher's into the ground," said Tara. "You almost did."

"But you're not going to," said Tony. "Jimmy doesn't want the company to go down the toilet, which it will if there's a criminal investigation."

"And I don't want sales of my book to go down the toilet," Tara echoed, "which they will if you don't show up at my book party."

"You're crazy," Stuart scoffed. "You're all crazy. I kissed off that bullshit when I faked my own murder."

"When you *tried* to fake your own murder," I said.

"And to think that you almost let us take the rap for it," said Tara.

"Whatever," he said. "I'm in Florida now and I'm starting over."

"Not before you tie up a few loose ends," said Tara.

"Why should I?" asked Stuart, whining like the child he was.

"Why should you? The easy answer is that if you don't, we'll have you arrested for fraud, larceny, and anything else the prosecutors dream up," said Tony. "Or we could just tip off Sergei and the other mischief makers to your new state of residence and let them come down here and rearrange your face."

Stuart didn't speak for a minute. Our waiter took the break in the action to hand us menus and tell us the specials.

"What do you want from me?" he asked impatiently. "Tell me and get it over with."

"I want a divorce," said Tara.

"My pleasure," said Stuart.

"First things first," said Tony. "What we want most of all is for you to make things right with your family. Your parents are worried sick about you, although why they should care is beyond me. They don't have any idea what happened to you, because Jimmy didn't want to upset them any more than they already are."

"My bro is such a sweetheart," he said sarcastically.

"I wouldn't be so cavalier about him," said Tony. "He

cares enough about preserving Lasher's reputation that he's willing to pay off your debts *and* not press charges against you. Of course, you'll have to sell the house in Mamaroneck to cover some of the debts."

"Yeah. Fine. But what's the catch?"

"That you come back to New York and have a nice long talk with your folks. Tell them they were right to put Jimmy in charge. Tell them it's taken you a while to face it but now you understand that you're not cut out for running the company. Tell them you sulked at first, made mistakes, left town to clear your head, but that you've gotten yourself together and are starting a new business in Florida. Say you're sorry, Stuart. Get it now?"

"Yeah, yeah. What else?"

"Put in an appearance at my publication party," said Tara.

He laughed. "Why in the world would I do that?"

"Tony just told you why," she said. "It's either a nice long prison sentence or a half-hour cameo at my party, during which you'll play the part of the loving husband I wrote about."

"I'm not that good an actor, hon."

"No? You fooled your own family. I think you can fool a few reporters."

"If this party of yours is getting so much publicity, how do I know Sergei won't find out about it and cause problems?" asked Stuart.

"It's a private party at her editor's apartment," I explained. "Strictly invitation only."

"And I highly doubt Sergei reads Page Six of the *Post*," Tara said dryly. "I don't know about Ho and Miguel, but he barely spoke English."

"So let me get this straight," said Stuart. "All I have to do is go home, make nice to Jimmy and my parents, be irresistible at the book party, and then I can come back to Florida? Free and clear?"

"Don't forget the divorce," said Tara. "Once my book tour is over and I've hit the best-seller list, I'm filing the papers and you'll have to sign them."

"And you'll have to stop peddling Caspian Classics," added Tony. "Jimmy won't drop the charges against you unless you set yourself up in a legitimate business."

"Caspian Classics is legitimate. A legitimate moneymaker."

"Sell caviar if you want to," said Tony. "Sell quail eggs, cow's udders, who cares what. Just do it legally."

"Okay. Okay. But I don't have time to sit here," he said. "I have things to do."

"Just two things," said Tony. "First, you have to talk to the cops outside and tell them your disappearance was just a silly misunderstanding. Then you have to pack. You'll be on the plane with us tomorrow."

"I can't leave tomorrow," he said. "I need to—"

"Run away again?" Tara said. "I don't think so. We're not letting you out of our sight until you show your face at my party."

"But I have to make arrangements, tell people I'll be gone."

"What people?" I said, having been fairly quiet up to that point. "Mandy?"

Stuart turned to me. "What do you know about all this, Amy?"

"I know that you're selfish," I said. "You were selfish four years ago and you're selfish now. The only difference is that Mandy is the one on the short end, not me."

"What's with the Mandy stuff?" he said. "She used to be my secretary. Big deal."

"Oh please," said Tara. "She's done a lot more for you than type your letters. We paid her a visit this morning."

He looked surprised. "You saw her here? In Palm Beach?"

"Well, she wasn't in China," said Tara.

"Then I guess she told you about the baby," he said.

Tara and I locked eyes—it was our turn to be surprised—but it was she who spoke. "The baby?"

"Yeah. We're expecting. Since you're so keen on a divorce, I might as well marry her."

"Now that you mention it, your girlfriend did look rather

thick around the middle. I just figured she'd been overeating, given the strain of living with you."

"Speaking of which," said Tony, "you and she are moving into her aunt's house?"

He wrinkled his nose with distaste. "Not right away. We're renting a condo until the house is habitable. It needs major renovation, as you must have noticed."

Tara laughed. "You're such a prince, Stuart. Nothing but the best for you."

"The best?" He looked at her, then at me, and his expression became uncharacteristically somber. Even regretful. "I had the best and I threw it away."

As the busboy arrived to refill our water glasses, I couldn't help wondering whether he meant Tara or if he meant me. Which of us had been his "best"?

Before I could give the question a single second more than it deserved, Tony reached under the table and squeezed my hand, as if to remind me that none of that mattered anymore.

38

Julie Farrell's apartment was the perfect spot for a publication party. It was three times the size of mine, so that even if everybody who'd RSVPed actually showed up, there would still be plenty of space for them to mingle, talk to Tara, and line up for signed copies of the book.

At two o'clock on the day of the party, the star author met me at Julie's. I had brought along my new assistant, a young woman named Lily, who was polite, efficient, and, above all, discreet—the anti-Scott, in other words.

Our plan was to bring the book to life by transforming Julie's apartment into a shrine to Tara. We created a total environment, complete with the candles, the scented oils, the incense sticks, the multicolored paper clips, and the volumes of poetry Stuart "wrote." There would be Enya on the stereo and flowers in little vases and waiters in aprons passing our special Simply Beautiful cocktails, which were basically white wine spritzers garnished with a truckload of herbs. And for an additional decoration, we hung posters of Tara's picture, a dozen of her suggestions for a simply beautiful life listed underneath. These included: "Hug a child"; "Grow a plant"; "Invest in a good moisturizer"; "Wear fushia when you need a lift"; and "Buy the man you love a musical instrument so he'll serenade you after work." When I'd mentioned to Tony that I was thinking of buying him a harp, he'd told me to save my money.

About two hours before the party, he called on my cell phone to see how things were going.

"Everything's fine here," I said. "The bigger question is, How's our hostage doing?" Ever since we'd dragged him back from Florida, Stuart had been under a veritable house arrest at Jimmy's, keeping a profile low enough to deter Sergei from camping out at the door and pummeling him.

"He's had the big talk with his parents, confessed his sins to Jimmy, and worked out some sort of financial settlement to avoid going to jail. All that's left is this party tonight."

"I'm ready," I said. "How about you? I know how you love L and T parties."

He groaned. "Like I love a bad cold. But I promise to be charming if it'll help you."

"I appreciate that. What will really help me is if Jimmy brings Stuart early, in case Barbara Biggs and her *Today's Woman* crew are the first to get here."

"*Today's Woman*. Now that sounds like hard-edged television. Is there a *Today's Man* you could get me on?"

"Don't be a wiseass. The show airs all over the country, and it'll be great exposure for Tara—if I can make Barbara buy the act."

"If anyone can, it's you, Amy. You'll get your publicity, and everything will work out better than you think."

"I hope you're as good a forecaster as you are a writer. See you later."

"Can't wait. I love you."

"And I—" Say it, I scolded myself. Say it back to him. Just say it already. "I—" Nope. Not yet. "I can't wait, either."

At five o'clock, Julie came home and was clearly impressed with what we'd done with her apartment. After she gave us a pep talk, we went over the guest list. It included a mix of L and T executives, book reviewers (even the snobby ones who wouldn't deign to review a book as mundane as Tara's but who'd never turn down a free drink), magazine and newspaper reporters, and the handful of opinion makers who seemed to show up for every publication party in New York.

"If these people all come, the word of mouth for the book will be tremendous," she said. "You and your husband will be the toast of the town, Tara."

"Either that or he'll just be toast," she muttered.

"What?" said Julie.

"A little joke," Tara said, flashing her big teeth, which were so white, they were blinding. In preparation for the party, she'd had them bleached.

She looked her usual gorgeous self, by the way. Her hair was up in an ultrasophisticated chignon. Her outfit was a red dress that went all the way down to her ankles (hiding the knock-knees). And her jewelry was exquisite—straight out of a fashion magazine. She really did have a talent for pulling herself together, and I defied anyone to guess that her life wasn't as beautiful as it seemed.

The guests started arriving just after 6:00 P.M., one of them Tony. He kissed me in full view of Betsy, whose eyes blazed with resentment.

"Break a leg," he said.

"Break your own leg," she told him.

"I was talking to Amy," he said.

"Good, because my legs are no longer any of your business," she replied. "And that goes for the rest of my anatomy."

"Why don't we let your husband worry about your anatomy," I said. "Right now, I have a job to do. You must have one, too, Betsy, although for the life of me, I can never figure out what it is."

Nostrils flaring, she wheeled and stormed off. Like my nerves weren't jangled enough.

As more and more people filled the apartment, I spotted the reporter from *New York* magazine and another from the *Post,* both with photographers, and went to play hostess.

"Where's the husband?" they both asked after getting a shot of Tara sipping her Simply Beautiful cocktail.

"He's stuck in traffic," I said, winging it. "He's on his way."

Where *is* the husband? I thought as I checked my watch. Jimmy should have had him here by now.

At that moment, Lily hurried over to tell me that Barbara Biggs and her crew had just walked through the door.

"Okay," I said, trying to stay calm. "I'll introduce them to Tara, give them all a drink and an hors d'oeuvre, and by the time they've set up, Stuart will be here."

I hoped I wasn't wrong. I'd turned myself inside out to snag Barbara's show for Tara, and I was not about to let that twerp ruin everything.

With a phony smile plastered on my face, I greeted Barbara and brought her over to meet Tara, who was in the middle of telling the *Post* reporter that one of her favorite tips for a simply beautiful marriage was to watch sunsets and sunrises with the loved one.

"Speaking of the loved one, Amy, where is he?" asked Barbara, a blow-dried redhead who looked like she'd just graduated from TV Anchorperson School. "My understanding was that he's part of the interview."

"Of course he is," I said.

"Fine, but I can't keep the crew here all night," she said, starting to act pissy.

"Let me see what's keeping him," I said, and slipped away to find Tony.

"We need Stuart," I whispered to him. "Can you call Jimmy and ask where the hell they are?"

"I know where the hell they are."

"Where?"

"On the Bruckner Expressway. Jimmy's car had a flat."

I felt my throat close up. "How flat? Like flat where it's got a huge rip in it and the car has to be towed and there's no way Stuart will get here in time?"

"No. Like flat where it's got a small leak in it and you take it off and put the spare on and Stuart will get here a little late."

"Okay, but what am I going to do about Barbara Biggs? She said she has to leave soon."

"I'll stall her."

"You? Usually, you just sit by yourself at these parties and growl at people."

"I know, but I told you I'd be charming if it would help you. So I'll go over there and rock her world."

Barbara was on her second cocktail when I introduced Tony.

"The mystery writer?" she said, putting down her drink so she could shake his hand. "I totally love your books."

"And I totally love your show. Never miss it," he said, giving her his sexiest smile.

"You've never watched *Today's Woman* in your entire life," she said, realizing she was being teased.

"Actually, I did watch it once," he replied. "You were doing a segment on women who take stripping lessons and feel empowered once their clothes come off."

"You saw that?" she asked.

"I saw *them*," he said. "I couldn't tear myself away."

"You're bad," she replied, enjoying their banter. While he kept her talking, I took Tara aside and broke the news about Jimmy's flat tire.

"Swell," she said. "If I hadn't made such a big deal about Stuart in the book, we could be doing all this without him."

"You can leave him out in the sequel."

"There won't be a sequel if this one doesn't sell."

We were interrupted by the *Post* reporter, who was getting fidgety. "Is the husband coming or not?" she asked.

"He had a flat tire," I said. "Just give us another few minutes."

Then, the *New York* magazine reporter said she couldn't wait anymore.

And finally, Barbara Biggs announced that she'd have to leave if Stuart didn't appear soon. "I'd love to stay and chat with Tony Stiles," she said, "but business is business. I thought we had this all arranged."

"We did," I said. "We do."

"He'll be here," Tara assured her. "Why don't you have another one of our delicious—"

Before she could ply Barbara with more alcohol, Stuart and Jimmy finally trudged in.

"Stuart!" Tara cooed as she raced up to him and threw her arms around his neck. His hair was still orange, but the Hawaian shirt had been replaced by his customary Brooks Brothers suit. "I was so worried."

"I'll bet," he said, letting her kiss him on the cheek. "Sorry we're late."

"Sweetheart, don't apologize," she said. She turned to Barbara. "That's one of the tenets of *Simply Beautiful*: Saying 'I'm sorry' too often can make for a sorry relationship."

"Very interesting," said Barbara. "Now, let's get the two of you set up for the interview."

"Here," I said, rushing over to pull up a couple of extra chairs so the three of them could sit together for the taping of the segment.

While the crew positioned themselves, I took a deep breath, glanced around the room, and smiled at Tony, who was standing nearby. Somehow, it was all coming together. Stuart was playing his part and allowing Tara to play hers, and L and T would sell lots and lots of books.

The interview got off to a promising start as Barbara asked Tara to talk about her hints for keeping the romantic fires burning. And then she turned to Stuart and asked, "Do you really write her poetry and read it to her at bedtime?"

I was leaning in to hear his answer, when a waiter carrying a tray of hors d'oeuvres nearly collided with me. He mumbled an apology and slunk away, but after a second or two, it dawned on me that I knew him. Well, not knew him, but recognized him. Yes, I'd seen him before, but I couldn't remember where. Oh, who cared, right? At least he hadn't collided with the camera and disrupted the taping.

"Yes, I do write Tara poetry," Stuart was saying, "and she returns the favor. She leaves me these amazing little love notes in my toiletry case, so that when I travel, she's always with me."

"That's special," Barbara enthused.

"It's the element of surprise that keeps things exciting in a relationship," Tara added. "It's the wonder of what might happen next that—"

She was in midsentence when the waiter, the one who'd nearly knocked me over, suddenly lunged at Stuart right in front of the camera.

My God, it's Sergei, I thought as the party guests screamed, scattered, or froze. Yep, it's Sergei, and he's wrapping his hands around Stuart's throat.

And then before anybody could react, another man entered the melee—an Asian man. At first, I thought he was coming to Stuart's defense, but he, too, wanted a piece of my ex-fiancé.

"Lasher is mine," he said to Sergei in broken English. "He owe me money and I collect."

"Who are you?" Betsy yelled at him from several feet away.

"Ho!" shouted the man.

"Well! I beg your pardon," said Betsy, clearly offended. "I will not be called names like that by you or anybody else. Now get out."

The Chinese truffles vendor ignored her and threw a punch at Stuart's head that landed instead on Sergei's torso.

While he and Sergei went after Stuart, a Latino man suddenly shoved them both out of the way, muttering, "Nobody forgets to pay Miguel, eh?"

Now we had an actual free-for-all going on, and it was pure bedlam. While the three interlopers clobbered Stuart and one another, the guests made a mad dash for the door. Some grabbed copies of Tara's book to use as shields. Some tore down the posters of her and stomped on them in their frantic efforts to get out. And some just threw up their hands as they fled, dropping their Simply Beautiful cocktails on the floor, soaking Julie's carpet, and leaving a trail of sprigs.

The photographers, on the other hand, weren't going

anywhere. Instead, they stayed to catch the bizarre scene that was taking place in front of their eyes. Worse, the *Today's Woman* cameraman kept shooting, with Barbara egging him on.

In an effort to rescue Stuart, Tony dove into the frey, grabbing a tray of hors d'oeuvres and smashing it over Sergei's head.

Following his lead, I snatched a copy of *Simply Beautiful* and spanked Ho's butt with it.

But it was Tara who really scored. She went for one of her candles—I think it was the vanilla with boysenberry—and seared Miguel's forearm with the flame until he shrieked.

"Good one," I told her as Tony gave Sergei another shot with the tray.

Luckily, Jimmy had called 911 the minute things had turned ugly, and the cops showed up just as Tara was singeing Miguel's skin again, this time with an incense stick.

After another twenty minutes or so, the bad guys were taken away in handcuffs, Stuart was whisked away to the hospital by Jimmy and Tony, and Tara and I were left with the mess—the literal mess and the media mess.

"So much for your job, Amy," Betsy taunted as she stepped gingerly over the debris. "The book's going to tank, and it's your fault. But cheer up. Maybe they have an opening in the publicity department at the World Wrestling Federation."

Before I could respond, Barbara was at my elbow.

"Well, this certainly wasn't what I anticipated," she said with a laugh after telling her crew to pack up. "I can't use it on *Today's Woman,* but I won't have any problem turning it over to the executives at my network."

"Turning it over to your network? What for?"

"For one of their reality shows."

"Oh, Barbara, I'm begging you not to," I said after moving her away from the shellshocked Tara, whose image, not to mention her career, had been trashed, along with mine.

"You can beg all you want, but they're always looking for reality programming."

"Come on, you're better than that," I said, trying a little flattery. "You're a journalist, not some sleezy tabloid reporter."

"Journalist, schmernalist. I've got your author right there on-camera, setting people on fire while a bunch of thugs are throwing punches at her husband. It's not my thing, but there's an audience for it."

"What about your audience? *Today's Woman*'s audience? Don't you care about them?"

"What's your point?"

What is my point? I wondered. I took a breath while I tried to come up with one. "Your audience wants human-interest stories that they can relate to," I said, the germ of an idea forming.

"Yeah? So?"

"So I think I've got one for them. Give me a sec, would you?"

I scurried over to Tara, who was sitting by herself in the living room. Her chignon had come apart, and she was staring off into space, twirling the end of a loose strand of hair.

"Hey, snap out of it," I said, shaking her shoulder.

"What's to snap out of?" she said. "It's over. Our entire campaign is over."

"Not necessarily," I said. "Not if you're willing to spin your story a little differently."

"You publicists and your spins," she said morosely.

"Listen to me. Barbara Biggs is about to walk out of here with damaging video of this party, and while it's perfect for some stupid reality show, it's the wrong material for *Today's Woman*. I say we give her the right material."

"Amy, we tried," she said. "We got Stuart to fly back from Florida and the plan backfired."

"Then we move on to plan B, like Tony always does."

"What's our plan B?"

"We turn this awful night to our advantage by making a deal with Barbara. We give her an exclusive interview with you, the controversial and charismatic author whose book party ended in a brawl, and in exchange she agrees to toss the Three Stooges video."

"An exclusive interview with me about what? That my husband and I don't have the marriage I pretended we did? That what I wrote in *Simply Beautiful* was a fantasy?"

"You guessed it."

"Are you crazy? That would kill book sales."

"They're already dead, Tara. But you have a chance to save yourself. Do an exclusive interview with Barbara and tell the truth for a change. Tell her you dreamed up the book to distract you from your miserable marriage. Tell her you made yourself happy by surrounding yourself with beautiful things. Don't tell her audience how to be perfect; tell them how to make the best of a bad situation, how to be *human*. I guarantee you that you'll be more sympathetic than you ever imagined. It's worth a try, isn't it?"

She nodded, her eyes tearing up.

"And don't cry, for God's sake," I said, handing her a cocktail napkin. "You're still going to be a role model for women, just not the one you expected."

"I'll do it."

"Good. Now fix your hair and makeup. I don't want you looking that human."

I ran to pitch Barbara the new slant on the interview. "If you don't want this, I'm going straight to Oprah," I said, back in publicist mode.

"Oh no you don't," she said vehemently. "I'm doing the interview myself."

"Then you'll hand over the footage you shot tonight? No tape, no deal, remember?"

"You got it."

There was a flurry of activity then as I straightened up a corner of the apartment so the crew could set up for round two.

"Now," Barbara began once the camera was rolling again, "what's the real reason you wrote *Simply Beautiful,* Tara?"

What came next was pure Tara Messer, which is to say that, even in her darkest hour, she shone. The minute the little red light went on, she was dazzling, sparkling, as compelling as ever. You couldn't turn away from her as she told her story. I had heard it all before, but I was riveted. She was the flawed Tara now, the fallible Tara, and she had a way of making even heartache and deception seem glamorous.

"I created the environment I wrote about because it allowed me to feel in control," she said, then admitted that her marriage was a sham and all the rest.

By the end of the interview, Barbara was totally in her thrall, just as I'd been for so many years.

"This will be dynamite television," she told me. "I'm airing it as soon as I can get it edited."

"I'm glad," I said, and I was. Glad for Tara that she'd been able to walk away from the evening with some dignity. Glad for me that I'd convinced Barbara to stay and shoot the segment. Glad that, no matter what happened with the book or my job, I had my best friend back.

"You know," I said as we strolled down the street after leaving Julie's, "we're not a bad team when we keep it honest."

"You were amazing the way you saved my ass with Barbara."

"Just working the media, as usual. You were amazing the way you nailed the interview."

"Just hogging the spotlight, as usual."

"As I said, we're not a bad team."

She hooked her arm through mine while we waited for the light to change.

39

"hearthebooksflyingofftheshelves," said Connie about a week later. She had stopped by my office between meetings.

"What?"

"I said, I hear the book's flying off the shelves. You must be pinching yourself."

"I am. I am."

Within twenty-four hours after Tara's interview with Barbara Biggs aired on *Today's Woman*, copies of *Simply Beautiful* started selling faster than booksellers could keep it in stock. A few days after that, it shot up to number one on nearly every list in the country and transformed Tara from a fallen lifestyle guru to a literary superstar. According to the readers who saw her on the show and flooded L and T's Web site with E-mails, she touched a nerve in a way she never would have if she'd done the interview as the deliriously happy wife. What they related to was her vulnerability, her pain, her valiant attempts at coping with disappointment and despair. That's not to say that they didn't love all the soft-focus stuff about taking baths and collecting seashells and filling the house with the scent of cloves. But mostly, they just loved her, and they wanted more of her.

"Julie's already talked to Tara about a follow-up book," I

told Connie. "I think they're playing with the title *Simply Beautiful for Singles*."

"Catchy." She rolled her eyes. "So she's getting a divorce?"

"The paperwork is in the mail to Stuart as we speak. Plus, she's got the Westchester house on the market. She's looking for a place in the city."

"Amazing how things turned out. The launch party's a media disaster, and your best friend's a media darling."

"Which goes to prove that there's no such thing as bad publicity," I said.

"I guess not, although you'd have a hard time convincing Tony of that. He'll go to pieces if the reviewers don't give him a break on the new book."

I felt myself blush. "I think the research he did for this one should change their minds about the Joe-Lucy relationship. It's more fully developed than it was in the earlier books."

"And what about your relationship? Is marriage in the future for you two?"

"Oh, Connie. Come on. Tony's never been the marrying kind."

"He's never been the dating one woman for more than a month kind, either, but look at him now. People change, Amy."

"I know." I smiled. "Remember how I used to say I didn't want Betsy's job? That I wasn't cut out to be marketing director?"

"Yeah?"

"Well, I do want her job. When Julie let it slip the other day that they were canning Betsy, I told her to spread the word that I was interested in a promotion."

"Now, that's showing some guts. Good for you."

"Thanks." I gave her a hug. I had aimed for her waist, but she was so short, I ended up hugging her teased-up hair. "There's something else I need to change about myself, though."

"What?"

"My reluctance about telling Tony I love him. I haven't

been able to do it, Connie, and it's got nothing to do with his fear of commitment. It's about mine. I'm afraid that if I expose my feelings the way I did with Stuart, I'll get crapped on again."

She put her hands on her tiny hips. "First of all, Tony is not Stuart. Second of all, he adores you. Third of all, you've gotta get over what happened in the past. As in move on already."

"You're right. It's just hard."

"Hey, it's all hard. You think being married to Murray is one long picnic? I'm crazy about him, but there are days when I want to chop off his—Well, what I'm saying is that there are no guarantees in life, not in love, not in work, not in anything. Could Tony end up crapping on you? Who knows? In the meantime, he makes you happy. That's something."

I nodded. "It is."

"Sostopbitchingandtrynottoblowit."

"What?"

"I said, So stop bitching and try not to blow it."

"Okay."

It was my birthday the following week. Not surprisingly, Tony wasn't much for the sort of scenes at restaurants where the waiters gather around the table and sing badly, so we celebrated quietly, just the two of us, at his loft. He ordered in from the Chinese place around the corner, and we spread all the little white boxes on his dining room table and dug in.

"So what's my present?" I asked, munching on Szechuan shrimp in black-bean sauce. It was so spicy, my lips were vibrating.

"What makes you think you're getting another present?" he said, snaring a shrimp off my plate with his chopsticks. "Isn't this dinner enough of a happy birthday?"

I looked up and noticed the twinkle in his eye and realized he was kidding. "Then there is a present?"

"There might be. Have you been a good girl?"

"A very good girl."

"So you think you deserve a present?"

"I do, yes."

"What kind of present, may I ask?"

"Something shockingly expensive, but not embarrassingly so. Oh, and it should be something personal—not a new set of sheets, for example."

"Sheets aren't personal?"

"They are, but no one except you and my cleaning lady would ever see them, so why bother?"

"Ah, so this present is supposed to impress people? Make them a little jealous?"

"Not necessarily, but it would be more fun if it did."

He nodded. "I've got just the thing." He bounced up from the table and disappeared into his bedroom.

I waited with great anticipation as I polished off the rest of the shrimp. What could he have gotten me? I wondered. I was guessing a pair of skis, since he'd talked about taking me to Aspen for the holidays. I was guessing a sleek new laptop, since he'd made jokes about my clunky old one. I was even guessing jewelry, although he wasn't big on flashy possessions, his flashy sports cars aside.

"Here we go," he said, emerging with a big gift-wrapped box.

I joined him on the sofa. "Wow," I said, shaking the box. "Whatever it is weighs a ton."

"Open it."

I tore open the wrapping and flipped off the top of the box. "It's a manuscript," I said, peering at the five hundred–plus pages inside. "Your manuscript."

He smiled proudly. "That's right. The next installment in the Joe West series. I wanted you to have a copy before I deliver the original to Connie next week. It fits your criteria for a birthday present, doesn't it? It's shockingly expensive—L and T paid me a hefty advance for it—but not embarrassingly so. It's personal—check the dedication page and you'll find out just how personal. And it's bound to impress other people—I do have my fans, and they'd be mighty envious of you for getting a peek at it. All in all, it's the perfect gift, I'd say. Happy birthday, Amy."

He leaned over and kissed me.

Okay, so I admit it: A copy of his new book wasn't what I'd had in mind. It just wasn't. Skis? Yes. Computer? Yeah. Jewelry? Why the hell not!

And yet, I was touched that he wanted me to share his sense of accomplishment about the book. And I was extremely flattered that he was dedicating it to me, to show his gratitude for my input. I told myself to look thrilled.

"This *is* the perfect gift," I said. "It's a part of you, and that's very meaningful. Really."

"Glad you like it," he said, still sounding mischievous. "Now open it."

I was confused. "I did open it."

"No. Take the manuscript out of the box and turn the pages."

"Oh, Tony. You don't want me to read the book now, do you? Don't get me wrong—I'm dying to read it. But we're in the middle of dinner. We haven't even had our fortune cookies."

"Please?" he said, sort of pouting.

"Fine." I lifted the manuscript out of the box and set it on my lap. I read the title page. Then I read the acknowledgments page. I'm sure I was doing a little pouting myself—why did I have to read the book during my birthday dinner?—when I came to the dedication page. "Oh." I blinked when I saw that there was something taped to it. "What's this?"

He shrugged. "Just the floppy disk, in case you lose the hard copy."

"It's too bulky for a disk." I pried the layers of tape loose from the page. Underneath it all, there wasn't a disk, but a Tiffany aqua velvet pouch. My eyes widened as I glanced up at him. "Tony? What in the world are you up to?"

"Go on. Open it."

I pulled the drawstring and reached carefully inside the pouch.

"Oh my God," I said as I held it up to the light. It was a gift that was shockingly expensive but not embarrassingly so, was personal, and would totally impress other people.

"Let me," he said, slipping the diamond ring on my finger, since I was too stupefied to do anything but gawk at it.

"But Tony, it's—"

"A ring. And I take it you're pleased. Or did you really want the sheets after all?"

I smiled. "It's gorgeous. Truly gorgeous. You have great taste."

He stroked my cheek. "I do, don't I? So what do you think? Should we get married?"

"Married? You?"

"Married. Me. And you, too, of course."

"But I haven't even told you I love you yet."

"I was hoping the ring would motivate you to do that."

I looked at the sparkling stone on my finger and could feel the hugeness of the smile on my face. Oh, I did love Tony. That much I knew. As for the rest? Well, Connie was right about there being no guarantees in life. Getting dumped was always a possibility, but so was being cherished. It was high time I went for the cherished, I decided.

"I love you," I said. "And, yes, I will marry you."

He pumped his fist in the air, then scooped me up in his arms. "Would tomorrow work for you?"

I laughed. "Couldn't we be engaged for a little while?"

"Haven't we done that already?"

"I mean, for real this time. Just so I can experience what it's like to have a fabulous fiancé, instead of one who marries my best friend, steals from his family, and winds up in Florida with orange hair and a pregnant secretary."

"Okay, you win." He kissed me. "Just tell me you love me again."

"I love you again. And again."

He nodded at the bedroom. "Want to see how many *agains* you have in you now that you're wearing the magic ring?"

"Lead the way."

TARA

EPILOGUE

You see that? I wasn't the villain of this story after all. I know you were dying to hate me, because I'm gorgeous and stylish and smart. Yeah, smart. (How many of you have a book on the *New York Times* best-seller list, huh?) But in the end, I turned out to be sort of the heroine. Amy got the man she wanted *and* the job she wanted, and I was the one who made that happen.

And no, I'm not being overly self-congratulatory. If it weren't for me, she wouldn't have gone after Tony in the first place, nor would she have garnered all that attention within the publishing industry. She owes me a lot, when you get right down to it. But am I keeping score? Please. I'm not that petty. What's important here is that she and I are best friends, just the way we used to be. While we still have our little bones of contention, we're there for each other. We really are.

For example, as soon as she and Tony set a date for their wedding, she asked me to be her maid of honor and I accepted. Talk about a long-overdue gig. And when the big event finally arrived, I couldn't have been more excited if I'd been the bride myself. Well, in a manner of speaking.

"I wish you two had picked a place with some panache," I said. Amy and I were standing in the back room of the steak restaurant in SoHo where she and Tony were getting married in an hour. The manager had done a fairly decent job of sprucing it up for the ceremony. There were a few rows of chairs, flowers at the ends of the aisles, and a makeshift altar at the far end of the room. But still. It smelled of slabs of beef, for God's sake.

"We had our first date here," she said, "so it has senti-mental value for us. And the waiters treat Tony like their firstborn son. He's comfortable here."

"Maybe, but people get married at quaint country inns, not at steak joints."

"Stuart and I were supposed to get married at a quaint country inn, and look how that worked out."

"Point taken," I said. "Besides, my job as maid of honor is not to criticize, just to help the bride prepare."

"Then let's prepare me already."

I shut up about the restaurant—you can't force people to have good taste—and concentrated on the crucial aspect of the wedding: what I was wearing. Well, okay, what she and I were wearing.

We carried our garment bags into the ladies' room and undressed, dressed, then admired each other.

"You look beautiful," said Amy.

You bet I did. I had chosen my own gown this time around, and it was smashing on me. It had a pale green silk top with matching—

Never mind. It was her night to shine.

"You look beautiful, too," I said, and made a huge fuss over the Vera Wang number I'd found for her at Neiman Marcus. "The gown, the shoes, the bouquet. The whole enchilada."

She smiled. She really was radiant and, thanks to my tire-less efforts, downright chic. I envied her happiness almost as much as I envied that rock Tony had put on her finger.

"Are you nervous?" I asked.

"Maybe I should be, but I'm not," she said, then giggled. "I can't wait to get out there, say 'I do,' and then party."

"I'm up for the party, too," I said, "although I have no idea if my date will be any fun."

"You have a date? Since when?"

"Since last night. Forgive the short notice, but you told me I could bring someone."

"Sure I did," she said. "Who's the lucky guy?"

"You know him, actually. He's an accountant at L and T. He runs the Business Affairs department."

She arched an eyebrow. "Michael Ollin?"

"That's the one," I said. "We met last week and I just started seeing him. He's a hunk, isn't he?"

"He's a hunk all right." She made a face. "A hunk of jerkiness. He calls women 'bodilicious' and cheats on his girlfriend."

"The girlfriend's history. He told me."

"Oh, Tara." She sighed. I felt one of her holier-than-thou lectures coming on. "Since the divorce, you've dated a string of men with absolutely no redeeming—"

Just then, there was a knock on the door. It was Tony.

"Time's up," he called out. "I'll be waiting for you two at the altar in five minutes."

Amy and I gave each other a hug and an air kiss (I can't speak for her, but there was no way I was smudging my lipstick).

"I'm so glad you're by my side tonight," she said.

"I wouldn't be anywhere else," I replied.

We clasped hands, then hurried into the ceremony area.

She took her father's arm, the keyboardist struck the chords of "The Wedding March," and the show began.

I walked down the aisle first, toward Tony and his best man (he had asked his car mechanic to do the honors, of all things). I glanced at the guests as I moved along, nodding at each of them, the way Miss America nods at her well-wishers as she glides along the carpet after her crowning. There was Amy's mother, of course. There was Amy's tacky friend Connie and her husband, Murray, the abstract artist/insurance salesman. There was Michael Ollin, my handsome and, according to Amy, disreputable date. And there was Marianne, Amy's therapist, who was now my therapist and was teaching me to deal with what she called my "grandiosity issues." Over on the groom's side sat Tony's father, his mother, and his three stepmothers, as well as his friends, some of whom were New York City cops in uniform. It was a motley crew, in other words.

Once I'd reached the spot where I was supposed to stand, Amy and her father proceeded down the aisle. She beamed when she reached Tony, and the current of love that passed between them was unmistakable.

After the justice of the peace delivered his remarks and Amy and Tony recited their vows, it was time for the Kiss. My big moment. Well, okay, their big moment.

I stepped forward and lifted Amy's veil for her. I was about to return to my corner, I swear I was, when it occurred to me that a maid of honor should have more to do. I mean, why rush off so damn fast, especially after all the time I spent on my makeup? There had to be other tasks for me to perform in front of those people, right?

I saw that a hair on the top of Amy's head was sticking up, so I smoothed it. And then I saw that one of her earrings was twisted, so I straightened it. And then I saw that there was a wayward piece of string hanging from her bodice, so I gave it a little tug and pulled it off.

I was about to check the skirt of the gown, when she leaned over and whispered, "Thanks, Tara, but I'll take it from here."

I smiled and went back to the sidelines like a good girl. But I've got to tell you: It was a kick strutting my stuff, you know?